ADIEU, VOLODYA

Adieu, Volodya

A NOVEL BY

SIMONE SIGNORET

TRANSLATED FROM THE FRENCH

BY STANLEY HOCHMAN

RANDOM HOUSE   NEW YORK

Copyright © 1986 by Stanley Hochman

All rights reserved under International and Pan-American
Copyright Conventions. Published in the United States by Random House, Inc., New York, and simultaneously in Canada by
Random House of Canada Limited, Toronto. Originally published in France by Librairie Arthème Fayard in 1985. Copyright
© 1985 by Librairie Arthème Fayard. This translation published
in Great Britain by Macmillan Publishers Ltd., London.

Library of Congress Cataloging-in-Publication Data
Signoret, Simone, 1921-1985
Adieu, Volodia.
Translation of: Adieu, Volodia.
I. Hochman, Stanley. II. Title.
PQ2679.I36A6613 1986   843'.914   86-19572
ISBN 0-394-54927-9

Manufactured in the United States of America
Typography and binding design by J. K. Lambert
9 8 7 6 5 4 3 2
First American Edition

CONTENTS

PART ONE

Someone's Assassinated Petliura *1*

PART TWO

Masques and Bergamasques *65*

PART THREE

The Yellow Leaflet *157*

PART FOUR

News of Volodya *231*

PART FIVE

Life Is Beautiful! *275*

PART SIX

The Family Picture Frame *335*

PART SEVEN

. . . Out of Mind *369*

I

SOMEONE'S ASSASSINATED PETLIURA

*T*HERE WERE NO legends about their first meeting. They had never actually met, because they'd always known each other. She'd simply come along a little later than he had, but it was in a stroller belonging to Maurice, who was now a toddler, that Zaza, a little Jewish girl of Polish parents, had her first outing under the sun of her first Paris spring.

He was Guttman, Maurice, born to Elie and Sonia Guttman—natives of the area around Zhitomir in the Ukraine—one morning in December 1919, on the second-floor left of a three-story building at 58 rue de la Mare, in Paris's XXth arrondissement.

She was Elsa (Zaza), born to Stépan and Olga Roginski—natives of the area around Lublin, Poland—one night in March 1921, on the second-floor right of a three-story building at 58 rue de la Mare, in Paris's XXth arrondissement.

He had stopped being a Ukrainian Jewish boy and she a Polish Jewish girl on the same evening in July 1925, when Messieurs Guttman and Roginski had brought home their fervently awaited naturalization papers.

With tears in their eyes, the two men had taken the documents from their pockets and presented them to Mesdames Guttman and Roginski, who had promptly fallen sobbing into each other's arms.

The papers were carefully stored in two honey-soft pigskin notecases personally made by Monsieur Guttman, a worker in fine leather, employed in a shop that supplied Lancel of the Opéra and Bond Street of the faubourg Saint-Honoré.

The notecases were passed from hand to hand during a small improvised celebration, in which the Lowenthals, third-floor right, Isidore Barsky, third-floor left and the Sterns, first-floor right, all joined.

The Lowenthals and Isidore Barsky had compared the brand-new documents with their own, which they'd been lucky enough to obtain five years earlier. They themselves, of course, were also much older. They'd arrived in about 1905, and during the "Fourteen-Eighteen War" their lives as aliens had not been easy.

The Sterns, from the first floor, had never worried about naturalization. Jews, and religious, they were only incidentally Polish, and they remained so.

A great deal of *tchaï* had flowed for the ladies that evening, and a little bit of vodka for the gentlemen (clearly too much for Isidore Barsky) in the two small second-floor apartments, whose front doors were always open onto the common landing; Maurice and Zaza, meanwhile, had gone downstairs to join the gang of neighborhood children as they did every summer evening.

Outside the house, Elie Guttman and Stépan Roginski had managed to get along in French from the very beginning. This was especially true of Elie: upon his arrival, he had found employment at Mercier Frères, fine-leather craftsmen; in his shop, the five other workers were French.

It was harder for Stépan. He had been hired even before arriving in France. His brother, Janek Roginski, a boss furrier who had set himself up in Paris on the rue d'Aboukir, had brought him from Poland. In that shop, everyone spoke a little of everything, especially Yiddish—except Janek, who spoke French and was now called Monsieur Jean.

Monsieur Jean was married to Nicole Zedkin, who was called "Madame Jean" on the rare occasions when she still showed up in the shop. His partner was Roger Ziegler, called "Monsieur Ziegler," and he was married to Liliane Leblanc, who was called nothing at all, since she'd never been seen at rue d'Aboukir.

Roginski and Ziegler were associated under the name "Fémina-Prestige." Fémina-Prestige specialized in the manufacture of fur-trimmed garments for ladies and girls.

Now, it's a fact that the manufacture of fur-trimmed garments for ladies and girls calls for finishing operations. One evening, Stépan had brought home some white collars ready to be attached to girls' coats. They were made of rabbit treated to look like ermine, and eyes had to be sewn on either side of their tiny snouts. It had occurred to him that Olga, his wife, could do this work easily, and he'd been right. Olga had called in Sonia, Elie's wife, to show her the little animals and their little eyes, and so it was that in 1923 Mesdames Roginski and Guttman became finishers who worked at home—only occasionally at first, when there was a sudden rush at Fémina-Prestige, then, little by little, as full-time professionals.

Garment bags made of black cotton cloth knotted at all four corners would arrive full in the morning and leave full that same evening. Depending on the season and the dictates of changing fashion, they were filled with dead foxes, whose sight Sonia and Olga had restored, or with moleskin neckpieces to which they had sewn small chains and large clasps covered with imitation silk.

Once, and once only, they had found a cape of real sable in one of the two garment bags, with a bronze taffeta lining they were supposed to sew in. That day they were in ecstasy. The cape went back lined. For a long time they were not to know for whom it was meant.

In any case, they were finishers who worked at home. That meant exactly what it said: they remained in their apartments at all times, never speaking to anyone but each other and always in Yiddish.

When they were at home, Messieurs Roginski and Guttman, who got along in French outside, reverted to Yiddish, to which Mesdames Guttman and Roginski replied in Yiddish and the children more and more often in French. Eventually the time came when the children no longer merely answered in French but also stopped asking questions in Yiddish. The fathers struggled to keep up with these questions. The mothers sighed and, eliminated from interesting discussions, took their revenge during sieges of measles and whooping cough, which Maurice and Zaza came down with at the same time, naturally.

Sonia Guttman and Olga Roginski could make no progress in French. Especially Olga, the younger of the two. Sonia spoke a little, but infinitely less well than Madame Lowenthal—third-floor right— who was the oldest.

Soon after arriving in France, Sonia Guttman had fallen into the habit of calling on Madame Lowenthal when the gasman, for example, came to read the meter or when Maurice, who was still in his cradle, came down with a bad cold and she couldn't do her own marketing.

Little by little, even if Maurice didn't have a cold, the custom took hold: it was Madame Lowenthal who did all the shopping on rue de la Mare and rue des Pyrénées, where her bulky silhouette was both familiar and feared.

Madame Lowenthal knew what she wanted, and especially what she didn't want. You couldn't palm off a slightly faded lettuce or a chicken without giblets on *her*.

To simplify things, Madame Lowenthal bought in bulk, and bought whatever appealed to her. Thus it happened that at the Guttmans' they ate whatever was being eaten in the Lowenthals', and—by extension —when the Roginskis moved into the building, whatever was eaten at the Guttmans' and Lowenthals' was also eaten at the Roginskis'. The only variations were to be found in the cooking time, the spices and the sauces, which Madame Lowenthal left to the invention or the culinary memory of Olga and Sonia, who had to give up their secret dreams of fish or *escalopes farcis* when Madame Lowenthal brought back the beef of the day.

It also sometimes happened that the Lowenthals, the Guttmans and the Roginskis would really eat precisely the same dish, down to the last grain of paprika. Those were the days when Madame Lowenthal woke up feeling *ruban bleu,* which was her version of *cordon bleu,* and set to work in the kitchen. She never gave any warning, and instead of raw materials, pots full of her native specialties—Madame Lowenthal came from Hungary—would appear in the small second-floor apartments. "Just taste this," she would say before vanishing, like a friend come to deliver a birthday cake for a family celebration to which she hadn't been invited.

Sonia and Olga lived in some terror of the regimen imposed by Madame Lowenthal, whose seniority in the neighborhood and status as a French citizen allowed her to be a bit dictatorial. They watched their children grow, and calculated that, soon, they would be old enough to do the shopping. . . .

But on that evening, the evening of the naturalization papers, they weren't calculating anything. They were smiling. Everyone was smiling. Even Madame Lowenthal—and especially Monsieur Lowenthal. But then Monsieur Lowenthal never stopped smiling. That way he didn't have to speak. Nobody was ever sure whether he spoke French, Yiddish or Hungarian, since the occasions for expressing himself were so sparingly doled out by his dominating wife and little encouraged at his place of work. Monsieur Lowenthal was a diamond polisher.

As for the Sterns from the first floor, though generally melancholy they were inspired by the little shot of vodka Isidore Barsky had forced on them, and began to hum softly. Unfortunately their monotonous Hebrew singsong had somewhat depressed the others—until the Prince made his entrance.

Prince Andrei Alexievitch Gromoff was what might be called the tag-along member of this group. The reasons that led him not to rejoin his Imperial regiment in 1905 had nothing to do with those that had inspired the tenants of the building to emigrate. They had more to do with the gaming tables of the casinos than with the convulsions of World History. After some fabulous bancos and some catastrophic bankruptcies, he now owned his own cab. He was resident of the Hôtel de la Gare, 42 rue de la Mare, and the card partner of Isidore Barsky, with whom he immediately began to sing *"Je sais que vous êtes jolie,"* accompanying himself on the guitar he'd taken care to bring with him.

The only tenants missing from the celebration were the Bonnets, first-floor left, opposite the Sterns. Without being really xenophobic, they didn't much like foreigners. Without being truly anti-Semitic, they didn't much like Jews. Without being absolutely chauvinistic, they detested new Frenchmen, especially if they were Jewish. The Bonnets had therefore abstained. In any case, Monsieur Bonnet, who was employed in the town hall registry office of the XXth arrondissement, liked to go to bed early. He had been gassed during the war. Since the windows on the second floor were wide open, the noise of the celebration probably disturbed him: Monsieur Bonnet had coughed more—and more loudly—than usual. But none of this had bothered the Bonnet twins, Charles and Lucien, who had gone off to join Maurice, Zaza, and the others in a half-demolished house at 21 rue Henri-Chevreau, where a fabulous treasure hunt had been going on for the last ten days.

It was shortly after this cordial evening, during which even old Madame Lutz had left her concierge's loge to put in a brief appearance, that an apparently innocuous incident had unleashed a flood of completely unforeseeable events.

: :

ONE EVENING at supper, when he had found Hungarian goulash, which he detested, on his plate yet again, Elie Guttman had become angry and slammed his fist on the table. Raising his eyes heavenward, in other words in the general direction of the third floor, he had shouted that he hadn't left his village, crossed half Europe and four frontiers on foot or chosen France as his country only to suffer within his own four walls at the hands of a *real Petliura* . . .

He had repeated the expression three times.

After which, as his dismayed wife and son looked on, he had emptied his portion of Hungarian goulash into the garbage pail. Sonia had wept.

The name "Petliura" had not fallen on deaf ears. Maurice had found the word, repeated several times, very funny, but as there was a lot of shouting going on in the kitchen at the time he hadn't dared ask any questions.

The next morning, however, he told Zaza that there was a *Pet-Lura* in the building. He couldn't tell her who it was, but a Pet-Lura was a sort of wicked witch who smelled as bad as the *pète,* or fart, in her name.

That very evening, when her mother refused her a second banana, Zaza threatened to go for Pet-Lura, and an uproar erupted on the second floor at the end of a supper that had until that moment been very peaceful.

When Olga knocked at the door of her next-door neighbors and shouted loudly, "Madame Guttman! Madame Guttman!" Sonia knew that something was very wrong even before opening it. They always used the Yiddish *du* between themselves, calling each other "Little Olga" and "Sonia, my dove," reserving the Madame Guttman and Madame Roginski, followed by the French *vous,* for their very rare moments of discord. The presence of a grave-faced Stépan standing alongside his wife confirmed her fears. Maurice was sent to play with Zaza on the other side of the landing, and the senior Guttmans and Roginskis sat down at the kitchen table. Stépan spoke first.

He was sure there were bastards in the neighborhood who were going to make trouble: the little girl had spoken the name of Simon Vassilievitch Petliura, and despite the vow they had made one another, this couldn't be ignored. Something had to be done, and fast.

The vow was simple, even simplistic. It went back to the time the two young couples had first met. Sonia had made them swear to it at the end of a beautiful March day, their first Sunday as neighbors, a day during which they had told one another many stories about their earlier lives. Their stories were so similar—and it surprised them so little! All four were in the Guttman kitchen, the window open on rue de la Mare, where nothing ever happened on Sundays. It was so calm, so reassuringly peaceful, so provincially Parisian, that Sonia, although naturally shy, had suddenly raised the liqueur glass half filled with vodka that Elie had placed in front of her and Olga—he had poured a full glass for himself and another for Stépan—and in a hushed voice had begun a little speech.

"Let's swear," she'd said.

And they had sworn.

As parents, they would be young amnesiacs, at least in front of the children. And she had pointed to the room in which Maurice was already asleep in his little iron bed, and then she had touched Olga's belly. Since they were in France, they would forget, or at least pretend to. They wouldn't be like their parents or grandparents, who had fed them the details of the pogroms of their day by the terrifying light of tallow candles, comparing them to those they had just escaped yesterday and leaving them in shuddering expectation of the next, which was sure to come. They would tell their children stories that began with "Once upon a time . . . " and not with "The last time . . . ," which never meant that it was really the last but only the one before yesterday—until, of course, the one tomorrow.

"And that's what I wanted to say!"

Embarrassed, Sonia had buried her face in her hands.

There had been a brief moment of silence, then all four stood up and sealed their pact with a chaste kiss on the mouth; they had kept their word throughout the five years that followed.

It hadn't been easy, surrounded as they were by the Sterns and the Lowenthals—to say nothing of most of the other inhabitants of rue de la Mare, who were also fond of counting off the memories of their youth.

When they felt the dangerous temptation stealing over them, Sonia and Olga would somehow get rid of the children, just as all respectable French families know how to do when that incorrigible, hardened-rake-of-a-bachelor-uncle raises his voice at dessert and announces: "And the one about the girl making her first communion? Do you know that one?"

There were no first communions in their youthful memories, but there were multitudes of violated young girls, a great deal of blood, many human screams mixed with the neighing of horses, an enormous number of burning houses, kicks, whips, stinging riding crops, flashing sabers and choruses of groans. There were also the names of brigands and gangsters, feared names handed down through the lost, dark mists of time. The sounds of the names differed, depending on whether it was in this or that part of Central Europe that these men had unleashed their drunken hordes. For every bloody Gilles de Rais or Beast of Gévaudan in French history—landmark figures in the childish terrors of French children—there were dozens and dozens of Cossack, Tatar, Polish, Hungarian or Ukrainian names that came up repeatedly in the memories of their youth.

The accidents of history came to the aid of their still-fresh memories, and Elie, Sonia, Stépan and Olga could point their fingers at the same name, that of their common torturer: Simon Vassilievitch Petliura, the hetman who had massacred thousands of his Ukrainian fellow-citizens between 1918 and 1920 and then gone off, the Red Army at his heels, to massacre thousands of Poles, especially in the Lublin region.

The truth was that it was above all to escape Petliura that the Guttmans had fled the Ukraine, just as it was above all to flee Petliura that the Roginskis had fled Poland. And that was why they had never told the children.

And now Zaza had brought up Petliura! If she recognized the name, it was because she'd heard it. And if she'd heard it, it could only have been in the streets. And if someone had mentioned his name in the streets, it was because there was pogrom in the air. And why should Petliura himself not be in Paris, crept into the neighborhood in the dead of night?

Stépan had dropped the news like a bomb, addressing Sonia, Olga and Elie simultaneously. At first he couldn't understand why, from the very beginning, from the words "Simon Vassilievitch P . . . ," Elie's face had contracted, as though in great pain, or why there followed the most thunderingly joyous laugh ever heard at 58 rue de la Mare.

Sonia, who had taken longer than Elie to connect yesterday's goulash with the imminence of a pogrom, in turn grew purple with wild laughter, which little by little spread to Olga, while the still-somber Stépan waited for an explanation.

They supplied it between gasps of laughter. Only then did Stépan understand the ridiculousness of the situation, and joined the others in a laugh all the greater because he felt in his guts the final dissolution of that old terror he'd believed he'd forgotten forever.

When they'd all calmed down they wiped their eyes, passing around the clean dishtowel used for polishing glasses. Elie confessed he'd gone a bit too far, that Madame Lowenthal wasn't all that bad. "I zaggerated . . . I zaggerated," he added—in Yiddish—to his *mea culpa.* He meant to say "exaggerated," a new word Maurice had brought back from school the week before. Then they decided something would have to be said to the children. Sonia agreed to handle it. She didn't have to call them from the landing, because they'd already come running to see just what crazy thing was going on with their parents.

Papa had said something silly yesterday evening when he'd lost his temper. He had spoken a word that must never, never be repeated. It was a vulgar word, or actually the name of somebody who was very wicked, and Madame Lowenthal was a very-very-nice lady. That Word was never, never to be used, in front of her or anyone else. It was the name of someone very bad who'd never lived—at least, he didn't live any longer. So that was that. Okay? The children didn't really think so, but they promised never to say The Word again and went back to their games. Apparently.

But only apparently.

They held a long confab in hushed voices.

First, Zaza scolded Maurice for not having told her that the building's Pet-Lura was Old Lady Lowenthal; Maurice, a bit shamefacedly, admitted it.

Then they decided they'd have to find another name if they didn't want to be spanked. But it would have to be one only they could understand: in other words, a secret.

They thought, hard. For a moment they were tempted by the idea of "Pet-Pet"—its suggestion of farting doubled them up with giggles. But they decided the code was a little too transparent.

From "Pet-Pet" they naturally slid to "Prout-Prout," which made them double up even more. They tested it for a long time.

Then suddenly Zaza thought of "Pouett-Pouett"! That broke them up.

And for good reason! They could even sing it, and all France, which was already singing a similar ditty, would join in. The only difference would be that when they hummed

> *She went "Pouett-Pouett" to me,*
> *I went "Pouett-Pouett" to her,*
> *We went "Pouett-Pouett" together,*
> *And everything was fine . . .*

as they met Old Lady Lowenthal on the stairway, they'd be the only ones in the whole country to know exactly what they were saying.

They had invented a double secret. By the time their parents sent them off to bed they were ecstatic.

: :

A MAN WHO WOULD have been astonished by Maurice and Zaza's rapture was at that very moment buying himself his sixth cognac at the bar of a *café-tabac* in the Vth arrondissement, where he had been living for quite a while. As he was leaving, the proprietor said, "Goodnight, Monsieur Boris." And the hetman Simon Vassilievitch Petliura went calmly home to sleep on the third floor of 7 rue Thénard, a small student hostel where he'd been lying low since 1921—ten minutes away from rue de la Mare, as the crow flies.

: :

ALTHOUGH THE parents' vow was strengthened by the episode, the children's secret quickly leaked out.

After two days, *"She went Pouett-Pouett to me"* was being hummed and whistled a lot on rue de la Mare, especially when the children went to buy fresh bread and just happened to come across Madame Lowenthal and her shopping baskets. In other words, after school and before lunch.

Maurice hadn't betrayed their secret, so it could only have been Zaza.

She admitted she'd given away half of it, or, to put it another way, the words and the music to hum in case one ran into Madame Lowenthal. Yes, she'd told that much to Myriam Goldberg during recess. But after all, as she pointed out to Maurice, she'd been the one who'd invented "Pouett-Pouett." As for the origin and transformation of the whole thing— from "Pet-Lura" to "Pet-Pet" and from "Pet-Pet" to "Prout-Prout" until the definitive formula was arrived at with "Pouett-Pouett"—no, she could swear to him she'd revealed nothing to that idiot Myriam Goldberg.

And it was true.

There was an important reason for Zaza's discretion, a reason that had nothing to do with the enlightenment of Myriam Goldberg: Zaza had simply forgotten the first link in the chain.

But Maurice had forgotten nothing about that evening. Not Stépan's somber expression, or his own eviction from the kitchen, or the vast amount of whispering from the other side of the landing, or the huge bursts of laughter that had followed, and especially not his mother's face when she'd delivered her speech—a speech that had been incoherent, contradictory, threatening, pleading and censored, all at the same time.

Above all, censored. Not once had his mother spoken the name she had forbidden them to speak. As a result, a little later, when he and Zaza were doubled over with laughter during their joint search for a replacement, without telling her and possibly without being aware of it himself, he'd firmly planted the three forbidden syllables in his memory.

Forbidden by their parents, who had not told them the truth, he was sure. He had felt scorned and excluded. As mysteriously excluded as on that night when, awake in the iron bed which was now unfolded for him every evening in the dining-room–finishing-shop because he no longer slept in his parents' bedroom, he'd overheard through the partition his mother and father speaking and sighing together in hoarse voices he'd never heard them use during the day. He hadn't asked them any questions the next morning, but he'd talked about it with Zaza, who admitted that both her mother and father sometimes seemed to be crying as if they were in pain, that suddenly they'd be quiet for a while and then burst out laughing for no reason she could think of. Zaza accompanied this information with a drilling motion of her index finger into her right temple, a gesture that said more than any commentary could. Maurice never talked to her about it again, but this, too, was something he'd never forgotten.

The months slipped by, and with them the craze for "Pouett-Pouett" whenever Old Lady Lowenthal went by.

Maurice had quickly tired of it, probably because, as the sole custodian of the real secrets of the rite's origins, he disliked seeing it celebrated by ignorant little parrots. Copying him, Zaza in turn ceased humming the refrain, and even went so far as to reproach Myriam Goldberg for making fun of Madame Lowenthal, who-was-a-very-very-nice-lady.

Myriam Goldberg, who much admired Zaza Roginski for her great intimacy with Moishe Guttman—which was how her grandmother, Madame Goldberg, 48 rue de la Mare, referred to Maurice—passed the word about Madame Lowenthal's great-great-niceness to Jeannot and Sami Nussbaum at number 22, who passed it on to the Novacks at number 29 and the Benedettis on rue des Pyrénées. The Bonnet twins, who had for a time whistled softly like everyone else without having in any way been let in on the secret, stopped too, even though they had not been given the good news about the great-great-niceness of Madame Lowenthal, whom Monsieur Bonnet never called anything but "the kike on the third floor"—no doubt to distinguish her more easily from the other tenants in the building.

The building in which there was soon to be something—someone—new.

O N THE SPRING of 1926, during Easter, the Clements moved into the entirely redone concierge's lodge, which for forty years had been occupied by old Madame Lutz.

Having reached retirement age—she was seventy-eight—Madame Lutz had been thanked and dismissed by Providence Urbaine, the company that owned a good part of rue de la Mare. With a great deal of urbanity—it would be hard to find a better word—Providence had undertaken the expense of repatriating the old woman to her native village in Lorraine, "which she will have the joy to find happily French once more," as Monsieur Bonnet had emphasized in a farewell speech he had written himself and personally declaimed in the name of all those he referred to as the *"occupiers* of the building."

A small ceremony had been held in the dining room-bedroom of the Bonnets; it should be noted that the whole idea and its execution had been conceived by Monsieur Bonnet, who, unwilling to enter into any personal contact with the "occupiers," had behaved like a true administrator. Taking time off during his working hours, he had handwritten a summons which he had then politely asked his colleague, Mademoiselle Bourron, to type out on the letterhead, adorned with the "Registry Office" stamp of the *Mairie* of the XXth arrondissement. The text was as follows:

Paris, April 13, 1926

Our dear Madame Lutz is leaving us! I suggest that we express our sincerest regrets to her. The function will be held on April 19 of the current year at precisely 19 hours, in the apartment of Monsieur and Madame Bonnet, first-floor left, in order to spare Madame Lutz's poor legs the effort of climbing the stairs. Since, as you know, the apartment is small, children are not invited.

Eugène Bonnet
(Military Medalist)

P.S. Madame Bonnet will see to arrangements for refreshments, and the sharing of expenses will be calculated on a pro rata basis at a later date. Thank you!

Monsieur Bonnet had simply initialed the postscript. The five summonses were slipped into five official envelopes from the *Mairie* of the XXth arrondissement, on each of which Mademoiselle Bourron had typed the names of the families, using a list prepared by Monsieur Bonnet.

When it came to the Roginskis, she had left out the *n*. That made it "Rogiski," but she skillfully corrected her error by squeezing a lower-case *n* between the *i* and the *s*, which made the patronymic of Stépan, Olga and Zaza look as if it were being strangled in the middle.

Monsieur Bonnet had sealed the envelopes, stamped them on the back with "Registry Office" and at 58 rue de la Mare turned them over to Madame Lutz with the request that she take his letters up to the tenants.

Though the arrival of the emblazoned and rubber-stamped gray-brown envelopes had at first perplexed them and made them vaguely uneasy, the reading of the invitations had delighted the Lowenthals, Isidore Barsky, the Roginskis and the Guttmans, who at eighteen hours fifty-five minutes had gathered at the Stern apartment on the first-floor right in order to be together when they made their entrance at the Bonnets', whose threshold they were to cross for the first time.

Monsieur Bonnet opened the door and, careful not to waste time in overly familiar words of welcome, rapped out a sonorous *"Bonjour,"* counted them quickly in one glance, declared, "Perfect! Since we are all here, I'll go and fetch the queen of the celebration," and rushed down the stairs.

It was Madame Bonnet who invited them in, with a simultaneously affable and charitable gesture accompanied by a loud "This way, ladies and gentlemen." The nine occupiers of the building filed in one at a time in a buzz of vague good evenings, thank yous, and very kinds that died of itself, leaving a mournful silence. Madame Lowenthal broke it by remarking that the room seemed to be larger than her own dining room.

Everyone rushed to fill the opening so judiciously offered by Madame Lowenthal, agreeing with her wholeheartedly.

Madame Bonnet then supplied an explanation: to prepare for the small crowd, Monsieur Bonnet had put all the chairs in the children's room and pushed the table, ordinarily in the center of the room, in front of the fireplace, so that she could set up the reception buffet there. She apologized for being unable to ask them to sit down, and, pointing to an enormous sofa embellished with two pillows representing a Pierrot and a Pierrette with black-satin ruffs—Isidore Barsky, an expert in secondhand furniture, immediately noted that the sofa hid a double folding bed—added with a smile: "Only our dear Madame Lutz will have the right to the pillows. *Noblesse oblige!*" The occupiers laughed politely, and silence fell again.

Sonia and Olga hadn't caught what was being said, but they had understood that in the Bonnet apartment the children had their own room, and this had bothered them.

Madame Bonnet in turn broke the silence. "I hope that my little, actually *our,* little buffet will meet with your approval, ladies and gentlemen. Monsieur Bonnet was particularly eager to have a quiche. I didn't dare make one myself, so I had this one prepared for us Au Blé d'or de Quimper," she said, all smiles.

Au Blé d'or de Quimper was a very good caterer–pastry-shop–bakery, everyone agreed—including the Sterns, who had noticed bits of ham visible under the yellow and brown swellings of the delicate crust and had already decided that they wouldn't even touch it.

"So much for the appetizer," continued Madame Bonnet. "Now, for the dessert, also from Au Blé d'or de Quimper, we have apple tarts, some 'nuns,' and both chocolate and coffee éclairs. Since I had no idea of what you like, I ordered a mixture."

Her comments were so gracious that they were on the point of saying "Thank you, it's too much, really too much," when they remembered in time that they were not only the guests but the hosts. They therefore limited themselves—at least, Elie Guttman limited himself—to congratulating her on her choice and thanking her for the trouble she had taken.

"It was nothing," she replied, adding that it had nonetheless taken several hours of work, but after all this was quite normal, seeing "Monsieur Bonnet and I were born in the neighborhood." Taking up where she had left off, she pointed out the two bottles of Julien Damoy champagne and the three bottles of Normandy cider, in the middle of which was placed a bouquet of wildflowers artistically selected to form a pretty little red, white and blue arrangement.

At this point Monsieur Bonnet made his entrance, pushing an amazed and breathless Madame Lutz in front of him. Madame Bonnet gave the signal for applause. She authoritatively seated Madame Lutz on the sofa-bed, and the old lady, wedged between the two pillows, burst into tears and hiccupped, *"Mein Gott, mein Gott."*

Madame Lutz, a Catholic from a little town in Lorraine called Kirchenberg, had for forty years made strenuous efforts to master the French language, but in moments of great emotion she relapsed into· her native tongue. She now used it only occasionally in front of the Bonnets, but was quite free with it when speaking to the others. After all, her Christian dialect wasn't so different from their Jewish one. Gasped out in her loge or on the different floors, her *Mein Gott*s would have inspired floods of tenderness in Yiddish, but here, in the Bonnet apartment, they were followed only by several suppressed sighs accompanied by slow shakes of the head, and it was Monsieur Bonnet who took the floor to read her his farewell, the peroration of which was the historical reference to Madame Lutz's return to her "little village happily once more French."

The phrase was pronounced with a circular movement of the head that indicated it was meant for all those present rather than just for the good lady from Lorraine, and was followed by a brief fit of coughing, a reminder of Monsieur Bonnet's personal contribution to the reannexation of Kirchenberg. His little cough, so familiar to the ears of the occupiers of the building, lasted only a moment, and Monsieur Bonnet ended with a charming picture of Madame Lutz surrounded by the warmth of her friends and relatives:

"And when you hear the ringing of the little bell of the tiny Quirchambert church, do not forget your friends here, who at the same time will be listening to the tolling of the great bells of Notre Dame."

This striking foreshortening, given the distance involved, enraptured his audience.

To cut short the first bursts of applause, he popped the cork on the two bottles of Julien Damoy champagne.

Twenty minutes later, the ceremony was over. Half a bottle of Normandy cider remained, along with some crumbs of the quiche

Lorraine, three éclairs—two filled with coffee cream—and two choco-late "nuns."

As they were all returning to the stairway in a polite little hubbub of thank-yous, Madame Bonnet stopped Sonia, the last to cross the threshold, and handed her the cardboard base that had been at the bottom of Au Blé d'or de Quimper's pyramidal package. On it was an assortment of bits of éclairs and "nuns," their fillings oozing from icing-covered shells.

"For the children's dessert," she said. "I've divided them up between yours and mine. As for our little accounts, I've kept the bills and we'll take care of it tomorrow."

: :

THE NEXT DAY, everything happened very quickly. At eight o'clock, Isidore Barsky and Madame Lowenthal went down to Madame Lutz's loge. She was waiting, dressed and ready, an oilskin shopping bag on her knees, sitting in a chair next to her wood-banded moleskin trunk, which Stépan and Elie had reinforced with a thick rope the previous evening, after the Bonnets' celebration. Her gaze was fixed on the floor, which was spotless because she had insisted on scrubbing it down with Eau de Javel one more time, just as she had done every morning for the last forty years.

At 8:05, Andrei Gromoff's taxi had stopped in front of 58 rue de la Mare. Prince Andrei Alexievitch had seized one of the deerskin han-dles, while Isidore Barsky grabbed the other. Between the two of them, they managed to settle the trunk on the roof of the taxi.

Madame Lowenthal took the arm of Madame Lutz, who, without so much as a glance at her buffet, her four chairs, her bed or her walls, left the loge. The women got into the rear of the taxi, while from the windows of the second and first floors, Sonia, Olga, Madame Bonnet and Madame Stern said goodbye, each in her own way.

At 8:30, Monsieur Nussbaum and Manolo, his associate at the Clig-nancourt flea market, arrived with a handcart to load the furniture Monsieur Barsky had advised them to buy back from Madame Lutz.

At 9:10, a team of two painters and a plumber, sent by Providence Urbaine, went to work in the loge, singing "O Sole Mio."

At 9:47, the train left the Gare de l'Est to take Madame Lutz back to finish her remaining years—not to say weeks—in the shadow of the belltower of Kirchenberg, where there was no longer anyone who knew her.

On the platform, Isidore Barsky, Madame Lowenthal and Andrei Alexievitch Gromoff waved their handkerchiefs. If they had tears in their eyes, it wasn't just because they were fond of Madame Lutz but also because, years earlier, a train one day brought them, too, first one and then the other, and for different reasons—to the great glass enclosure of the Gare de l'Est. In Paris, France.

At 10:15, when Gromoff and Barsky set Madame Lowenthal down on rue de la Mare, "Santa Lucia" was being sung, and pieces of brown wallpaper already littered the freshly scrubbed floor. Both men then headed for a destination which, though unknown to most, was nevertheless legendary in the neighborhood: the racetrack at Vincennes.

At eighteen hours, the two rooms plus kitchen of the loge had been primed. By nineteen hours on the next day, Sunday, a special emergency team from Providence Urbaine, no doubt handsomely rewarded, had finished doing the walls in an off-white sized paper.

In the kitchen, near the polished yellow stone sink, five small tiles of flamingly bright new porcelain had been set in among the old ones. They depicted navy-blue boats against a white background, and swore a bit at the lavender windmills on an ivory background that were all that was left of Madame Lutz's stay in the capital.

Zaza, Maurice, the Bonnet twins, Jeannot and Sami Nussbaum, Coco and Lulu Novack, Myriam Goldberg and especially Bruno and Gino Benedetti, from rue des Pyrénées, had all followed the progress of this marathon metamorphosis, achieved in forty-eight hours by the fabulous transalpine team that had good-humoredly put up with their constant intrusions.

When the job was finished, the long, black silhouette of the man who was erroneously known as the Landlord on rue de la Mare turned up. Aristide Cloutier was nothing more than a modest employee of Providence Urbaine, one among two hundred and fifty.

He inspected the site, seemed quite satisfied, took a bottle of red wine and four jelly glasses from his expandable satchel and very democratically shared a drink with the workers.

He scattered the children crowding around the open windows with a gesture, nevertheless taking time to tell them:

"Tomorrow, you'll find two new friends here, a girl and a boy."

: :

THOUGH THE BOYS on rue de la Mare shared their games, their treasure hunts, their transitory catchwords, their recreation period, the same landlord and—with the exception of the Bonnet twins—parents who had accents, kitchens that emitted the same cooking smells, the same Dr. Kauffman and—the Bonnet twins once more excluded—the same Monsieur Florian, the admirable Monsieur Florian who never stumbled over foreign names and who, in the memory of all of them, would always remain their irreplaceable first teacher, it was with Zaza and Zaza alone that until then Maurice had shared what grownups pompously call their inner life.

Nocturnal terrors related in the morning, their first amazement about birth, death and sex, the flowers and the seasons, the moon, the snow, money, the big soap bubble that suddenly bursts while the next very fragile one floats out the window and must certainly have flown to join the red balloon that one let go the other day on the Buttes, just to see . . . and why you didn't have a grandmother the way Myriam Goldberg did, and why Monsieur and Madame Stern don't cook on Saturdays, and what the catechism was, and why the rabbi never comes to our house, and just what was a rabbi? and why does the big sister of the Novacks have a big belly? All these observations, all these personal questions, all these things one asked the grownups, their answers and lack of answers, their omissions and "becauses," Maurice shared with Zaza, just as he had shared his whooping cough, his stroller and his diapers. And even if she sometimes betrayed the shared secrets, it was with her, nonetheless, that he first tried to share them.

Maurice, at seven, was an only child with a small five-year-old sister and friends his own age, and he was really the only one who properly understood Aristide Cloutier's magic words. Tomorrow, in a tiny but dazzlingly white palace, would appear a girl and a boy looking for a friend.

: :

IT WAS VERY EARLY one morning, at the Gare de Lyon, that the Clément family entered Paris. They were from Savoy: Jeannette, a housewife, was twenty-seven. Félix Clément, a postman, was twenty-eight, and his appointment to Paris's XXth arrondissement was a handsome promotion. Robert was going on eight, and Josette was six.

As they got out of the train, Aristide Cloutier, who had immediately spotted them in the crowd of travelers thanks to the tag sent by Providence Urbaine when they were hired, was delighted to see that all four were sturdy, sun-tanned, reserved and smiling. And well organized, to boot: no little bundles, no valises, just knapsacks. Their furniture had been shipped and registered forty-eight hours earlier, and the Paris-Lyons-Mediterranean Company would deliver it early that morning. Aristide Cloutier gave them their first Métro lesson, and at 7:30 they entered their apartment—as Monsieur Cloutier had been asked to call the loge henceforth, given the fact that Félix was a postman and not a concierge. Cloutier began to recite the list of their duties as concierges anyway, but Félix interrupted him and completed it on his own. He knew exactly what Jeannette would have to do, what he would have to do when he wasn't busy at the Post Office—and he also knew what could not be demanded of either one of them. Apparently they had studied the problem carefully, weighting the pros and cons before accepting the offer, which had the special advantage of providing them with a rent-free apartment in Paris. He smiled, speaking slowly in a mountain accent. Jeannette smiled too, and said nothing. The children smiled and watched their father. Monsieur Cloutier realized the interview was over when he saw Jeannette undo her knapsack and, without having to fumble around, take out a thermos she set down on the kitchen sink, saying, "Come along, children." He then opened his own expandable satchel and took out a green folder on which was written, in big, black letters, "La Mare, Building Number 58." He withdrew a sheet of Providence Urbaine stationery listing the names of the tenants, followed by the floors they lived on and whether they were to the right or left of the landing. He handed it to Félix, who glanced at it as Cloutier started to say something about how difficult it was to decipher certain spellings, but once again Félix cut him short with a smile.

"I'm a postman, Monsieur, and I'm used to family names."

"Well then, I'll be getting along," said Monsieur Cloutier.

"Fine," said Félix, opening the glass-paneled door.

Somewhat frustrated at having been unable to give his usual fine paternalistic performance, generally so well received elsewhere, Aristide Cloutier called out to these four Savoyards who were setting foot in Paris for the first time:

"Until next week, then. I'll drop by to see how you're getting along."

And he left. Jeannette opened all the windows. The smell of paint was really very strong.

Their arrival was so unobtrusive, the unloading and installation of their furniture and the two big packing cases of clothing and dishes so rapid and silent, blending with the familiar early-morning noises, that nobody on the floors above was really aware of the new presence—that of the Cléments—in the building. Elie, Stépan, Monsieur Lowenthal and Monsieur Stern had left for work at seven, as they did every morning. And as he did every morning, Barsky slept on. Mesdames Stern and Lowenthal were busy with their housework. Madame Bonnet was giving the twins breakfast, Sonia was giving Maurice breakfast, Olga was giving Zaza breakfast and no one was in a hurry because it was the Easter vacation break.

And so it was Monsieur Bonnet—who always left for work at eight-thirty because, in every kind of weather, for the good of his bronchial tubes, he made it a practice to walk along rue des Pyrénées as far as Place Gambetta—who was the first to knock at the pane of the glazed door and give the final touch to Jeannette Clément's new functions. He knocked, partially opened the door, and called out:

"Bonnet! First-floor left. Good morning. Please give these envelopes to the persons named thereon. Have a good day!"

Félix had already gone off to introduce himself to his superiors at the Post Office. Jeannette was standing between two open packing cases. She had scarcely caught a glimpse of Monsieur Bonnet, who'd already closed the door, when she found the five envelopes in her hand. Sky-blue and ornately addressed in mauve ink, they bore the names on the list Monsieur Cloutier had given to Félix, who had tacked it up near the door. Every name except Bonnet. The envelopes were embellished in the bottom right-hand corner with the word "local," which left her bemused.

It was Robert who was given the task of distributing the letters among the three floors, which she as yet lacked the courage to confront. Robert took his little sister Josette by the hand and went off to knock at the doors of these unknowns to whom they were bringing the results of the scrupulous calculations—prorated down to the last centime and accompanied by copies of the bills from Au Blé d'or de Quimper and Julien Damoy—of the contribution due from each for Madame Lutz's farewell celebration.

Maurice opened the door at the Guttmans'.

By ten o'clock, Josette had joined Zaza and Myriam Goldberg in a game of hopscotch, and Robert was playing prisoner's base on the empty lot that had now replaced the completely demolished house at 10 rue Henri-Chevreau. On the large blind wall of the building next door someone had painted a giant portrait of Dr. Pierre, the illustrious toothpaste creator: Robert's first lesson in advertising. By noon, white curtains, crocheted and starched, adorned the three windows and the glazed door of the loge.

*T*HE SNOW, the thicket, two grandfathers and two grandmothers, an uncle Charles, aunts named Marie, Germaine and Louise,
boy and girl cousins, climbers' huts that smelled of pine, fireplaces with
big logs, a postman who made his rounds on skis, ski wax, mulberry jam,
Englishmen who fell through crevasses, eggs slurped down raw, a wolf
slaughtered by the villagers one day, a frozen creek you could walk
across, last year's avalanche, the hurricane lamp, clotted milk, overshoes,
wedding breakfasts, German campers who swam in the raw, socks knit-
ted by your great-grandmother, "monks"—hot-water bottles you put in
your bed to warm it—the big round loaf of bread that lasted a whole
week, snow that iced over, the feel of grappling irons beneath
snowshoes, the reappearance of grass and cows and sheep, sheepskin
worn under your hooded cape, the porcelain stove in the classroom, the
Post Office in the *Mairie* and the house alongside the Post Office and the
school in the *Mairie*, too, and the class with only nine pupils . . .

To Maurice, who was beginning to read the books Monsieur Florian
had lent him, Robert Clément was a combination of Jack London and
Charles Nodier, two writers who'd taken a firm hold in both his house
and his life. He listened over and over again to the singsong voice and
the strange new accent—and to the new words: monks who weren't
monks, cracks that weren't caused by chilblains, a wolf who didn't
come out of La Fontaine; wax *(fart)* that wasn't the cold cream *(fard)*
used by the Novacks' big sister. He listened because he himself had
nothing to say—it was all there, right in front of him, there between

rue des Pyrénées and rue Henri-Chevreau and in the three floors of their building.

Maurice was inseparable from Robert, who was amazed at his amazement, and still more amazed that he was the one doing the teaching in this big city that had so frightened him before he'd joined the game of prisoner's base, just three hours after arriving in Paris.

Where the girls were concerned, things were very different. You had to have asphalt on which to chalk Heaven and Hell for hopscotch. From the beginning of the game, Zaza had taken over Josette and almost simultaneously rejected Myriam Goldberg. The latter's disfavor was made clear early in the afternoon, when Zaza asked only Josette to come upstairs "to see our mamas work," saying casually to Myriam Goldberg, "You've already seen, and anyway it would be too crowded."

And so it was that the little mountain girl discovered the world of open doors on the second-floor landing—Olga and Sonia together in the Roginski dining room; all the different-colored bobbins and left-over scraps of gray and navy-blue sateen from the linings of girls' and ladies' coats; and the pile of six carefully folded heavy blue-black peter-sham coats with gilded buttons—and on such a hot day!—waiting on the large square of black cotton, while those still to be finished lay in a heap at the feet of Olga and Sonia, who took turns doing the buttons and buttonholes.

These mamas had accents of a kind Josette had never heard—and Olga gave her a present: an unmatched fox eye she took from a Florent licorice box where, among the black-headed pins, she kept a scrap of white tulle and one of Zaza's milk teeth.

: :

THE ADJUSTMENT was not quite so fast for the older Cléments. Félix had been assigned a route elsewhere in the arrondissement, and was learning the streets. Jeannette, who'd been horribly worried about her status among all these well-established Parisians, found them very kind and understanding toward a "foreigner." At the beginning, she had, of course, fallen into the clutches of Madame Lowenthal, who tried hard to have her take over where Sonia and Olga had left off. Jeannette did so, but in a very different way from what was expected by the pensioned-off administrator. She took into account Madame Lowenthal's recommendations and ukases for and against the storekeepers she pointed out to Jeannette during an introductory trip along rue de la

Mare and rue des Pyrénées—an excursion they made the day after the Cléments arrived, during the course of which, interestingly enough, Au Blé d'or de Quimper was denounced as a "den of thieves." Very quickly, however, Jeannette sorted things out for herself and, having done so, turned over to Robert the little lists which, though he didn't have to translate them as Maurice had to do with Sonia's, nevertheless sent the two boys in search of the same items—minus paprika, cumin and Malosol pickles for Robert.

They quickly got into the habit of leaving the girls to themselves. This was a first for the boys. And for the girls, too.

: :

THE MORNING of May 26, 1926—it was only many years later that they verified the exact date—Maurice and Robert set off to do some errands. As they passed the Auvergnat's café, it seemed to Maurice that there was something of a hubbub inside, centering around Barsky, although it was quite normal for him to be in the bistro at this hour. On the other hand, at the corner of rue des Cascades, Messieurs Nussbaum, Goldberg and Katz were gravely discussing something, which *was* very unusual. At ten in the morning, that crew were generally working.

If he'd been alone or with Zaza, Maurice would have listened in on their conversation, which was in Yiddish, but with Robert around he didn't feel like it, so the boys went on up the street.

When they reached rue des Pyrénées, they heard a voice shouting words they couldn't quite make out at first, except for a kind of continuously repeated refrain: "Get *Le Matin*!" As they got closer to the Métro entrance, they heard the rest: "Political assassination right here in Paris! Get *Le Matin*! Scores settled between foreigners! Get *Let Matin*! White Russian assassinated in Paris! Get *Le Matin*! Fanatic takes his revenge! Get *Le Matin*!"

The vendor was hoarse and overworked. Bundles of newspapers were still tied up on the sidewalk, and a dirty piece of torn blue paper hid the headlines. On a folding chair in front of him a loose stack of newspapers was shrinking rapidly. He collected the money with one hand, thrusting it into a wallet that he wore bandolier style; with the other hand he held against his chest a copy of the paper, on which the latest news was displayed in banner type.

Maurice stopped hearing the street noises, the clink of coins, the barking of the vendor. Alone in the crowd, muffled in a cottony silence, he deciphered the name which, just for him, shone like the flash of a dagger in the middle of the headline. "YESTERDAY EVENING IN PARIS, HETMAN PETLIURA ASSASSINATED BY A COMPATRIOT." When he was able to hear the street noises again, the clinking of the coins as they fell into the wallet, the barking of the vendor, he also heard Robert's voice asking "What's the matter?" But he didn't answer.

: :

HE DIDN'T ANSWER because what was clashing in his head was unutterable, communicable to no one. It was such a diverse mixture of ideas that he was unable to arrange them in any order of importance, and it wasn't until many years later—in fact, not until that day when he and Robert looked up the exact date on which Petliura was executed by Samuel Schwarzbard—that, helped by the passage of time and a grown man's vocabulary, he could finally tell his friend about that moment they had lived through together yet worlds apart.

He remembered it so well that he even went so far as to say to Robert, "When you asked me what was wrong, I almost answered, 'I know him.' "

It was true. And perhaps that was really the problem—the enormous shock he had received reading the name forbidden and censored by Sonia. In that choked-back "I know him," replaced by silence, there was a kind of pride in being personally involved in a bloody assassination, pride for no other reason than that he knew the name of the victim before, suddenly and for everyone, it became famous. At the same time there was the discovery of the missing *i*, from Pet-Lura to Petliura. The incongruity of the invention of "Pouett-Pouett" would not shock him until later.

But what dominated this chaos of impressions above all else was the fact that his mother had lied. Petliura existed. And the proof was that he'd been killed.

But that morning he said nothing to Robert. They went off to do their errands, and he didn't buy the paper. Elie Guttman and Stépan Roginski took turns bringing one home when they came in from work each evening.

When they got to the house, Maurice told Robert he'd be right back, and climbed to the second floor with his shopping basket. All the way home he had tried to think of some simultaneously striking and accusatory phrase to hurl at Sonia. He'd found nothing. He'd hesitated between the style of "Unhappy woman! You are lost! I know all!"— picked up from a caption under an illustration showing a woman weeping as a man brandished a letter in front of her—and the more sober style of "The Pope is dead," from a eulogy Monsieur Florian had read them before the Christmas vacation.

When he went into the kitchen, Sonia was busy washing the floor. She was on her knees, and her back was to him. He had time to say only: "Petliura has been . . . " On the word *been*, the damp, twisted rag stung his bare legs at Sonia's level; hearing him pronounce the forbidden name, she had whirled around in a fury without giving him time to explain. Just then a loud, familiar voice was heard on the landing. He ran out of the kitchen and down the stairs. Robert was standing in front of the windows of the loge, watching the girls jump rope. Josette and Myriam Goldberg—once more returned to a state of grace—held the handles, and Zaza, in the middle, was jumping "vinegar."

: :

THE CRIME of the day had been discussed at Mercier Frères when the five leather workers, one after another, arrived at the shop in the morning, but it was given no more emphasis than any of the crimes that had occurred weeks or months earlier. In fact probably a little less, since both the protagonists in the drama were foreigners. Only Levesque had read the headlines—the others had merely heard the vendors shouting. From what he'd read, Levesque had been especially struck by the fact that it had all happened on rue Racine. He greeted Dubos, who lived on the Cour de Rohan, with a "So they did someone in, in your neighborhood, huh?"

"You'd think they could do their dirty work in their own country," Dubos had replied.

When Elie Guttman arrived a little later, they were already talking of something else. He'd read the paper, and was relieved not to have to explain things about which the others were apparently incurious. They had never been curious, and Elie was grateful for that. From his first day at Mercier Frères they had grown used to his silent working habits, his questions about vocabulary and his requests for explanations when he wanted to join in the laughter over a joke he had failed to grasp. They called him neither Elie nor Guttman, but "Lilyich," a single, affectionate reference to his distant origins—and perhaps unconsciously also to Vladimir Ilyich Lenin, whose glorious destiny was not, however, a major concern of the Mercier Frères employees: for the Mercier brothers never gave their workers reason to contemplate revolution.

They were what is called good bosses. They had a model to follow. In the middle of the last century, Grandfather Fabien Mercier "had left Cahors on foot, wearing wooden clogs and rolling his tanner's barrel before him. And since he and his barrel had arrived safely in Paris, it proved two things: Grandfather Fabien was a man of courage, and his barrel was made of sturdy stuff." Elie had heard these words so often from the lips of Paul Mercier that, despite his halting French, he could recite them faultlessly. Fabien had progressed very quickly from barrels to wooden trunks, and then from wooden trunks to leather ones. His son Adrien had taken over the leather trunks, abandoned the street stall on rue Papin and set himself up with a worker and an apprentice on the first floor of an old private house near the corner of rue Blondel and rue Saint-Martin. From leather trunks he had progressed to valises, dressing cases and women's handbags.

Adrien's sons, Paul and Julien, had become Mercier Frères. They employed six specialized workers and no longer handled the leather themselves. And though in the large workshop to the right of the landing one could smell the skins of animals from all over the world, as well as lanolin and glue, in Paul Mercier's office to the left of the landing the air was heavy with the perfume of pepper and sandalwood. A trunk of light-colored wood with brass fittings rested on the dark-red pile carpet, alongside the imposing desk and the two mahogany chairs. Since it was open, one could see into the pinkish-brown interior, and the mingling of the two odors spoke of distant voyages. The trunk— made by the first Mercier and no doubt forgotten or never paid for by some captain of the Imperial Navy who had been absentminded or had died at sea—stood there to remind the saddlers who came from fancy neighborhoods to place orders with Mercier Frères that members of the Mercier family, before they had taken to playing with Waterman pens with retractable points, had worked with their hands.

Julien Mercier was rarely seen. He was responsible for the acquisition of skins from all over France, even from Europe. But whenever he passed through Paris, he'd begin by closeting himself for a few hours in the office with his brother; then, in the late afternoon, he'd sail into the workshop carrying three bottles of Cahors, of which there was a constantly renewed supply in the cellar of the old house. He came to have a drink with the men. He'd feel the skins suspended from nails, look over a new model that was being worked on, examine sketches for work being specially ordered, have one last drink and announce soberly: "And now I'm going to take Popol to the circus." This invariably made the whole workshop resound with laughter.

The first time he'd heard Monsieur Julien's little joke, Elie had joined in the laughter just to be like everyone else. A month later, after Monsieur Julien had left, he plucked up enough courage to ask for an explanation. Dédé Meunier undertook to supply it. No, Monsieur Julien wasn't going to take his brother Paul to the Cirque Médrano. After Monsieur Julien had gone downstairs, he'd "go upstairs" . . . with a little rue Blondel tart he knew well and never failed to pay his respects to after settling accounts with his brother. That's the way it was—she was a good kid, and everybody thought it was rather nice.

Elie had smiled and nodded his head politely, but actually he'd been shocked. He'd never completely forgotten the smirk with which a cop had pointed out the way to rue Blondel after he'd deciphered the slip of paper held out to him by this young man—mute and obviously a foreigner—on the first morning he'd presented himself at Mercier Frères. Nor had he forgotten his surprise when, on leaving at six o'clock that evening, he'd found that same street, which had looked so innocent in the morning, transformed into a human cattle market by nightfall. He'd gotten used to it; naturally, he knew the girls at the end of the street and would smile at them as he passed, but he'd sworn never to let Sonia come and pick him up after work, as she'd suggested in the early days. He himself had never "gone upstairs." One evening, however, he thought he had spotted Barsky having an amorous exchange a little further up the street, and he'd been shaken: he'd never mentioned the matter to anyone back on rue de la Mare—except of course to Stépan, but then Stépan worked on rue d'Aboukir . . .

And so the Merciers were what are called good bosses. They had a model to follow: Grandfather Fabien had been a Communard, and their father, Adrien, a Dreyfusard. Julien, who didn't just visit brothels on his travels, had learned to know the world, and people from other countries. He was no xenophobe, and he and Paul had speeded up the joint naturalization of the Guttmans and the Roginskis considerably by asking their cousin Martial Mercier—a Socialist deputy from the Lot —to help the process along.

And since Paul Mercier was a good boss and had read the newspaper, on that particular morning he'd stuck his head into the workshop and called out "Everything okay, Guttman?", which let Elie know his employer had fully understood the importance the news item might have for him. A little later, Dédé Meunier, noticing his friend looked a bit down in the mouth, had tried to make him smile.

"So the Russkis are killing one another off, are they? Why the fuck should that bother you? After all, you're not a Russki anymore, you're a Fransusski now!" he'd said, giving Elie an affectionate jab in the ribs.

: :

AT FÉMINA-PRESTIGE there was so much talk, and all of it so loud, that by the time Stépan got to rue d'Aboukir nobody could understand anybody else. He'd left Elie at the exit of the Strasbourg–Saint-Denis Métro, paid no attention to the newspaper vendors and, unlike Elie, hadn't stopped at a newsstand; in short, he got the news in bits and pieces by asking precise questions of the eight furriers, who for all intents and purposes had already decided what charges would be brought against Samuel Schwarzbard at his trial.

Initially, Stépan retained only one piece of information from the babble of commentaries and explanations, and that was not the name of Samuel Schwarzbard, which he scarcely heard. No, the terrifying and insane fact, unimaginable and yet something he'd imagined several months earlier, was the materialization of Petliura in Paris, a piece of news of which Zaza had actually been the innocent herald. At the time Guttman had treated him like a madman and, to calm him, had invented that grotesque story about the Lowenthal goulash, but now it was all clear: if the child had really spoken, it was because there was never smoke without fire. He went over all this in his head and, having asked the name of the assassin again, began to wonder if this Schwarzbard wasn't that cousin of the Novacks, a bright-eyed, dark-haired young man whom he had seen one day emerging nervously from the Auvergnat's and who, for no apparent reason, had raced off and disappeared down rue Henri-Chevreau. From that point it was but a single step— which Stépan's feverish imagination had no difficulty taking—to conclude that Petliura's execution had been conceived on his very own street, and that the plan, still in embryo, whispered about by Coco and Lulu Novack, hawked around and repeated to Sami and Jeannot Nussbaum, had finally been picked up by Zaza. And the enormous fear he'd felt the year before gripped him once again. Because if Petliura had been able to get to France, the others, all the others, were there too, and were going to emerge from the shadows. He told himself all this as he stood alone in his corner and slipped on his work smock.

The cutters and furriers made more and more noise, impudently putting off the moment when they would have to pick up the big scissors, the razor blades, the small hammers and the tiny nails that awaited them on the shop's large tables. Monsieur Jean appeared.

Twice he called out "Quiet!" in French, and in the immediately rees-tablished silence he said, "And now let's get to work!" rapping it out curtly and in Yiddish. He went back up to the offices he shared with Roger Ziegler on the floor above, and half an hour later Mademoiselle Anita, the administrative secretary of Fémina-Prestige, came into the shop and murmured to Stépan that Monsieur Jean wanted to see him. Stépan got up and followed her. This was so unusual that the whole shop watched him leave, staring the way schoolchildren do when a monitor comes to take somebody in the class to the principal's office.

It was common knowledge that, though Stépan was the brother of Janek Roginski, who was called Monsieur Jean, he had no familial contact with the bosses. Those who'd been with the firm longest well remembered Stépan's arrival at the shop one day in February or March 1921. Roginski had just established a partnership with Ziegler. Those were still the days when the proud Venetian-blond head of Madame Jean could be seen bending over the account books at the end of the month. That morning, Mademoiselle Anita had ushered a blushing young man into the shop. Monsieur Jean followed behind and made a short speech, half-French, half-Yiddish, to inform them that he had brought in a new man, whose name was Roginski but who was to be called Stépan—that he hoped he would make a good furrier but that, if he didn't, he would be told so in no uncertain terms and, if necessary, have his ass shown the door. Stépan was a good furrier, he had not had his ass shown the door, he was never called Roginski, Madame Jean had never been seen to say so much as a word to him and he had never been seen to go up to Monsieur Jean's office.

: :

JANEK HAD had two reasons for bringing Stépan to France: an urgent need for specialized craftsmanship, linked with the somewhat tardy fulfillment of a promise made one night in a small Polish village to a little eleven-year-old brother, who sobbed because he was leaving.

Against his wife's advice, despite his wife's angry outbursts, ignoring his wife's fits of sulkiness, Janek ended up sending off a letter offering employment as well as money for Stépan's trip.

Seeing that she had been unable to win out over what she called the "shtetl Polacks," Nicole Roginski had taken the matter in hand. She had instructed Mademoiselle Anita to find an apartment as modest as it was distant from Neuilly-sur-Seine, where the Roginskis had just moved. Mademoiselle Anita had turned to the Providence Urbaine agency and settled everything herself after a personal visit to rue de la Mare. When Janek had told his wife the date of his brother's arrival and urged her to accompany him to the Gare de l'Est, she had refused, and requested Mademoiselle Anita to be so kind as to join Monsieur Jean in what she had smilingly called the welcoming committee.

That morning, leaving the apartment on rue Charles Laffitte, he had slammed the door. He'd left behind a superb, dazzling and perfumed Nicole, spreading her toast with an orange marmalade that went well with the lace of her salmon-colored dressing gown. He'd met Mademoiselle Anita, who had already purchased the platform tickets. And it was in the company of this modest creature dressed in gray, her lusterless chignon knotted at the nape of her neck, that he saw a smiling young man wearing boots and a leather cap descend from a third-class carriage. In one hand he held a big garnet-colored bundle, with the other the hand of a child-wife whose face could barely be seen under her white cotton babushka, but whose swelling belly was very much in evidence beneath a black skirt.

The boots, the cap, the wine-colored bundle, the girl's big belly, the dust and odor of the train clinging to their clothes, the gratitude and the fearful timidity in the eyes of these strangers, made it quite clear that they'd come from a little daily hell, whose details Janek immediately realized nothing in the whole world would make him want to hear. And thinking, "The bitch was right," he embraced his brother and sister-in-law—who, assuming that Mademoiselle Anita was their own sister-in-law, had already clutched her to their bosoms. The misunderstanding was quickly rectified. Mademoiselle Anita had been very pleased by the mistake, but Janek explained that, since his wife was not well, his secretary would show them to their Paris home. He left them at the Métro entrance and took a cab to rue d'Aboukir.

Years had passed. Olga had never met Nicole. Nicole and Janek had never seen Zaza.

: :

JANEK WAS STANDING behind his desk, on which, among the samples of cloth, the invoices and a leather blotting pad, a place of honor had been assigned to a silver frame, of which Stépan saw only the back. Mademoiselle Anita left, closing the door behind her, but she could hear Monsieur Jean's angry voice asking Stépan a question; she had no trouble realizing it wasn't very pleasant, even though she didn't understand any Yiddish. Translated, it meant, "Who's the young fool who's made the shit hit the fan by killing this old idiot right in the heart of Paris?"

Stépan made no reply, and Janek continued, "He's not only spread the shit around the country generally, but on top of that he's dragged it into my place. And that's not all! You tell your friends in the shop that they'd better not draw attention to themselves, because since this little prick of a Ukrainian crossed the border illegally just so he could gun down another Ukrainian prick who also got in illegally, in about an hour rue d'Aboukir will be swarming with cops who'll make them sweat when they start checking papers. And I'll be doing some sweating myself. You're not all legal down there, either!"

Stépan was about to reply that he'd been a French citizen for a year now, but Janek didn't give him the time.

"If fools like myself have gone to the trouble of seeing to it that idiots who weren't able to take care of themselves in their own country have something to eat, it wasn't so some good-for-nothing fake Ukrainian could mess things up by playing hero because he unearthed some Cossack prick whose name nobody even remembers!"

"Shut up, Janek! Shut up or or I'll kill you!" said Stépan, bursting into sobs.

Stupefied, Janek stared at his weeping young brother, who, little by little, began to talk.

Everything came back to him. He finally blurted out what he'd had on his mind for so long—so long that it almost went back to the time he was eleven.

It was a hodgepodge that included their parents, his fear, the long wait in the shtetl, the time before Petliura and the time during Petliura, Stépan's happiness with Olga, their unbelievable joy when the letter came from Paris, Olga's belly, which was as big as the bundle that had been quickly put together for their departure, the unbelievable unhappiness of their arrival, and Mademoiselle Anita and the first Métro ride, Olga's belly, which Sonia had touched so tenderly when they had all four sworn that they'd never tell their children of the horror but would continue to recount it to one another because it was impossible to forget, and the information that that prick of a Cossack whose name Janek couldn't remember was called Pet-li-ura—he rapped out the syllables, repeating them three times—and that he might very well have cut Janek's balls off if he, Janek, hadn't already left the country, and more power to Schwarzbard who had avenged them all, those down-stairs in the shop, their grandparents, the people on rue de la Mare, where Janek had never wanted to set foot and where Olga and Sonia were going blind sewing those shitty phony eyes on his goddamned silver foxes so that when he got home he could still smell the fur—and all of it just to make money for Fémina-Prestige, which didn't deserve to be avenged by Schwarzbard, neither him, Janek, nor his bitch of a wife!

His bitch of a wife! His bitch of a wife! He was shouting. He had come around to the other side of the desk and was pointing his finger at Nicole, smiling in her silver frame.

: :

HE WENT back to the shop and started to work. He felt better. Curiously enough, he was no longer afraid, but he was eager to get home.

: :

AFTER STÉPAN had left the office, slamming the door behind him, Janek stood motionless for a while. Opening the window, he had stood gazing down at the cheerful and sunny rue d'Aboukir for a long time. Then he had closed the window and sat down at his desk. He hadn't called for Mademoiselle Anita, hadn't tried to find out if Roger Ziegler had come in. He had placed his hands on the black leather blotter, into the four corners of which, every morning, Mademoiselle slid a new sheet of pink blotting paper bearing the name and address of the firm. Sandwich men on the Grands Boulevards had for some time been distributing these blotters every Thursday to schoolchildren enjoying their half holiday. It was one of Nicole's ideas. A good one. For a moment he considered his wife's admirable face. The bitch, his brother had said as he slammed the door. He too had often slammed the door. But that bitch, that slut—he loved her, and he owed her everything.

*C*Y FATHER left St. Petersburg because Lucien Guitry ran off with him the way some men run off with ballet dancers . . . " This was one of the favorite sayings of Nicole Judith Victoria Anna Zedkin, now Madame Roginski. She'd already been dropping it into conversations in the days of the small shop on rue Pierre-Demours, in the XVIIth arrondissement, when her father had his back turned and she was helping customers pass the time while Janek was in the back preparing to fit a moleskin or squirrel coat.

Now that old Zedkin was dead, the rue Pierre-Demours place sold, rue d'Aboukir prospering and the association of Roginski Furs–Ziegler Garments flourishing, there were more frequent opportunities to relate the astonishing odyssey of the late Piotr Zedkin. Nicole seized them with charm and skill at moments when conversation lagged during the business dinners Ziegler and Roginski organized for buyers from the provinces, or when Augustin Leblanc, a Troyes hosier who had financed Fémina-Prestige and was Liliane Ziegler's papa, took the two young couples out to dine at Lucas Carton.

But, after 1926, given the new five-room apartment in Neuilly and the uniformed maid, she was able to entertain, and as an accomplished hostess she considered it her duty to enliven her dinners, and she did so with family stories that became more and more Imperial Russian as the aides-de-camp and the ladies-in-waiting of the unfortunate Romanovs descended on Paris and were to be found in every home. As they were also to be found in the homes of resellers of furs, silver and jewels,

Nicole Roginski had picked up several Siberian sables that were still in good shape, and some signed objets d'art by Fabergé. The sables were disassembled on rue d'Aboukir, the Fabergés repatriated to Neuilly.

As a result, when the Roginskis now gave dinners it was always around a circular table covered with a white embroidered cloth from the center of which rose a large egg of champagne-colored enamel that seemed to be suspended in the air, smooth and hermetic, because the three claws of fine gold on which it rested were so unobtrusive. Even less obtrusive was the small, unfaceted cabochon ruby hidden under the base of the egg, by means of which it could be made to open into four equal sections, like an orange. Nicole would wait until everybody was seated, and then, as casually as she might have removed her napkin ring, she would press on the ruby. The large egg would open slowly to the sound of three distinct harpsichord notes, and reveal its secret in the form of totally anachronistic midnight-blue ramekins containing nothing more than salt, pepper and various mustards. Everyone would go, "*Oh,*" and Nicole would modestly acknowledge the general amazement.

"An old thing from Papa's days . . . but using it for condiments was my own idea," she'd say.

And, quite naturally, she'd follow this up with St. Petersburg, Lucien Guitry and rue de la Paix.

According to Nicole Judith Victoria Anna, Piotr Zedkin had been the best furrier-tailor in all the Russias. He had so charmed the actor Lucien Guitry with the cut of his long fur-lined cloaks and his dramatic collars that when it came time for the great artist to bid his last farewell to St. Petersburg's Grand Theatre, he had implored the czar to grant him the unique privilege of having the man he called "the Rodin of fur" go along with him to France.

The discussion with the sovereign had been a heated one, and since no one at court wanted to see this rare bird fly the coop, the response to the petition had been delayed. As a result, in one of those whimsical gestures so common with him, Lucien Guitry had shown up at Piotr's house one dark night, roused him from bed, dressed him and literally propelled him onto the back seat of a troika in which a small child lay asleep; then, with the crack of a coachman's whip and a gallop down the Nevski Prospect, they were in the train, which had already started. The child on Piotr's knees woke up. Needless to say, it was little Sasha.

In Paris, the news had spread like wildfire that Lucien Guitry had brought a genius back with him after his long stay in the City of White

Nights. There were schemes to get Piotr away from him. Piotr, somewhat bored with always working in the same style and weary of the whims of the great actor, had finally broken with him and chosen old Charles Frédéric Worth, who opened his prestigious upholstered salons on rue de la Paix to him.

At this point in her story, Nicole Judith Victoria Anna Roginski would rattle off the names of all the society women and demimondaines over whose shoulders our Rodin had poured cascades of chinchilla, mink, ermine, squirrel, broadtail, leopard, astrakhan, panther, otter, opossum, nutria and—needless to say—sable. She would by now have reached 1894, the date she'd more or less determined on as when Piotr Zedkin had set up on his own at the "Palais de l'Hermine."

After that the chronology became a bit misty, the topography of Paris more imprecise. They were no longer on rue de la Paix but they weren't far off, and then at a given moment, which was never assigned a date, she made her own entrance. She was born. She described herself as being already half grown as she wandered through her papa's fitting rooms. Of her "poor Mama," "who was so beautiful," she said very little, but always while letting her fingers slip dreamily over a gold serpent bracelet she wore coiled above her elbow, its flat, triangular head sparkling with two little emerald eyes. Everyone understood that, though the egg came from Papa, the bracelet was Mama's. She often ended with an amusing anecdote that explained three of her names (she censored the Judith).

Nicole, which was so French—right out of Molière—had been chosen because Piotr, who was still very attached to his native land, had wanted to give his daughter a name that was the feminine version of Nicolas. Victoria was in honor of the Worth family, which was itself very attached to its native Albion, and Anna was once more the steppes, the birch forests, Karenina and—needless to say, above all—her poor Mama: "Anna, Aniouta, Aniouchka, as Papa used to say, and as I am still sometimes called by my great Slav of a husband . . . "

The business about the Slav husband was the final touch that buried the truth as to the true origins of Monsieur Jean, whose accent, for those who were not connoisseurs, could as easily evoke the pageantry of the Winter Palace as the muddy lanes of a shtetl on the outskirts of Lublin.

And to indicate that the meal was really about to begin, she would coo, "*Douchka*, suppose you give our guests some wine. Enough of these old stories!"

Her audience, generally consisting of two or three traveling salesmen from Elbeuf, Lyons or Tourcoing, accompanied by their wives, would turn, still dazzled, to the great Slav and hold out the cut-crystal glasses, and the little maid would make her entrance—just when one was really expecting gypsies.

: :

. . . JANEK LOOKED at the ten-year-old photo of his wife's wonderful face. The picture was in sepia, but nonetheless he could see in it the copper of her heavy, endlessly long hair that would spill over the white pillow, the green eyes that closed when the red mouth spoke those Yiddish words he'd taught her when they made love at night, whispering so as not to wake her father when they used to do it in secret, or in the morning, and again in the afternoon, and once again at night. The red mouth that sighed in a language she forbade herself to speak anywhere else but in bed. In bed in that room, which was a little dark because it was between floors, and where the scent of apples, lemons and bay lingered, deeply imbued in the walls of what had for so long been a fancy fresh-fruit-and-vegetable store before becoming the Palais de l'Hermine—a scent that mingled intimately with the odor of furs and the aromatic vetiver grass used to store them.

And her father's hearty laugh when he had finally caught on. And the lesson in his beautiful, deep voice. The lesson, free of the long-abandoned old Jewish puritanism, gorged with a lechery gleaned from the bedroom legends of the Second Empire, yet at the same time still charged with the voluptuous souvenirs of adolescence.

"She's a Païva! My friend, I'm giving you my Païva. Take her! She's beautiful, bitchy and a liar—like the Marquise de Païva of the old days. Love her well! Fuck her well! The way only we know how. Teach her, teach her well, and you'll be able to keep her. Make her jealous, but don't cheat on her! I love you, Janek! Thank you, Janek! She's so pretentious that she might have gone off and done it with the son of the man who runs the bookstore on avenue Niel! Luckily, you came along. Thank you. You've spared me the bookseller and you've spared yourself boredom. We three are going to have a fine time, my son."

The joy, the happiness and the laughter of all three during those years of complicity with the father, passion with the daughter and apprenticeship to France—or, more accurately, to a tiny, peaceful, petit-bourgeois shop-tending bit of it.

"BEAUTIFUL, bitchy and a liar," the old man had said with tenderness and pride. Beautiful everyone could see. Bitchy he had once heard her be—and in a manner that had chilled him—when she had chased a first cousin of the poor Anna, her mother, from the shop—a cousin who'd come straight from the Gare de l'Est to rue Pierre-Demours, as custom dictated when you left the shtetl. She had chased him away in Yiddish without even giving him time to ask for the glass of water every emigrant has a right to. That was in the early days of their love affair. Before he could even emerge from the back of the shop, the cousin was out on the street. What had struck him most about this fleeting incident had been the sound of Nicole's beautiful voice saying crude words in the language that she used only in her pleasure and tenderness with him. She'd blushed when he'd asked the identity of the man who was leaving. "A chicken thief," she'd answered in French.

A liar . . . Yes, that she was—every day that God gave. And proud of it, too.

Useless, childish, inoffensive lies, but always linked to a kind of reality, they'd make old Zedkin burst into laughter at table while she served them. In those days it was, "The Baroness de Rothschild came in to ask the price of the muff in the window," "The Bonnot Gang held up Mademoiselle Grandval's candy store, and I had to bring her out of a faint," "Madame Guynemer is going to order a fur coat for her son," "The tenant on the third floor is Mata Hari's sister. . . . "

Useful lies, like when he was in his volunteer regiment and she'd come to meet him disguised as a Red Cross nurse in a uniform old Zedkin had made up for her.

Old Zedkin had died too early to hear the astounding dime-novel account that claimed to recapture the exciting days of a life he had never lived and that was nevertheless the only one of his Païva's lies that had really paid off, was still paying off and would pay off for years to come —for the simple reason that its protagonist was no longer around to slap his daughter and make her shut up.

Janek himself had considered giving his wife a good slap the first time he had surprised her in her role as a spinner of completely unbelievable tales. Then, to his great amazement, he had seen her audience won over, and his own affairs become profitable.

Michael Strogoff and Marie Bashkirtsev, the troikas, balalaikas and *douchkas* found favor. All the more so because the October Revolution that had shaken the world in ten days had, oddly enough, served

Nicole's ends too, by obscuring every genealogical, geographical and denominational track.

And so he hadn't slapped his wife, and since then he'd let her tell her tales. He no longer listened; he played the great Slav, though at times his heart ached for old Samuel Zedkin—who had not been Piotr any more than she was Victoria, the Païva of this father who wanted her to be called Nicole but who himself always called her Judith, and never Anna.

His heart ached because the true story of young Samuel Zedkin's actual escape from Russia—hidden in bundles of bearskins at a St. Petersburg fur fair and traveling clandestinely across so many frontiers before finally reaching Paris—was a hundred times more wonderful than the kidnapping attributed to the famous "Chanticleer," Lucien Guitry.

His heart ached when he thought of the old accomplice he had loved so much, who had thoroughly detested all the Nicolases—First, Second or Fourteenth—for the same reason he had detested Ivan the Terrible, Peter the Great, and all those Great Catherines of all the Russians who had continually subjugated, beaten and often slaughtered his people. But rather than tell Janek about it, Samuel had preferred to teach him to sing Paul Delmet's *"Les Petits Pavés."*

His heart ached, but he let her talk. He smiled and served the wine. He looked at the big Fabergé egg and the snake bracelet, its cruel eyes blazing above his wife's satiny white elbow. He'd paid that fellow too much for them, that Isidore who kept coming round with his friend the taxi-driver—a real Russian, he was—offering him all kinds of stuff. They would barge in when the workshops were closed and that idiot Anita had gone home, and though they'd really got the better of him with the Fabergé, the Fabergé too was paying off. And then there were those sables that had been reworked into an evening cape with a hand-sewn bronze-taffeta lining, a cape ordered by Augustin Leblanc—with the understanding that his daughter, Liliane, and his son-in-law, Roger Ziegler, wouldn't know about it—and delivered to a young lady named Maddy Varga, lyric artist, 24 rue Pergolèse . . . That had certainly brought in a good profit!

: :

BARSKY HAD never dared admit to Stépan and Olga that he did business with Monsieur and Madame Jean of Fémina-Prestige. Neither had Gromoff.

It had come about quite by chance through Gromoff one day, when an extremely beautiful woman had hailed his taxi and, because Prince Andrei's accent made her extremely talkative, confided to him through the glass divider that she had a liking for Russian exiles and didn't mind helping them out when they wanted to unload certain personal souvenirs.

He had dropped the woman in Neuilly on a very quiet street right off the Bois de Boulogne.

As she paid her fare, to which she delicately added a royal tip, the young woman had murmured, "Spread the word among your friends. I live here. Madame Jean, third-floor left. *Dosvydanya!*" And she had disappeared through a thick, solid oak porte-cochère.

For the next two hours the interior of the taxi had smelled so good that successive customers congratulated the driver.

Gromoff had noted the address and—as the lady had suggested—passed the word on to his friend Barsky. Barsky had immediately scented a sucker, and what with the Clignancourt flea market, the Salle Drouot neighborhood haunted by Barsky, the exits from the nightclubs and large hotels cruised by Gromoff and the racetracks they frequented together, the two of them had quickly found stuff with which to nourish the Russophile charity of the unknown perfumed lady from Neuilly-sur-Seine.

A brass samovar, a garnet ring and a lapis-lazuli snuffbox made up the first haul, sufficiently modest to evoke the extreme distress of the man or woman who was reduced to parting with them.

They had gone to Neuilly, and through a half-opened door a timid maid had told them to go to rue d'Aboukir, where Monsieur worked.

They were about to get into the taxi when Gromoff spotted his mysterious passenger coming home. She was overwhelmed that he had not forgotten her. He introduced Monsieur Isidore, a friend who had helped him look around. The lady tried on the garnet ring, went into ecstasies over the lapis lazuli of the snuffbox, felt the solidity of the samovar, and the deal was concluded, without bargaining, on the sidewalk of rue Charles-Laffitte. Gromoff and Barsky had set their prices very low, having decided that a first deal, if it was to be followed by a second, must always be made at a loss. The lady, delighted in having put one over on them, left with the suggestion that henceforth they ought to concentrate on items of greater importance. Which is what they did that very evening, going off to have a drink in a Montmartre cabaret where Gromoff knew the doorman.

The day they laid hands on the big sable cloak, it was Madame Jean herself who advised them, from the doorway, without inviting them into the apartment, to take the item—which Barsky had spread on the landing as he sighed, "It's a museum piece, a museum piece, Madame" —and show it to her husband, who knew more about these things than she did.

It wasn't until they were in the stairwell at rue d'Aboukir, in front of the first-floor door bearing the "Fémina-Prestige" nameplate, that Barsky and Gromoff realized they were at the shop run by Stépan's brother. They had promptly redescended, installed themselves in a bistro across the way, waited until closing time and then gone upstairs again.

When they left half an hour later—having concluded the deal with the harsh man in whose handsome face one could nevertheless see traces of Stépan's charming and vulnerable features—they had been a little ashamed. Then they had had a lot to drink and decided to keep their business relations secret. They had from time to time, over the past two years, gone back to rue d'Aboukir—always at suitable hours.

And despite the remorse that overcame them some evenings when they saw Olga and Sonia desperately trying to complete their work before the carrier tricycle returned to pick up the wretched black cotton garment bag, in an odd way they relished the fact that the two of them were the secret link—the only link—between rue de la Mare and rue Charles-Laffitte, in Neuilly.

ONIA WAS STILL kneeling on her damp floor, the avenging rag in her hand, when, petrified, she once again heard the abominable and forbidden name, but this time in a sort of dull, incantatory groan: "Petliura, that jackal! . . . Petliura, that stinking hyena! . . . Petliura. . . . It was God's will! . . . " Sonia looked up; Madame Lowenthal, monumental and out of breath, was standing in the kitchen doorway, and behind her Olga was signaling Sonia not to be frightened. But Sonia was already frightened when Madame Lowenthal, having regained her breath, terminated her imprecation with "It was God's will. . . . The Beast is dead!"

Madame Lowenthal was expecting a variety of reactions from her two neighbors, whom she had always considered brainless young things, but she was certainly not expecting the inexplicable, unpardonable and unquenchable mad laughter that had immediately convulsed both of them. One was so doubled over that her forehead touched the basin of grayish water between her knees; the other, leaning against the doorway, had buried her head in the crook of her bent arm. Madame Lowenthal could see nothing but two necks and two backs, shaking spasmodically. They weren't laughing out loud—they were gasping softly. It was something between a fit of coughing and the sound of great sorrow. Then they caught their breaths in long, sonorous moans that announced a new wave of gasps, increasingly stifled, apparently painful.

Initially surprised, then indignant, and finally incredibly wounded,

Madame Lowenthal was turning to leave when Olga stopped her and sputtered, "Let us explain, Madame Lowenthal. . . . "

At the idea of the impossible explanation so lightly suggested by Olga, Sonia, who had risen to her feet, leaned down to pick up her basin, which she emptied into the sink as she said, with some difficulty, "You must excuse us, it's just nerves. Sit down in the dining room, Madame Lowenthal, I'll make some tea. Olga! Make Madame Lowenthal sit down."

Madame Lowenthal, sitting down heavily at the table, couldn't help taking a rapid inventory of the provisions in the basket Maurice had abandoned in his flight. This was such a direct reminder of the menus of yesteryear now no longer under her control—and consequently of the unfortunate goulash—that Olga returned to the kitchen to smother a new fit of laughter, which was immediately communicated to Sonia, who had just managed to calm down.

An hour later, Madame Lowenthal was still there. She was drinking her fifth glass of tea—having asked Sonia to put on some more water —and crunching her tenth sugar cube as she began a new, detailed description of one of the innumerable pogroms she kept stored in her memory. She had long since finished with Petliura. His hash had been settled. The jackal was dead? Well and good! But all things considered, he wasn't the worst. For example, when her own mother was only eight . . . And she went on with an interminable list of local torturers, often called by their first names followed by ones related to their personal sadistic traits: "The Disemboweler," "The Sodomizer," "The Eye-Gouger," "The Emasculator," "The Drowner," and even the name of a woman, "The Whip Lady," and of dates, names of villages, names of cousins left blind for life or missing a right hand, or of babies burned alive and virgins split in two.

That late-morning session in the sunny little dining room turned into one of those lugubrious and bloody wakes Sonia and Olga had sworn would never take place in their homes. It was impossible to make Madame Lowenthal shut up: obviously, the announcement of the death of the hetman had been just the excuse she'd been waiting for to finally tell her story to these ungrateful ignoramuses who had consistently rejected her right to do so.

Their eyes still reddened from tears of laughter, Sonia and Olga let her talk, and trembled at the idea that the children might come in, especially at some moment when Madame Lowenthal was dwelling on the physiological details of a new rape, previously overlooked but now suddenly brought to mind.

Never, even in their most terrifying stories, had either their mothers or their grandmothers surrendered to the verbal debauchery to which Madame Lowenthal now succumbed as she related those ignoble deeds. She used words the meaning of which Sonia often didn't know, and which the old woman explained in detail and with the help of gestures as soon as she realized she hadn't been properly understood.

As a result, to the horror inspired by the rapes themselves was added the horror of observing the obvious joy Madame Lowenthal experienced in recounting them. And little by little, because too much is too much, Olga and Sonia began to feel the first pangs of a new fit of wild laughter. Simultaneously and without prearrangement, both women began to concentrate hard on imagining what exactly went on at night with the always-smiling Monsieur Lowenthal.

Only the muffled, padding entrance of Madame Stern saved them from a second catastrophe. It was not the custom of the timid and reserved Madame Stern to leave her first-floor right and invade her neighbors. She had come up because she had a question to ask. As she saw it, it was the one question that could rightly be asked at this time. She had caught snatches of the shouts in the street from her open window, and simply wanted to know, "Who is the man who had the courage to kill The Beast and offend God?"

Madame Lowenthal didn't know. Neither did Olga or Sonia, who both suddenly realized the extent to which Madame Lowenthal had led them away from the only preoccupation that should logically have been theirs.

> *Ah, the salad*
> *Will be eaten*
> *With some oil*
> *And vin-e-gar!*

Zaza jumped very high, and the other two counted, turning the rope as fast as they could. It cracked: One! Two! Three! Four! And then they went back to a slow "Rock the Cradle" movement.

> *Ah, the salad*
> *Will be eaten . . .*

"They're dumb," decided Maurice, without looking at Robert, who was watching the girls.

He wanted very much to cry, but he would have had to find a corner in which he could cry all alone. There was no one to whom he could tell his story. What was it he actually wanted to say? That his ankles still smarted from the blow with the wet rag? It was a lot more complicated than that. So complicated, in fact, that he himself couldn't untangle the skein of reasons he had for being so unhappy. Unhappy at not understanding and at being completely misunderstood. Unhappy and hurt at having been treated like a disobedient brat just when he was getting ready to deliver a serious message that would finally allow him to learn the real truth, which was also serious, and which he had always suspected was being hidden from him precisely *because* there were serious reasons.

He kept looking at Zaza. He hated her for jumping rope at a time when, together, they might have shared the extraordinary news that "Pouett-Pouett" had never been Old Lady Lowenthal, and that both of them were somehow involved in a crime committed by grownups. But Zaza went on jumping, and anyway, she'd forgotten everything about the secret she had once betrayed.

He didn't look at Robert, because he was afraid Robert might see he was on the verge of tears, and because he was desperately trying to figure out a way to tell him this long story that now went back so far, months before the Cléments arrived in Paris. He couldn't think how. And somehow—this too made him want to cry—he felt that, all things considered, this story was no concern of Robert's. It was *theirs*. But who were they? *Us. Us?*

The street was empty.

There was no one in front of the Auvergnat's. And besides, he didn't want to learn the truth from just any old grownup.

Since his mother was good for nothing except lying or spanking him, he would wait for his father and Stépan. He would wait until evening.

"Suppose we get our lunch and eat it in the empty lot?" Robert suggested.

"Sure, but without the girls," answered Maurice, returning from a great distance.

: :

THE REST of the day was surprising for more than one reason.

First of all, without saying anything to Zaza, who hadn't heard about the picnic, he climbed up to his own apartment, crossed the dining room without saying hello to either Old Lady Lowenthal or Madame Stern, went straight to the kitchen pantry and halved the big piece of

Gruyère that had been the special of the week, took two oranges from the fruit bowl that sat on the little table and returned to the dining room to break off a large chunk of the baguette in the basket now lying at Madame Lowenthal's feet. When Sonia asked him why he was behaving so strangely, he replied, "I'm not eating here. Madame Clément said it was all right."

And on this half-truth he left, slamming the door—which was never closed during the day—loudly.

He found Robert in the loge. Jeannette Clément had in fact given her permission. She was busy screwing a tin cup onto the neck of a funny-looking big red bottle. Taking the piece of Gruyère from Maurice, she said, "Wash your hands," and while he was inspecting the brand-new little boats above Madame Lutz's sink, she wrapped the cheese in a piece of folded-up paper from the Blanchot dairy that she took from a drawer in the sideboard, where Maurice had time to catch a glimpse of different-colored papers, bits of string and carefully rolled ribbons.

Another Blanchot package already lay on the table alongside two apples. Robert was holding wide open a large, dark-brown cloth bag, from which hung a white cotton cord and two tan leather straps that trailed on the ground. Into this bag Madame Clément put the two packages, Maurice's two oranges and the two apples. Then she took a clean blue-and-white checkered dishtowel from the buffet cupboard and a partially eaten round loaf from the pantry, from which she cut two thick slices, setting them on the dishcloth with Maurice's big piece of baguette before wrapping it all up carefully. "Be sure to bring this back," she said to Robert, as she stuffed the cloth into the sack. Then she added the big bottle, having checked to make sure the tin cup that sealed it wasn't leaking. "Don't break it. It's expensive," she added.

Knotting the white cotton cord so that the sack looked like a skirt, she flipped over a sort of flat, square hood bordered in tan leather and ending in a tan leather strap pierced with little holes. She inserted it beltlike into a brass buckle and said, "Turn around, Maurice." Then she fixed the two leather straps over his shoulders.

"Off you go, my raggle-taggle crew! Have a good time!" she called out, as she opened the door to adventure for them.

They passed the girls, calling out, "So long!" Maurice slipped his thumbs under the straps at about the level of his armpits. The pack was three quarters empty and flopped against his buttocks, but it appeared much heavier because the carrier's stride was so deliberate and rhythmic.

Zaza stopped turning the rope, and Myriam Goldberg, who'd been allowed to have a shot at jumping vinegar, stumbled. The three girls watched Maurice and Robert go down rue Henri-Chevreau, and Zaza, seeing them plunge into the yellowish prairie of the empty lot, made her usual gesture—drilling her index finger into her right temple.

They didn't decide immediately where to bivouac.

"We'll have to look around," said Robert, "and undo the pack when we're sure."

In the light and silence of noon, this no man's land that they knew so well because a dozen or more of them played there day after day— Maurice had first known it when a house stood there that had progressively become a ruined house, then a demolished house—took on all the charm and mystery of a clearing discovered by explorers, though it was charted on no map.

Finally they found exactly what they wanted. It was at the end of the lot, at the foot of a giant portrait of Dr. Pierre in a hole-pocked corner they usually avoided so they wouldn't fall into it while playing ball.

Two stone steps, all that remained of a stairway that had led to cellars now filled in and cemented over, struck them as being miraculously suited for bringing to the country the latest in modern comfort.

"This'll be great. It gives us a table, a bench and a floor. We won't have our asses in the grass, and we can see what's going on," said Robert.

Maurice put down the pack.

Once they were seated on the second step, they were in a comfortable little trench, the first step offering them a backrest to lean against. They were also in a racing car, and a little bit in a submarine.

The checkered towel served as a tablecloth. They had carefully spread it on the top step and set out the two Blanchot packages, an orange, an apple, a slice from the round loaf, half of the baguette and the big red bottle, which they had trouble standing upright on the worn granite. They had done all this while seated on the second step, the pack open at their feet, and it had taken a lot of twisting and turning. Everything was finally ready, and they could sit down at table, though of course the table was behind them.

"It's better, because of the ants," Robert had explained when they'd considered the problem. "With grass you're never sure."

They began with the two halves of a cold breaded cutlet Jeannette Clément had put into the Blanchot package, each piece placed between two lettuce leaves. Robert put his half on the slice of bread, and Maurice split his piece of baguette and slid his cutlet inside.

"That gives me a seven-layer sandwich," said Maurice. "Yours has only five." And he counted: "The crust, the bread, the lettuce, the meat crust, the meat, the meat crust again, the lettuce again, the bread again, the crust again. No, nine layers," he rectified.

"It's not called meat crust," Robert corrected. "It's called breading. It's made by rolling a bottle over stale bread."

But Maurice's first great discovery was the licorice taste of the kind of golden liquid Robert poured into the tin cup for him.

"It's coconut mixed with water my mother lets run a long time so it will be cold. If it had been hot water, then hours from now it would still be boiling. That's because of the bottle's lining."

The bottle's lining was Maurice's other magic discovery. Not only for its properties, but also because of the way it looked, like one of the balls Monsieur Florian made them hang on the Christmas tree.

"The thermometers they use when you've got a fever are something like that. It's mercury, that's why its so fragile," explained Robert, as he carefully poured himself a drink.

They wanted the oranges, not the Gruyère, after the taste of coconut.

Robert replaced the apple, the Blanchot cheese package and the folded-up Blanchot cutlet paper in the bag; after removing the second orange, he reknotted the white cotton cord. They left the cloth and the bottle.

"That way, when we're hungry again, everything will be ready," said Robert.

"Yes, that's better," agreed Maurice, who decided Robert was a really terrific organizer.

Just as Maurice was about to bite into the orange skin, Robert said, "Not like that. Wait a minute," and from the small sidepocket of the pack, which Maurice hadn't noticed earlier, he took an eight-bladed knife such as nobody on rue de la Mare had ever owned. It was brownish, and had an inlaid silver cross on it.

"Don't say anything about this, because it's my father's," said Robert.

They shared their oranges, one of which was a blood orange. Then, for the first time, silent and motionless, they really looked at Dr. Pierre in a way they'd never done before. His curled toupee started at the fifth floor of the windowless wall, and from where they were now they could have touched the bottom button of his brocaded vest, if said vest, which began on the second floor, had still been visible. It no longer was; it had disappeared under the layers of filthy plaster and the superimposed posters that dotted it.

On the other hand, the affected face of the young dandy of dental care was like new, being closer to the sky.

Still, if you looked at the face more carefully—which is what Maurice and Robert had been doing with increasing intensity for some time— you could see here and there, in those apparently perfect features, some unfortunate irregularities due to the unevenness of the surface they'd been painted on. Seen this way, it resembled a jigsaw puzzle right after it's finished—you look at it close up and you can see the marbling where the pieces fit together.

"Oh! . . . Look," said Maurice suddenly, "he's got a window in his eye."

They heard a distant noise in the silence surrounding them, and something in Dr. Pierre's right eye moved. High up on the fourth floor, a hand had opened a small window daubed with blue.

Then they began to look for other windows. There turned out to be four of them. A black one in Dr. Pierre's hair, a blue one in his eye, a pink one on his chin, and a gray one on his shoulder.

"Those must be the toilets," said Robert.

The very idea that you could make pipi and caca and smash the toothpaste-merchant's eye whenever you wanted to delighted them.

They were a little afraid, too. A man they had never seen in the neighborhood suddenly appeared from nowhere, took a few steps into the lot, peered toward the rear, saw them huddled in their encampment, stood motionless looking at them and then, with a fine sweep of his hat, returned to rue Henri-Chevreau, his long coat floating behind him.

"Maybe it was the assassin," said Maurice.

"What assassin?" asked Robert.

"The one in the newspaper."

"What newspaper?"

"It doesn't matter," said Maurice. "Look, here come the others. Let's show them the toilet in his eye."

A football, kicked from a distance, came very close to the thermos. Robert quickly removed it from the stone step, folded the cloth and shoved everything into his pack just as the Novacks, the Nussbaums, the Benedettis and the Bonnet twins swarmed toward them, yelling like savages.

"There's really no need to show them, they can just find it by themselves," decided Maurice, changing his mind.

AS THE exhibitionist approached Zaza, Josette and Myriam Goldberg, he hadn't noticed Jeannette Clément's silhouette behind the white curtains of her loge. She'd had her eye on him from the time he'd walked by across the street, obviously fascinated by the little panties that appeared and disappeared as the girls jumped rope. And so when he suddenly decided to cross over, unbuttoning his big coat as he walked, Jeannette was already on the threshold of the door to the building. "Are you looking for something, Monsieur?" she said, in a voice that sounded so strange to the girls that they watched him curiously as he strode energetically away.

"Who was that, Mama?" asked Josette.

"A disgusting man. If he ever shows up around here again, come and get me, Josette."

"Well, then, he's not a 'Pouett-Pouett' lady, but a 'Pouett-Pouett' *man*, right?" said Zaza, and Myriam Goldberg burst into shrieks of laughter.

Zaza went on, "Why did they go off to eat without us?"

"Because they're big boys," said Josette.

"Would you like to eat with Josette?" suggested Madame Clément. "And you, Myriam, would you like to eat with Josette and Zaza?"

Myriam Goldberg glanced at Zaza for permission before answering.

"Her grandmother will never let her," replied Zaza.

"Well, she can go ask anyway," said Madame Clément. "And you, Zaza, go ask your mama. I'll make egg toast with some stale bread."

: :

MADAME LOWENTHAL was busy telling Sonia Guttman that she could only expect trouble ahead if she let her son behave as rudely as she had just seen him do. Sonia, who had already been unable to explain her first outburst of laughter, as well as the beginning of the second, was also at a loss to explain her lack of discipline with Maurice, whom she had so unjustly punished thanks to Madame Lowenthal, without whose goulash none of this would have happened.

Madame Stern had left as she had come, and Olga Roginski, exhausted by Madame Lowenthal's verbal outburst, worn out by the frustrated desire to laugh and also deeply upset—because Madame Stern's question about the identity of the assassin had made her think of Stépan—glanced at the black garment bag they had not so much as unknotted, and told herself that if things went on this way, neither she nor Sonia would be able to finish their day's work.

Just then Zaza burst in.

"I'm not eating here! We've been invited by Madame Clément. We're going to eat toasted eggs and we've seen a disgusting man."

"Better and better!" sighed Madame Lowenthal. "And this is only the beginning, you poor things . . . "

And she finally left them.

AT JUST ABOUT the same time Stépan had been yelling "bitch" and pointing at her photo, Nicole Judith Victoria Anna Roginski in person, even more beautiful than her picture, was comfortably enjoying the admiring cries being shouted gaily in her direction.

"Ah, what a beauty! What a beauty! What a peach! Come closer, little lady, you can touch, they're all fresh. My apples are as firm as yours, and when it comes to apples, I'm an expert . . . "

This morning her beautiful face was crowned with a soft triple braid pierced by tortoise-shell pins, which gave her a charmingly old-fashioned look—though belied by the boldly made-up mouth and the casual charcoal-brown jersey outfit, with its low V-neck and a skirt that stopped well above the knees. The opulence of her hair excused the absence of the little cloche hat, which should normally have been on her head instead of in her gloved hand. She had a way of keeping it in view that showed a respect for the conventions, though they'd been thwarted by her overgenerous nature.

She responded to some calls and ignored others, and when she'd decided on a purchase she would put it, using her ungloved right hand, into the wicker basket carried by Armelle, whose starched coif and long black mantle contrasted prettily with her own flamboyance.

Ever since Monsieur and Madame Jean had moved to rue Charles-Laffitte, Nicole had been careful to conform to the customs of the house.

Twenty-two rue Charles-Laffitte was a four-story house, too old to have an elevator but sufficiently antiquated to boast an imposing stairway covered with dark-red carpeting that was bordered with a mustard-and-black scrolled design, fastened with brass stair rods and protected by unbleached linen from the ground floor to the mezzanine.

A service stairway rose from the courtyard, climbing up past the kitchen doors and ending at the maids' rooms in the garret under the slate roof; the fanlights of these rooms could only be seen from the opposite building at the rear.

Most of the tenants in the front apartments had lived there a long time. One often passed their grownup children on the stairway; they would politely move aside to make room, and once a young man in a Saint-Cyr military academy's uniform even carried Nicole's net bag of groceries up to the third-floor left, having greeted her when they met on the mezzanine landing.

Nothing like that had happened since she had taken Armelle into her service.

Armelle and Gildaise were sisters who came from Ploërmel in Brittany's Morbihan region.

It was Madame Le Gentil who had found Armelle for Nicole. Joëlle Le Gentil and her husband, Edouard, an engineer in a tire company whose main office was in Clermont-Ferrand, lived in the second-floor-left apartment. Madame Le Gentil had been born in the building and had taken over the apartment from her parents when they had retired to their little manor house in Arzon, Brittany.

One day, shortly after Monsieur and Madame Jean had first moved in, Joëlle had rung their bell, and when Nicole had shown her into the salon—still almost empty but already carpeted with black and white squares—she had made a suggestion.

"I've a Breton girl who's coming to me straight from her farm. She's got a sister—do you want her? If you agree, they could share the maid's room that goes with your apartment and then I wouldn't have to put out my husband's young employee, to whom I've sublet my own maid's room. I can't promise you a polished lady's maid, but Breton girls are honest, and from the moment you pick her up from her train—before she can be seduced by the Gare Montparnasse pimps and provided you keep her on a leash during the Neuilly festival—I don't think you'll have any reason to regret it."

That was how Gildaise and Armelle Baud, aged eighteen and twenty respectively, entered into the service of the Le Gentils and the Roginskis and slept snuggled up in a little bed on the top floor of 22 rue Charles-Laffitte.

And that's why no one had to cart Nicole's provisions up the stairs for her. Taking her cue from Joëlle Le Gentil, she had them carried by Armelle, who lugged them up the back way after saying, "See you in a few moments, Madame," while Nicole took the large main staircase to rejoin her maid, who had already reached the third floor and was opening the front door for her.

Sometimes Armelle carried the two shopping baskets, Nicole's and Joëlle's, after they'd decided to make what they called a raid on the souks. The expression was one Joëlle had picked up from her brother, who was doing his military service with the spahis at Senlis.

The two neighbors had quickly become friends, a development encouraged by the fact that they had to join forces to train Gildaise and Armelle. Joëlle knew the procedures. From early childhood she'd had a lot of experience with Breton girls, and even used some Breton words picked up at the Arzon manor house. She had drummed these into Nicole, who knew the right moments to use them. A nice *Kénavo*—the meaning of which she didn't actually know—made up for a larger than usual number of dishes or a button that had to be sewn on just when the floor was being washed.

And it was Joëlle who had known how to cope with the Sunday Mass problem, which developed soon after the arrival of the Baud girls. At ten o'clock, after doing a little light housekeeping, they would go to Saint Jean's at the end of avenue de Neuilly, near the bridge. It was a bit far, but it would make a nice walk for them.

"I don't know about you, but Edouard and I attend church only occasionally. When we do, we go to Saint Pierre's, on avenue du Roule. They'd feel awkward if they ran into us there. And as for the distance, you'll see—they won't find it too tiring when the gypsies invade avenue de la Porte-Maillot at Puteaux."

Nicole had felt she was a little too obsessed with dangerous street-fair entertainers, but since Joëlle had already lost three maids to the merry-go-round, sentimental songs and Theresina, the Three-Hundred-Pound Fat Lady, she tried to understand her point of view.

She had, however, appreciated the extreme delicacy with which her neighbor avoided questions about her own religious practices, and when she gave Armelle instructions about when and where she could go to church, she pretended that she herself had set it up this way.

Their intimacy grew, but was limited to the two of them. The men knew each only other by sight. They nodded on the staircase, but had never spoken.

Joëlle Le Gentil had spoken to Janek only once, on an evening when he had returned home earlier than usual, and she had apologized for still being there. She had lingered to admire the Fabergé egg, which Nicole had refilled with salt, pepper and mustards as she watched. Armelle had been given strict orders never to touch the egg that had belonged to Madame's father.

Janek had murmured "Good evening" in his beautiful bass voice, kissed her hand and quickly left the dining room.

"I'll send you Gildaise as soon as she's finished the dishes," Joëlle had said, as she left Nicole to her preparations; on evenings when one or the other gave a dinner party, they would graciously lend out one or the other sister.

They had never dined in each other's homes. It was one of those things they'd probably do some day—or, more likely, some evening. Nicole wasn't impatient: she was happier than she'd ever been.

She was in the process of acquiring everything she'd always wanted, and at the same time had got rid of everything she'd always hated—in other words, other people's memories.

There was no longer anyone around to remind her of the sickly ugliness of her poor Polish mother, illiterate and timid, whom she'd always been afraid of finding at the door of the Saint-Ferdinand elementary school when she was still very young, and whose discreet death she'd found such a relief when she was fourteen.

Now there was no longer anyone left to remind her of how, when she was six, she'd hidden, sobbing, in the bakery, while the League of Patriots, armed with sticks, had come to break the tiny-paned displaycase windows in the Palais de l'Hermine.

No longer anyone to remind her of Janek's first appearance as her father's workman.

No longer anyone to remind her of the years when Janek's papers had still not arrived from Poland and she was the mistress of a workman and he was the lover of the boss's young daughter—to the silent disapproval of the neighborhood, which was even more shocked by the fact that old Zedkin so openly enjoyed the situation.

And no longer anyone to say, "Good morning, Judith, how's business?"

True, there was also no longer anyone left to say, speaking of the dead man, "We were very fond of him." Perhaps that was the only thing she felt was somewhat lacking, because she missed her handsome, strong, joyous father terribly. In a way, she had resurrected him with her fantastic tales of a life that had never been his, and in her more inspired moments she could hear the distant, thundering laughter of the man who had always been amused by her girlish lies, both big and small.

She would have been very surprised if anyone had spoken of betrayal. She never betrayed her true fantasies. She merely kept them for herself. They were the ones no one could remember and, in doing so, remind her about. They were not to be shared.

Never again anyone, anywhere, to remember a crowded little room on rue du Roi-de-Sicile where her father sewed and her mother wept, while she herself played on the floor with a rag doll.

Never again anyone to remember crossing the threshold of the old fruit-and-vegetable shop on rue Pierre-Demours that day when, as a four-year-old girl, her hand in her father's, she had heard him read "Commercial lease available" aloud to her before entering to ask the price.

Only she knew why the smell of fresh spring vegetables brought such a tender smile to her face as she promenaded her beauty and her little Breton slavey through the Neuilly market.

But she was also the only one to know why she never went past the Sablons Métro when she made her joyous raids on avenue de Neuilly. Beyond that frontier lurked a great danger. She had brushed up against it one morning when she had carelessly followed Joëlle Le Gentil, who had absolutely insisted on showing her Charlot's stall—Charlot, the Secondhand King. The bargains here weren't in Dutch potatoes or Mediterranean fish, but in shoes, handbags, belts and fine lingerie, always "marked" in both senses of the word: marked because they always bore the label of a leading manufacturer, and marked because they were always slightly imperfect. Too imperfect for rue de la Paix, but astonishingly luxurious for the sidewalk of avenue de Neuilly, where they were displayed on a cloth spread on the ground.

Luckily for Nicole, Charlot, even from a distance, was noisy and conspicuous. He was turbaned in a pair of lady's pink peau d'ange panties, the lace falling over his eyes as he harangued his exclusively feminine clientele. Surrounded by eager women and blinded by lace ruffles, Charlot hadn't recognized the terrified Nicole, who had just identified him as that cousin of poor Anna's, the cousin whose fate she had dismissed from her thoughts when she'd so brutally chased him from the Palais de l'Hermine all those years ago.

She never crossed that frontier again. To Joëlle, who'd been amazed at her lack of enthusiasm for Charlot's bargains, she'd said, adjusting the bracelet that snaked above her elbow, that she hated secondhand merchandise.

EVERYTHING piling up that morning in Armelle's basket was of top quality. The dinner Nicole was giving that same evening was special, and it excited her imagination as a hostess as well as her penchant for romance and intrigue.

She was opening her house to the clandestine amours of Augustin Leblanc, the Troyes hosier in his sixties and, until then, the irreproachable husband of Marie-Jeanne, mother of Liliane Ziegler. By placing a secret order with Janek for the making of a sable cape—which, as a precaution, Nicole was to deliver personally to Mademoiselle Maddy Varga, lyric artist, 24 rue Pergolèse—Augustin Leblanc had gotten snared in the accursed trap of complicity.

Overcome with joy and tortured by remorse, he had accepted the invitation whispered by Nicole as they stood outside the Lucas Carton cloakroom after the regular monthly dinner given for the Zieglers and Roginskis by an Augustin Leblanc whose dress had suddenly become more fashionably youthful, but who was strangely vague in his comments as a Fémina-Prestige stockholder.

"There'll just be the two of us and the two of you," Nicole had specified, in a barely audible voice.

And since then she'd been seething with impatience at the idea of finally getting to meet the frigid little nightingale who, Augustin Leblanc had told her in confidence, was shy, came from Saint-Etienne and was only twenty-two.

She could think of nothing else as she pushed open the massive oak door of her building. As a result she paid no attention to the conversation between the concierge, Madame Lamblin, and Madame Vanesse, first floor, right front. She got the impression they'd been talking about some unfortunate foreign aristocrat who'd been assassinated by some hooligan or other. As Nicole started up the stairs, she heard a name: it meant nothing to her, and anyway she hated such stories.

When she reached the third-floor landing, two thoughts made her smile: the vision of Mademoiselle Maddy Varga arriving wrapped in sable when it was almost June, and the memory of one of her father's young mistresses, who had been so wild about him that she'd always brought violets to their romantic assignations—violets Papa Zedkin would bring back to the shop and present to her, Judith, in a small glass he would place, laughing, on the cash register.

TÉPAN WAS IN such a hurry to get home that he hadn't waited for Elie on the Strasbourg-Saint-Denis platform the way he usually did. As he walked down rue de la Mare, he was relieved to see him in the distance, sitting on one of the chairs the Auvergnat would set out when the weather was good and his bistro crowded.

Neither Stépan nor Elie generally stopped at the café in the evening. They always went straight home. They preferred the little glass of Polish vodka Sonia or Olga would occasionally pour out in one or the other's kitchen to the peasanty white wine or Amer-Picon the Auvergnat generally served his customers and which they themselves had never really grown to like. They would, however, enjoy it with pleasure every Sunday morning, almost as a ritual, on their return from the public baths on rue des Pyrénées. They liked the Amer-Picon on Sundays because its taste was associated with the unusual silence of their street and with the clean smell of their well-scrubbed skins.

Nor was it Monsieur Stern's custom to hang around the bistro, nor old man Benedetti's to leave rue des Pyrénées. But it was them, nevertheless, Stépan saw sitting on two chairs near Elie, who was signaling him to come and join them.

Standing around in the street or at the bar of the bistro, the door of which was wide open, Nussbaum, Katz, Goldberg, old Lowenthal, Novack and a few men he had never seen in the neighborhood listened in silence as Benedetti spoke to them quietly.

As he came closer, Stépan studied the *tableau vivant* made by this village meeting and found it couldn't be more peaceful, compared with the disorderly and noisy agitation to which he'd been subjected all day long at rue d'Aboukir. First before and then after the terrible scene with Janek.

He was worn out. Worn out by the screaming of others, worn out from having screamed himself. Exhausted, he willingly accepted half of the chair offered him by Elie and the Amer-Picon held out to him by the Auvergnat. He listened to the Italian.

Benedetti was telling them that in America there were two men who had been in prison for six years and were now condemned to the electric chair, two Italians, and all the Italians everywhere in the world —except Mussolini, of course, but there were Italians and Italians— were joining forces to keep them from being killed. And now all the Jews in the world had to join forces to protect this *"Chouassbarre"* and keep the French from guillotining him.

Monsieur Stern, who was well acquainted with the story of the two Italians in America, told him that it wasn't at all the same thing. The Italians in America had been condemned without proof. Schwarzbard had committed murder. He had killed a monster, but nevertheless he had killed. There was no need for proof. He had furnished it himself. He had killed, and it wasn't with French justice that he had to settle accounts, but with God.

Monsieur Stern spoke no louder than Benedetti. His condemnation was voiced with a very sad smile, but condemnation it was, and, as such, incontrovertible. He had got it from Rabbi Blau, with whom he had spent the afternoon, as he did every day, since he was helping him decipher some sacred texts that had come to them from a representative of an Abyssinian tribe. And as he had closed his eyes to make his condemnation more solemn, he missed the anger, the sorrow and the indignation that his Orthodox sentiments brought to the faces of his listeners.

"You're worse than my son of a bitch of a brother," said Stépan loudly in Yiddish. And without offering any further explanation, he turned to look inside the bistro. It was only then he noticed Maurice, who was leaning against the bar listening, a lemonade in his hand.

"He was waiting for me at the Métro," said Elie, as though to excuse his son's presence at the bar.

The stumbling silhouettes of Barsky and Gromoff emerged from the dark rear of the bistro like two awakened dragons. Monsieur Stern, who'd had nothing to drink, rose and waved goodbye with the sad, indulgent gesture common to those who know they're right despite what others may think.

Benedetti, who hadn't understood Stépan's brief comment, nevertheless understood that his presence was embarrassing, especially after
Barsky collapsed on the chair vacated by Monsieur Stern. He thanked
Elie for the drink and got up too. Stépan took his chair. Elie could read
in his friend's eyes that he already regretted having mentioned Janek
in front of the others—this brother about whom he never spoke except
to Elie, and about whom no one on the street knew anything.

Gromoff sat down on the doorstep. Nussbaum and all the others left.
Barsky had for all practical purposes spent the entire day in the bistro.
They weren't interested in hearing him ramble on.

"Where's Zaza?" Stépan asked Maurice, as he watched Novack walk
away.

"She's playing at dressing up with Josette and Myriam," answered
Maurice, shrugging his shoulders.

"Like a czarina? The way her aunt does?" guffawed Barsky, looking
at Gromoff, who studied his shoes.

Silence.

"You're drunk, Monsieur Barsky," said Elie, when he saw the stupe-
faction in Stépan's eyes. "You're drunk, and so you'd better not talk
about people you don't know."

"You're right, I'm drunk. But Gromoff isn't. Ask him, ask Prince
Andrei Alexievitch if the wife of his son-of-a-bitch of a brother doesn't
get herself all dolled up like the czarina or the Grand Duchess Pavlova.
You'll see whether or not we know them!" replied Barksy, bursting out
laughing.

Gromoff used Zaza's familiar little gesture to show Barsky no longer
knew what he was talking about.

"Don't take me for an asshole, Gromoff!" said Barsky, who had
spotted the gesture. "Not today. Today we can say anything. Tell him,
tell Roginski, that we know them. Him. Her. The Bois de Boulogne.
Even the maid with her embroidered cap. Her fine carpeted staircase.
Her red hair, her perfume, her *dosvydanyas*! And how much they've
paid us since we began supplying them two years ago. Do you know
what she wants now? Icons! Yes, my friend, icons to go with her
mechanical egg for which we made her husband shell out more than
you make in six months on the job. And there's more, but I won't say
because I'm not really sure, but that big cloak, the big fur cloak, eh,
Gromoff? I'll bet you got it from Petliura . . . "

He choked with laughter.

"Oh no, none of that!" shouted Gromoff, who hadn't said anything
until then. "None of that, Isidore! Not you. I've had to take enough

shit all day from fares who wanted to know if maybe Petliura was my cousin. It's funny—they never talk about Schwarzbard, never! No! Petliura, Petliura all damn day! When the last one began, "You must know that hetman . . . " I turned and said, 'You can say that again! I'm Schwarzbard's brother!' He got scared and didn't say another word."

"Don't try to change the subject!" said Barsky, with a knowing wink at Stépan, who didn't answer. He was pale, grave and silent.

"Let's go home," said Elie, already on his feet. "Come on, Maurice. Let's go, Stépan."

As he watched the three of them move off, the boy between the two men, Barsky wondered if he'd been right to speak out. Gromoff didn't think so.

: :

IT WAS ABOUT a hundred yards from the Auvergnat's to the house. Maurice walked between his father and Stépan, who looked at each other without saying a word, either to one another or to him. Another few steps and it would be too late. He never had any luck, he said to himself.

He'd had a very definite idea in mind when he'd suddenly decided to leave the others on the empty lot and go off alone to wait for his father at the top of the Métro steps. He wanted to ask a question and get an answer. To be listened to and understood. To listen and understand. If he hadn't been able to get anything out of his mother, it must have been because he'd asked the question badly. He'd be more careful about the one he was going to ask his father.

He'd repeated the definitive version over to himself as he watched for Elie at the top of the Métro stairway, at the very same spot where, that morning, he'd read the extraordinary news of the death of someone about whom they'd now have to explain why he'd been told he didn't exist, after he'd originally been made to believe that he was Madame Lowenthal—who wasn't dead at all.

From "Who is this Petliura?" he had gone to "Who was this Petliura?" and finally settled on "Who was this Petliura who's dead?"

That at least was clear.

His father, head raised, had been smiling at him, surprised to find him at the top of the stairs, when a "Ciao, Guttman!" had resounded behind Maurice, so his father had talked to Monsieur Benedetti as they walked along the street to the Auvergnat's. At the café, he'd heard everything. And even if he hadn't understood it all, he'd understood enough to know that now he had thousands of questions to ask. To ask his father, Stépan, the whole world. He just couldn't figure out which question to begin with.

They were almost at the door. Elie took Maurice's hand and, bending down, said:

"You're very quiet, son. Everything okay?"

"I've got a sore throat," answered Maurice, without looking at his father.

He wanted to cry so badly that in a way it was true. But he was as brave as he had been that morning with Robert. They entered the building hand in hand. Elie thought Maurice's was very hot, and he told Sonia so when they reached the second floor.

"It's almost a hundred and one" said Sonia, shaking down the thermometer and pulling up the sheets of the big bed in their room, where she'd put Maurice.

"Show me, Mama," said Maurice, reaching for the thermometer.

"It's too delicate, and it costs a lot," answered Sonia. "I'm going to make you some hot lemonade with sugar and aspirin."

She went next door to ask Olga for a lemon. Stépan was in the kitchen talking in a low voice. Zaza was in the dining room.

"It serves him right. They ate all sorts of junk at the lot," said Zaza, when she heard Maurice had a fever.

"We'll come back as soon as he falls asleep," Sonia told Stépan.

: :

THE PILLOW smelled of his mother's hair. His father sat on the edge of the big bed and held his hand. Maurice closed his eyes. His throat wasn't sore at all anymore, but he decided it was too late to say so. He just seemed to hurt a bit all over, the way you do when you've had a fall, but he was so comfortable in the big bed it was almost pleasant. His mother and father spoke in whispers and then tiptoed out of the bedroom.

Maurice had the delicious impression of having punished them. And to punish them still more, he decided to think only of his own secrets, the ones he now shared with Robert. If he hadn't felt so sick, he would have shrugged his shoulders with pity for his mother, who thought she knew more about mercury than he did.

He therefore went over all the discoveries of that afternoon in his head, smiled at the idea that tomorrow he would go and look at Dr. Pierre's glass eye, and put the vision of the man in the long coat out of his mind. Then, thinking about the taste of coconut, which would have been good mixed with the lemonade, he fell asleep.

Elie transferred him to his own little bed when they returned from the Roginski apartment.

He had no fever when he woke up, and went to school with Robert the way he did every morning. Just before they entered the schoolyard, Robert hit his forehead with his open palm:

"I almost forgot . . . You know, he was a son of a bitch, that guy who was shot down yesterday. I hear he wanted to kill all of you—you, your father, your mother, Zaza, her mother and father, Sami, Jeannot . . . all of you. My father explained everything to us last night. He was glad the bastard was dead."

"And you, would he have killed all of you?" asked Maurice.

"Well, no. . . . We're not Jewish. Come on, get moving, there's the bell," said Robert.

: :

FROM BEHIND his classroom window, Monsieur Florian was watching all his little men scurry to be on time. He had taught them about the Gauls, Joan of Arc, Henri IV—and, naturally, about Henri's assassin, Ravaillac. Today some of them would maybe ask him to tell them about Schwarzbard.

He was ready. But it wouldn't be easy.

Ravaillac had been wicked because Henri IV had been good. Schwarzbard was good because Petliura had been wicked—and anyway the Saint Bartholomew Massacre was lost in the night of time, which was already the time of pogroms.

But the pogroms weren't in the French History syllabus.

And it was just this that, since yesterday, had been troubling Monsieur Florian, who was responsible for their souls as well as their minds.

He went out into the schoolyard and had them line up. As he clapped his hands, he was still wondering if it was up to him to pass on to them a history that was theirs alone, and of which they were the young survivors. He was irritated with himself for not having talked to their fathers about it, when he'd seen them in the distance, on both sides of rue de la Mare, deliberating among themselves.

He was all the more irritated when Guttman lowered his head as he took off his beret and walked in front of him. The boy really didn't look well.

II

MASQUES AND
BERGAMASQUES

*M*ADEMOISELLE Maddy Varga had proved neither as shy as Augustin Leblanc had described her nor as dumb as Nicole Roginski had supposed her during the course of that long-ago evening in 1926 which both pretended to have forgotten was their first meeting.

"It's lost in the mists of time," they would say to the curious who wanted to know how Victoria Jean and Madeleine Varga—the two inseparable managers of "Masques and Bergamasques," which occupied the entire first floor of a Directoire building in the little Allée Chateaubriand, 11 rue Chateaubriand, in the VIIIth arrondissement—had got to know each other.

Lost in the mists of time . . . except for Armelle Baud, who still trembled when she spoke to her sister Gildaise about the terrible evening "when Monsieur had wanted to break the egg that had belonged to Madame's father and had yelled the way Papa does when he comes back to the farm drunk."

Because that was how things had started that evening on rue Charles-Laffitte, as Armelle and her mistress were putting the final touches to setting the table that was about to receive the nightingale of Saint-Etienne and her Maecenas from Troyes.

Janek, who had come home very early, still swollen with grief after Stépan's outburst, had announced himself with a violent slam of the front door. He had erupted into the dining room and, shouting words that Armelle took to be Russian, seized the Fabergé, which Nicole just managed to rescue. She had sent Armelle to the kitchen and, shouting even louder, asked for an explanation.

Nicole admitted that with all the household chores to oversee, she hadn't opened *L'Echo de Paris;* that day's issue was indeed still waiting on the hall table. She tore off the subscription band and thought she recognized the name of the former Ukrainian dictator as the same one she had vaguely overheard that very morning on her way upstairs. Glancing through the article, she shrugged her shoulders and dismissed the affair with a comment to the effect that trouble always came from the same source.

Then, having advised Janek to take a bath and change, she had pressed the little ruby to make sure that the Fabergé mechanism hadn't been harmed, breathed a sigh of relief when she saw the ramekins weren't broken, carefully wiped up the spilled mustards, gathered the salt and pepper into the hollow of her hand and had gone to renew her stock of spices.

She cut three roses from the large bouquet that decorated the grand piano in the salon, set them in the middle of the table, and placed the imperial egg on the buffet, having suddenly decided the less it was seen the better, especially on an evening when events threatened to make the conversation slide dangerously in the direction of Cossacks and pogroms.

Then she'd gone off to scratch at the bathroom door and, in a perfumed mist, kissed Janek's angry brow and mouth. She had whisperingly advised him to steer the table talk in the direction of the Rif war and the rebel Abd-el-Krim, whose surrender Marshal Pétain had just demanded in the name of the French government. She even had a vague regret, which she didn't mention: that of depriving herself of having Joëlle's brother, who was dining with his sister, put in an appearance. He would have looked so splendid in the salon in his spahi uniform. "It would be too cavalier," she told herself softly, and laughed aloud. The linking of "cavalier" with "fantasia"—a word used to describe Arabian displays of equestrian skill, which was frequently sprinkled through that young man's stories—put her in a good humor.

"What's so funny?" asked Janek, as he slid into his terrycloth robe.

"I was thinking of Papa," she replied, as she rubbed his back.

"The hell you were," said Janek. "But this would certainly be the right day for it."

AUGUSTIN LEBLANC and Mademoiselle Maddy Varga rang the bell at precisely eight o'clock.

She was not wrapped in sable. She slipped off a light navy-blue, three-quarter-length surah coat bordered in the same white piqué as her dress. Nicole had time to read the label, but wasn't surprised because she'd already identified the cut. But then one never knew with all those imitations . . . No, if the girl really came from Saint-Etienne, she hadn't lost any time and must have gone directly from the "Dames de France" to Paul Poiret.

A brown-eyed brunette, she wore her hair in a Spinelly bob, with bangs and two locks skillfully shaped to form a half kiss curl over each ear. Seen from the rear, the small, well-shaped point on the nape of her neck made her look like a graceful adolescent.

"Thank you for having us, Godfather and me," were her opening words, spoken in a low voice that gave the seemingly banal phrase a hint of clandestine passion and complicity.

Nicole might just as well have left the egg, the czarina's tiara and even a Star of David and a seven-branched candelabra on various pieces of furniture in the apartment; she could have put the Sidi Brahim record on the phonograph and hung the Foreign Legion flag on the dining-room wall—nothing would have distracted Mademoiselle Maddy Varga, or even Augustin Leblanc, who listened to her, enchanted and mute with bliss, from the only two subjects that interested her: her passion for the lyric and dramatic arts, and her attachment, apparently filial, to her graying benefactor.

She always used the formal *"vous"* when speaking to him. As she enumerated the shows they'd seen together, Nicole and Janek learned of the hitherto unsuspected cultural cadences to which the old provincial, who they would have thought knew nothing of Paris nightlife but the dining rooms of Lucas Carton and the lobby of the Hôtel Terminus, was being subjected.

And she spoke of Saint-Etienne. Of her father, who'd been killed in the war and who'd begun working in the mines when he was only eleven. Of her mother, who worked in a small factory that made bicycle chains. ("But that's all changed over the last six months . . . ") Of the mine-sponsored young people's choir in which the curé always gave her a solo part to sing. Of the job she might have ended up with in the bicycle-chain factory. ("But I had a stroke of luck, and I came to

Paris.") She announced that her real name was Madeleine Vargougnan, but that was too much of a mouthful for the stage. Then she asked what time it was, and decided she had to leave. She had an audition at the Capucines in the morning.

She embraced Nicole in the hall, shook hands with Janek and said, as she slipped on her three-quarter-length Paul Poiret coat, "I'm so alone in Paris when Godfather isn't here, but now I know I've found a family."

She urged Augustine Leblanc onto the landing.

"Come along, Godfather. Let's go. You're going to walk me as far as my door. It'll help you slim down," she added, in a whisper loud enough to be overheard.

"What energy!" said Janek, when Nicole had closed the door.

Without replying, Nicole returned to the salon, Janek following her.

"She may not even be sleeping with him," he commented, finishing off the cognac in his glass.

Nicole went to the liquor cabinet to get the bottle of vodka she had refrained from serving all evening. She poured herself a small shot.

"She is doing better than that. . . . She may not go to his bed, but she knows where she's going all right. And she's not wasting any time. But I like this Mademoiselle Vargougnan," she concluded, tossing back her thimbleful of Polish vodka.

Dear Family,
   You've brought me luck. I've got a part at the Capucines.
Godfather and I thank you.

Maddy

The message was carefully written out in a simple, clear hand on the lace-paper collar surrounding a charming, romantic bouquet. The bouquet had been lying on the doormat when Armelle, replying to a discreet ring, had opened the door and found no one behind it.

It had been the following day, about three in the afternoon. When Armelle knocked, Nicole was in the salon with Joëlle Le Gentil, who was telling her about her mother's cousin, who'd just been named public prosecutor in Lorient.

"Our Armelle and our Gildaise know who he is. Do you remember our Henriot cousins, Armelle?"

"Oh yes," said Armelle, blushing. "There was nobody there, Madame," she announced, holding out the bouquet to Nicole.

Nicole deciphered the message as she slowly turned the lace paper, and suddenly Joëlle Le Gentil's conversation struck her as unbearably boring.

Though she didn't know it yet, Joëlle had had her day and been replaced. A daughter of Stepanois proles, ambitious, spiteful, charming, honest and mercenary all at the same time, had just dethroned the insipid heiress of Celtic gentry, trainer of Breton maids, engineer's wife and spahi's sister. With Madeleine Vargougnan, Adventure had made its entrance in Neuilly. Or, rather, its reentrance, after an intermission devoted to middle-class apprenticeship.

Nicole twirled the little bunch of stems between her fingers, but so rapidly that Joëlle was unable to read the message, which she suspected came from a lover's pen. Too well-brought-up to ask questions, she awaited the confidence as she gave a detailed account of the magisterial career of Public Prosecutor Henriot.

Sitting opposite her, La Païva was no longer listening, she was smiling the way Samuel Zedkin used to smile when he'd say to Janek, "You've saved me from the bookstore clerks. You'll see how much fun the three of us will have!"

: :

THE HIGH ROAD to Adventure that tempted Nicole's greedy curiosity turned out to be more like a path across brush-filled, marshy terrain.

The role of leader of the expedition Maddy Varga had given her when she named her mother of their morganatic family consisted mostly, in the early days, of filling in ditches, locating and flagging quicksand, laying snares and seeing to it that no badly extinguished cigarette butt set fire to this little underbrush of lies. Lies indispensable to the maintenance of the balance between the Roginski-Ziegler, Ziegler-Leblanc, Leblanc-Varga, Varga-Roginski associations on which henceforth depended—though only she knew it—the very existence of Fémina-Prestige.

And Nicole's imagination, so long at the service of a counterfeit past, rediscovered all its vitality in the daily invention of lie after lie. Not only was it necessary to lie to Liliane Ziegler, who thought her father looked very tired and her mother very sad in her house in Troyes, and to Roger Ziegler, who never ran into his father-in-law at the Hôtel Terminus, but also to Augustin Leblanc, who sometimes failed to find Maddy on rue Pergolèse.

Unfortunately at the same time it had also been necessary to lie to Maddy, and it was this that had really bothered her.

COMPLETELY LOST on the Capucines stage in her tiny role as a Louis XVI shepherdess who sang *"Il pleut, il pleut, bergère"* to a very décolletée and self-assured Marie Antoinette, Maddy Varga, as an actress, was extremely disappointing. Nicole found in her nothing of the mixture of aplomb, innocence and childlike perversity that made Madeleine Vargougnan so charming offstage.

Armed with a mandate from Augustin Leblanc, who still didn't quite dare show himself in the wings of a theater, Nicole—without Janek, who for his part still didn't want to compromise himself openly with the Zieglers—had gone alone to the last rehearsal of *L'Autrichienne et le Serrurier* (a French adaptation of an enchanting American musical comedy by Clarck and Simpson that had triumphed on Broadway as *The Merry Mary Antoinette*). It had been agreed between Augustin Leblanc and Nicole that she would phone him in Troyes, as late in the evening as possible so as not to arouse the suspicions of Madame Leblanc, who went to bed at about ten. The password, taken from the vocabulary of hosiery manufacture, was "pure silk" for a triumph, and "mixed cotton" for a demi-success. The possibility of a fiasco had not even been mentioned.

A quartette sang out "Come in!" when Nicole knocked at the door pointed out to her by the backstage doorman. Maddy Varga shared a tiny dressing room with three other girls Nicole could hardly recognize as haughty court ladies; she had found them, unlike Maddy, very convincing in their little sketches. Relieved of their monumental powdered headdresses and fancy crinolines, still outrageously made up, their heads gripped by the black silk stockings that had served as a base for dozens of white hairpins designed to hold their wigs in place, they looked, in their cotton smocks, like schoolgirls changing after a costume ball in which they'd been Pierrettes. They said, "Good afternoon, Madame," an inquisitive and disarming smile playing in the depths of their kohled eyes.

Maddy was the only one wearing an elegant Chinese silk kimono. She wasn't smiling, and Nicole read a panicky fear in her eyes, which had already been cleaned of makeup.

"Bravo!" said Nicole at the top of her voice.

A gigantic basket of flowers, disproportionate to both the size of the dressing room and the insignificance of the shepherdess's role, cluttered up the portion of the makeup table at which Maddy sat. This floral tribute made the three little bouquets the ladies of the court were keeping fresh in toothglasses seem all the more touching.

"Really bravo!" repeated Nicole.

"Thank you very much, Madame," said the three girls.

"Thank you, Nicole," murmured Maddy, rediscovering the beautiful contralto that had so tragically abandoned her in *"Il pleut, il pleut, bergère."*

Nicole just had time to catch a glimpse of the sable cape suspended from a hanger.

"Well, ladies, I'll leave you. Thank you for a pleasant evening, and once more bravo!"

And she fled.

On the telephone she improvised a mélange of pure cotton mixed with natural silk: it didn't meant anything, but it reassured Augustin Leblanc, who must have been sitting on top of his telephone judging from the speed with which he responded to the Troyes operator, who wasn't used to putting late calls through to 122.

L'Autrichienne et le Serrurier ran for two weeks.

There were other auditions, other small roles, other baskets of flowers, other disappointments and other lying bravos from Nicole, who to her own surprise got no pleasure in proffering them.

Then one happy day lucidity won out over a love for the dramatic art that was as immoderate as it was sincere—or perhaps *because* that love was sincere—and Maddy Varga decided to abandon the profession and, at the same time, relieve Nicole of her obligation to invent charitable lies.

Maddy had come to her decision after reading the reviews of what was to be her last role. She'd had enough humor and courage to read the cruelest of them out loud to Nicole:

" 'As for Mademoiselle Maddy Varga, we had been led to expect Joan of Arc and Antigone. We were given the Madelon of barracks ballads. We are returning her to the sender!' "

"That's nasty," Nicole had said.

"It's nasty, but it's very true," Maddy had replied. "I'm going on to something else, and my Tintin will have to pay up. At least my friends in the theater will have got something out of it."

And it was on that day in 1930 that the seed of what was to become the firm of "Masques and Bergamasques" had germinated.

For some time now, Augustin Leblanc had gone, in Maddy's confidences to Nicole, from being "my Godfather," to being "my Tintin" or just "Tintin," when he wasn't "that old idiot Tintin." Her confidences were of all kinds, and often complicated the programming of lies. Because Maddy also had her sentimental moments . . . and sometimes they went on for weeks.

There had been several young actors, a Spanish guitar player, a chief scene-shifter from Bagnolet and two lightning trips to a Lausanne clinic. And most recently, right in the midst of the Saint-Etienne–swan-song number, there had been a costume-and-scenery designer.

They were all young, handsome, nice, disinterested and in love. In love and forewarned.

Forewarned that there was "Tintin." That she loved Tintin a great deal, and that she would never do anything to hurt Tintin, she would never leave Tintin.

And so eventually they left her. She was unhappy for a while, and then it passed. It passed more or less quickly.

But the affair with the costume-and-scenery designer seemed to be lasting.

As for Nicole, because she'd frequented the dressing rooms, the wings and bistros near the theaters in which Maddy—though she had never taken on another part—maintained warm friendships, she had become familiar with a world in which people knew how to play, sing, dance, laugh and weep—and lie like children.

And she had finally found a justification for what, in other days, had mysteriously urged her to choose His Majesty Lucien Guitry rather than His Excellency the French ambassador to the czar to spirit Piotr Zedkin to Paris.

Although she'd enjoyed discovering the world of children, she hadn't wasted her time, either, because she'd also discovered the world of adults on whom the fate of the children depended. They, too, had their dressing rooms backstage, often on the same floor as those of the children. But whereas, depending on the vagaries of success or failure, the children merely passed through these rooms, the adults held onto theirs. Besides, they didn't call them dressing rooms, they called them "offices." And *they* weren't children.

And since Nicole wasn't a child either, she soon learned what made a show and what didn't, or why it would sometimes even be canceled in rehearsal—in which case, the same forlorn words always exploded in the ears of the victims: "We're calling a halt, people, *my* backer has let *us* down. . . . *My* suppliers won't deliver anymore."

Nicole had never been tempted to become a Backer; the term covered invisible creatures who drew from far-off and likely-to-run-dry sources —about which little was generally known—the funds that they promised, lent or didn't lend. On the other hand, "Supplier"—in the exalted sense of "By special appointment to the King," "By special appointment to the Court," "Exclusive Supplier"—carried in its wake a romantic tradition of craftsmanship that appealed to her.

It was therefore by way of the trademen's entrance that Nicole had made her first official appearance in the bosom of the large show-business family, shortly before Maddy Varga had made up her mind to say goodbye to it.

The young lover–set-designer–costumer had helped to speed things along considerably.

The action of *The Dispossessed*—the title of the drama in which Maddy Varga was to lay siege to fame one last time—took place in a Rhineland castle. Inspired by his growing passion, Alex Grandi, the new lover, had designed an evening gown for Maddy that required so many yards of pailletted tulle and hand-embroidered silk that the theater management had balked at the cost. It was then Nicole intervened. She took on the responsibility for the materials, the sewing and the finishing. Free.

She had announced the news to Maddy, who passed it on to Alex Grandi, who communicated it to the management, which was delighted, congratulated the young actress on having such prestigious connections and asked to meet this incomparable and benevolent partner.

For the first time in her life, Nicole found herself sitting in front of a theater manager, who offered her a glass of port at the corner of a desk as encumbered with bills and invoices as Janek's. Only the faded posters tacked to the walls reminded her that she wasn't on rue d'Aboukir.

Yes, she really was offering the costume as a gift. And very willingly. She adored the play! As a matter of fact, for a ridiculously low rental fee, barely enough to cover the cost of insurance, she would also make available a very beautiful accessory that would put the finishing touch to the necessary opulence and ease of the character interpreted by Maddy Varga, who during the second act had to move about under the humid vaults of a Rhineland château. A real sable cape, which the heroine could slip off after her second line so as to better show the audience her sumptuous evening gown . . . She had only one request to make in exchange, a very modest one.

And from her handbag she took a little slip of paper on which she had written out a paragraph directly inspired by the blotter/sandwich man operation that had worked so well for the Roginski-Ziegler firm. She read it to the manager.

"The gown and sable cape worn by Mademoiselle Maddy Varga in the second act are the exclusive creations of Fémina-Prestige."

Delighted at getting off so cheaply, the manager accepted. Nicole Roginski and Fémina-Prestige were about to change their professional status.

And so was the sable cape. Thanks to the modest role it played every evening in the second act of this drama about "the dispossessed," it had come out of retirement and the camphor-smelling garment bag in which its owner had kept it for years. Nicole and Maddy shared its prop fee, which was listed on the theater invoices under the heading "Fémina-Prestige Rental," while the pailletted gown appeared in the column "In Return for Publicity."

*S*ONIA AND OLGA were also about to change their professional status, though they didn't know it yet.

Thousands of gold, silver and purple paillettes had invaded the second floor at rue de la Mare one day. They were everywhere: in the grooves of the parquet, in the sheets of the children's folding beds, on the stairways and even in Josette Clément's hair.

The women had to sew them, one at a time, along arabesques outlined in different colors on the turtledove-gray tulle, which was both delivered and returned in separate pieces. Then the pieces came back to them again, sewn together, ready for finishing. Once skillfully assembled, these pieces of tulle, disparate and dull before they had made them brilliant, fashioned a gown such as they had never seen except in the illustrated magazines Monsieur Katz would give them to leaf through while he was cutting Zaza or Maurice's hair.

They had set in minute snaps, sewn hems and oversewn ruffles with gossamer thread, and the gown had left them yet again—finished. Just as the girls'-coats-with-gilded-buttons and the women's-suits-with-fur-collars left them every day, never to be seen again except in newspapers during advertising campaigns, when there would be entire pages covered with the slender silhouettes of incredibly distinguished and haughty women and children who had been the models for the clothes Sonia and Olga sometimes recognized and whose prices left them perplexed.

It wasn't on ordinary newsprint, but on a full page of expensive glossy paper that the women rediscovered their gown, about three months after it had left rue de la Mare, when Barsky and Gromoff came to Sonia's apartment one afternoon and held out the photo of a very beautiful young woman.

The evening before, Prince Andrei had found in his taxi a theater program left on the back seat by a fare he had picked up at the Café de la Paix and taken to the XVIth arrondissement. Interested in the value of everything, he had leafed through it, and, remembering the leaping paillettes that had recently settled on the building like fleas, he thought he recognized—he now explained—the gown that had required so much work from the two young women. In addition, Barsky had added, looking at Olga who had just come in, there was *that*. *That* was a sort of big fur animal the dark and lively-looking young woman, photographed full-length by Piaz, nonchalantly trailed behind her.

"Exclusive creations of Fémina-Prestige," Barsky murmured, thinking that perhaps they couldn't read the words under the photo of Maddy Varga in the second act of *The Dispossessed.*

Barsky and Gromoff made them a gift of the program and—pleased with their generosity—left them to their own thoughts.

For a moment, the women were tempted to go and see with their own eyes how their new gown and the already venerable bronze-gold lining of the unforgettable cape would shine under the stage lights. They immediately dismissed the notion, just as one might dismiss the idea of a mad spree in some exotic country. They had made no more trips after arriving under the glass-enclosed shed of the Gare de l'Est.

Sonia clipped the photo from the program, and since she wanted to share ownership of it with Olga, they decided to insert it in The Family Picture Frame.

The Family Picture Frame was a large rectangular passe-partout mounting edged with four delicate dark mahogany rods, and it occupied a place of honor over the mantelpiece in the Roginski dining room. Elie and Sonia Guttman had presented it to Stépan and Olga after the birth of Zaza.

It was a modern version of a family album—there were no pages to leaf through. By leaning slightly over the photos that had accumulated under the big piece of glass—at first tidily and then untidily—you could recognize Zaza in her stroller, pushed by Maurice; Sonia, Olga and Stépan standing in front of the building; Olga and Stépan as a rural bridal couple; Elie, Zaza and Maurice on the terrace of the Auvergnat's café; Zaza on Elie's knees; Maurice and Robert with Monsieur Florian on Prizegiving Day; Zaza by herself, wearing a pretty lace collar; Madame Lutz and old Madame Lowenthal at the window of the concierge's loge; Félix and Jeannette standing on the doorstep; and a few unknowns, recognizable only by their mothers and fathers.

By crowding and by overlapping them a little, Olga and Sonia had always been able to make room for a new entry in The Family Picture Frame as the years passed. The Frame was housed in Olga's rather than Sonia's apartment only because they worked in Olga's place more often than in Sonia's.

And so Maddy Varga entered the family circle. They looked at her sometimes, then forgot her and busied themselves in hemming sateen, sewing false eyes on rabbitskins, and putting imitation ivory buttons on sleeves without buttonholes.

Until one day they found in the two big black cotton garment bags pieces of off-white heavy crepe, which they were instructed—in a pin-attached note marked "very urgent," underlined three times—to cut according to the indicated measurements, assemble according to the attached sketch and embroider at the hems, armholes and necklines with gold braid, the necessary yardage of which they would find wrapped around two big wooden spools at the bottom of each garment bag. The handwritten note was signed: Illegible. Jeannette Clément had deciphered the long message for them.

Though they had never been to Greece, never visited the Louvre, they realized from the sketch that they were being asked to make the kind of costume worn by the people depicted in Maurice's Ancient History textbook. Accordingly, they cut out the first peplum, but stopped working when the time came to stitch on the braid.

When the carrier tricycle stopped by that evening, the messenger found a letter waiting in the Cléments' loge instead of the two garment bags he'd come to pick up.

They'd spent all day concocting the letter in their heads. Jeannette Clément had helped outline its general content, which Felix Clément then put into the correct form. Maurice recopied it on a sheet of lined paper and slipped it into an envelope addressed to "The Head of Personnel, Fémina-Prestige" (By Messenger). It read:

Messieurs:
    Hired as "finishers," we have for many years worked for your firm at rates of which you are aware.
    Your last shipment calls for dressmaking skills. As you know, we

have already done work of this kind for you. We are prepared to do it again, but under other conditions than those established by your company for "finishers."

Sincerely yours

It was signed Sonia Guttman, very legibly; and Olga Roginski, barely legible.

The next day, the carrier tricycle returned with a typewritten letter on paper engraved at the top—between two Mardi Gras masks—with the words "Masques and Bergamasques, Period Costumes and Creations." Zaza deciphered it for them.

Mesdames,

As you note, our firm has grown.

Madame Victoria Jean has just created a new department in our company.

She has turned over its artistic direction to Monsieur Alexandre Grandi, a very talented scenery-and-costume designer, for whom you have already worked.

It is at his request that we have chosen you to execute the order for the Greek tunics, the material and sketches for which you have been sent, and which are most urgently needed.

Your salary will, of course, be calculated according to new rates. It has only been lack of time that has, until now, kept us from taking the subject up with you.

Good luck in your work!

It was signed: For the Management, illegible.

Olga and Sonia, very proud of their promotion, set to work happily, and in the evening they showed the formal communication to Stépan and Elie, confessing that it was in response to a letter they themselves had written without telling their husbands. They had, however, kept the rough draft.

The men in turn were very proud of their wives. Especially Stépan, who asked to reread the letter written on the firm's stationery. He snickered when he came to the passage about "Madame Victoria Jean," and belatedly understood why he had, for some time now, so often run into his hated sister-in-law on the staircase at rue d'Aboukir, always with a tall, rather likable, dark-haired man. That must have been Alexandre Grandi. Stépan reread the last paragraph out loud and said: "We'll see." Then he handed the letter back to Sonia, who put it with the rent receipts.

TWO DAYS LATER, instead of one of the anonymous, indifferent and interchangeable carrier-tricycle champions who for years had delivered and picked up the black cotton garment bags, a tall, handsome, dark-haired young man showed up at the second floor of rue de la Mare in the late afternoon.

"Hello, Sonia; hello, Olga," he said, stretching out both his hands with a smile. "From now on, you're going to work for me. My name is Alex. Make me a cup of coffee and I'll explain everything."

And he explained. He expected from them the same fine work they'd done on the pailletted gown. Very few people were capable of doing it; the skill was disappearing. He'd established a fair rate of payment for them. The tunics were just a little order to get the firm going: after that, orders would come fast and furious. He was going to buy them a tailor's mannequin—and also a real Italian coffee maker, since he expected to be there often. Then he'd looked at Maddy's photo in The Family Picture Frame and said, "Beautiful, right?" Before Sonia and Olga could decide if he was talking about the gown or the girl, he'd left, saying, "See you tomorrow."

The next day he had returned with a mannequin, some petits fours, a package of ground Corcelet coffee, and a funny aluminum cylinder with a black ebonite handle. He'd placed the mannequin in Sonia's dining room and demonstrated the use of the Italian coffee maker in Olga's kitchen. Then he was gone again, leaving behind him that aroma which only yesterday had been unknown to these tea drinkers, and that padded bust Maurice and Zaza called "The Old Lady."

Three days went by without any news at all. Sonia and Olga, jobless for the first time in their lives, looked at the mannequin, wondered if they'd been dealing with a swindler and, without admitting it to themselves, began to regret the boring but punctual daily garment bags.

Alex showed up on the fourth day at about nine in the morning, his arms loaded with bolts of multicolored satins and velvets. From a suitcase he took some muslin, a lot of little bags filled with beads and three sketches. Olga put water on for coffee, while Sonia helped Alex tack the sketches to the flowered wallpaper of her dining room. And the Adventure began.

Neither Stépan, Elie nor Maurice really followed it. On the other hand, every day at about four o'clock Zaza would drag Josette and Myriam over to see "The Old Lady" 's sartorial progress.

Ten days later, three sumptuous courtesans' dresses—designed for

Lorenzo de Medici's companions in debauchery—left rue de la Mare in Alex's arms.

Before taking them away, he had carefully India-inked "Masques and Bergamasques—Sonia-Olga, 9/3/32" on three little pieces of white selvage Sonia and Olga had carefully sewn into the dresses, like mothers marking the outfits of children going off to boarding school for the first time.

"You'll see, girls—if everything goes well, we'll soon have real *griffes* especially woven for us," Alex had said as he went down the stairs, leaving Sonia and Olga trying to elucidate the mysteries of his vocabulary.

And since things went very well, there was soon a second "Old Lady," this time in the Roginski dining room. And *griffes* turned out to be labels.

Then, returning from school one day, Maurice found a real lady in the dining room. She was undressing as Olga, his mother and Alex looked on.

Eventually, since neither he nor Zaza ever found a clear space on their tables so they could do their homework the way they always used to, they got into the habit of working in the Cléments' loge: Maurice with Robert, Zaza with Josette, under the placid supervision of Jeannette, who took the opportunity to relearn with the girls what she had already forgotten, or to learn with the boys, who were now in the A section of the Fourth Class at the Lycée Voltaire, what she had never known.

*O*H MY INCOMPARABLE, my abominable, irreplaceable and adored bitch! Janek thought in Yiddish while Nicole guided the hand of the old lady to whom she had just given an ornamental cake server.

"The honor of blowing out our first candle and serving us pieces of our cake belongs to our godmother," she had said when the waiter at La Cascade in the Bois de Boulogne had set an enormous chocolate-mocha confection on the table.

The icing was decorated with two almond-paste masks—one smiling and the other sad—and a vanilla-and-strawberry marzipan design that evoked the dancing silhouettes of the inhabitants of Bergamo on this July 29, 1933. A candle blazed in the center. *"A la Russe,"* Nicole had announced.

Madame Augustin Leblanc blew, and the nine guests applauded.

In a manner of speaking, it was the final curtain of a comedy that had been rehearsed for months, had just opened and seemed assured of success.

The lucky author and director, Nicole Judith Victoria Anna, smiled at her husband and the rest of the troupe. Her face radiated that indulgent gratitude common to playwrights who know a great deal more about the end results of their work than the actors, who merely play the roles assigned them.

In Nicole's play, there was a mixture of Marivaux, Feydeau and Alexandre Dumas, *fils;* and if Janek had been thinking in French instead of daydreaming in Yiddish he might very well have sighed: "Well done, Marguerite!"

Invited to commemorate the first anniversary of the legal foundation of the firm of Masques and Bergamasques, the following were seated around the table:

Its honorary president, Augustin Leblanc, accompanied by his spouse.

Its administrator, Roger Ziegler, accompanied by his spouse.

Its associate directress, Maddy Varga.

Its artistic director, Alexandre Grandi.

Its legal advisor, Maître Dubâteau-Ripoix, accompanied by his spouse.

And its directress, Victoria Jean, accompanied by her spouse.

The dramatic conventions that had made this peaceful masquerade dinner possible—it would have been inconceivable only a few years earlier—were actually extremely simple. They were based on the classical system of misunderstanding.

With the exception of Nicole, Janek and Maddy, everyone around the table was mistaken about everyone else.

For example, Augustin Leblanc thought it a stroke of sheer genius on the part of his young mistress to have found a bold way to throw people off the scent by making a display of her dubious intimacy with young Alexandre Grandi, whom he, Augustin, had every reason to think was actually Nicole's lover. Hadn't she been the one to introduce him to Augustin?

Alexandre Grandi—to whom Maddy, in order to keep him longer than her other lovers, had never revealed there was a Tintin in her life —was wondering if Augustin wasn't Nicole's rich old lover.

Liliane Ziegler asked herself if Maddy wasn't Janek's mistress— which would have explained that theater program in which she'd happened to see a publicity photo neither she nor Roger had ever been told about.

Maître Dubâteau-Ripoix, a newcomer brought in by Roger Ziegler, leaned toward a Liliane Ziegler–Janek Roginski liaison because he found them both very subdued.

As for old Madame Augustin Leblanc, extracted from Troyes for the evening at Nicole's express request, she thought that all these Parisians were very nice and cheerful—especially Maddy and Alex, to whom she referred throughout dinner as "our young couple," pointing out to Augustin how well matched they were.

When it came time to say goodbye on the terrace, Madame Augustin

Leblanc, exhilarated by two glasses of champagne, let her spirits over-flow and issued a general invitation.

"You must all come to see me in Troyes," she said. "There's no lack of love nests in that big old house in which my jealous bear of a husband keeps me prisoner."

Augustin Leblanc had to push her into Ziegler's Hotchkiss. Maddy offered to drop Alexandre Grandi off in her little Talbot, and the Dubâteau-Ripoix had their chauffeur, who was already opening the Panhard's door for Nicole when she declared, with a charming though nevertheless pointed casualness, "We're going to walk home. It will help us slim down."

Maddy laughed, and Augustin Leblanc, about to get in alongside his son-in-law, who had already started the motor, whirled around.

: :

JANEK AND NICOLE crossed avenue des Acacias and turned down a small, dark path. They were silent. Nicole gently took Janek's hand. He squeezed it, stopped walking and after a quick look around pulled Nicole into the woods, where he made fierce and tender love to her, the way people used to back in the old country on a summer evening.

: :

"SHIT! I ALMOST forgot about poor Joëlle," said Nicole, when she saw the windows of the Le Gentil salon on the second floor still lit at this late hour.

Joëlle Le Gentil had progressively slipped into the category until then reserved for "poor Anna." Not because she was dead, but because she simply didn't matter anymore. Or rather she wasn't worth beans. Or, better yet, she was only worth a couple of beans, given the role as steward in charge of food-purchasing Nicole had assigned her because of her own new artistic occupations.

Poor Joëlle had taken for gestures of friendship and personal confidence what Nicole, no longer finding the raids on the Neuilly market at all amusing, had willingly abandoned to her, and it was therefore Joëlle alone, followed by the two Baud sisters, who bought in quantity and according to her own whim the beans that were purchased for both the second- and third-floor households. As was true elsewhere, it was not at all rare that the Roginski-Jeans ate what was being eaten that same day at the Le Gentils' . . .

In return, without going so far as to say *kénavo* as she did to Armelle, Nicole knew how to get around her with a "Thanks, you're a dear. With all I've got to do, I don't know how I'd manage if I didn't have you..." which she would toss her way when they met on the staircase as Joëlle was coming back from the market just as Nicole was leaving for Allée Chateaubriand.

Since they now hardly ever saw or spoke to each other, it was easy for Joëlle Le Gentil to remain completely unaware of the total indifference Nicole felt toward her at the moment.

However, they had seen each other that morning, and the two windows, shining into the Neuilly night like beacons in the Breton sea, reminded Nicole of this as Janek picked off the twigs that still clung to her somewhat disheveled braids.

Poor Joëlle had rung her neighbor's bell very early that morning, and with a schoolgirl's familiarity had stood at the foot of Nicole's bed, nibbling her toast and sharing her tea. She had a request to make.

"I'm sure you remember Public Prosecutor Henriot, my cousin, actually my mother's cousin, of whom I've so often spoken?"

"Of course," Nicole had answered, though actually the name meant nothing to her, and all she could think of was the dinner ordered at La Cascade for that evening.

"Good, then I won't beat around the bush. What I'm going to ask is a bit cavalier. We're expecting my cousin Michel, actually my second cousin Michel, the son of the public prosecutor, who's passing through Paris after a long stay in Germany, where he was studying . . . "

"He was studying law in Germany?" asked Nicole.

"No. He was studying animal farms. Fox farms. He adores animals."

"German foxes?" asked Nicole with a smile, thinking of the late Samuel Zedkin.

"I can't really say. You know, when it comes to fur . . . In any case, German or not, they're silver. My cousin Michel is a very timid young man. He's always lived in Morbihan, and it took a great deal of courage on his part to make such a long trip. I was wondering if your husband could give him some advice? For outlets, that is, since he's going to set up for himself on a beautiful estate he has near Loch-en-Guidel, a marvelous place with acres and acres facing the sea. . . . "

"If he loves animals, the poor darling is going to suffer!" said Nicole, who was beginning to be amused. "All those silver fox cubs raised by hand and bottle-fed only to end up as collars, muffs and trimmings . . . How sad!"

"I doubt if he'll do the slaughtering himself," replied Joëlle. "But that's none of my business, is it? I'm only interested in doing a good turn for his father, the public prosecutor, who's a kind man, and worried about his son's future . . . Could you and your husband take pot luck with us this evening? They could talk shop."

"Dinner is impossible this evening, we're not free, but we'll stop by afterward for a drink," Nicole had promised. She hadn't cared much for the word "shop."

She'd promised, then forgotten. Only now did she remember. Obviously, they were still awake on the second floor because they were still waiting for them.

"We'll only stay five minutes," she said to Janek, who hadn't the slightest desire to end his evening this way.

They had no sooner entered the Le Gentil salon than Nicole realized the disaster they had escaped by not being free for dinner that evening.

The son of the public prosecutor, who was collapsed in a wing chair, made no effort to rise. He extended a limp, damp hand to each in turn, then let it fall on his knees. He didn't look at them, either. His head was bent forward, and a long lock of black hair escaped from his already balding pate to hide his right eye and join the skimpy mustache covering his upper lip—under which there was a kind of vacuum swallowed up by a starched, grayish collar.

Contrary to the impression one often gets when belatedly joining a family group—of intruding on a conversation which has been going on for some time—Nicole and Janek had the strange feeling that they'd interrupted nothing at all, unless it was the silence that had evidently weighed for hours on the unfortunate trio formed by the Le Gentils and their cousin Michel, sprawled on the Louis XV chair. His large, sluglike body and sharklike head made him resemble one of those sea monsters a heavy tide sometimes deposits on the beach, where it decomposes until the sea returns to reclaim whatever is left of its carcass and deposit it elsewhere.

"I'm afraid we were delayed . . . My apologies for being so late," said Nicole.

"We had really given you up," admitted Joëlle, handing them two small glasses from a bottle of second-rate vodka Edouard Le Gentil had just opened especially for them.

"Our cousin is still exhausted from his trip," began Edouard Le Gentil. "Germany is exhausting, isn't it, Michel?"

Michel Henriot was staring at the carpet and didn't hear.

"Just what did you see in Germany?" asked Janek, who was eager to get it all over with and therefore attacked the topic for which he had apparently been called in.

Michel Henriot still didn't hear.

"Monsieur Jean is asking you what you did and saw in Germany, Michel," said Joëlle loudly, her high-pitched voice betraying all her regrets—especially having been weak enough to have invited this cousin and stupid enough to ask strangers in to see the family idiot. "Well, tell us . . . What did you see in Germany?"

The shark raised its head. Its eyes were very blue, very globular and very innocent.

"I saw . . . I saw foxes, German shepherds and Jews," he said, with a sad little smile.

"Stupid nitwit, you're just talking nonsense," scolded Joëlle.

"That's not true. I saw Jews down on all fours like dogs. They were funny," repeated Michel Henriot.

Edouard Le Gentil gestured helplessly toward Nicole and Janek, who gulped down their glasses of bad vodka, murmured "It's getting late," and followed poor Joëlle to the front door. She was almost in tears.

"I hadn't seen him for five years," she whispered, "and his unhealthy timidity hasn't improved at all. It's been awful. Anyway, thank you for stopping by."

: :

CONVINCED that Joëlle was listening behind her door, they climbed to their floor in silence.

"If I had a cousin like that, I'd keep him out of sight!" exclaimed Nicole, pouring out two hefty shots of real vodka for Janek and herself.

"Imagine going off to finish your education in Germany at a time like this! You should have suspected something!" said Janek. "He's either a son of a bitch or a madman."

"Why? I hope you're not going to jumble everything together again —silver foxes and politics . . . "

"I repeat—anybody who chooses to spend months in Germany the year Hitler has won the election can only be either a son of a bitch or a madman, or both. Or a son of a bitch who's pretending to be a madman. You know, he didn't just invent what he saw in the streets. Hitler's got booted toughs who kick Jews around as though they were dogs."

It wasn't the first time Janek had brought up the topic of Hitler in Nicole's presence. When he did, things always ended badly.

"Keep that kind of talk for your brother," she said, and immediately regretted it.

"I don't have 'talks' with my brother, as you very well know," he grumbled bitterly. And he headed for the bathroom.

What a shame, thought Nicole. It had been such a wonderful evening until then. And since she was irritated with herself, she became particularly irritated with Joëlle Le Gentil.

They went to bed in silence. In the dark, Nicole cuddled up to Janek.

"You've never really understood," she said into his ear. "It's not that I hate them. It's only that poor Jews frighten me."

"Well, then you should have taken a Rothschild into your bed," breathed Janek in Yiddish, his mouth so close to hers that the little singsong sentence ended in the kiss she was already giving him.

"Not at all," he heard indistinctly, as she slid over him.

And they made love subtly and skillfully, as they had expertly done for many winters, springs, autumns and summers.

: :

THE NEXT morning, Armelle Baud had puffy red eyes and a scratch on her nose. She wouldn't say why she'd been crying, claimed that the fifth-floor cat often wandered about at night and went back to her kitchen.

Nicole knew nothing about a cat on the fifth floor, just as she knew nothing about anything that lived up there.

She'd gone up only once, a long time ago, the day when, accompanied by Joëlle, she'd settled the two Baud sisters in the tiny room they shared. She remembered, before going down the service stairs, having turned the brass faucet of the little zinc tap on the landing to assure herself that the water flowed freely. Her ears had told her that the water closets—which she imagined were of the Turkish, hole-in-the-ground variety—must be at the end of a very long corridor.

She counted on her fingers. That must have been seven or eight years ago.

Armelle's red eyes and suspicious-looking scratch suddenly reminded her of a macabre joke Maddy, doubled over with laughter, had made several weeks earlier. They were on the staircase. Passing the Le Gentil door, they'd become aware of Joëlle's voice sternly scolding Gildaise, who was sobbing. They'd stopped a moment before continuing their climb. On the third step, Maddy had energetically wiped her feet on the carpeting and said, "If you and your neighbor continue to make those girls live like the Papin sisters, the next time people come up these stairs they'll be wading through miladies' brains."

: :

BY BRUTALLY murdering their two mistresses at Le Mans on February 2, 1933, the two Papin sisters had acquired a celebrity that outshone the fame Adolf Hitler had legally laid claim to when he'd taken power in Berlin the month before.

Ever since that tragic evening of February 2, all of France's real or would-be criminologists, sociologists, psychologists and erotologists—as well as several surrealist poets—had had something to say about Léa and Christine Papin, who after having committed murder had chosen to spread over the stairway of their pleasant little suburban villa the eyes and brains, scalps and teeth of the Lancelin ladies to whom they had been afraid to confess that the fuses had blown because Léa Papin had incorrectly plugged in the new electric iron . . .

True enough, it gave one a lot to think about. And people indulged themselves. They indulged themselves even more because the nature of the relationship between the two young sisters provided the curious with touches of fantasy that proved extremely lucrative for those who commented on the case in certain newspapers.

It turned out that for the seven years the Papin sisters had been servants in the home of the Lancelin ladies they had always slept in the same room and in the same bed . . .

: :

"WAS IT REALLY a cat that scratched you last night?" asked Nicole, as she entered the kitchen.

"Yes, Madame," replied Armelle, her head bent over the sink.

"Then if it slipped into your room, did it scratch Gildaise as well?"

"No, why should it? Gildaise doesn't . . . "

The sentence stopped short. She'd said too much or not enough. She all but imperceptibly shrugged her shoulders as though to emphasize the obvious.

"Gildaise doesn't . . . what?" Nicole asked softly.

There was a long silence. Armelle's hands were submerged in a blue-enameled basin in which the two cups and saucers from her employers' breakfast were soaking. Without wiping them, she crushed her palms against her eyes and began slowly and silently to shake her head from left to right; then her entire body began to rock from one leg to the other to the rhythm of a dull groan that exploded into an enormous sob.

"Now, Armelle, you must tell me everything," ordered Nicole, who was in fact expecting just about anything.

And so the double confession began.

For years now, Gildaise hadn't slept in her sister's bed. She slept with Monsieur Lucas, the driver of the delivery van for the tire factory of Mademoiselle Joëlle's husband, in the room that Mademoiselle Joëlle sublet to him. And that was why the cat couldn't have scratched Gildaise and Armelle at the same time.

As for the cat, since Madame wanted to know everything, there was none on the fifth floor. There never had been. But there had been a visit to the fifth floor yesterday by Madame Joëlle's cousin.

Armelle unbuttoned her checked blouse. Her shoulders, her forearms and the tops of her breasts were crisscrossed with thin blackish slashes and punctuated by purple pinch marks that were beginning to turn a sulphurous yellow.

"I knew it would happen as soon as I heard he was coming yesterday. He used to do things like that to girls even when he was a boy, whenever he and his parents came to visit the manor house owned by Mademoiselle Joëlle's parents. And not just to girls, to animals too. He does it with his fingernails, and with those fingers that seem so flabby . . . "

She was crying less now, and her tone had become informative.

"Yesterday evening he took advantage of the fact that Monsieur and Madame weren't dining at home, that I was in Gildaise's kitchen, and that I went to bed early. He followed me upstairs at about seven o'clock. He didn't even want to go to my room; none of that business interests him. He just enjoys doing these nasty things, things that are a part of him, right in front of the door, where somebody could come along at any moment."

Simultaneously horrified and relieved, Nicole swore by Sainte Anne d'Auray that she wouldn't say anything to Mademoiselle Joëlle about Gildaise and Monsieur Lucas.

As for Cousin Michel, she couldn't promise. She'd see. She'd see later. Anyway, he'd already taken the train back to Morbihan.

She put arnica on the little cuts and kissed the burning cheeks of her servant, whose sensuality was evidently still unawakened, since neither the misconduct of her sister nor the Neuilly festivals that for so many years had taken place only a short walk away had managed to arouse it.

AS SHE HAD told Armelle, she delayed until later the report she never-theless promised to serve up to Joëlle Le Gentil some day about the surprising practices indulged in by the son of her honored cousin, the public prosecutor of Lorient.

The news might come in handy, she told herself, if poor Joëlle's mania for social discrimination should one day push her to make unfor-tunate use of the word "shop" once too often. . . . She'd see. Later.

Given what happened very shortly afterward, it struck Nicole as completely superfluous to add to the affliction that overtook the second-floor left-front tenant of the house on rue Charles-Laffitte.

The Papin sisters were dethroned. The entire press now was writing about nothing but the moors killer.

But whereas the Papin sisters had had the elementary decency to sign their names to their crime and sagely retire to their little bed to await the police, the moors killer had led the authorities on a wild-goose chase. And in the press, his epic story had taken the form of a serial thriller.

Initially, the front pages of all the newspapers had shown a young and inconsolable widower standing among a group of armed volunteers ready to go off on a search party. "I'll find the man who destroyed my happiness," said the caption under the photo which that morning served as a double announcement to Nicole—the announcement of both the marriage and the widowhood of Cousin Michel.

Another and larger photo, taken on the day of the widower's mar-riage, illustrated the "happiness destroyed by the infamous crime of the ignoble prowler."

At Nicole's request, Armelle identified the men in evening dress, the ladies in long gowns and the little bridesmaids in lace the local Nadar had positioned according to importance around the enormous tulle veil that formed a snowy pool at the feet of the young bride.

She pointed out the notables and rattled off the names from the Morbihan Almanach de Gotha. Nicole finally got to see what Joëlle's parents looked like, and she recognized, but only barely, the face of the brother, the former spahi. Freed of his military obligations and simul-taneously deprived of his gold-crescented sky-blue kepi and his embroi-dered burnoose, he looked just like a shop attendant. On the other hand, the young groom's father wore his dress clothes with the ease of a man accustomed to togas and ermine.

Nicole left a card with the concierge to be delivered to the le Gentils: " . . . sharing the sorrow that has overtaken your family."

The next day, the search party having turned up nothing, the prowler was still prowling, and the front page had a picture of the widower and his father at the head of a long funeral procession. The destroyed happiness was buried in a granite cemetery.

Two days later, the Loch-en-Guidel moors murderer was identified.

It was learned that the widower himself had pumped six carbine bullets into his young nineteen-year-old bride, married six months earlier thanks to matrimonial ads that had described her as having a dowry of two hundred and fifty thousand francs.

It was also learned that her long bridal veil had hidden a paralyzed hip and that her wreath of orange blossoms had covered a botched trepanning operation—the after-effects of a nasty fall that had rendered her forever unmarriageable.

And it was above all learned that, a month before her disappearance, an eight-hundred-thousand-franc accident insurance policy had been taken out on the cracked head of the young handicapped girl. With a clause covering murder.

An unfortunate step by the public prosecutor—no doubt explainable by his taste for order and the sense of discipline inherent in his duties —had raised the hare even as the search party was being organized to flush out the infamous prowler.

While the young body of the deceased was still warm, the insurance company's office had received a telegram, sent from the Lorient Magistracy and signed by the public prosecutor, in which it was requested to disburse the sum due his son. The company, finicky as all insurance companies are, had asked for more time and, during that time, had passed on the telegram to another division of the Lorient legal authorities.

The last photo published in the press showed the moors killer smiling into his victim's Baby Kodak. Booted, capped and carrying a whip, he stood facing the sea, surrounded by his silver foxes and German shepherds. In the foreground was a barbed-wire fence intended to keep the beasts from escaping, and in the background were the carefully aligned little wooden huts that served as their burrows.

: :

NICOLE DECIDED there was no point in letting this document lie around where Janek might see it. She therefore threw it into the wastebasket. Armelle retrieved it, and clipped out the photo.

On the second floor, they were lying low.

According to Armelle, who got it from Gildaise, Mademoiselle Joëlle was prostrate in her bed. And, still according to Armelle, who again got it from Gildaise, who in turn got it from Monsieur Lucas, at the factory, Mademoiselle Joëlle's husband had to be handled with kid gloves.

The household menus were suffering because poor Joëlle no longer went out, and Nicole decided to strike a blow—an exact metaphor, since she went to knock at the kitchen door rather than to ring at the front, which Gildaise had received orders to open to no one.

The murderer's cousin was unrecognizable when Nicole entered her bedroom. In her turn, Nicole now sat familiarly at the foot of the bed and served up the sort of banal comfort offered the grief-stricken. In a soft voice, she threaded together phrases: "Courage . . . Get a grip on yourself . . . It will soon be over . . . We're not responsible for our relatives . . . There's always an uncle or a cousin in every family who . . . " She had gotten that far when by a lightning association of ideas she realized that of all the commonplaces she had spouted, the truest—and the only constructive one—was the last. And so, with brutal good humor, she pulled off the blanket and wrinkled sheets.

"You're going to get up, wash, dress and go off to the market and do me a great favor. Go see what your friend Charlot has to offer, and buy his whole stock for me. Shoes, handbags, underwear, belts—I'll take it all. We're short of supplies at Masques. Get up! Go work for my shop!"

And thus it was that poor Joëlle became both an unpaid buyer for Masques and Bergamasques and "poor Anna" 's poor cousin's best customer.

Then Charlot no longer saw her at his big display, where, to tell the truth, good buys were more and more rare.

Then one day Charlot himself was no longer seen at the Neuilly market. His spot was taken over by an Argenteuil vegetable peddler.

Nicole, an ardent believer in the "from the producer directly to the consumer" system, had done away with middlemen. Henceforth, she bought directly from the big firms, which—responding to the interest in their labeled but imperfect merchandise by another big firm that was rapidly growing—offered "Masques and Bergamasques, Period Costumes—Creations and Rentals" prices that were as friendly as they were unbeatable.

"We'll meet at Masques" was a phrase more and more frequently heard, backstage and in the bistros near the theaters, during rehearsals.

At Masques, they sewed, rented and repossessed—they never sold.

For every new show, the costumes spent some time on the backs of the actors to whose measurements they had been tailored; then, after the last performance, were promptly returned to the firm, where they were carefully cleaned before being sent to increase the stock.

At Masques could be found the wherewithal for costuming the burghers of Calais, Alcestes, golfing tomboys, lady martyrs, firemen, chambermaids, gypsy violinists, Agrippinas, chanteuses from the Belle Epoque, chimney sweeps and St.-Vincent-de-Paul nuns.

At Masques, they first cut to measure and then made many alterations. They did an enormous amount of assembling, disassembling and reassembling, and it was not unusual to find the Misanthrope's famous green ribbons on the cabriolet of a grisette and the sackcloth of a sister of charity in the pants worn by a fireman. Everything at Masques and Bergamasques was made and remade; nothing was ever wasted.

But for those who came to Masques, the sudden recognition in a new costume for a new role of a fragment of material—a bit of lace, or two or three embossed buttons already worn in other roles—was like finding fragments of old love letters, and they were charmed.

Moreover, when they came to Masques *everything* charmed them, starting with the very fact of being there. Because if they were there, they'd been sent there, and if they'd been sent there to have a costume fitted or refitted, it was an irrefutable sign that they'd very definitely been hired.

So, whether very old or very young, the days they came to play, like children, at dressing up, they smiled the way people do when they know their future is assured, at least for a while. And that made them very happy.

They were charmed and happy from the moment they entered the delightful little Allée Chateaubriand, which looked as if it had been specially laid out in a garden to serve as a backdrop for costume balls. The spell was prolonged on the stairway, which smelled of fresh wax polish and led to the first floor, and continued into the salons that had been decorated with all of Alex Grandi's fine taste and Victoria Jean's boundless cleverness.

On the inlaid parquet, which creaked somewhat, the artists were greeted by ottomans, padded velvet tub chairs, beveled cheval mirrors, and delicate little chairs with gilded legs, picked up at a Versailles auction of Second Empire furnishings.

On the walls, portraits of their great predecessors gave the impression that they too had previously prepared themselves in this same sanctuary for their prestigious creations. "I want only dead actors. That way there'll be no jealousy," Victoria Jean had specified. And so it was Talma, Mademoiselle Mars, Frédéric Lemaître, Mademoiselle Georges, Réjane, the Divine Sarah Bernhardt and, of course, Lucien Guitry, who provided encouraging examples to the youngest actors and revived bitter resentments in the oldest.

Beneath the portrait of Lucien Guitry, a small oval console provided a pedestal for a glass cover under which Victoria Jean had placed the Fabergé egg, whose salt-pepper-mustard functions were unnecessary on rue Charles-Laffitte.

The relic sat there, hermetic and enigmatic, exposed to the curiosity of visitors. The more erudite remembered Lucien Guitry's seven years of triumph at the court of the last of the czars, and they explained to the uninformed the history and origin of this imperial gift, which they felt had found a better home among show people than in some old museum.

Victoria Jean let the erudite ones rattle on. She waited until some leading light showed up before taking the trouble to remove the egg from its cover, press the little ruby and start the precious mechanism. Accompanied by the sharp harpsichord notes, the blossoming of the egg, now empty, gave rise to admiring murmurs compared with which the noisy exclamations that had greeted the earlier exhibition of condiments resounded in Nicole Roginski's memory like so many peddlers' cries.

The little ceremony had taken place only once or twice. Stars were still rare at Masques. They would surely come later. For the time being, it was the secondary actors—the walk-ons and extras—who came to Allée Chateaubriand.

They were received by Ginette. Ginette had been one of Marie Antoinette's three ladies-in-waiting in *L'Autrichienne et le Serrurier,* the most promising of the trio. But the years had gone by, and she had never risen from the ranks. One day, sick of playing small parts, she had dissolved into tears at Masques while trying on the 1900s soubrette costume she was supposed to wear in another of those fleeting, wordless roles that were making her so sad—so desperately sad that she stuffed herself with pastries. Both the impossibility of hooking up her whalebone corsage and her grief at never being able to latch onto a real part got the better of her nerves.

It was then that Maddy had suggested she come and work for Masques. Relinquishing the role of soubrette, she accepted that of receptionist. She had finally found steady work. And since then, without bitterness, with a great deal of good humor and the wisdom of those who have been through everything, she was able to share the hopes, anguish and disappointments of her former colleagues.

It was she, too, who welcomed the directors and the costume designers who accompanied their overgrown children when it came time to choose from the stock. At such moments she had the delicious sensation of being their equal. She was no longer the one to whom they could say, "Thanks, but no thanks," she was the one to whom they said, "Thank you, Ginette."

On a smaller scale, she experienced what Maddy Varga experienced on a larger one. The people who had often auditioned and rejected her for their shows now said "Dear Maddy," or better still, "Dear Madame."

Maddy Varga appeared only for custom fittings, and she was always followed by Mademoiselle Agnès. Mademoiselle Agnès was another old acquaintance of Maddy's, from the time she got her clothes at Paul Poiret's. When Mademoiselle Agnès had gone over to Molyneux, Maddy had followed her, and when she'd left Molyneux, Maddy had again followed her, this time to Jeanne Lanvin, whom Maddy had eventually persuaded her to leave—to follow her, Maddy, to Masques.

Mademoiselle Agnès was a true *première d'atelier* and saw to it that she was paid accordingly. She never smiled, unless it was with formal irony at certain moments—moments that were actually always the same. She adjusted, pinned up and unbasted in a silence that Maddy filled in. Until, finally, she would say in a colorless voice, "Now you can call in Madame Victoria Jean."

Then Nicole would appear. With a somewhat curt "Good day" that overawed many of the younger actresses, she would study the costume at length and nod her head thoughtfully. After a brief silence, she would extend her hand to Mademoiselle Agnès and murmur, "My chalk, please." Mademoiselle Agnès would take a thin flat piece of mauve chalk from the pocket of her black twill and give it to her. Then Victoria Jean would swiftly trace two or three straight lines and, sometimes, bold St. Andrew's crosses, a few millimeters from the white basting on the seams and buttonings.

"Doesn't it seem better to you this way, Mademoiselle Agnès?" she would say quietly, returning the chalk.

"Much better," Mademoiselle Agnès would answer, putting her smile on her face and her mauve chalk into her pocket as Victoria Jean disappeared.

"It's almost nothing, but it seems to change everything," Maddy would sum up.

Mademoiselle Agnès neither acquiesced nor disapproved. Silently undressing the actress, she, too, would disappear, the unfinished costume carefully folded over her forearms.

Two apprentices waited for her behind the scenes. The most important part of their job was to immediately erase all traces of mauve chalk, lest the false markings be confused with the real ones by the seamstresses in the Masques and Bergamasques workshops, to whom the costumes were sent after their hasty transit through Allée Chateaubriand. There were three or four of these studios on the outskirts of Paris. The firm provided work for many people never seen on its premises.

Alex wasn't seen very often, either. The setting he had so lovingly imagined and arranged had ceased to amuse him. For that matter, so had his love life. It all began the day he understood Tintin's real role in Maddy's life. It hadn't been tragic for either of them, and even less so for Augustin Leblanc, who never had to suffer the repercussions of a break in a relationship of which he'd been completely ignorant.

Alex had become Maddy's best pal and Nicole's amused accomplice. It was he who had taught her the mauve chalk routine, picked up from some character one evening at the Cheramy restaurant on rue Jacob;

the fellow's name was Prater or Prévert, but they all called him Jacques. Nicole had made it her own, and everyone was satisfied. Especially Alex, who was thus relieved of his function as artistic director–fitting supervisor for costumes he himself had not designed.

He lost all interest in the stock and what happened to it. "I'm not a museum guard or a salesman renting out tuxedos at Cor de Chasse," he'd announced at the company's last meeting.

When it came to the costumes he designed himself, he preferred the badly equipped dining rooms on rue de la Mare—where he was met with the smiles of Sonia and Olga, and where his coffee was always ready in either the Guttman or the Roginski kitchen—to the velvet upholstery, the portraits of the famous dead, the Fabergé egg, the sullen competence of Mademoiselle Agnès and the elegance of the VIIIth arrondissement.

NOTICE TO TENANTS: INVITATION

The Bonnets are leaving you! They invite you to share a last farewell glass, Saturday, June 29, 1934, at precisely 19 hours, in their apartment on the first-floor right.

EUGENE BONNET
*(Chief of the Registry Service
at the Saint-Mandé Mairie)*

T HOUGH MONSIEUR BONNET'S style hadn't changed, the way he chose to deliver his friendly message was decidedly modern. He had done things "American style," as he himself explained to Jeannette Clément, when at about eight o'clock that morning, he'd politely asked her to post his typed text on the glass door of her loge. "Of course, you're included too," he'd added delicately, and as usual disappeared without awaiting a reply.

Madame Lowenthal was the first to read the notice-invitation when she came down to do her marketing. She was so surprised that she immediately went back up the stairs. She paused for a moment at Madame Stern's door on the first floor, but instinct told her it was more urgent to take the astonishing news to Sonia and Olga first, and she continued her climb, confident that this time the importance of her message would justify her intrusion.

The last time she'd knocked at her neighbors' door—it was at Olga's apartment—things had gone badly. Finding them busy making Hungarian peasant dresses, she'd felt legitimately authorized to offer a few suggestions gleaned from personal memories of her native Puszta. This was all right for a bit, until, all of a sudden, it wasn't. Especially with that badly brought-up Alex, whose family name she could never remember and who seemed to have settled in there these days. He'd listened to her with a smile and then gently taken her by the arm, shown her to the door, kissed her on the forehead and said, "Dear Madame Lowenthal, you're a delicious pain in the ass, and so I suggest you be even more delicious still by going to give someone else a pain and leaving me and my lady friends to our work." And he'd closed the door.

Madame Lowenthal had been particularly shocked by the words "my lady friends." She knew enough about the subtle ambiguities of the French language to draw the proper conclusions from the incident.

Since then, therefore, she'd been reserved, contenting herself with smiling sadly at Elie Guttman and Stépan Roginski when she met these two blind husbands on the stairs.

After all, it was their business, and if there was one thing Madame Lowenthal hated, it was interfering in other people's lives. And heaven knows, she certainly could have said a lot! She wasn't like the Sterns, with their prayers and their rabbis, but even so . . .

Never celebrating Yom Kippur or Rosh Hashanah, never a circumcision or a bar mitzvah, nothing, never anything Jewish. It really was too much! To say nothing of how the children were brought up . . . if you could call it bringing children up, considering that even when they were small they'd had things their own way, sang and snickered at you for no reason, and that now they were big—because there was no room at home—they spent their days with these concierges whom she personally had never completely forgiven for replacing Madame Lutz . . .

The fleeting image of Madame Lutz, queen of the farewell celebration held at the Bonnets', reminded her of the reasons that had urged her back up the stairs. The astonishing news she had come to bring was not so much that the Bonnets were leaving, nor about the fabulous hierarchical advancement that was transforming this office worker of the *Mairie* of the XXth into a department head of the Saint-Mandé *Mairie*. No, the astonishing news concerned the Bonnet pardon.

Obviously, Monsieur Bonnet no longer held them responsible for the rifle-butt blow dealt him by the security police in the Place de la Concorde last February. To be precise, during the night of the sixth to the seventh.

The healing of his scar had been long and difficult, not only with regard to Monsieur Bonnet's skull, but in his heart and mind as well. He had sternly made the whole building aware of this, nor had Madame Lowenthal thought he was entirely in the wrong. As a result, she had strictly forbidden Monsieur Lowenthal to hang around the Auvergnat's café, where the Stavisky Affair and its consequences were gone over in detail every evening. Before February, during February and after February.

Madame Lowenthal felt herself to be much too French not to condemn foreign swindlers, and much too much of a Hungarian Jew not to despise Russian-Jewish swindlers. It was a little complicated, but that's the way she saw things. She knocked at the Guttmans.

: :

SONIA GUTTMAN retained only one thing from Madame Lowenthal's long monologue: the beginning. If the Bonnets were leaving, the first-floor left would be vacant. That and only that was the astonishing news which began to light up like a flashing neon sign, and seized by panic at the notion that someone else might—before she and Olga could—lay claim to that space so desperately needed to allow them to work without spoiling the lives of their husbands and their children, Sonia stopped listening to Madame Lowenthal, left her on the landing and knocked at Olga's door, and together they raced down to see Jeannette Clément, the only official representative of Providence Urbaine to whom they could immediately present their candidacy.

Lacking other listeners, Madame Lowenthal fell back on Madame Stern.

Madame Stern, very discreet and too abstracted to inquire, had always believed that the bandages worn by her neighbor on the landing were due to a traffic accident. So she didn't immediately understand the significance of the "Bonnet's pardon" as it was explained to her by Madame Lowenthal. On the other hand, her temperament, which was little inclined to optimism, wrung from her two remarks concerning the hazardous future faced by the entire building: "It's not until the blind man replaces the one-eyed man that we know what we have lost," and "Three thieving magpies are worth less than a hen that's a bad layer."

Discouraged by having been understood by no one, Madame Lowenthal decided to put off her errands till later. Climbing back to her own apartment on the third floor, she left her door open and watched for Barsky's awakening, which, as she knew, would be belated.

In the meantime, on the ground floor, Jeannette Clément, who was in a position to know, explained that she had no authority other than to transmit the request to Aristide Cloutier, who himself had no authority either, and she advised Sonia and Olga to write immediately to the main Providence Urbaine office. Seeing the dismay frozen on their faces at the announcement that they would have to write a letter, she suggested they wait until evening.

"Félix can easily do that for you," she said. "But when you send letters to Providence," she added, "you know when they leave, but you never know when they get there. Nor if they get there, nor who reads them, nor even if they are read up there . . . "

And when she said "up there," you might have thought she was talking about the summit of Mont Blanc.

: :

SONIA AND OLGA returned to their own apartments. For a moment they studied the lock on the Bonnets' door, which seemed to mock them and say "Find the key . . . " as in those puzzle drawings they could never figure out but which were mere child's play for Maurice and Zaza.

Just as they'd done with the only other letter they'd ever sent off, they composed a mental draft. And now they began to wonder if Félix Clément was the right man for this particular letter.

Should it be in the style of "it's my right" rather than a straight forward request? They knew Félix well enough to be somewhat leery of his denunciatory tone. Although he'd managed admirably when it came to demanding what was due them, it wasn't necessarily true that he would do as well when it came to obtaining a favor . . . And then, since the Bonnets weren't Jewish, might not Providence want to re-place the goy who was leaving with another goy?

"And what about the rent?" Olga said suddenly.

They began to make calculations from which it became clear that if the new rent was shared by both households, given what they were now making, they could manage . . . And it was then that they realized they were busy planning a new future without even discussing it with their husbands.

It was the second time they'd done such a thing. They felt a little guilty, and decided not to repeat what they'd done earlier. No, they'd wait for the return of Elie and Stépan before sending the letter, which still had to be written by someone who they weren't sure would know how to write it, to people they thought might very well not bother to read it.

The women set to work. According to the sketch, this time they were making two "Winterhalter" costumes. They didn't know who this Winterhalter was, but they weren't all that pleased with him. For the past two days, they'd been fighting with crinolines that made the mannequins so cumbersome that they'd had to move them to the kitchen before the children's beds could be unfolded.

They heard a truck draw up to the house. On the floor below, furniture was being pushed about. The main part of the Bonnet move was already under way. They began to dream about the emptiness being created beneath their feet, one they could so easily fill if only they were given authorization.

"The Croix de Feu seems to be deserting!" said Alex, whom they hadn't heard come in.

Because of the rustling of the taffeta they were adjusting on Olga's crinoline, he had trouble understanding the real reasons for the fever that appeared to have gripped them. Ordinarily so calm, they were speaking in loud voices, interrupting each other to explain to him a situation that had initially seemed so simple and about which he now understood absolutely nothing.

"Quiet!" he ordered. "Let's begin again from the beginning. The apartment below is available, right? You need space in which to work for me, right? The landlord is the divine Providence, right again? . . . I assume that Vercingetorix's place has a telephone? . . . Put on some water for coffee, I'll be right back!"

Fifteen minutes later, Alex was there again.

"It's all been taken care of," he said quietly, putting the sugar into his coffee. "The Little Boat has sounded its foghorn. Providence is on our side."

Sonia and Olga always had trouble understanding Alex. But it was especially true that morning. They had no more understood that Vercingetorix was the Auvergnat than they had understood that the little boat was Maître Du*bâteau*-Ripoix, whose very existence was unknown to them.

On the other hand, they understood immediately that the Bonnet apartment was theirs.

Speechless, they looked at this man, who was calmly drinking his coffee. They looked at him the way you might look at those great travelers who come from places so far away you're so sure you'll never go that it's pointless to ask where they come from. Those "elsewheres" peopled with telephones, semaphores, green lights and underground passages. Universes in which there are no numbers handed out to those waiting at ticket windows, no forms to be filled out in triplicate, no send-in-your-requests-we'll-let-you-knows, no return-with-the missing-documents, no your-permit-expires-tomorrows, no speak-up-I-don't understand-you-Madames, no " . . . gins-ki? With an I or a Y?"

"Let's get to work, princesses!" said Alex, who had finished his coffee.

He gave them some advice about the lawn bodices and the velvet boleros to be embroidered with golden arabesques, and when he left, they were both still behaving like sleepwalkers.

Shortly afterward, a breathless Jeannette Clément came to announce that Aristide Cloutier had just left her loge, having made a special trip to instruct her that she was to reply negatively to all applications for the now-vacant first-floor left. Orders from the main office . . . which must have its own protégés.

Sonia and Olga reassured her and told her the great news.

"Oh, so *you're* the protégées? Well! . . . " she said, with a big smile.

"It's us . . . Actually, it's our shop," replied Sonia, who was much too sensitive not to have seen in Jeannette's smile a glimmer of incredulous disapproval.

"Well, that way Félix won't have to write a letter to God . . . I'd just as soon he didn't," she said.

There was a little silence. Then she embraced each of the women in turn.

"Fine! It's going to make a change in your lives," she added, racing off.

: :

" . . . AND SINCE the burden of my new responsibilities unfortunately calls me far from here, it is with a somewhat heavy heart that Madame Bonnet and I abandon you. A strange fate has united us under the same roof, like pollen gathered here and there by a bee and carried to the hive. And like bees, we too had our queen. She has long since left us for her dear Lorraine, but she has never left our hearts, as is shown by the presence in the center of this table of her favorite treat. It is therefore to her that I will raise my glass, to her and to France, once again threatened by great misfortunes. At 58 rue de la Mare, we do not all agree on the remedies for treating this great invalid, my dear Country that is now also yours. Do not forget that . . . Good luck to all of you!"

Monsieur Bonnet refolded the paper from which he had just read his speech, placed it in his pocket and, picking up the only full champagne glass remaining on the table, joined in a toast with his guests, who already had their glasses in their hands.

The whispered "your healths" and the clink of the glasses against each other resounded in the completely empty apartment as if it were a cathedral.

The buffet was laid out on a plank resting on two trestles that Monsieur Bonnet had borrowed from the concierge of the XXth's *Mairie* and that Madame Bonnet had covered with a tablecloth. On it, she had placed some blue cornflowers, three white daisies and two red poppies, which were already losing their petals. The etched glasses, too, came from the *Mairie;* the four bottles of champagne came from Julien Damoy; and the quiche Lorraine from Au Blé d'or de Quimper. Plenty to eat and drink.

Plenty to think about in Bonnet's speech, too, as was later pointed out by Félix Clément, whom Jeannette had had to beg to accompany her to the farewell ceremony and the solemn return of the keys. He had come, seen, heard and drunk. And nothing had escaped his analysis.

Bonnet's speech had been a jingoist, paternalistic and reactionary provocation. He should have been challenged, but unfortunately it was not the right time or place to speak up, and Félix had regretted it. Nevertheless, he had clinked glasses with Eugène Bonnet—without, however, saying a word about being sorry to see him leave the building.

As for Elie and Stépan, they had heard a different speech. That of a Frenchman speaking to other Frenchmen. They even thought they'd caught a direct allusion to the Nazi peril in Bonnet's prophecies. After all, they pointed out, Hitler the German was an enemy of both the Jews and the Bonnets. Félix, however, maintained that Bonnet had only one enemy: the Left—and consequently the Soviet Union.

Madame Lowenthal had been so moved by the evocation of her old friend Madame Lutz that she'd lost the end of the speech, about which Monsieur Lowenthal had nothing to say.

The Sterns too had nothing to say, except what they would later say in private, and that concerned only the quiche, from which after eight years they had again managed to escape.

Barsky, once he had read the notice-invitation, had kept repeating, " 'We will share the *last* farewell glass . . .' actually only the second in eight years. Or maybe he meant the condemned man's last!" And it had been in this frame of mind that he'd approached the ceremony and listened to the speech. He'd had two extra helpings of quiche—"since Monsieur and Madame Stern are having stomach trouble"—and drunk three glasses of champagne.

As for Sonia and Olga, they hadn't heard a word of the speech. It was with a courteous smile but a deliberately critical gaze that they had attended the ceremony, which they found endless. They'd forced themselves to remain in the circle that had formed around the Bonnets, in front of the buffet, even though they were dying to move about the unfurnished space, whose proportions, despite being familiar, struck them as having increased tenfold—or, better still, as having returned to their true dimensions, those true dimensions that had so enchanted them when each in turn had discovered them years earlier. Now, while they were already mentally furnishing the space, they saw themselves as very young women arriving from the Gare de l'Est and setting their immigrants' bundles down on this very spot.

: :

THE CHILDREN who lived in the house hadn't been invited. In any case, the Bonnet twins had said their own farewells to the neighborhood long ago, when Florian had made the selection that broke up the rue de la Mare children's community at the close of the 1930 school year.

With tact, charity and firmness, Monsieur Florian had called in his pupils' parents separately to give them the results of his reflections on the proper orientation of their children's education.

Maurice, Robert and Sami Nussbaum were all three recommended for entrance into the sixth class of the Lycée Voltaire as scholarship students; the others were to continue their education at the school on rue Henri-Chevreau or be placed as apprentices. Monsieur Bonnet had decided he'd rather send his boys to a boarding school in Meaux, the home of his unmarried sister, who was an assistant bookkeeper with the French railways.

The twins, wearing their gold-buttoned uniforms, had been seen once or twice in the neighborhood, but generally it was the Bonnets who did the traveling when they took the boys out on Sundays. They went by train, since they could get reduced-rate tickets.

"We prefer to go there. Meaux has a good restaurant, and the beautiful wide avenues are a change from the streets here, where we'd just as soon they didn't spend too much time. And then it makes a nice outing for us," Madame Bonnet had confided one day to Jeannette Clément, who wondered why she never saw the twins in Paris.

"They must have a hell of a time in Meaux, all five of them, including the aunt!" Robert had said to Maurice, who couldn't imagine Elie and Sonia coming to wait for him at the gates of a prison to take him to lunch in a restaurant. The idea was so crazy he wanted to communicate the humor of it to Zaza. It had been a long time since they'd shared a good belly laugh—such a long time since they'd begun to hum, together and without thinking, *"She went* Pouett-Pouett *to me . . . "*

The same evening the Bonnets left, Maurice and Zaza asked about the speech, the champagne and the quiche, and then both of them went down with Sonia and Olga to see what would henceforth be their mothers' exclusive domain. A little intimidated by the professionalism with which the two women decided just where to put the big tables, the mannequins, the ironing board, the mirrors, the sewing machine Alex had talked of and the curtain they'd have to hang up to form a small dressing booth, they felt vaguely dispossessed of their mothers and excluded from a world they'd always shared with the two women.

"Couldn't I have my folding bed in one corner?" asked Maurice. "It would give you more room upstairs, and it would make it easier for me to work with Robert in the evening."

"And what about me?" said Zaza.

"For all that you and your pals do in class, you don't really need a place for extra studying after dinner," snapped Maurice, as he went upstairs to his father and Stépan.

He had the feeling he was interrupting a conversation that wasn't any of his business. They were talking of someone called Volodya.

"Who's this Volodya?" asked Maurice.

"Nobody. It all goes back a long way. It's because of what Félix was talking about a little while ago. You were saying that you're going to take your bed and set up bachelor quarters downstairs? What does your mother think about it?"

"She hasn't said anything yet—that's why I'm telling you, so you can both talk it over," said Maurice.

"Well, that's something new! What do you think of that, Stépan? Suddenly they're talking to us. If things go on like this, you think they might even ask our advice?" joked Elie.

There was just a little bit of truth in this pretense at bitterness.

Overwhelmed by the initiative of their wives, Elie and Stépan were also overwhelmed with admiration for their energy. Particularly for the energy they'd shown in restoring to their former husbands the tranquillity that had formerly been theirs when they left work and returned to a real home and not another shop. During all the years they'd worked as finishers, Sonia and Olga had always seen to it that the four corners of the black garment bags had been tied up and that all the scraps of cloth and bits of fur had disappeared well before the footsteps of Stépan and Elie could be heard on the staircase. The men had always been aware of this. Yet they had never said anything about it.

Since the women had become "disguisers," as Stépan put it, however hard they tried they never managed to completely hide the traces of whatever they were working on, and since the two mannequins had been moved in, they no longer even made the effort. Elie and Stépan, who couldn't have helped noticing, never said anything about this either, but sometimes they'd come home and then go out to have a drink at the Auvergnat's while they waited . . .

Henceforth, as though by magic, everything would go back to normal, thanks to their wives! Those women were fantastic, really fantastic —all the same, the men would liked to have been the first to hear of the departure and replacement of the Bonnets . . . Just on principle. However, they hadn't said anything about that either.

"All right, Mama and I will talk it over, and we'll tell you tomorrow," Elie went on soberly.

He looked at Maurice, to whom he hadn't said anything at all, for that matter, about his pride in having a son who spoke Greek, Latin and English in addition to French, which he had so much trouble speaking himself. A son who would be a *bachelier*—Maurice had had to spell the word out for him when he explained that it wasn't a profession, like being a leatherworker, for example. Playing on the word "bac," which meant both ferry and "baccalaureate," Maurice had made them believe, for the whole of one dinner, that to become a *bachelier* you had to write out endless assignments for two days running, but that that wasn't the worst of it: the worst was that they had to be written on a kind of cabinless flat-bottomed boat that went back and forth between the shores of an immense river until you finished writing. They hadn't laughed quite as much as he'd hoped they would. Nor had they completely believed him when he told them it wasn't true.

Everything had become mysterious and often incomprehensible since Maurice stopped going to Florian's classes.

It had begun when he'd moved from the sixth to the fifth. "In other words, you were left back?" "No, I was promoted," Maurice had explained. "It's an upside-down world!" Elie had told the others at Mercier Frères. Since then, they'd ask him every year: "Say, Lilyich, has that kid of yours finally reached the basement?" "He's getting there, he's getting there," Elie had replied that morning. "He's going into the second . . . "

"As I understand it, you want me to tell Mama that to get up to the second more easily you have to go down to the first. Right?" said Elie, happy to have contrived a French pun that made Stépan burst into laughter.

"You've got it, Papa!" Maurice exclaimed, embracing his father.

The idea of turning the first floor into a folding dormitory for Maurice and Robert hadn't come from the Cléments. Sonia had been the one to think of it.

"That way, it will change your lives, too," she'd said to Jeannette, who, too sensitive not to have grasped the allusion, had enthusiastically accepted: even with a screen, it was becoming difficult for Robert and Josette to share the same bedroom.

: :

THE TWO BEDS were placed in what had for so long been the Bonnet twins' bedroom and what Sonia and Olga now called the undressing salon. They liked this arrangement so much that it was decided not to fold them up again. Their function as folding beds had changed. Banished were the springs and little wheels that always peeked out from beneath the heavy tablecloth that covered them; forgotten their unattractive look of big bins—bulky, rectangular, useless and yet too often used as handy surfaces on which to place things that always had to be taken away in the evening; gone the squeaky symphonies that always accompanied their unfolding at night.

Unfolded and coquettishly covered with orange throws, they now served as couches during working hours. Sonia and Olga had used the same orange cloth to make curtains for the little booth that had been set up in a corner of the room. It was behind those curtains that the women undressed, and it was on those couches that they sat half naked, waiting for their fittings.

At night, the couches once again became beds. Beds for adolescent boys.

Even with the window open, the perfumes and the odors left by these unknown women lingered on; but it was those orange curtains, pulled across a narrow, free-standing mirror, that particularly excited the imagination of Maurice and Robert. They never talked to each other about this. To hide it, they'd say, "It stinks, it stinks"—and then turn out their lights.

These were two small lamps that clamped onto the pages of the books they read before falling asleep. Both had tops like mushrooms, one red, the other yellow. A present from Jeannette, they were lamps for a children's room, and they were used to read men's books before sinking into the incredibly lonely sleep of sexually uninitiated boys.

It was there they spent all their nights after they went into the Second. They ate in their parents' apartments and then met on the first floor, where Sami Nussbaum would join them for long cramming sessions.

Indifferent to what was in preparation on the large work tables, to what half clothed the mannequins and what was suspended from the hangers hung on a large rod, they'd cross the workshop without even switching on the lights and settle themselves at what had once been a kitchen table, where they'd work until bedtime under the light of a pulley lamp whose rippled opaline shade they brought down as far as possible.

With its single pot hung from a nail on the freshly painted wall, its one-burner stove—sufficient to boil water for tea or coffee—with the Latin, Greek, English and math books aligned on a shelf that had long supported large boxes of salt, sugar, chicory and cocoa, the room now resembled an austere chemistry lab, the sink a sterilized washbasin.

But in the mornings they were children again, and the laboratory was transformed into a shower room. Laughing heartily, they'd spray each other with cold water and splash around wildly—being careful not to turn the rubberized jet on their books. Before leaving, they'd mop up the floor tiles and carefully stow their toothbrushes, toothpaste and towels in the lattice-fronted pantry that served as a bathroom cupboard, then quickly make their beds, which would once again become dressing-room furniture. Maurice would go upstairs for his breakfast, Robert would go downstairs for his, and then they'd leave together for school.

Sami would be waiting for them at the corner of the alley and rue de la Mare, and all three would head for the Lycée Voltaire together, on foot when the weather was nice, by Métro when it was raining. Often, they would pass Monsieur Florian, on his way to their old school. They were a little surprised to meet him so early in the morning, but never suspected that the old teacher arranged his own schedule just for the pleasure of seeing them leave—simultaneously joyful and serious—for the inexhaustible well at which they drank deep every day: the secular and republican secondary education for which he had nominated them. By doing good work at the Lycée Voltaire, Maurice, Robert and Sami kept alive Monsieur Florian's dreams of scholarship; the oldest child in a large family headed by a widow, the universities had been closed to him in earlier days. So he would pretend to meet them by chance, his birds who had flown from the nest on rue Henri-Chevreau. He kept a close watch on them, from a distance.

They worked hard, even very hard; this was particularly praiseworthy at a time when students had all sorts of excuses to put politics before lessons and homework. Politics was an everyday presence on all the streets surrounding the large lycée. It entered the classroom through the closed windows. The cries, the slogans that came and went and were drowned out by the whistles of the riot police, the fragments of the "Internationale" and the "Marseillaise"—sometimes they overpowered the voices of the teachers and broke the legendary silence of the study halls. Politics also awaited them in the streets at the end of the day; as they left, the first marchers would be forming for the big parades. Politics crowded the entrances to the Métro, emptied the café terraces and made shopkeepers lower their metal shutters.

If, in other Parisian neighborhoods, the adolescents in the higher classes were active in politics, at Voltaire, from the eleventh to the Philo, they had to study it. It was called politics: in fact, it was really the History of France, but no one knew that yet.

It was being written under their eyes, it resounded in their ears; it was so conspicuous and noisy that it masqueraded under simple words: marches, popular outbursts, riots, disorder and racket—depending on the politics you did or did not support.

At Voltaire, it was a little like everywhere else, but less so: there weren't many representatives of the rightist Camelots du Roi; like everyone else, Maurice, Robert and Sami had once gotten into a fight after classes, but it hadn't made them join the Faucons Rouges.

The History of the present France kept them from concentrating on the histories of the past. All the histories of the past.

Old Florian had chosen the image of a well, but they preferred to think of the sources of rivers. They had had to seek these out, and since then they'd followed the rivers' courses joyously, marveling at the dizzy heights that transformed them into rapids, at the tributaries that came to swell them, at the locks that restrained and regulated their caprices.

The corrupted Greek word that became the Latin word and would become the French word; Aesop, Plautus, and La Fontaine; the Ides of March in Mallet and Isaac, and Shakespeare's *Julius Caesar*; Galileo and Jules Verne; Romulus and Mowgli; Perceval and Parsifal; the same words carved in Breton and Cornish granite; the Greek child in the poem and the French child in the song; Easter Island and Karnak; the Jeu de Paume and the tennis-court oath; the Iphigenias in Aulis, in Tauris, in Greek drama, in Racine, in Goethe; and the little broken bench of the slightly dishonest cobbler who was expelled from the Windsor market in 1603, that broken bench which gave us the word "bankrupt" for the great swindlers of modern times; colonialism and the box of cocoa showing a grinning black saying "Banania very good"; Catiline and Stavisky; African tomtoms and the drums of the Hot Club —these were the things they'd come up against every day since they'd first been given the keys to the great territory known as culture and which they themselves called school, or the sweatbox.

They weren't solemn; they played with yo yos, exploded into wild laughter, used dirty words and told filthy jokes; they weren't pedants, didn't take themselves too seriously, but they did take seriously the things they were asked to do.

Since they also ate lunch there, they spent the whole day in the sweatbox. Back at rue de la Mare they had dinner with the family. On the ground floor, as on the second, the parents asked questions.

"Did you learn anything today?" asked Elie.

"What are you up to in History?" asked Félix.

Their answers were evasive. Heads still buzzing with the day's discoveries, they sometimes tried to share them, but it was becoming more and more difficult. So they'd keep their mouths shut and let their fathers do the talking.

Their fathers talked about the present. Félix talked about the Post Office, Elie about Mercier Frères—and both, of course, about politics. About the politics that had been discussed at the Post Office and at the Mercier shop.

At the Post Office, everyone saw red, except Félix's boss, who saw blue, white and red and wanted a France for Frenchmen.

At Mercier Frères, Eli's co-workers saw things in terms of the beiges, coppers, buffs, and blacks of the animal skins from which they cut elegant leather accessories, and it was with mocking affection that they watched their boss treat himself to the luxury of going down into the streets to attack the reactionaries, to defend the claims his workers had never made and to demand in their name a liberty that he himself had never, never deprived them of.

"We'll march with you, Monsieur Paul," Meunier would say, "but only because we like you. Right, Lilyich?"

And so Lilyich went along and dragged Stépan with him, but they had a lot of trouble picking up the rhythm of the slogans, and they weren't at all sure that they really belonged among all these grandchildren of Communards, who were often surprised by their accents.

That's what was talked about at dinner that year. Downstairs, Jeannette would agree with Félix, and Josette would be bored. Upstairs, Sonia and Olga had things explained to them, and Zaza was bored.

Maurice and Robert listened, remained silent, said good night, kissed everyone and raced away.

They still lived at Papa and Mama's, but they weren't really there anymore.

: :

ON THE other hand, the girls were there more and more, especially in "Mama's place."

Zaza and Josette may have been restless at the dinner table, but they were dying of boredom at the girls' school on rue de la Mare. They had never had a Monsieur Florian to bend over their schoolgirls' cradles, and now their teacher was a Mademoiselle Delacroix.

Mademoiselle Delacroix had no interest in cultural activities, and no interest in culture for herself. She thought education for women was a waste of time. Mademoiselle Delacroix was that rare specimen, an accidental teacher. She had never meant to be one.

Widowed before her wedding day by a fiancé who had died on the field of honor and never been replaced, she had become an employee of the public education system because she had a high school diploma and because, in her world, if you had a diploma and no looks, you didn't become a salesgirl even if you wanted to. As a salesgirl in a shop, she would have met people and perhaps even found a replacement for the only man who had ever told her, "I love you." As a teacher in a girls' school, Mademoiselle Delacroix had never met anyone, and she had wasted her life. She attributed this waste to the war, to her social milieu and to her diploma.

She was bored dispensing boring lessons that never went beyond the frontiers of the rigidly defined syllabus. She was a conscientious woman, who demanded from her pupils perfect spelling, faultless memorization in geography, history and recitation, and mental arithmetic at lightning speed. She was neither strict nor permissive. She was indifferent and punctilious with the girls, whom she never got to know. She didn't want to know them, and anyway she never had the time. Mademoiselle Delacroix was often transferred.

And that was why, in the school year 1934–1935, while Maurice and Robert gamboled in the great spaces opened to them by their professors in the Second at Voltaire, Josette and Zaza wallowed in the marsh of boredom squandered on them by Mademoiselle Delacroix, temporarily assigned to rue de la Mare.

During prescribed hours, therefore, Josette and Zaza were bored, but as soon as the liberating bell sounded they ran to the workshop on the first floor and they enjoyed themselves hugely.

They also learned a lot.

Unlike the boys, who only took over the place at night, when nothing was happening anyway, the girls occupied the terrain during the day, when a *lot* was going on; none of these things were ever referred to at the dinner table, but very little about them escaped the curiosity of these thirteen-year-old adolescents. This was especially true after work had started on *The Moon Is Naked*.

The Moon Is Naked was a spectacular musical revue that a rival of the Bal Tabarin cabaret was putting on at great expense. The theme of the work was clearly indicated by its title.

"The Moon is ours," Alex had announced, the day Masques had been chosen to make the costumes that would be artistically stripped off by actors and actresses who were also required to know how to sing, speak and dance.

The least nude had their fittings at Allée Chateaubriand. The most nude, at rue de la Mare.

Four women. Four superb "phases of the Moon," according to the inscription under the sketches Alex had handed to Olga and Sonia, and which they had studied, blushing.

At first sight, the sketches appeared to show four completely nude female bodies, shadowed in places by gradations of tones ranging from the most silvery of grays to the blackest of blues. Initially, Sonia and Olga didn't understand just what there would be to sew—or, once they had understood that, what to sew it on.

"On transparent body stockings, obviously," Alex explained. "Since we can't very well sew paillettes to the skins of these nude dancers, we'll make them a second skin that will fit like a glove. They'll be dressed from head to toe, but they'll seem completely naked . . . Funny, huh?"

Paillettes, funny? Neither Olga nor Sonia would have chosen quite that word.

"It will be difficult, but it will be pretty," Olga admitted.

"Most of all, it will take a long time," put in Sonia.

"We have two months," Alex specified.

This was the first time they didn't tack the sketches to the wall. They put them in a portfolio Maurice had once used for his geography maps.

The Four Phases of the Moon were called Lucienne, Magali, Albertine and Yvette. They came every afternoon between two-thirty and three o'clock, wearing no makeup and looking a little tired. They had performed the evening before, and taken dance class that morning.

They were very tall girls, each exactly the same size. They had small breasts, high round buttocks and interminable thighs. They were between seventeen and nineteen years old, had childish faces and laughs, and one of them even had a child. The child was Magali's. He was four months old, she brought him along with her, his name was Bruno and he almost never cried.

The girls called Olga "Madame Olga," Sonia "Madame Sonia," and Alex, whenever he was around, "Monsieur Grandi."

From their big cloth carryalls they'd take out white terrycloth robes—immaculate, but indelibly stained with makeup at the collars and cuffs—and sequined shoes with two-and-a-half-inch heels. They'd undress completely behind the orange curtain, and put on their "stilts" and their robes. They never walked around nude while waiting for fittings.

At 4:07, Zaza would appear. She was almost always with Josette, sometimes with Myriam Goldberg.

"We've come to help," she'd announce, in a tone of clandestine complicity.

No one at school knew that the four towering girls who were often seen in the neighborhood—dressed in gray and navy-blue wool, one carrying a baby in her arms—were really "nude dancers"; no one either at school or in the building, because Sonia and Olga had made the girls promise to keep the secret. They kept it. And, keeping it, knew the delicious sensation of having become accomplices. Especially Zaza.

This was the first time she was her mother's accomplice in keeping a secret whose reason for staying secret her mother didn't explain.

Olga didn't explain it to Zaza because she had trouble explaining it to herself. Just as she had trouble explaining it to Sonia, her only true accomplice in the execution of work they both thought was completely reprehensible but which they performed with a conscientiousness and an inventive genius that first surprised and eventually shocked them.

Sheathed in their silky, milky and transparent second skins, Lucienne, Magali, Albertine and Yvette succeeded one another in front of the shop's standing mirror.

The making of the body stockings had been a long and painstaking job. You might say it was Phase One of the "Phases of the Moon" operation. Josette and Zaza had watched it all, after asking and being granted permission.

"You won't see more than you can see in your own mirror in the morning, my darling!" said Lucienne, who was called Lulu and who was the most talkative.

On the day the four body stockings were finished, they had stood hand in hand in front of the mirror. They looked like four marble statues in a garden. It was very beautiful, and Alex's arrival had shocked no one.

"We'd just as soon have danced like this, but it seems that's not enough to make anyone buy a ticket. So let's get to the dirty bits!" Lulu had said that evening, as she was getting dressed again. Her friends had begun to giggle.

"In future, let's call them the *erotic* bits," Alex had corrected.

"What's the diff?" Lulu objected, obstinately, from behind the orange curtain.

This little exchange had not gone unnoticed by either Zaza or Josette, who were busy dressing Bruno in his playsuit while Magali was dressing herself.

They had searched the dictionary for the word Alex had used, the only one they'd really remembered from the conversation and which they'd never heard before in their lives. They looked under "H" first, because the word was pronounced something like *héros* and because complicated words often began with an H, and finally they found, under "E," an explanation that then forced them to look under "P" for the definition of "pathological." Their research was becoming dull and boring, and the mystery remained impenetrable.

Then they decided to find out for themselves, with the help of Lulu, Magali, Titine and Vévette, from whose muffled and rambling gossip around the laundry basket in which Bruno had been installed between the two dressing-room couches they learned something new every day.

The information contained in these whisperings invariably concerned the girl who was taking her turn as Olga and Sonia's prisoner in front of the mirror. For example, they heard that Magali had no husband and Bruno no father; that on the days they had the curse they were uncomfortable when they danced but happy nevertheless, because it meant they hadn't been caught that month; that Vévette's eyes were still all red because she was always falling in love with someone impossible; that Magali's mother was a bitch because she wouldn't take care of Bruno; that if you wanted beautiful breasts you had to sprinkle them with ice water every morning, even at their age, because you had to begin as soon as they began to bud; that Albertine had become a dancer just to please her mother, who had wanted to be a star at the Opéra; that Lulu was learning English in her dressing room at the Casino because she wanted to go to America, to Radio City, where dancers kicked in cadence; that Lulu was mad about dancing and had lost her virginity by doing a split long before she'd had a lover, and that anyway Lulu wasn't that interested in lovers; besides, when you think about what happened to Magali—and what about Maryse! But then Maryse had let them use a probe on her when she was already two months gone—two months was the worst, you had to have it done at three weeks or three-and-a-half months. Maryse had waited too long or not long enough, and that's what killed her, not the probe—a probe was the best thing—or maybe boiling milk with lots of saffron, or steaming footbaths every day for eighteen days, but right at the beginning. Magali had tried it, but it hadn't helped. That's how little Bruno came to be here, and he was a darling, but still! All that for a shitty love affair which didn't last four days, and with a man who didn't even like women. Actually, that's why she'd never told Ricardo, because for a kid it's better not to have a father than to have a father who's a fag. But that Ricardo sure was handsome. Where are they now? They're doing the winter season at the Palladium, in London . . . London? Ricardo must be in seventh heaven, because it's all Fag and Company in London. No chance of Ricardo making another Bruno in London! And doesn't Bruno already look a lot like Ricardo? You know, she tried to breastfeed him, but it made one of her breasts larger than the other. How she cried when she had to give him his first bottle! Speaking of bottles, it must be about time . . .

It was time for the bottle, but above all it was time for Zaza and Josette to shine, the only time when they could justify their "We've come to help!" Finally, they could *help*.

They took turns doing things. When it was Zaza who took the already prepared bottle, swaddled in a clean diaper, from Magali's big bag, it was Josette who took out, first, the triangular diaper lined with terrycloth and then the talcum powder, and while Zaza was warming up the milk in the kitchen-laboratory's only pot, Josette was changing Bruno on Robert's couch.

"Make sure you dry his little bottom and birdie carefully, my darling," Lulu would say. "We don't want it to get chapped, do we, Bruno? He's going to need that little stick of barley sugar later, won't you, my sweet . . . "

Bruno would be in seventh heaven while Josette, shaking the box of talcum as though it were a giant salt cellar, powdered his bottom and his angelically innocent sex.

The bottle-pause in no way interrupted the bustle of Sonia and Olga, who, wearing work smocks buttoned to the neck, were about to begin Phase Two of Operation *The Moon Is Naked*.

This was the phase that Lulu had called "the dirty bits."

It consisted first in laying out and then in tacking on designs made of silver sequins, clusters of tiny beads, teardrops of paste gems and glittering jet, all designed to cover the natural but forbidden shadows. As it happened, spurred on no doubt by the authors and the producer of *The Moon Is Naked*, Alex's imagination had taken off at a gallop. Instead of going about it simply—the embroidered G-string-and-brassiere-routine, to call things by their right names—he had designed night birds in full flight, entwined serpents, man-eating flowers, and mounted butterflies, which when properly applied where it was most proper to apply them, dazzlingly and suggestively emphasized in a most equivocal fashion just what they were supposed to hide.

Each Phase of the Moon had its basic theme, and each theme had its ramifications: bolts of lightning, raindrops, shooting stars—even a sunbeam in a night of eclipse. These decorations still had to be embroidered on the tights, from the ankles to the necks of the tall, patient girls, who were amazed at the blushes that reddened the faces of Olga and Sonia when one or the other instinctively placed a fake jewel or a jet beauty mark on a part of the body undreamed of, even by Alex, as needing adornment.

"Well now, Madame Olga, you're very sly today," Zaza had overheard as she came out of the kitchen, testing the temperature of Bruno's bottle on her forearm.

: :

THE DAY when the last sequin was irrevocably attached to the mauve nipple of Vévette's breast, all four girls dissolved in tears. Lulu opened her carryall and brought out three bottles of Veuve Cliquot and a large box of Marquise de Sévigné chocolates.

"From us to you, Madame Olga, Madame Sonia. And you too, darlings. We weren't too Jew about it, there's plenty for everyone. Come on, good health—and thank you!"

: :

MAURICE AND ROBERT had shared in none of this.

Among the faint scents that lingered, even though the windows were open, scents they couldn't name, the most tenacious was the violet fragrance of Bruno's talcum powder.

It took a long time to fade away.

ON THE BONNETS' time, the first-floor left was called "the first-floor left." After their departure, and despite the Masques and Bergamasques card thumbtacked to the door, no one in the house ever called the first-floor left anything but "the Bonnets'."

Sonia and Olga went down to "the Bonnets'" and came up from "the Bonnets'," Jeannette Clément sent customers to "the Bonnets'," the boys slept in "the Bonnets'," the girls hung around "the Bonnets'," Madame Lowenthal rang—Sonia and Olga had kept the expensive installation worked by an elegant brass pull that was set in a slab of black marble and had often tempted Maurice and Zaza as they passed—at "the Bonnets'" instead of knocking and entering without warning as she had always done on the second floor; but she always chose a time to ring at "the Bonnets'" when she was sure not to run into Alex: she knew his schedule.

So did Barsky. And because he knew it, unlike Madame Lowenthal, he always rang at "the Bonnets'" when he thought Alex would be there. He had an idea. He also had his reasons, and they weren't always as self-centered or greedy as might have been expected. To his way of thinking, they were of a high moral caliber.

He and Gromoff had long since been shown the door at rue d'Aboukir by Mademoiselle Anita, who had given them to understand that her employer no longer collected secondhand merchandise. One day he decided on a little reconnaissance of his own at Allée Chateaubriand.

He announced himself as "Monsieur Isidore." Ginette had made him wait in the pretty vestibule, under the portrait of Lucien Guitry, in front of the Fabergé egg. Three minutes later, she returned. "I'm sorry, but Madame Victoria Jean is very busy. What is it you wanted to see her about?"

Reduced to being a mute spectator of a metamorphosis of which he vaguely felt himself one of the spiritual progenitors, Barsky sank into gloom. "It's not right," he told Gromoff. And he would go over the chronological chain of events, from the first jaunt of the Neuilly sister-in-law in the prince's taxi to the posting of the Masques and Bergamasques card on the door of the Bonnet apartment. One or the other of them was somehow involved all along, and Barsky wanted to be recognized as a link in the chain. It was only right.

The idea that had dawned on him was less complicated.

Because they always hung around the Vincennes racetrack, he and Gromoff had become friendly with the stableboys who took the horses out for early morning runs at Saint-Maurice. Across the road there was a bistro, and alongside the bistro, the main entrance to the Paramount-France movie studios. The guard at the studio gates frequented the bistro, and one day he invited Barsky and Gromoff over—in other words, to go through the imposing doorway and wander around the sidewalks. "Don't try to get on any of the sets or you'll be thrown out," the guard had warned them. Then, like the proud gatekeeper of a château, he had returned to his elegant lodge.

Guided by instinct, they found themselves in front of the bar-restaurant, which overlooked a pretty little pond surrounded by a lawn in the middle of this magic enclave. It was there that everyone, irrespective of class, from the machinists to the most famous actors—in other words, all those who "worked in the movies"—gathered at mealtimes or during breaks. They knew one another, recognized one another or adopted one another without knowing one another, since they were all citizens of the same small town.

The first time they had charged into the bar, Barsky and Gromoff felt quite at home. Russian was being spoken. A conversation was being carried on between a man and a woman—already middle-aged, but well preserved—while an indifferent barmaid, who didn't understand a thing they were saying, looked on.

"She's been unbearable this morning! If this goes on, I'm quitting the baggy-eyed bitch," the man said in Russian.

The woman sighed and nodded.

"Something wrong?" Barsky asked suavely, and in Russian.

His tone might have been that of a producer, a director, a script-writer, a film editor, an actor or maybe an extra offering help to a member of his professional family—certainly not that of a chance visitor.

"She's been giving him a hard time every morning for the past five years . . . Thinks she doesn't look young enough on screen! As though it weren't her own fault that she grows older every day," said the woman, calling on Barsky and Gromoff to bear witness to the obvious.

"Those women are terrible!" hazarded Barsky, and he offered a round of drinks by way of consolation.

"It makes me lose my appetite, but it doesn't stop her, she eats enough for four," said the man, raising his glass.

He jerked his chin toward the guilty party, whose famous profile Barsky now recognized bent over a cheese platter on the other side of the glazed door that separated the bar from the restaurant. Swallowing hard, Barsky continued, "Everybody knows she's trouble, but what talent she has!"

"What she has is a good makeup man and a good dresser," said the woman, laughing.

"Everybody knows that too, beginning with herself . . . Your health, my friends!" said Barsky, who finally understood whom he was talking to. "And what about costumes? Is she difficult about those too?" he continued in a sympathetic voice.

"Never satisfied . . . Nothing's ever right," sighed the woman, in turn saluting him with her glass. "What a profession, eh?"

"And how are things with you?" Fedor Boulansky asked politely. "I know we've worked together, but I can't remember on what film . . . "

"Was it *L'Epreuve*? In Joinville?" suggested Tania Boulanska.

"No," Barsky answered firmly, after a pause in which he pretended to scour his memory. "No, it wasn't Joinville, it was somewhere else . . . "

A breathless and worried-looking young man sailed into the bar.

"Has she finished stuffing herself?" he asked Tania.

"Go and ask her," replied Fedor. "Why? Are you ready to shoot?"

"Just about," said the young man, turning toward the restaurant, more worried-looking than ever.

"I'd better get her into shape," said Fedor wearily, as he slid off his bar stool.

"And I'd better dress her again," sighed Tania, getting off her own.

"See you later!" they both said to Barsky and Gromoff.

"See you later!" the latter chorused, and Prince Andrei kissed Tania Boulanska's hand.

"WHAT ARE their names again? I've completely forgotten," Barsky asked the barmaid after the others had left.

"Oh, that's Féfé and Tata Boubou!" she said, as though stating the obvious. "And who are you?"

"Why, Isidore!" Barsky replied, adopting the same tone. "Have a good day, Madame!" he added, turning to the famous actress, who was dashing out of the restaurant followed by the young man, now smiling and relaxed.

"Thank you, thank you . . . See you later, Adrienne!" they heard above the creaking of the door the young man held open for the star.

Barsky and Gromoff ordered another drink.

"What are you playing at?" Gromoff whispered softly in Russian.

"Amusing myself," answered Barsky. "What do we owe you, Adrienne?"

Adrienne pushed the bar slips toward Barsky. He left a big tip.

"Thank you, Monsieur Isidore. See you tomorrow," murmured Adrienne, with a charming smile.

As they walked toward Gromoff's taxi, a little redheaded man ran out of one of the studios and asked if he could share the cab at least as far as Paris.

"Of course," said Barsky, getting into the back seat with him. "Driver, drop the gentleman off at Château de Vincennes," he said to Gromoff.

"At your service, Prince," Gromoff answered in French. "Always at your service, asshole!" he added in Russian.

"Everything all right?" Barsky asked the little redhead, after a moment's hesitation.

"Everything would be better if it wasn't already midday, if we weren't in Seine-et-Marne and if my van hadn't had a breakdown! Because it's not going to be easy to find a Virgin of Guadeloupe in Joinville-le-Pont before four o'clock! A Virgin of Guadeloupe no one will even see, thanks to all the pompoms and gewgaws they've hung everywhere. It's already hard enough to make out the actors buried in all that crap . . . If only they'd told me yesterday! . . . It's always the same, always the last minute. My prop shop is crammed with virgins and saints—Saint Annes, black Virgins, Bernadettes, Thérèse of Lisieux, Joan of Arcs—but no Virgin of Guadeloupe . . . And if I don't find one, I'm in big trouble!"

He was really desperate.

"You should try the fleamarkets," Barsky suggested. "Especially the Clignancourt ones. Do you know the Nussbaum stand?"

"I always go to Saint-Ouen," answered the redhead.

"Let's try Nussbaum," said Barsky. "Driver, to Clignancourt, please."

"*Pajalsta,*" grumbled Gromoff.

"Let's try," agreed the redhead. "But I'll pay the whole fare, right? It's for the production. She's going to cost them a bundle, their Virgin of the Islands . . . *If* we find her!"

They found her.

Not at Nussbaum's; but, at Nussbaum's, Manolo remembered he'd seen one in the market five or six months ago. He took them to Old Lady Dupraz. Old Lady Dupraz had no trouble remembering the Virgin of Guadeloupe they'd been asking too much money for. Loeb must have bought it. Loeb had indeed bought it and immediately resold it to a customer who collected religious artifacts. Loeb went through a notebook he kept in a Bank of France cashier's bag and found his collector's address.

"I'll call and tell him you're not thieves, if you like."

Loeb, Barsky, the redhead and Gromoff went off to a bistro, and Loeb put in a call from the bar.

"He's expecting you. He's crazy about the movies."

At 2:30, Barsky and the redhead rang at the door of Monsieur de Bello, Quai Voltaire.

At 2:40, Monsieur de Bello exchanged his Virgin of Guadeloupe for a receipt signed by Pierrot Mérange, propman, which guaranteed that his virgin would be returned intact the day after next. De Bello would have liked to point out that she didn't come from the islands, as might be thought, but it would have taken too much time. Isidore and Pierrot were already out the door.

At 3:35, the Prince's taxi drew up at the Saint-Maurice Studios for the second time that day. The little flower-covered Virgin was on time. As for Barsky, he was the man of the hour.

Throughout this treasure hunt, which he had at first considered merely an amusement designed especially to get a laugh out of Gromoff, Barsky had sensed a passionate excitement growing in Pierrot, one he had previously encountered only in poker players and racetrack gamblers, and it had communicated itself to him in turn. He recognized it, and was amazed. He was amazed that it could also be connected to a job.

"It's thanks to my friend Isidore that I found your exotic little

Madonna, Monsieur," Pierrot had said when he introduced Barsky to the director as he congratulated his propman.

All this happened on the A Stage. Féfé and Tata Boubou came up to congratulate him in Russian, and from a distance the star called out, "Thank you, thank you."

: :

BARSKY RECLAIMED his usual seat alongside Gromoff, and for a long time they drove in silence through the Bois de Vincennes.

"That was fun, eh, Andrei?"

"You're the kind who cleans up the first time he plays at the casino . . . You'd better not go back," Gromoff advised.

Barsky said nothing.

Go back? . . . He could think of nothing else—to go back before they'd forgotten him.

So he went back, without Gromoff, for the simple pleasure of hearing Adrienne say "Hello, Monsieur Isidore," and Pierrot Mérange toss him a "Hi, buddy." Now that he was a familiar face, they talked freely in front of him, either in the bar or on the sidewalk. No one wondered what he was doing there because everyone thought he had an official position in some production or other.

The miracle of the Virgin of Guadeloupe having failed to repeat itself, Barsky had waited. And one day, while he was gossiping with Tania Boulanska, who was complaining about the badly sewn buttons on a costume delivered that morning, he saw the light.

"People don't know how to do decent work anymore," the dresser had grumbled.

"That depends on the people. I know some who still remember how," Barsky had said.

"Send them to us then, because we don't want to use the others for our next movie."

There was something imperial about Tania Boulanska's "we"; she sounded decisive and determined.

"I'll see what I can do," Barsky had said.

He hadn't tried to find out who those unwanted "others" were. It was enough for him that they weren't wanted.

"The next movie—what is it?" he asked casually.

"I don't know yet. Let's hope to God there'll be a next one. In this business you never know." And Tania had sung the first few bars of an old Russian song, whose words meant, more or less: "Like a bird on the branch, I wander with the will of the wind . . . "

Barsky had been shaken by her cynical fatalism. He suddenly had a mournful vision of this place deserted by the people he knew and who knew him, a place that would soon be full of people who had not witnessed his hour of triumph.

He told himself he'd have to act quickly if he wanted to be the one to bring the movies to rue de la Mare before the movies had a chance to discover Allée Chateaubriand.

And that's what he'd wanted to tell Alex Grandi.

Things worked out beautifully: Alex had just broken with Masques and Bergamasques for good.

T WAS IN HER big and beautiful house in Troyes, where she had vainly awaited those gay Parisians who never came to see her, that poor Madame Augustin Leblanc gently slipped from life as she slept.

The sudden disappearance of the old lady—whose charming ghost had appeared, like the token godmother you permit to cut the birthday cake, only once within the bosom of the Masques and Bergamasques family—nevertheless shook the firm from top to bottom.

Contrary to what had so long been believed about the company's finances, it wasn't Tintin who'd shelled out: it was Madame Tintin.

Thus, somewhat abruptly, Nicole summed up for Maddy the substance of the conversation she had just had with Maître Dubâteau-Ripoix, who had called her from Troyes. The lawyer had been with Liliane and Roger Ziegler, to whom the will of the deceased—who was to be buried the next day—had been shown.

After a few comments about the cruel fate that had overtaken them all at Masques, Maître Dubâteau-Ripoix had felt it necessary to point out that he was not only the legal advisor of the firm, but—above all —the Ziegler-Leblanc family lawyer and, consequently, the lawyer of the heirs. In the present instance, the lawyer of Liliane Ziegler, henceforth half owner of the estate with her father, the only other heir of Madame Leblanc. "But we'll have time enough to speak of all that tomorrow. Dress warmly—the cathedral will be glacial . . . " he had advised, before hanging up.

Maddy was in the middle of a fitting when Nicole had come to tell her the news. Mademoiselle Angès had quickly thrown together a black outfit for her that was sober enough to be suitable for a friend of the family while elegant enough to keep her from being taken for a member of the family.

"The veil will come later," said Nicole, looking into the mirror and straight into Maddy's eyes.

Hearing herself make this strange comment, which had escaped her involuntarily, Nicole would have found it impossible to say whether she'd meant a bridal veil or the veil of a future widow.

Maddy hadn't replied. But Mademoiselle Agnès had smiled and nodded her head in a way that expressed simultaneously the subtlety of her understanding and the deep-seated complicities and secrets that linked these three women when they thought they were alone.

They weren't. Alex, who had stopped by to pick up his travel instructions for the pilgrimage to Troyes, as he put it, was still hanging around when everyone thought he'd already left. He'd heard and seen everything. He appeared.

"Dress warmly, Alex my friend, because apparently it'll be very cold down there tomorrow," Nicole said, more Victoria Jean than ever.

Alex didn't answer immediately. He studied all three of them: Maddy, whom he had loved very much; Nicole, who had always amused him; and Mademoiselle Agnès, whom he had always found deadly boring. To each of them he might have said something: something tender, funny or nasty. But he couldn't separate them anymore. It was a group, a sect, an organization that he faced now—a small army preparing for attack. He no longer wanted to have anything to do with these people, he told himself as he searched for some way to announce his departure. Ordinarily so witty, he refused to allow himself the luxury of humor.

"I won't catch cold because I won't be there. I'm leaving you, ladies. I'm no longer part of the Firm."

Passing through the vestibule, he took time to recenter the Fabergé egg under its cover; it was a bit too far to the left. "As for you, I'll miss you," he said affectionately to the egg.

Then he crossed the threshold of Masques and Bergamasques and gently closed the door behind him.

: :

BETWEEN the George V and Les Pyrénées Métro stations, Alex went over the years he had just said goodbye to. The professional summing up could be made in a single word, "idiocies," whose four syllables perfectly caught the various rhythms of the train's movement: rapped out jerkily during the fast runs or stretched out into sighs during the slow opening of the doors at the stops.

Idiocies, nothing but idiocies since that idiocy of *The Dispossessed*, which had snared him partway. And now the rest of him had followed.

He'd been led astray. Wandered off among beads, laces, embroideries and frills, gewgaws and feathers, braids and brocades; gone astray among silly operettas, peasant folk-tales, phony great plays, petit-bour-geois melodramas and porno-cosmographic revues like that inept piece of pretentiousness, that moonstruck trash which had gone over so well that it was now playing in London.

" 'My kingdom for a horse,' said that other asshole; no, goddamn it, I'd trade all my stupid successes for a stupider one, but Pitoëff would have to act in it; even lace-up corsets and crinolines, but just for Chekhov; broads without a stitch on, why not? But only for Aristo-phanes! . . . "

That's what Alex was thinking, watching people getting on and off the train as he hadn't done for ages. Not since the idiocy of *The Dispossessed*, in fact. He started to laugh, imagining a woman getting on at the next station wearing the famous pailletted gown, dragging the sable after her as though it were some enormous poodle.

That's what had been idiotic: he'd got out of the habit of observing his contemporaries, because the contemporaries he had to dress never took the Métro, never did housework, never did the marketing or really made love, never had to keep office hours or deal with unwanted children. The contemporaries he'd had to costume were the contempo-raries of no one in this world. They were fashion plates, with not even a tuxedo button missing.

The image of the button caught his imagination, and he began to take stock of how his rediscovered contemporaries were dressed. He saw frayed cuffs that had just been trimmed with scissors, much more obvious than those that had been carefully edged in a color that almost matched; ear clips, plus matching necklaces and rings, a red-gold wed-ding ring that was wide, thick and rounded, and had sunk into the fat of an old ring finger; shapeless but supremely elegant tweeds, and a brand-new, cardboardy Prince of Wales check; preknotted ties attached to celluloid collars; coats that had been turned; mended silk stockings, stockings that were running or had run yesterday, the run stopped with a dab of nailpolish that had been colorless the day before but by now looked grubby; darning that was guaranteed invisible; soles of honey-colored crepe and their poor little ersatz sisters; phony "Burberry" coats from the "Fashionable" store; the girdle pulled down over a woman's buttocks when she stood up; immaculately white ankle socks that fit tightly—so tightly that they made the calf bulge; unmatched shoe laces; an astrakhan collar so worn at the crease that the bald black leather looked polished; a short jacket refashioned from a man's suit coat; a pretty white blouse under a handknitted bottle-green cardigan worn with a gray jersey skirt; a navy-blue beret only half covering a barrette over the right ear; and, of course, buttons: buttons hanging by a thread, buttons too small for the split buttonholes, two mother-of-pearl buttons sewn on with cross stitches instead of with a parallel stitch the way their twins were, and especially one button—a big, heavy, pistachio-green, Bakelite diamond-shaped button, too heavy for the artificial silk of the short black coat it was supposed to close at the waist, jiggling with every step like the maharajah's pendant in *Around the World in Eighty Days.*

: :

ALEX ALMOST forgot to change trains at Châtelet.

It had also been a long time since he'd taken the Métro. Not since the idiocy of *The Dispossessed,* in fact!

At the beginning, he'd had the use of Maddy's little Talbot, then there'd been a period when he'd taken taxis, and finally there'd been the firm's Citroën. The Masques' Citroën with Lucas, who was sometimes the chauffer, sometimes the delivery man, sometimes the floor waxer and sometimes the man who changed blown fuses. Lucas was a bit too talkative, but nice—well, not nasty. But he too was probably a little corrupt: another of Nicole's recruits, that Lucas! Completely devoured by Madame Victoria! And to think that he would be the one to trot the new boss round to management meetings: the sad, colorless, boring Liliane Ziegler, who'd been born Leblanc, the mischievous Lily! That Lucas! He who never took the trouble to raise his checked cap . . .

Come to think of it, he hadn't noticed any caps in the Métro. Either he hadn't taken a good look, or it wasn't the season for caps. He spotted four of them, though, in the interminable corridors leading to his train connections. He walked slowly, taking long strides. The strides of a stroller.

He dropped some coins into the bowl of a beggar singing "Ramona," his eyes shut tight behind navy-blue glasses rimmed with steel. He took his time getting the coins out of his pocket, bending down to the bowl, listening to a few bars of the song, photographing everything in his head. Everything: from the infantry boots with their battered, worn, crumpled, blackish-green and moldy bronze uppers to the trousers of a department-store section manager, with their dirty-white stripes over sewer-rat gray and the six-button but buttonless blazer worn without a shirt and held around the waist by a Boy Scout belt.

He walked off whistling "Ramona." It had been a long time since he'd heard that song. It went back to his days at the Beaux-Arts. Before all these idiocies had begun!

He stopped at the bottom of the stairs to the platform and nearly went back to check out what he'd just seen. And then he told himself that the blind man might not be all that blind, and that he might upset him by going back to look at him more closely.

He also told himself they hadn't waited for him before filming *Boudu Saved from Drowning*. More's the pity. They hadn't waited for him before filming *L'Atalante*, either. Without him, there had been that cheerless wedding party heading for the rocks! Without him, they'd had a white satin dress, so disarming with its mock chic, and the devastating white tulle veil, being both too short and too long at once! He was dead now, the guy who'd created *L'Atalante*. He'd just gone and died without waiting for Alex.

"He couldn't have known I'd be along," Alex murmured in a low voice as he went down the stairs. He made it onto the platform just before the automatic door closed.

: :

HAVING LIQUIDATED his past by the time he had changed trains at Châtelet, Alex now had to construct his future between Châtelet and Les Pyrénées. Especially his immediate future: what he was going to tell Sonia and Olga and how he was going to say it.

After closing the door at Allée Chateaubriand, it had been quite natural for him to buy a Métro ticket and head for rue de la Mare— not mechanically, just the way you rush home when you've got good news to tell.

But now, only a few versts from the Les Pyrénées station, he began to wonder if the news he was bringing would be as well received as he hoped by his two beloved spangle-Stakhanovites.

"They're not going to understand a thing, poor darlings, if I tell them the truth as I see it. I'll have to disguise it for them somehow," he told himself.

He loved them with all his heart, today more than ever; and though he saw them almost daily, he was moved by the idea of soon being with them. He was going to see their beautiful, blue, childishly believing eyes, always a little questioning and so eager to understand. To understand everything—the work to be done as well as the new words. He didn't want to have to read fear in those eyes, as had already happened once or twice. Nor dismay or worry about tomorrow, nor the bitterness of seeing the work they had done yesterday rejected by him today.

His own private truth was not the thing to tell them. They needed another, just as true, but simpler and more reassuring. He searched for a formula. Time was growing short; he had to get off at the next stop. He found it.

"I've turned in my apron, but not yours. I'm leaving them, but you're keeping me. And I'm keeping you. And you're keeping them, and they're keeping you. And you won't have a minute's rest, because it's all going to make a lot more work for you!"

That was it! That's what he was going to tell them. He was in such a hurry to get there that he leaped from the still-moving train.

Alex had forgotten only one thing, but it was understandable, since it was the one thing no one ever spoke of. That no one had ever spoken of. No one except old Anita, once, once only, years ago, when he had asked her where to find those mysterious dressmakers who had done such a perfect job on Maddy's gown. She had blushed and let out, as though it were a secret, that Madame Olga was Madame Jean's sister-in-law, "but that's none of our business . . . " At the time it had made so little impression on him, his heart and head were so full of love and future projects, that he had scarcely listened to Anita and had remembered nothing but the address of those two women and their combined first names.

Sonia-Olga, Onia-Solga, as he sometimes called them to make them laugh, had never referred to the firm for which they worked other than by its commercial name or by the banal expression "the Bosses." He remembered that one of them was vaguely related to Victoria, but he wouldn't have been able to say if it was Sonia or Olga. And when he ran into Stépan, it was at Olga's husband, Zaza's father and Elie's friend that he smiled when he said hello, not at Janek's brother.

That's what Alex had forgotten while he walked down rue de la Mare whistling "Ramona" and mentally rehearsing the little speech he'd just perfected.

And he was thinking about the look of the next day's enormous funeral wreath, bannered with MASQUES AND BERGAMASQUES in gold on violet watered silk as he untacked the card on the door of "the Bonnets'."

He'd always hated that name, which had been Maddy's idea. He'd had a great deal of trouble getting her to acknowledge that it wasn't borrowed from Baudelaire. She'd taken it badly, and before the inevitable "Just because I'm a miner's daughter . . . " he saw coming into her eyes, he'd clasped her in his arms and sworn he was telling the truth; they'd made love, and the name had been kept because Maddy liked it so much.

Now, with a little distance and knowing what he knew, it occurred to him that the idea had probably come from poor Madame Leblanc; that one day, as she reread poor Verlaine under the leafy trees of her solitary and sunny park in Troyes, she had noted it, then breathed it to Augustin Leblanc, who had brought it back to Paris.

"Off with the Masques!" he murmured—a pity he couldn't share the joke—as he tore the card to bits and dropped them in his pocket. Then, as usual, he pounded three times on the door, now stripped of its professional identification.

: :

WHEN ALEX had smilingly asked them to take Maddy's photo out of The Family Picture Frame, Sonia and Olga began to wonder.

Like everything else, The Family Picture Frame had been moved down to the Bonnets'. No one ever looked at it, but without it something in the background of their daily work would have been missing. So the thing was enthroned, just as it had been on the second floor, in the middle of the mantelpiece. Sonia and Olga had often worked the four little brass fasteners that held the back of the frame to the mahogany borders of the passe-partout mounting. The operation was a painstaking one, and there was something ceremonious about it. When The Family Picture Frame was dismounted, it was always to introduce a new and precious souvenir, never to remove an old and devalued one.

The women had no devalued souvenirs.

In the days when they still looked at what Alex called the photo of Maddy they'd always called it "the photo of the beautiful gown," never anything else. It was a long time since they *had* looked at it, but considering it again, since they were obliged to, they didn't see why it should have lost the virtues that had once destined it for The Family Picture Frame.

But Alex seemed so set on it that, to please him, they removed the picture, which Olga put in the sewing-machine drawer.

There was now something like a white hole to the left of the frame —a big empty rectangle that would have to be filled. They filled it by rearranging the other pictures, which slid like cards under a fortuneteller's fingers. Some, which had been completely or partly hidden by others for so long that they'd been forgotten, now reappeared.

"Who's this?" asked Alex, leaning over the photo of a man extending his hand toward the camera lens in a vain attempt to hide his smiling, saber-scarred face.

"That's Volodya," said Sonia, after a slight hesitation. "He's a cousin," she added, as she adjusted the brass fasteners and returned the frame to the mantel.

"Make me a cup of coffee and I'll explain everything," said Alex, just as he had done on his first visit.

: :

THEY KEPT silent. He had spoken for some time, had drunk two cups of coffee. They'd had trouble following what he was saying. There was this "apron" that he was handing over but they weren't: but Alex wasn't a cobbler, and they weren't cooks! . . . Next, there were all those "I'm leaving them, but they're keeping you, we're splitting up, we're quitting one another but we're remaining together . . . " It was really too complicated.

They had felt something very serious was happening when he had insisted they get rid of the photo of the beautiful gown, as though to erase the memory and proof of what they could do. Of what they had known how to do even before it was their real profession. If it was over, he should have said so. But he shouldn't have done that, it wasn't very nice. He must be very unhappy to be so unkind.

He waited for them to speak. They said nothing. Olga stood up. She went off to check on something she thought she'd fleetingly noticed a little while ago, when she'd opened the door.

"He's even taken down the card!" she whispered to Sonia in Yiddish, as, without looking at her, she went back to her place at the little kitchen table where the three of them had been sitting.

"If you're going to talk behind my back, we'll never understand one another," scolded Alex with a smile.

"There's nothing for us to understand anymore, Alex, now that *she* has made us go back to being finishers," said Olga, staring at him.

He saw neither fear nor dismay in her face; nothing but the exhausted resignation of someone who really isn't surprised at misfortune, merely a little startled that it had arrived a bit earlier than expected.

"Who's this *she,* and why *go back to being finishers*?" asked Alex, who'd not understood a word—except that he was beginning to understand that they themselves hadn't understood anything, either.

Olga didn't even bother to answer.

"Who is this *she?* What do you mean?" Alex repeated gently.

"You know very well," replied Sonia, who until then had said nothing.

"No, Sonia, I *don't* know," Alex said impatiently.

Sonia looked at Olga. Olga looked at the table.

"Well?" said Alex.

There was another brief silence. Sonia finally made up her mind.

"She . . . is them . . . I mean, it's his wife, Stépan's brother's wife. She's the one who's making us go back to being finishers, the way we were at the start. In other words, right back to square one."

To make him understand better, Sonia had copied the gestures and inflections Maurice and Zaza had used on rainy Thursdays when they were younger and would fight bitterly about who'd get to go first in a game the rules of which completely escaped her.

"That's it—back to square one, like when we'd just arrived!" said Olga, looking up in agreement.

To their great astonishment, Alex began to laugh. They waited patiently until he'd calmed down—which took a couple of seconds—and then Olga asked him, with considerable dignity, just what was so funny about what had just happened to them. Or was it what they'd said? They spoke French as well as they could . . .

"Everything's funny," he answered, pulling a handkerchief from his pocket to wipe his eyes.

Three fragments of the torn card drifted silently to the floor. Olga picked them up and, in the hollow of her hand, restored a piece of the puzzle.

"And this? . . . Is this funny, too?" she said, shoving the torn card under his nose.

"And the pretty picture of our first costume that we've been forced to take away so we can be made finishers again at Fémina-Prestige, is that funny too?"

Olga had spoken so loudly that the veins in her neck stood out.

"Help! Help! I'm drowning. Put me ashore, I'm lost! Saint Misunderstanding, pray for me!" yelled Alex.

It was the first time they'd heard him raise his voice. They were stunned. There was a leaden silence, during which Alex looked from one to the other.

"All right, here's how things stand! We'll begin from the beginning . . . I'll explain everything to you . . . "

His everyday smile had come back.

"Explain—but for once, Alex, please, use words that we understand, not the way you just did. We didn't understand anything!" said Olga, going to put on water for fresh coffee even before he asked for it.

"I'll explain. But first you'll have to explain to me how anyone goes about being 'finishers, the way you were at the start,' okay?"

He'd imitated their accent so perfectly that they in turn burst out laughing. Olga set the little coffee maker on the table, sat down again and for Alex's benefit told the story of their arrival.

The arrival under the glass enclosure of the Gare de l'Est.

She also told about the departure, before the arrival.

And she also told about before the departure.

And she told about Petliura in Poland.

Then Sonia told about Petliura in the Ukraine.

And Sonia told about her own arrival, before Olga's, under the glass enclosure of the Gare de l'Est.

And so Alex entered a world even more foreign to him than the one he'd reestablished contact with in the Métro a little while before. This world wasn't one he'd simply forgotten: he'd never even known it existed.

Then Olga told again about getting out of the train under the glass shed, the terribly dirty bundle, her big belly, the dust, Stépan's cap, Janek's panic, Anita's kindness and Nicole's absence.

And about the birth of Zaza, and Nicole's absence.

And about the first imitation weasel eyes, and the sable cape, and the death of Petliura, and Stépan's anger, and the beautiful gown, and their letter, and Nicole's continued absence and the present absence of Victoria Jean.

And the more Olga spoke of the absence of that absent woman, the more Nicole-Victoria grew in importance and the more Alex realized that the shadow of that unknown woman had never ceased to haunt this house—a house into which she had never set foot.

Invisible from the very first day, immense and all-powerful, it was she who rolled the dice that made them either move ahead or go back to square one as if she'd never forgiven them for coming. And still less forgiven them for coming from where they came from.

All this was a great revelation to Alex. And while Olga evoked her feared, inexorable shadow, Alex had a vision of the panicky face of the real Nicole as he had left her less than an hour ago. Nicole, in the mirror, between her two accomplices, caught with her hand in the cookie jar and slapped for it when he resigned. Nicole at bay, threatened by that wretched will, in great danger of finding herself *right back at the start.*

The disparity between this busy little ant and the omnipotent lioness described by Olga was such that he began to laugh again, and Olga stopped talking.

"How old is Zaza now?" Alex asked.

"Thirteen and a half," Olga and Sonia said together.

"And this has been going on for thirteen-and-a-half years! It's unbelievable!" exclaimed Alex.

"What is?" asked Olga.

"That after thirteen-and-a-half years you still haven't understood that without you and your work she would be nothing, Madame Nicole Victoria Jean, NOTHING, do you hear? Without you, without me, she's nothing! She's already lost me, and you're going to see how she'll try to hang onto you. Without you, they've had it at Masques, whereas you—you exist without Masques! That's why I tore up the card on the door. You're free. Do you know what that means? You're free, free to say yes, free to say no! You're at home, at 'the Bonnets',' and you work for whomever you want. That's what I was trying to explain. As for this other business, about the photo, it's not the pretty gown I didn't want to see anymore, it's the beautiful lady—or rather the lady's beautiful face. And I can't explain that to you, because it would take too long, it's too complicated, and not very amusing."

"Are you leaving because of her?" risked Sonia.

"A little—but it's not only that . . . " said Alex.

The doorbell rang. The women looked at each other and Sonia went to open it.

Alex recognized the voice of Lucas, the chauffeur. Sonia came back with an envelope in her hand, and Alex heard the Citroën start up.

"What did I tell you! They didn't waste any time!" Alex laughed.

But his smile died. It was still fear that he read in Sonia and Olga's eyes. In spite of everything he had just said, they were afraid. So intensely afraid that their fear spread to him.

Sonia held the envelope in her hands without opening it. He took it from her, opened it, glanced through the letter hastily and, without allowing them to see anything of his deep joy, asked them in a solemn voice to please seat themselves comfortably. He took his time before he began to read the letter the way you might read a story to children.

Mesdames,

The Management is happy to inform you that following an administrative reorganization our Firm is finally able to offer you the exclusive contract (as cutters–dressmakers–embroiderers) that it has long desired to submit for your approval.

We also take this occasion to make known to you that Monsieur Alexandre Grandi is no longer a member of the Firm, and that in the future you will no longer be dealing with him.

However, as in the past, Masques and Bergamasques remains, more than ever, one big family.

Good luck!

signed: For the Management,
illegible

The women looked at Alex, who had placed his hand over his heart as he declaimed the last lines.

"Why are they talking to us about family all of a sudden?" asked Olga after a moment. "This is the first time . . . "

"They're not really talking to you about 'family,' at all, Olga! They're talking about the Great Big Family. . . . When things go badly, the bosses always talk to their employees about the Big Family. They talk that way to all their employees, even those who are part of the real family. . . . You see, the real family has nothing to do with the Great Big Family. They don't want you in the family, but they need you in the Great Big Family. Me, I'm not part of the family, and I've quit the Great Big Family. And so Madame Illegible writes to you in the name of the Great Big Family so that I won't take you with me to another Family, you who are my real family, even though I'm not a member of your family. Come on, now—you don't have to be a university graduate to understand that!"

He had begun his long speech in a slow voice, then, as he became aware of the incomprehension growing in Olga and Sonia's eyes, his delivery speeded up, until he finally saw that little gleam that he loved so much—the one which preceded laughter.

"Are *you* satisfied? We haven't understood a thing," said Sonia, trying to contain her laughter.

" 'bsolutely nothing!" said Olga, giving way to hers.

"Well then, I'll explain . . . " sighed Alex.

"Oh no! Not that!"

And finally, together, they burst into laughter.

: :

None of them had heard the sound of the key in the lock.

"Well, it's a lot more fun here than at school!" Zaza cried as she entered the workshop, followed by Barsky, who had been waiting outside for a good quarter of an hour, uncertain whether to ring the bell. The disappearance of the Masques and Bergamasques card had stopped him dead in his tracks. He had a feeling great changes were going on, and wondered, his heart beating wildly, if he hadn't arrived too late.

"Well, what's new here?" he asked jovially.

"Lots, Isidore my friend," Alex replied with a smile. "What's with you?"

"Oh, I'm in films now," Isidore declared easily.

"You'll have to tell us all about it tomorrow, Isidore," said Alex.

OU CAN WEAR it while we're driving in the country, but as soon as we get near the city, put on the new one."

"Very good, Madame Victoria," replied Lucas, raising a finger to the brim of his checked cap.

Beside him on the empty seat was the new cap. Pearl-gray, rigid and flat, it looked like a pancake, and its stiff black-leather visor shone in the darkness like patent. Lucas shot it a nasty look. "A good thing I can still use my own head," he thought. "I can't feel my legs at all." His gabardine uniform was tight under the arms, at the collar and at the waist, but it was the long brown-leather gaiters that particularly tortured him: they rose to mid-leg and stopped his circulation at the curve of the calf. He wriggled his toes to get rid of the pins and needles.

It was seven in the morning. There were only a few trucks on the road, and when Lucas had to pass them he sounded his horn twice by way of thanks. They must be laughing their heads off, he told himself, imagining the jokes as the hanging garden he'd had so much trouble stowing on the roof of the Citroën loomed in front of their headlights. The wreath was so big it hung over the luggage rack behind, in front and at the sides. "We'll be in a greenhouse when the sun comes up," he added, looking at the palms falling gracefully over the windshield wiper.

It must have cost a bundle, a monster like that, all those gladiolas, white roses and lilies in the middle of November. Lilies in November? I'll have to check when we get there. They must be artificial, like those flowers they sew on hats. It'll be funny if they are—in a week, everything will have rotted except the lilies.

What sense did that make?

What sense had anything made since yesterday? He didn't get it. Why hadn't they taken the train as planned? Why had they sent him off at top speed to old Anita on rue d'Aboukir to pick up a letter that he had to rush over to those old ladies in the XXth, and why, when he got back, had they decided to dress him up like a cavalry lieutenant?

Christ, what a circus! First Big Ginette had had to rummage through the stock: there'd been no private chauffeur's uniform his size. Too tall, too well built, he was. What a weird feeling it'd been to find himself in shorts, like all those hams who were always stripping down in the Allée Chateaubriand shop. Old men, young men, all carrying on like a bunch of skirts, prancing around and ogling themselves in the mirrors for hours on end. It had made Ginette laugh when she'd seen him there. Not him.

At least at Latreille's it had been frank, honest and quick. A work outfit? Of course, Monsieur, see the "Chauffeur" rack. It might just as well have been the "Pastry Cook" rack, or the "Plumber" 's. After all, a job's a job!

Still, he'd been wrong to let them get away with these gaiters. *Leggings,* the Latreille salesman had called them, in English. He'd liked the other model without the *leggings* better, but Ginette had put in a phone call: pearl-gray gabardine cap, *leggings,* rust-red boots. Packed, it weighed a ton!

Gildaise was still fast asleep when he got into harness this morning at five on the dot. He'd gone to pick up the car at the garage on avenue de Neuilly, and then he'd loaded the fucking wreath, which was being kept fresh in the courtyard. Luckily Armelle had come down in her robe with Gildaise, because the three of them together had hardly been able to load the "Eternal Regrets of Masques and Bergamasques." Armelle had kept saying "the poor lady, the poor lady," even though she'd never laid eyes on her.

It was true that nobody knew the old lady who'd died. She'd never even been seen at rue Charles-Laffite. The old man, yes, he'd been seen —or at least Armelle had seen him with Maddy, years ago. One evening the boss and his wife had gone at each other in that gibberish of theirs, and Armelle had been scared and told Gildaise about it.

But all that was long, long ago.

He passed a big trailer truck. The driver returned his two whacks on the horn.

He'd have to make some time one day to go see his pals at the plant. He'd heard there was a lot going on at Courbevoie. It all kind of tickled him. What an easy life he had these days! No more meetings, discussions, delegates, dumb votes, all the rest of that crap! All in all, he'd been lucky when Le Gentil had been transferred to the Clermont headquarters. In a way, though, it was really Le Gentil who'd been lucky. Because in Paris, after that business of his killer cousin, there'd been a lot of talk in the building and at the plant. They didn't follow these things so much in Clermont. As a matter of fact, they didn't follow much of anything in Clermont, not even that there was something going on at Courbevoie—if there was. Anyway, in Clermont it was as if the workers were in a city within the City. They got a silver cup when they were born and a gold medal when they retired. Everything that happened in between happened inside the company, so it takes a hell of a lot before you can stir them up . . . !

How she'd bawled, Mademoiselle Joëlle, when she had to leave Neuilly! Gildaise a bit, too, but not as much. She was a tough one, that Le Gentil dame. Luckily she'd never found out about Gildaise and him up there on the fifth floor. That was thanks to Madame Victoria, who'd kept her trap shut. "She swore, she swore by Sainte Anne d'Auray . . ." What a laugh those Breton girls were, with their Sainte Anne d'Auray. In any case, it had worked. She'd been a real sport.

She'd been a sport, too, about taking over the room that went with the apartment on the second floor. They called it "keeping the *enjoyment*" of the room. Exactly! . . . The look of those new tenants! They were too broke to have a maid, but with four kids they might have put two of them up there, those boches. Boches and Jews to boot!

And it had been nice of her to hire Gildaise to clean costumes. That way, nothing had really changed. But it still didn't explain the panic yesterday.

And it didn't explain why Grandi wasn't with them now, either. At least when he was in the car there were a few laughs.

Back there the women had stopped whispering. As usual, he didn't say anything . . .

It was beginning to get light. Lucas caught a glimpse of Nicole in the rearview mirror. She was whispering something to Maddy, who didn't seem to be listening, then suddenly she began to laugh. That woke Janek, who was asleep, leaning against the door.

"What's so funny?" asked Janek, his voice even deeper than usual because he was sleepy.

"Nothing, darling. Grief is making us nervous. Go back to sleep . . . How much farther, Lucas?" Nicole asked.

"About half an hour, Madame Victoria, if we don't end up in a ditch," Lucas replied, smiling.

"My poor Lucas, this isn't the day for that," sighed Nicole.

"Well, maybe they'd give us a good price for whatever's left," Maddy murmured.

"Please, Maddy!" said Nicole sharply.

Lucas pretended he hadn't heard.

They look tired, but not all that sad, he thought, after another glance in the rearview mirror. It was daylight now, and he could see them quite clearly. Tired and a little old. It must be the black. They usually wore light colors. And then those hats—they really didn't suit them, especially Madame Victoria. She could still be pretty sexy, with that long hair that seemed to go on forever. It must be all over the bed when he jumps her. Because when it comes to fucking her, he fucks her, even though they're not that young anymore. From what he'd heard, sometimes they'd even go at it right in the middle of the day, with poor Armelle stuck in the kitchen, afraid to poke her head outside. Then she had to remake the bed, like in some two-bit hotel. Poor Mémelle, who doesn't want to have anything to do with screwing around! Funny, these Breton girls. Gildaise had wanted it as soon as she got to Paris, even though there'd been no fucking going on in the Le Gentil apartment. With Armelle, there was nothing doing, even though it was a regular whorehouse on the third floor! That's why Victoria had kept quiet: she gets a kick out of fucking, and there'd been no need to make her swear by Sainte. Anne d'Auray . . . She must have put the hat on because of the cathedral, but she should've done what he was doing with his new cap and wait till they got into the city. He almost felt like telling her just how dowdy she looked with that stupid lid on her head. Maddy's hat suited her a lot better. But he didn't give a fuck about Maddy. That one was all skin and bones, not a good piece. Besides, imagine taking on that old fart in the early days, when she'd been so young . . . Well, maybe it wasn't true: Joëlle had told Gildaise that because she'd been jealous when Victoria had dropped her. Nobody really knew for sure. But wouldn't that be something, getting into black and making all this fuss to come and bury the wife of her old lover! He'd soon see, when all the playacting began. That was going to be some goddamn spectacle! . . . Like everything else he'd seen since he'd stopped busting his balls at the factory! The things he'd seen in the last year! Things he'd never have known about if he'd just gone on punching a time clock. Jaunts around Paris without having to keep an eye on the time, and even the hours spent at Chateaubriand fixing this and that and feeling up all those naked dames in the corners. Because it wasn't only the guys who stripped down—luckily there were compensations! And always something unexpected—that was what he liked. Even this trip, except for the dumb cap and leggings, and the uniform that was strangling him . . . How and with what would he have ever been able to treat himself to an outing in Troyes! Things must really be buzzing at Troyes, too, since the place was full of factories . . . Underwear, mostly. Come to think of it, while they were at Mass he might look around in the stores and maybe he could pick up some snazzy lace panties for Gildaise. Black lace, so they could have a ball on the fifth floor . . . They must cost less here, near the factories.

They weren't going to make him attend their Mass, were they? Once he'd unloaded that wreath, he'd leave the family to itself. If you could call it a family!

He glanced in the rearview mirror again. Janek had gone back to sleep. Maddy stared absentmindedly at the countryside through the window. Nicole opened her pocketbook, took out her compact and inspected herself in the mirror.

"Oh, shit, look at that! I'll never be able to carry it off . . . " she said in a low voice. She removed her hat and with one hand fluffed up her flattened hair. Maddy went on staring through the window. Nicole took out a lipstick and carefully began painting her mouth. She smiled into her compact, then put it back into her bag, from which she removed a large square of black chiffon. "I'm glad I thought of it," she sighed, knotting it under her chin.

Now the bitch looks like a Madonna, thought Lucas.

"Doesn't this look simpler?" asked Nicole, elbowing Maddy so she'd inspect her.

"You can say that again! I'm going to look too dressed up, next to you . . . You look like a real Polack!" said Maddy, bursting into laughter.

What an idiot, thought Lucas.

"We'll soon be there, Madame Victoria. Where do we stop first?" he asked, taking a map of the city from the glove compartment.

"First at the Hôtel de la Poste, where Maître Dubâteau-Ripoix is waiting for us. Afterward, we'll see," replied Nicole.

"Won't we look odd parked in front of a hotel with this wreath on the roof?" Lucas asked.

"Poor Lucas, the whole town will be full of wreaths! Everybody loved our godmother . . . Wake up, darling, we're there," said Nicole, giving Janek's cheek a little pat.

She's beginning to get my goat with this "poor Lucas" crap. That's the second time she's done it, thought the chauffeur. The idea of meeting Maître Dubâteau-Ripoix suddenly put him in a bad mood. There would be that chauffeur of his, a guy he couldn't stand the sight of. A real flunky. High-hat and a snob to boot. You could hardly get him to say hello when he came to Allée Chateaubriand. Wore gloves, too, as well as his uniform. Shit, I should never have let them do this to me, Lucas told himself, furiously adjusting his livery cap.

They were in the suburbs of Troyes.

"It looks like Saint-Etienne," said Maddy.

: :

"ISN'T GRANDI with you?" asked Maître Dubâteau-Ripoix, who was waiting for the travelers in the hotel lobby.

" . . . No," replied Nicole.

"What time is he coming?"

"To tell the truth, he's not coming at all."

"What do you mean, he's not coming? Is he sick, too?"

"Why? Is someone else sick?" asked Maddy, who thought Dubâteau was behaving very coldly.

"Yes, Mademoiselle Varga, someone is sick . . . Very sick. But let's not stand here. I've ordered *breakfast* for all of you," he added, using one of his favorite English words. "Come along to the *lounge*. Octave, see to it that my friends are served, please, and call Madame Dubâteau-Ripoix to let her know where to find us."

"Of course, Maître," said the man with the gold keys.

Dubâteau preceded them. They found themselves in an English-medieval–style salon with an enormous fireplace, in which a tree trunk was blazing. An elderly lady was writing at a little secrétaire in one corner.

Dubâteau made sure she wasn't listening and went back to what he'd been saying.

"Very, very sick. A man struck down by fate, crushed by sorrow, stupefied—I say *stupefied*— by grief. Our poor Augustin hasn't said so much as a word since he lost his life's companion. I spent part of the night at La Bonne Chanson, with Liliane and Roger. Neither she, nor he, nor I, nor his old friend Dr. Roussin—despite the fact that he was the one to close poor Marie-Jeanne's eyes—nor Monsignor Ziegler, Roger's uncle, who came all the way from Strasbourg for the funeral service, were able to get a word out of him. I really don't think he will be up to attending the funeral, which will complicate things strangely for . . . Thank you, Gustave, you may go, my friends will serve themselves . . . "

Gustave bowed. Janek buttered a piece of toast, while Nicole filled the teacups.

" . . . I was saying, it will complicate things strangely for the officials, who have all prepared speeches addressed to the widower. Well, the important thing is that he not saddle us with a real attack. Anything can happen."

"But he did recognize you, didn't he, Maître?" asked Nicole, her eyes on Maddy.

"We don't know," replied Dubâteau.

"Was he like that when you phoned me yesterday, or did it happen afterwards?"

"After *what,* my dear Victoria?" the lawyer asked softly.

"What I mean is that when you phoned me you didn't seem worried. If we'd known, we would have come sooner!"

" 'bsolutely," agreed Janek.

Maddy said nothing.

"A few hours wouldn't have made any difference . . . We are faced with a total collapse. Is it temporary or definitive? Only time and science can tell. Yesterday, I saw no reason to add to your troubles prematurely . . . *Wait and see!* . . . But facts are facts, and we must face them. Maître Parbot and I . . . "

Dubâteau fell silent and looked at all three of them.

"Maître Parbot?" Nicole inquired softly.

"Maître Parbot is poor Marie-Jeanne's notary, and it is he who, yesterday, introduced a new element," replied Dubâteau, lowering his voice and consulting his watch. "This new element happens to concern our friend Grandi, whom you now tell me is not coming. It's too much! . . . Is he really sick?"

"Exhausted," Nicole said feebly.

"That's unfortunate, because our Casanova is going to have a lot to do!" exclaimed Maître Dubâteau-Ripoix, his eyes fixed on Maddy. "The fact is that these old provincial ladies of ours are more fantastic and unpredictable than you can imagine! Well, since we have only a little time, I had better read you the copy of a letter that Maître Parbot unsealed in our presence yesterday evening, a letter that left us all dumbfounded."

Dubâteau took a slip of paper, folded in four, from his crocodile-skin wallet, then put on his tortoise-shell spectacles. Nicole, Janek and Maddy set down their cups. Maddy was studying the rug. Dubâteau read tonelessly, as though he were dealing with a police report:

Healthy in body and mind, today, the second of November 1935, All Souls' Day, I have given thought to my death. By these lines confided to my notary, Maître Parbot, I wish to modify certain terms of my will, which was written a year ago and which will be found in the righthand drawer of my vanity table in the bedroom of my dear house, La Bonne Chanson.

This will remains unchanged and valid insofar as concerns my goods—real estate as well as bonds, stocks and jewels—with the exception of Masques and Bergamasques Inc., of which I now desire to make different disposition. The artistic goals of this company, of which I am the sole owner, have greatly enriched the last days of one who is the wife, daughter, and granddaughter of hosiers. I therefore bequeath Masques and Bergamasques to Monsieur Alexandre Grandi: this young artist seems to me more fit to continue my work than my immediate family or that of my husband. While I lived, I was greatly misunderstood.

Done at Troyes,
November 2, 1935, 10 P.M.

"There you are," said Maître Dubâteau-Ripoix, removing his spectacles. "And this"—he waved the paper before refolding it—"is what we have been unable to communicate to our sick friend, who is the only one to know nothing about it . . . Except for Alex, of course. Confusing, isn't it?"

"Jean-Gaétan! . . . We are very late," announced a feminine voice.

Madame Dubâteau-Ripoix crossed the lounge, arriving at just the right time. Everyone stood up.

"I do hope you are all warmly dressed, because the cathedral will be glacial," she said, pecking Nicole and Maddy twice on both cheeks. Janek kissed her hand. "As for the cemetery . . . "

"They know, they know, I've already warned them, Jennifer," said Maître Dubâteau in an irritated voice. "Let's go, children!"—and he led the small group toward the lobby.

"The bastard calls that a warning!" Nicole swore between her teeth.

She was livid. Only Maddy heard her. "My poor Tintin," she murmured. She wore a strange smile, both sad and tender.

"Two hours and forty-five minutes, but there was nobody on the roads," Janek was explaining to Jennifer Dubâteau, who turned to wait for Nicole and Maddy.

"Has Grandi taken the train?" she asked, when they were all in front of the concierge's desk.

No one answered her. Maître Dubâteau-Ripoix had started talking again.

"Let's not get separated," he advised, glancing through the glass of the revolving door. He recognized Lucas at the wheel of the Citroën. "Let's not get separated, or we'll lose one another in the city. To La Bonne Chanson first, of course, but I suggest that before then we relieve ourselves of this amazing wreath. So we'll stop in the cathedral square. We'll take the lead, your car will follow, Hubert will give your man a hand unloading the flowers, which we can turn over to those in charge so they can find their rightful place on the catafalque, and then on to the deceased's home, where we will descend from our automobiles and follow our old friend's remains on foot. We will drive to the cemetery in our vehicles, however, so they will have to follow slowly behind the cortege and pick us up near the cathedral when Mass is over. Does that suit?"

Maître Dubâteau-Ripoix didn't wait for an answer. He went on:

"Octave, please be so kind as to tell my chauffeur we are leaving," he called out to the concierge.

"Monsieur Hubert is in the couriers' waiting room. I'll call him, Maître," said the concierge, picking up the house phone.

"I so often appear in court in this region that I have my little habits, I should say obsessions, just as I do at home. This is hardly the time for it, but I'm sorry that you didn't really get the chance to enjoy the *marmalade*"—he used the English word— "with your breakfast. Octave has it shipped from London especially for me, don't you, my good Octave?"

"For you, Maître, and for Madame," said Octave with a bow. "And for poor Madame Leblanc, when she would have tea here . . . I hope the flowers sent by the management were delivered to La Bonne Chanson?" he sighed, his look questioning and stricken.

"They came yesterday, and Madame Ziegler was very touched by them," said Jennifer Dubâteau-Ripoix.

I'll bet, thought Maddy, I'll bet these particular *dispossessed* were thinking about flowers yesterday!

She hadn't made the connection intentionally. The idea had simply slipped into her head.

"I'll be back in a moment," she said with difficulty, a wild laugh stuck in her throat, and she headed toward a door marked LADIES to the right of the elevator. Nicole followed her.

"A wise precaution! All this will go on for hours! Coming, old man?" said Maître Dubâteau-Ripoix to Janek, who followed him toward the door on the left marked GENTLEMEN.

"This is hardly the time for that sort of thing!" exclaimed Nicole, when she discovered Maddy doubled over with laughter in front of the mirror in the little anteroom.

"The dispossessed . . . the dispossessed! . . . " Maddy gasped painfully. "Doesn't that remind you of something?"

Nicole shrugged her shoulders. She doesn't even remember, thought Maddy, meeting Victoria Jean's hard, absent and determined eyes in the mirror. She doesn't remember a thing . . . And Maddy realized that they didn't even share the same memories. She felt abandoned, and wanted to cry. About Saint-Etienne and her mother, about Alex's lost love, about Tintin's grief, about the good Marie-Jeanne's smile, about her own failed career, about the nasty look on Dubâteau's face, about her connivances with Agnès, Lucas's livery, the silliness of funerals and the little crow's feet at the corners of her eyes.

"Are you coming?" asked Nicole, her voice covering the discreet flush of water.

Maddy followed her without replying.

The two cars started up together. Monsieur Hubert, who seemed not to recognize Lucas, helped him unload the wreath in front of the cathedral. Lucas returned to the driver's seat, and that was when Maddy made up her mind.

"I'd rather wait here," she said suddenly.

And she got out of the car just as it was starting up. Lucas braked.

"Let's not lose the others," said Janek.

Lucas started up again, and Maddy just managed to catch a glimpse of Nicole turning to look at her questioningly through the rear window of the departing Citroën. For a moment she stood rooted to the spot.

"The railway station, please?" she asked an elderly couple walking by arm in arm.

The woman had a small bouquet of flowers in her hand. In a low voice, she gave Maddy directions. Maddy thanked her in the same tone and watched the couple move slowly toward the opening in the immense black hangings surmounted by a silver coat of arms emblazoned with the letters "M.J.L." Funeral sheaves and wreaths were set out on either side of the arched door, and before being swallowed up in the large nave of the Cathedral of Saint Peter and Saint Paul, the couple stopped for a second to decipher the eternal regrets written across the largest wreath. "Masques and Bergamasques" shone in all its glory of golden letters on the medieval paving stones. The man and woman exchanged looks: the name meant nothing to them.

Maddy waited until they had disappeared, then resolutely set off in the direction they had indicated.

 *M*y love,

I'm writing to you from the Brasserie of the Gare de l'Est. It's a very sad railway station, and before going into the café I looked carefully at the mural showing the soldiers leaving in '14. I even thought I recognized Papa.

I've had three cognacs and I'm a little drunk.

When I've finished my letter, I'll mail it and then go home to kill myself.

On the trip back, I saw you all again, all those whom I've loved. But I can say this only to you. Though I tried to think of the others, I always came back to you. You, in the shadows, behind a stage flat, with your sleeves rolled up, smiling at me for the first time when we still didn't know each other and I was reading my part on the stage. I stumbled over the words, and you smiled.

You, the first time I saw you.

I lost you to keep from losing Tintin.

Poor Tintin who loved only his old wife, whom he's now lost.

And I, who am losing everything. I who am today losing you forever because if I were to tell you now that I never stopped loving you, you wouldn't believe me! You can imagine how convincing that would sound, now that everything is going to be yours!

I thought it all over in the train. I've really messed up my life. But I'm not going to mess up my death. It's the only way I have left to tell you the truth and make you believe me.

Goodbye, my love, and don't forget me.

Maddy

P.S. I've reopened my letter after having sealed it. They've given me another envelope, and the waiter is looking at me strangely.

It's going to cause you a lot of trouble, but I want it to be *only you* who'll take me to the cemetery in your neighborhood. No fancy trimmings, and in a pine box. *Only you.* Not even with Ginette. To console her, I'm making her a gift of my sable, which she envied so much when we were in *L'Autrichienne et le Serrurier.* Don't worry about getting in touch with my mother. She died two years ago, but I didn't tell anyone.

Maddy paid for her cognacs and her stamp, put down a big tip and left; the waiter watched her out of the corner of his eye. She slipped the envelope into the slot of the mailbox near the station exit.

She took a taxi home, called out her name as she passed the concierge's loge and double-locked her door, leaving the key in the lock.

: :

AROUND eleven o'clock the next morning the concierge at rue Pergolèse had the firemen break open the door.

There was no blood on the bed, just a small circle around the blackened hole that looked like a cigarette burn in the pink crepe-de-Chine nightgown. Maddy's eyes were closed. The little revolver was still in her hand, which the recoil had sent flying over to the right side of the bed.

A note, printed in capitals on the cover of a shoebox, was on the night table.

> GOODBYE. I'M FED UP. NOBODY'S TO BLAME, NOBODY, NO-
> BODY. IT'S ONE IN THE MORNING.

The concierge said that her voice had seemed strange when she had come home at about ten o'clock the previous evening. And she testified that no stranger had entered the building during the night.

The coroner called it a suicide.

The police emergency service took the body to the morgue.

The letter posted at the Gare de l'Est was delivered at noon. Alex found it under the door of his studio on rue Campagne-Première at about four in the afternoon.

ALEX STOOD UP, wiped his hands on his handkerchief, stepped back a little and looked at the twelve forget-me-not seedlings he had just stuck into the freshly turned earth. Bounded by a fence of painted black wood, squeezed between two stone vaults, the small rectangle was like a tiny garden in the middle of a dead city. He kissed the palm of his hand and touched it to the inscription, which he caressed gently. The white paint was still as fresh as the upturned earth. He took out his handkerchief again to rub off the slight smudge his caress had left on the black background. He made the carefully inscribed letters sharp again with a little saliva: MADELEINE VARGOUGNAN, 1904–1935.

It looks like a schoolgirl's slate, thought Alex. With long strides and without turning around, he threaded his way among the graves until he reached the central path of the Montparnasse cemetery.

He had to stand aside to let a very fancy funeral cortege go by, and for the first time in forty-eight hours he thought of Troyes.

Of Troyes and all the others, whom he had refused to speak or listen to until he had done everything as Maddy had wanted.

The cortege went on forever. Exhausted from lack of sleep and too much coffee, he tried to advance against the current. A man wearing a silk top hat pushed him back. "A little respect, young man," Alex thought he heard. He really didn't feel like arguing. He waited and looked at the tombstones around him.

One especially caught his attention. It was an admirably maintained monument that had been covered with flowers just yesterday or possibly even that very morning. Under a Cyrillic inscription, he deciphered a name cut into the stone: Simon PETLIURA.

It vaguely reminded him of a recent conversation. But the dates—1879–1926—meant nothing to him, and besides, it wasn't important; tired of waiting, he cut across the tombstones and went out the little door onto rue Froidevaux.

Back at rue Campagne-Première he took the phone off the hook and ignored the mail that had piled up at the door over the past two days. He went to bed to get some sleep at last.

Six hours later he woke up, showered, carefully washed and brushed his hands to remove the earth that had dried under his fingernails, shaved, put on a clean shirt and placed the phone back on the hook.

Though it was five in the afternoon, he did everything one usually does in the morning when beginning a full day. He wasn't at all surprised.

Everything had come to a standstill the moment he had found the letter. Now he had done what the letter asked of him, it would all begin again.

He was back. He had come from far away, for forty-eight hours had lived elsewhere. Ravaged, stupefied, unbelieving, a stranger in a strange land, he had watched himself do the strange things ordered by an absent someone whose departure he would never understand.

And, since he was beginning a new day, he went to the door to pick up the envelopes he'd been stepping over for the past two days. Under various catalogues he found two telegrams. Both came from Troyes, had been sent a few hours apart and were not at all alike.

The first one he opened was signed Dubâteau-Ripoix and had been sent the day before yesterday at about one o'clock in the afternoon.

NEW SITUATION, YOUR PRESENCE INDISPENSABLE. CONGRATULATIONS. WE WILL WAIT FOR YOU AT THE HOTEL DE LA POSTE.

The second had been sent the same day at about five in the afternoon and was simply signed "Victoria":

MADDY'S FLIGHT INEXCUSABLE. SEND HER BACK TO US, OR BETTER STILL BRING HER BACK YOURSELF. WAITING FOR YOU.

And then he discovered a third, plus a *pneumatique* from Ginette— *Your telephone out of order, please call* . . . . *Impossible to get you on phone, call*— but from that point on, he had already known. . . . That was when he himself had broken contact.

And now that he had reestablished it, he decided to start up the current again, and dialed Dubâteau-Ripoix's number. Despite everything, he wanted to know why congratulations were due him and why, at the very moment when he was himself preparing to bury the mutilated body of a young woman whom he had once loved very much, his presence was felt to be indispensable at the edge of a hole into which they were lowering the mahogany coffin of an old woman who meant nothing to him.

He let the phone ring for quite a while, hung up, redialed the number with no better luck, promised himself to call the next day, slipped on his trench coat, and left.

He walked to La Coupole, where he found the usual people who were there almost every evening at about the same time.

"Were you off on a trip?" asked Rodriguez, the painter, without raising his eyes from his newspaper.

"A kind of trip . . . " replied Alex as he ordered a double scotch.

"Telephone call for Monsieur Vladimir Ulyanov . . . Monsieur Ulyanov . . . call from Monsieur Leon Bronstein . . . telephone call for Monsieur Ulyanov . . . " repeated the voice of the cashier over the loudspeaker.

"They never seem to get tired of that joke," sighed Alex, greeting from a distance a young man, handsome as a gypsy, whom everyone watched as he smilingly walked toward the telephone booth.

"There are variations. Yesterday it was Colonel de la Rocque for Captain Bordure!" said Rodriguez, folding his newspaper. "There was a table full of Croix de Feu hooligans in the rear, and we nearly had trouble . . . "

"I've got to make a call," said Alex, suddenly remembering rue de la Mare, which had not heard from him for two days.

He found the Auvergnat's number in the phone book. The handsome young man turned the booth over to him.

"You seem pretty happy." Alex grinned at him.

"You can say that again! My brother's just told me they've taken our screenplay! Want to eat?"

"Fine, tell Rodriguez . . . I'll be back in a minute," answered Alex, as he closed the door of the booth.

When the Auvergnat answered, Alex asked if somebody could take a message to Mesdames Sonia and Olga, at number 58. The Auvergnat gave him Barsky, who happened to be at the bar.

"Tell them not to worry. I've had some trouble, but everything's fine now. I'll stop by tomorrow . . . "

" . . . Tomorrow without fail," repeated Barsky. "I'll go tell them now . . . That way I can see you tomorrow too. I may have some business for you . . . "

"You can tell me about it tomorrow, Isidore. Goodbye!"

Alex hung up and went back to Rodriguez and his untouched double scotch.

: :

AT MIDNIGHT they were all still sitting around a table at Chéramy's on rue Jacob. Laurent and Louis Verdon had taken turns reciting their screenplay. Rodriguez and Alex were listening. It was a lovely story, simple, sad, and gay; much of it took place in the streets, some of it in a bedroom, on the banks of the Marne, in a bicycle factory, and on the pebble beach at Etretat. It was also the story of a love affair that ran its course over a Saturday and a Sunday between a boy and a girl who said goodbye on Monday.

"I wouldn't mind doing your costumes . . . " Alex said to Laurent Verdon, the brother who would be directing the film.

"My ladies won't be decked out in lace, you know," replied Laurent, a smile in his green eyes. "You people at Mamasques are much too fancy and much too expensive for us!"

"I'm not with Masques anymore, and I'm finished with lace," said Alex blandly.

The three looked at one another. There was a silence.

"And you never said a word!" exclaimed Rodriguez. "When did this happy accident take place?"

"A few days ago. It wasn't an accident, still less a happy one, and I don't want to talk about it."

There was another silence.

"But I'd very much like you to tell me more about your film, Laurent," said Alex. "Will there be women in your bicycle factory?"

"Some . . . Why do you ask?"

"Because of Saint-Etienne," answered Alex.

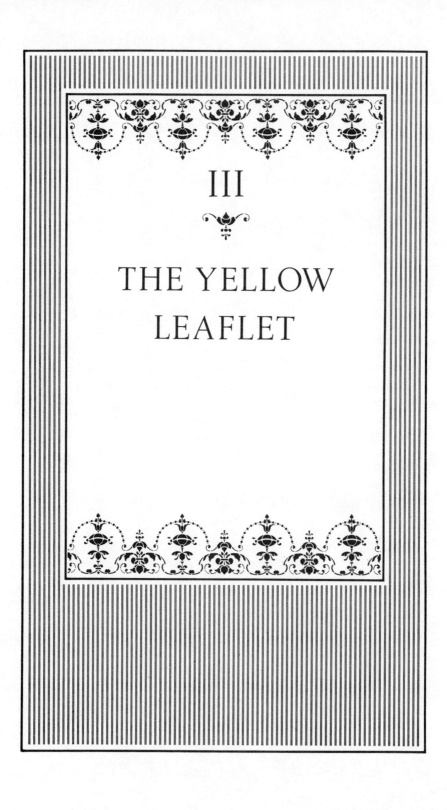

III

THE YELLOW
LEAFLET

*T*HE WOMAN WOKE with a start. She was afraid again. Just as she had been the day before yesterday.

The day before yesterday, it had happened early. It was still dark, but already morning when the doors had banged under the windows on this usually quiet street. Next to her, Kurt went on sleeping. Frieda Neumann had looked at the luminous hands of the clock set on the trunk that served as a night table. It was a quarter to six. She had remained motionless, her eyes wide open, and hadn't breathed normally again until she heard the car start up.

Only then had she laughed at herself. They were in France. It was time she got used to it.

In France, when the doors banged, it didn't mean they'd come to get you. It meant that people did what they wanted to, where they wanted to, when they wanted to. That's what Kurt would tell her again, just as he had for the last two months, and she decided not to mention her early-morning fright.

But tonight it was beginning all over again. And it really was the middle of the night. Two-twenty, said the hands.

There had been three bangs, steps on the sidewalk, then a ring at the street door, which had been slammed violently.

And the car had not started up.

Frieda got up in the dark, noiselessly left the room, went out to the hallway and, without turning on a light, put her ear to the door.

Someone was going up the main staircase. Slow steps, muffled by the carpeting. Someone was also going up the service stairs. Only one person, a bit faster, but the sound rang out frighteningly in the metal stairwell.

Now she was sure they were going to knock at the two doors simultaneously. But the quicker footsteps continued on up, and so did the muffled ones. She heard a woman's voice sigh, "How exhausting!" and the door on the third floor closed.

It was only then that Frieda Neumann realized she'd understood the woman's words. She'd spoken in Yiddish. The idea made her laugh so much that she almost ran into the bedroom to wake Kurt up and make him laugh with her, but decided it would be a better story when told over breakfast.

She turned on the lights, went to drink a glass of water in the kitchen and listened to the silence. There was no sound of movement from the other rooms of the apartment. The children weren't awake, either. I'm the only one awake, she thought—me, the house madwoman.

"I'm mad, the house madwoman," she hummed gaily in her head to the tune of a little Mozart sonata the family often played. "I'm the camp madwoman," she murmured without music, passing through the former Le Gentil salon, where her two oldest lay in sleeping bags.

If we stay, we'll have to buy box springs, she told herself again, as she slipped carefully back alongside Kurt on the big mattress resting on the floor.

Box springs and pianos. The two rented pianos were very bad and too expensive.

Once again she felt like laughing. Her Aunt Hannah always used to say, "Be a violinist, never a harpist and especially not a pianist. If you're a violinist or a flutist, you can even play in the trains." Aunt Hannah! She was the only one in the family who spoke Yiddish. The others didn't like that. German and English. English was very chic. A pity they hadn't made her learn French when she was a girl. It would come in handy now.

If they stayed . . .

She really didn't want to stay. In any case, she didn't want to stay here. Not in this garden district, not in this house, where no one seemed aware of their presence except the concierge, who never replied to the stammering *"Bonjour, Madame"* of the four children.

These French weren't even interested enough to wonder, Frieda told herself, about six people who had moved in without furniture, knew no French but had two pianos brought up three days after their arrival! Not interested, very discreet, totally indifferent or willfully ignorant, these French. However, despite the fact that she was the house mad-woman, she wasn't mad. That woman from the third floor had really spoken Yiddish just now, when she'd sighed, "How exhausting!" She at least must know these piano players weren't tourists.

: :

"THE BASTARDS won't catch me again!" said Lucas, as he kissed Gildaise, who was waiting for him on the fifth-floor landing. "I haven't put their car away . . . Here, don't say I never think of you," and he gave her a box with a fancy coat of arms on it. "I thought of you, and believe me I deserve some credit for it, because at that snazzy funeral they had me hopping around Troyes like Rouletabille at the kidnap-ping of the Begum."

He was in the hallway, speaking softly. They went into the room, and even before unbuttoning the collar of his tunic Lucas attacked the buckles of his leggings and the laces on his ankle boots.

"Damn, that feels good!" he breathed, before beginning his story.

The story of the "hunt for Maddy" that had begun after the Mass, when the bosses found she was missing. "Will she be at the cemetery? No! And so we begin racing around. Back to the cathedral we go, look-ing everywhere—including the confessionals and the sacristy. Then the hotel again, in case she's got sick. Then back to the old lady's house, and back to the hotel, a check on the hospitals and finally the police station. And then they decide we'll sleep in town, though nobody even asked if it was all right with me. And then to the drugstore. Do you have tooth-brushes, please? Toothpaste? What brand? No, they didn't say. Dr. Pierre? Okay for Dr. Pierre! . . . Meanwhile, the boss lady is stewing away, still grinding her teeth. She'd given orders for her to wait. Not that I could understand it all, because once they were in the car they pretty much kept their traps shut, except she said, 'If that little bitch and that little pimp think they're going to pull something off behind my back, they've got another think coming! I want them here, both of them, right *here*.' Period: we stay here. And *here* I had to share one of those so-called couriers' rooms with that fucking idiot Hubert! The next day the same routine, except that we go to the railway station to check on trains from Paris. *¡Nada!* Nobody. Then a trek out to the sticks to find a little inn the concierge at the hotel knows about, and it's no cinch finding it either—we circle around for about two hours. It seems the hosiery big shots go there to shack up, and Maddy knew about it. Maybe she went there with this Grandi so they could see the notary in private. I get all this poop from Hubert, whose boss talks a blue streak when he's in the car. But no sign of them at the fuckodrome! And back we go across the beet fields. It's already dark. And back again to the house of the dead lady, where things aren't going too well—the old man still hasn't said a word. As for that Maddy . . . "

"She's dead, and they buried her today," said Gildaise, who hadn't dared interrupt her lover. He looked at her in amazement. "Buried today. Ginette came to leave a note for Madame Victoria . . . You were already on the way back. She gave it to Armelle, who put it on the pillow so that her mistress would be sure to find it."

"Holy shit!" said Lucas.

: :

A WAIL and some long childish sobs pierced the silence, just as Frieda Neumann was beginning to fall asleep again.

"Well, these French seem to have nightmares too," she told herself. And she cuddled up to Kurt, who hadn't stirred.

: :

THEY WEREN'T having nightmares on the third floor. They were living through horror. Her eyes wide open, Nicole had just come up against grief. Real, irreversible, irreparable grief.

Out of his depth, helpless, Janek watched from a distance this voiceless madwoman who refused to let him near her. Collapsed on the floor at the foot of the bed like a bundle of black rags, she had fought him off with unsuspected energy when he had tried to take her in his arms; and when he had tried to speak to her, she had drowned his voice with groans so hoarse and so deep they seemed to come from the bellows of a forge. Then she had stood up suddenly and with closed fists hammered against the wall of their bedroom like a prisoner in a cell.

Janek summoned all his courage, and the two slaps he gave her were so violent that Nicole sank unconscious to the bed.

Her faint lasted a few minutes. Janek, leaning over and looking at his wife's closed eyes, wondered if it was vexation, rage or sorrow that had driven her wild. He'd know as soon as she opened them.

She did, and he recognized the little light.

The little light of tenderness and despair that, until then, only two people in the whole world—old Zedkin and himself, Janek—had known how to bring into those eyes that always looked so proudly triumphant to everyone else.

Henceforth there would be three.

There was no doubt it was grief that had driven her wild.

He felt vaguely reassured and strangely jealous.

: :

AT THAT very moment, Alex was trying in vain to fall asleep. "If it hadn't been for their nonsense about the bicycle factory, I wouldn't be thinking about it so much!" he said aloud. He knew he was lying to himself. He turned on the bedside lamp and, in the same movement, took a cigarette from a package on the ashtray. There were six butts in it. "Let's hope it's not going to be like this every night for the rest of my life!" he muttered, striking a match. He got out of bed, and as he had done the night before and the night before that, went to the drawer where he had placed Maddy's letter.

By now he knew it almost by heart, having reread it so many different ways.

The first time he'd glanced through rather than read it, and, convinced that it had been thought, written and carefully mailed so as to reach him in time, had rushed, unbelieving and almost cheerfully, to the aid of someone crying "Wolf!" . . . someone whom he'd make pay for it.

The second time was when he had returned from the morgue, where amidst the racket of the elevated railroad, he had officially identified the face of the corpse as the attendant had, very formally, requested him to do before lowering the sheet. That second time he had read it the way it deserved to be read, the way a farewell and a will that must be respected have to be read.

And then he had reread and reread, as if to force out the secret hidden behind that little sentence she had doubtless thought so clear when writing it; but he had completely failed to understand it, and he still could not understand.

" . . . You can imagine how convincing that would sound, now that everything is going to be yours! . . . "

And, as had happened yesterday and the day before yesterday, it was his last image of Maddy alive that came back: Maddy in black in the beveled mirror, between Nicole and Agnès; Maddy grave, a little cynical, a little guilty, watching him leave.

Where, to whom, had she imagined he was going, in such a hurry that he hadn't taken the time to turn to her? To her alone, for the quarter of a second necessary to say goodbye to her alone, before disappearing from the sight of all three of them.

All three, indissolubly welded together in his memory *in flagrante delicto,* and whom he hadn't turned to for a goodbye he hadn't wanted them to share, since he never wanted to see them again—ever.

She must have watched his retreating back in the mirror, and he hadn't looked at her face and so would never know what it had been like when she saw him leaving her life.

He refolded the letter, put it back in the drawer and returned to bed.

He crushed out his seventh butt and turned off the lamp, only to relight it almost immediately. He got up to get the charcoal lying on his drawing board, and noted on the package of yellow Gitanes: "Call Dubâteau without fail," then, underneath, "Remember sable Ginette," and turned off the light for good.

*A*LEX WAS STARING at the ceiling while Dubâteau-Ripoix listened to the sound of his own voice in his large circular office on avenue Mac-Mahon. The ceiling was rigged to form a sounding board, so skillfully rigged you had to be in on the trick in order to notice it. It wasn't the ceiling Alex was staring at: he knew about it; he'd been the one to think it up and have it constructed, installed, painted and matched to the light woodwork that served as a reflector for the vocal tricks of the illustrious tenor of the Paris bar. Alex was staring at the ceiling because he didn't want Dubâteau-Ripoix to see the tears that were filling his eyes. They had welled up abruptly as Dubâteau-Ripoix opened his mouth to reveal to him what he had called his enormous good fortune.

"Yes, my dear Grandi, it's all yours: the walls, the real estate, the stock and the keys, everything! . . . One might say that you really caught her eye . . . And by catching her eye, one might also say that you've latched on to thousands, not to say millions . . . " Dubâteau had concluded with a ribald smile that made very clear the admiring contempt in which he held the young beneficiary of the late and last whims of old Madame Leblanc.

It's all yours, Dubâteau had just said. So that was what Maddy's little sentence had also meant. It was just that: the walls, the stock and the keys. What horror, what misfortune, what sadness, what mockery— enough to make you weep!

But if he notices a tear, one single tear, if I lift my hand to wipe my eyes, if I say one word in my broken voice, this idiot is going to think I'm breaking up like someone who's just won the National Lottery . . . I mustn't cry, I mustn't cry, I mustn't cry, Alex told himself, as he continued to stare at the ceiling.

There was a rather long silence.

"Are you counting flies . . . or millions?" Dubâteau-Ripoix asked impatiently.

"I'm not counting anything, because I don't want anything," Alex replied when he was sure he had regained control of his voice and could assume his everyday expression. "Nothing," he said, fixing his dry eyes on those of Dubâteau-Ripoix, which were still sparkling at his own last little joke.

"What do you mean, nothing?" said the lawyer, stunned.

"Nothing. Nothing, as in nothing at all . . . Or all, if you prefer: I refuse all of it, that's all," said Alex, learning to laugh all over again.

Dubâteau-Ripoix, his eyes riveted on Alex's, tried to gauge the truth of what he had just heard.

"You're joking, aren't you, my dear Grandi?" he eventually managed to get out, *mezza voce* for once.

Alex gave him a sad smile.

"Do I really look as if I'm joking, my dear Dubâteau?"

He had almost called him Little Boat.

"No," admitted Dubâteau-Ripoix. "No . . . But in that case, what are we going to do?"

"We? But we're going to do nothing, my dear Maître. It's *you* who are going to do something. You are going to inform your clients and friends that the legacy hunter, the usurper, the thief, the former young lover of the defunct young mistress of the old widower of the old and regretted donatrix is sorry for the trouble he's caused them, the extent of which he only now appreciates, and that he'd be grateful if they would reclaim an inheritance he wants nothing to do with. That's what you're going to do, my dear Maître. And I—I'm going to leave."

Alex rose at the end of his speech, which he had managed to deliver in a very calm voice.

Dubâteau-Ripoix didn't stir.

"Sit down, Alex," he asked, almost humbly.

Alex sat down again.

"If you refuse, we will inevitably go into escheat . . . "

Dubâteau had resumed his beautiful voice.

"Excuse me?" said Alex.

"I said into escheat. And if that happens to Masques and Ber-gamasques, it *would* be a bit of a cheap cheat, now wouldn't it?"

"I don't see . . . " said Alex, who nevertheless saw farandoles of crinolines, of peplums, of musketeers without bodies or heads wander-ing pitifully over moonscapes . . . "No, I don't see at all," he repeated.

"I'll explain it to you," Dubâteau-Ripoix said, as if he were talking to a child.

He's beginning to sound like me, thought Alex.

"I'll explain it to you," repeated Dubâteau-Ripoix. "My clients and friends, the Leblanc-Zieglers to be precise, will not accept your gener-ous offer, to which in passing I take off my hat. They will be touched, I can assure you, but they will not accept it. And they will not accept because they have no interest in agreeing to manage what Liliane and Roger Ziegler have always considered expensive playacting. Playacting attributable to the combined but nevertheless diverse whims of old Monsieur and Madame Leblanc. Excusable whims, of course, since they stemmed from the amorous disorder you yourself just referred to —but caprices nevertheless. Because, in the final analysis, it was to satisfy his own caprices that Augustin Leblanc gave in to the caprices of Mademoiselle Varga, and it was to please Augustin Leblanc that Marie-Jeanne Leblanc innocently indulged in the caprice of playing Maecenas . . . Fine! Let's say no more about it, since, by a sad caprice of fate, both women have now departed this world . . . All that remains is poor Augustin Leblanc, or rather, what remains of him. In short, my clients Ziegler, and especially Roger Ziegler—who must henceforth take over for his father-in-law, now unable to ensure the smooth func-tioning of both the Tricotine and the Labour–Confort plants (and when I say the smooth functioning it's hardly the word for two facto-ries that have to limp along every other day because of the caprices of three hundred workers)—Roger Ziegler, I say, who has his hands full at Fémina-Prestige, where displaced persons are beginning to make the same kind of demands as Breton idiots of longer standing from our own plains of Brie, idiots who ought to be pleased that they were able to turn in their muddy farm clothes for overalls and run machines instead of milking cows . . . "

"Suppose you skip these digressions. . . . " interrupted Alex.

"What digressions? I'm trying to explain to you . . . "

"You're busy telling me about the misfortunes of the Zieglers, the troubles of the Zieglers. Nothing could be more interesting, I'm sure, but you were supposed to explain why Masques, that expensive play-thing, was inevitably going to be consigned to an uncertain fate."

Since he was obviously ignorant, Alex was treated to a masterly course on escheat and its tragic consequences: to wit, that an inheritance refused by one and repudiated by another falls into escheat and, subsequently, into the hands of the State.

But despite the fact that Jean-Gaétan Dubâteau-Ripoix had carefully aspirated the "h" when he said *déshérence,* in escheat, Alex continued to see crinolines, peplums and musketeers still in *errance,* still wandering, but now caught in the nets of uniformed hunters, court clerks, process servers, customs officials and appraisers: caught, rounded up, evaluated and tagged before being knocked down to greedy, indifferent people who would take them far from those who loved them, those who had known how to design them, sew them and wear them. Far from actors, Alex thought.

"What have the Zieglers got against actors?" he asked.

"They don't belong to their milieu and they are expensive," Dubâteau-Ripoix replied without hesitation. "Much, much too expensive."

"Like ballet dancers," said Alex, helpfully.

"Exactly," Dubâteau answered, smiling. "And in their world, it is unheard of for the legitimate offspring to support the bastards their fathers have had by dancers. Especially once those dancers are dead . . . and, I'm told, already buried," Dubâteau added, in a tone of melancholy reproof.

Alex said nothing.

"You might have alerted me, my dear Alex . . . "

"No," replied Alex, who was already getting up.

Dubâteau didn't insist, and he too got up.

"Well, are you going to adopt this bastard or abandon it to public welfare? Maître Parbot, of Troyes, is expecting your visit and your instructions."

"I don't know anything else," murmured Alex.

"Think it over, my dear Grandi, think it over, and when you go to Troyes—because you will have to go there one day or another—be sure to stop at La Bonne Chanson . . . "

"La Bonne Chanson?" asked Alex, already at the door.

"It's the name of the house where poor Marie-Jeanne waited so long for you . . . 'The hour of steaming tea and closed books . . .' 'Reveries by lamplight . . .' 'A finger against the temple . . .' I'm sure you know all that."

"I know, I know it very well. Damn Verlaine! As for Maître Whatsis, I mean the Troyes notary, I'll phone you. I have to think about it," Alex said, as he opened the door.

"Don't wait too long. The State is not very patient, and it is greedy!" concluded Dubâteau-Ripoix from the threshold.

The lawyer's beautiful voice had lost much of its vibrato.

I should have redone the ceiling in the corridor while I was at it, thought Alex, slipping into the trench coat held out for him by a majordomo in a striped black-and-yellow waistcoat.

: :

IT WAS THANKS to the movies that Alex found the solution to all the problems posed by the absurdity of his situation—the movies and the memory of something that had happened scarcely two weeks earlier.

There were only about twenty of them that evening in the movie theater where *The Crime of Monsieur Lange* was being shown. Rodriguez had brought him along. He was seeing the film for the fourth time in two days, as much for Jean Renoir, who had directed it, as for Florelle, Jules Berry, René Lefèvre, Guisol, Sylvie Bataille, and all the unknowns— except to the habitués of Chéramy's—who spoke the dialogue. What dialogue! "Shut up!" Alex had had to whisper to Rodriguez when he could no longer bear hearing him say the lines ahead of the actors. The words, the funny, sad words of real life, and the song of the Belle Etoile: *"Au jour le jour, à la nuit la nuit . . . "*—the dialogue and the words of the songs happened to be by that nutsy character everyone called Jacques, the one who had told the story of the mauve chalk . . .

"Let's form a cooperative!" said the film's sympathetic protagonists, and they formed their cooperative, and it worked, and they sang: "It's Christmas Eve and the snow is falling in big flakes . . . " and the little comic who was always seen at Chéramy's with his cello was here seen on his bike, weaving through the streets of Paris to distribute the newspaper they had successfully put out as a cooperative.

Alex had stayed for two showings. And Rodriguez, proud of being able to share this pleasure with his friend, had seen the film for the fifth time.

That was two weeks ago. Now *The Crime of Monsieur Lange* wasn't being shown anywhere. Alex couldn't remember anything but the songs, the pretty laundresses, Jules Berry as a phony priest, Florelle's organza smock, Duhamel's butterfly bow, the fox worn by Sylvie Bataille and Nadia Sibirskaïa's squaw outfit. He thought he had forgotten the legend of the Cooperative. It came back to him.

It came back to him right in the middle of avenue Mac-Mahon, which he was walking along, deep in thought, after having left Dubâteau-

Ripoix. And instead of going to the Etoile to get his Métro to Les Pyrénées, Alex turned back.

"I'll take it!" he said, as he might have said *Eureka!*, after having pushed aside the majordomo, who wanted to announce him. "I'll take it! And I'll take them all with me! The Zieglers and the Jeans, the workers, the jobbers, the dressmakers! We'll all take one another, we'll form a cooperative!"

He was breathless from having run up the three flights.

"I gather that you accept, my dear Grandi, and I am pleased for you," said Dubâteau, who had recovered his beautiful voice once more. "Since you accept, you are henceforth the boss and you may do as you please, isn't that so? But, given present conditions, I sincerely doubt that Fémina-Prestige, Tricotine and Labour-Confort are in a cooperative mood, or even in a mood to cooperate . . . The great guild of owner-workers, moving along hand in hand, is hardly a likelihood these days! In any case, I will tell them . . . "—and Dubâteau saw no need to get up and see the young madman to the door a second time.

: :

ALEX DIDN'T have to go to Troyes. Maître Parbot sent him his deed of ownership by his own clerk, who took the opportunity to visit Paris for the first time in his life. Alex therefore never saw the large park or the follies of La Bonne Chanson.

On the other hand, he got to know the liabilities and assets of Masques and Bergamasques, and thus discovered—once the clerk's jargon had been translated—that some of the items entered in the accounts came close to a "misappropriation of funds," not to say "fraud." It was obvious that Victoria Jean's mauve chalk adjustments were easier to obliterate than the unpaid bills of her steady suppliers. The list was long and repetitive. It included hairdressers and perfumers, gourmet food shops, florists, a garage in Neuilly and sleeping cars on the railways, entered in black and white in a most uncompromising ink, under the column headed "Entertainment Expenses."

Alex was thus forced to admit that life wasn't like the movies. In the movies, the sympathetic protagonists of *The Crime of Monsieur Lange* set up their cooperative in two shots requiring three camera movements. In Alex's life, it took more than three weeks. Twenty-five days, to be exact.

Twenty-five days to convince, sign up and reconvince those without whom the adventure was not viable.

Twenty-five days in which to cut through the red tape of corporate law, compared to which the jargon used by Maître Parbot's clerk was as limpid as a sonnet by Ronsard.

It was Mademoiselle Anita who did it. To Alex's great surprise, she had showed up one morning at Allée Chateaubriand without warning and had volunteered for the Coop. Discreet as she had always been, she gave no details as to what had brought about her decision.

"I've left Fémina-Prestige. Business administration and I are old friends," she announced simply, and, discreet as he had always been, Alex did not ask why she was leaving the well-established bosses she had been with for so long in order to work for their adventurous bastards.

It was she, therefore, who wrote up the bylaws of the new company, she who explained in writing to all the cooperators how, instead of a guaranteed salary, they would henceforth share in the profits, when there were any.

Mademoiselle Anita's letters were simple and clear. She was well aware that she was addressing people more skilled at sewing than at reading, more timorous than enterprising. She took great pleasure in writing these letters, and an even greater pleasure in signing her full name to them: Anita Bourgoin, very legible.

"It's a good feeling, a change for me," she had sighed happily as she set her carefully written signature to the first of these letters.

Alex hadn't said anything. He had smiled, too, as he held the blotting pad out to her. She had just told him the story of her life in one sentence.

The staggered return of the replies indicated the degree of surprise or incredulity the letters had inspired. Of the twenty-seven mailed, only three went unanswered. The twenty-four positive replies always looked the same, Mademoiselle Anita having taken the trouble to add to her letter a slip of paper with a typed acceptance that required only to be signed and placed in a stamped, self-addressed envelope.

The first two responses bore the postmark of the XXth arrondissement. The reply coupon was only a formality: the women at rue de la Mare hadn't waited for Mademoiselle Anita's letter before joining the Cooperative.

: :

SONIA AND OLGA had been Alex's first confidantes—except, of course, for Jean-Gaétan Dubâteau-Ripoix, if it can be said that Alex had confided in him when he had burst in unannounced and, under the rigged ceiling on avenue Mac-Mahon, had cried breathlessly, "I'll take it!"

He was also breathless when he got to Sonia and Olga's place. Breathless because he had run down rue de la Mare so quickly—but he was much calmer than when he had gone back up avenue Mac-Mahon an hour earlier.

As calm as Guisol had been in *The Crime of Monsieur Lange,* because Sonia and Olga resembled the protagonists of the film, and Dubâteau-Ripoix didn't.

He had told *them* everything. Everything right from the beginning, slowly and in simple words for once, without the metaphors or the more-or-lesses or the omissions that had caused so much trouble the last time.

They had listened, making him repeat when they didn't understand, go back when he went too fast.

They had listened to the story of Maddy in Saint-Etienne and Maddy in Paris, of Maddy and Tintin, of Tintin and Fémina-Prestige, of Alex and Maddy, of Fémina-Prestige and Madame Tintin, the deaths, the morgue, the inheritance, the escheat, *The Crime of Monsieur Lange* and his cooperative.

"The poor girl!" said Sonia, who had been particularly struck by Maddy's story.

"What a pity we never knew her," Olga had said, looking first at The Family Picture Frame and then at the sewing-machine drawer. "You should never have left her," she'd added, fixing her eyes on Alex.

"But I no longer loved her," Alex had murmured sadly.

"She probably didn't understand . . . That sort of thing often happens with you," Sonia had replied, and went off to pour water into the little coffee maker.

"It happens with everyone," Alex had concluded.

Then he had explained about the Cooperative, and they had understood everything. Except for one thing: why a cooperative?

"So that no one will ever again find himself right back at square one," Alex had answered, taken aback by a question he hadn't yet asked himself.

Then there had been a ring at the door.

"That must be Barsky," Sonia had said.

It was Barsky. He had a terrific deal for Sonia, Olga and Grandi. Two men he'd met through a friend, the Greatest Makeup Man of the Greatest Movie Star, he couldn't tell them the man's name, but the two men were brothers, young people, who were getting ready to make a movie that would be shot mostly in the streets, some of it in a bedroom, among workers, in a factory, and on the seashore. The Star had just about said yes, and the Makeup Man and his wife—who was the greatest Dresser in the Movies—could get her to do whatever they wanted. And so, for the costumes . . .

"Thanks, Isidore," Alex had replied kindly. "My associates and I will look into this tomorrow."

"Oh, you've got new associates?" asked Barsky, who, ever since the disappearance of the Masques and Bergamasques card from the door of "the Bonnet place," had been consumed with curiosity.

"We're a *cooperative* now, Monsieur Barsky," Sonia had specified, with the blasé assurance of a member of management.

" 'bsolutely!" Olga had confirmed, looking at Alex, who had smiled. Barsky had also smiled, but without knowing why.

"We're going to form a cooperative, Isidore, *become* a cooperative—in other words, work as a group."

"You mean a kibbutz!" Barsky had exclaimed, before bursting into laughter. "Like that nephew of the Sterns, the madman of Lake Tiberias. And you think it'll work?"

"We're going to see to it that it does, my friend," Alex had replied.

"And is the Grand Duchess Victoria Roginska also going to become a kibbutznik?" Barsky had asked in his most innocent voice.

Sonia and Olga had turned to Alex. It had taken Barsky to raise that fearful shadow, and ask the only question they hadn't as yet dared pose.

"We'll know tomorrow, but I'd be very surprised," said Alex, who had just remembered Dubâteau-Ripoix's "I'll inform them . . . " "Tomorrow at the latest," he had repeated, to banish the anguish he had suddenly seen reborn in the eyes of both Sonia and Olga. "But how is it you know Madame Victoria Jean so well, dear Isidore?" Alex had asked, after a brief silence.

"Gromoff and I did business with her a long time ago, a very long time ago," Barsky had replied, smiling mysteriously. "Well, what shall I tell my two friends in the movies?"

"What I told you a little while ago, my dear Isidore. What are these two friends called?"

"I can't tell you their names yet, but I'll be able to tomorrow without fail."

"Fine, you'll tell us tomorrow! Tomorrow we'll know everything about everything. Till then, my friend!" And Alex had shown Barsky to the door.

"WE COULDN'T form a kibbutz with her," Olga had murmured after Barsky had left.

"There's no danger," Alex had reassured her, wondering how the path of the two Verdon brothers could have crossed that of Isidore Barsky. Then after a moment he'd said, "What did Barsky mean by the madman of Lake Tiberias?"

Sonia and Olga smiled.

"He's a young man, a nephew of Madame Stern, and he spent a week in Paris last year. Before, he had been a student in Germany, but now he's a fisherman . . . " Olga had begun.

"A fisherman in Palestine, in a kibbutz. He sent some photos showing himself on a sailboat, and Monsieur and Madame Stern invited all of us in to see the photos. Barsky was a bit drunk, and he made jokes about the young man being in short pants like a little boy, and Madame Stern was upset . . . And that's the whole story," Sonia had concluded.

"And is the kibbutz working out all right?"

"Monsieur and Madame Stern never told us any more about it, so we don't know. It must be a hard life, the sun and fishing, when you come from a cool climate and books," Sonia replied.

"Can we put up our card now?" Sonia had suggested. "The door looks so sad without anything on it."

"It looks as if we don't have legal papers any longer," Olga added.

Five minutes later, the eleven letters of the word COOPERATIVE had been written across a sheet of lined paper. Drawn in red crayon, posted like a challenge, it made the Bonnet apartment once more their own, and it conferred a completely new identity on Sonia Guttman and Olga Roginski.

:   :

ZAZA WAS THE FIRST to discover the flamboyant announcement when she came home from school at four o'clock. Scarcely listening to the explanations offered by Sonia and Olga, she had gone down to the Cléments to do her homework with Josette, and had incidentally announced that from now on her mother and Maurice's mother had no bosses. They *were* the bosses.

Jeannette Clément, a little surprised, not to say hurt, that such social upheavals could take place upstairs without the arbitration and advice of Félix, impatiently awaited his return. He got back from the Post

Office at about five o'clock. Once informed, he decided to go upstairs and verify the accuracy of the child's news.

Félix had understood everything even before he reached the landing. The door of the Bonnet place said more than a leaflet, was more scarlet than a pennant, and his heart beat fast as he rang the bell.

"That's good, very good," Félix said quietly. "It's an example for the neighborhood, and when all the workers in the world have understood your example, the world will be a better place. Bravo, my friends, and long life to your cooperative!"

And Félix went back down to the loge, where he spoke of kolkhozes.

In the Auvergnat's café they were talking about kibbutzim. It was Barsky who had spread the news. First he had monopolized the telephone at the bar by calling the Saint-Maurice studios and always getting a busy signal. Barsky was as impatient as a boss who tries to call the office and finds that his employees are always on the phone, and was very curt as he said "Give me Adrienne" when the operator finally answered. No, Adrienne didn't remember two fellows who were at the bar the other day with the woman Féfé and Tata Boubou worked for, but if he'd like to call back later, she'd ask them . . .

"I'll call again in fifteen minutes," he said to the Auvergnat, who was serving him an Amer-Picon.

Just then Barsky saw Monsieur Lowenthal through the window. He invited him in for a drink and told him about the kibbutz.

Monsieur Lowenthal said nothing, just smiled as he always did, but when he got home he told Madame Lowenthal about the kibbutz.

"And it's written on their door?" asked Madame Lowenthal.

"No. What's written is 'Cooperative,' " said Monsieur Lowenthal.

"That's worse!" exclaimed Madame Lowenthal. "It's politics, worse than Zionism! . . . It's Zionist politics in France! . . . Just what we needed!"

After a moment's reflection she added: "So that was the reason for the wax! . . . "

Accustomed to the chaotic paths taken by Madame Lowenthal's thinking, Monsieur Lowenthal didn't comment on this astounding remark. Despite appearances, however, she was alluding to a real fact, one that had—last Tuesday or Wednesday—greatly troubled Mesdames Stern and Lowenthal. On coming down in the morning, Madame Lowenthal had surprised Madame Stern busily searching under the doormat in front of the Bonnet place. Without saying a word, Madame Stern, who hadn't found whatever she was looking for, had pointed to the four little holes left in the door by the thumbtacks that only yesterday had held the Masques and Bergamasques card. They had been worriedly whispering about this disappearance when the door opened. It was Olga.

"Did somebody steal it?" Madame Lowenthal had asked.

"No, it's because of the waxing . . . " Olga had stammered, blushing.

Later, both she and Sonia were seen working on the door, slowly and carefully applying the wax, then leaving it, sticky and dull, overnight. The stairway smelled of polish.

The following day they were seen with woolen cloths, slowly and carefully rubbing and polishing the door, which remained, though shining, desperately anonymous. The good smell of polish lingered in the stairway.

"What it really smells of is a closing!" Madame Lowenthal said to herself.

And that hadn't particularly surprised her. Anything might be expected from that badly brought-up Alex. You begin with czardas dancers and you end with naked women . . .

The comings and goings of Lucienne, Albertine, Yvette and Magali had aroused Madame Lowenthal's curiosity. Having heard them one evening as they were leaving, noisily exchanging some blunt comments about the *The Moon Is Naked* libretto, she had drawn her own conclusions as to what was going on in the workshop, where she was no longer admitted during the hours when fittings were taking place. Still, Madame Lowenthal hadn't said a word to anyone. Especially not to Monsieur Lowenthal, who had been imprudent enough to remark one evening on the air of health and youth emanating from the four tall girls and the pretty baby he'd passed in the doorway as he was coming home.

But she hadn't been able to keep herself from questioning Zaza.

"They're acrobatic gymnast artists," Zaza had replied, as agreed.

"Just as I suspected," Madame Lowenthal had thought; in her youth she had heard talk of Austro-Hungarian orgies spiced up with *tableaux vivants*. "Not surprising that it didn't last long, that den of iniquity. And when you no longer know what to put on your door, you polish it until something turns up. And when nothing turns up and there's no employer, you form a kibbutz . . . a kibbutz of artistic gymnasts!"

"I'm going down to see," said Madame Lowenthal to Monsieur Lowenthal, who indicated with a smile that there really wasn't much to see.

Madame Lowenthal went down anyway. She studied the placard, verified that it really had been pasted on, hesitated a moment and then rang.

No one came to the door. Madame Lowenthal went back up to her own apartment.

: :

SONIA AND OLGA had also gone back to their apartments. They were waiting for their husbands to return.

The desire to go back and wait in their own kitchens rather than in their workshop had come to them a little while after Félix Clément's brief visit.

Barsky's gibes and his variations on the cooperative-kibbutz theme left them unmoved. On the other hand, their role as exemplars for the working classes of the XXth arrondissement and their striking contribution to the building of a better world—evoked by the postman in his brief but stirring testimony—had left them thoughtful and, to tell the truth, a little uneasy.

They would never have suspected that a word which sounded as simple and innocent as the word "cooperative" did when pronounced by Alex Grandi would be charged with such revolutionary overtones when rapped out by Félix Clément. They'd only just become aware of it, and, at the same time, aware that they'd once again made decisions without first consulting their husbands.

Once again might become once too often. Not knowing how Stépan and Elie would take all this, the women decided to do everything they could to make things weigh in their own favor. They figured that if the two men took the time to decipher their troublesome sign, it wouldn't be a bad idea to give them time to climb another flight of stairs before they demanded explanations.

The women therefore went back to their own apartments and set out little glasses of vodka in Sonia's kitchen, just as they used to do when they were still finishers and not yet kolkhozniki.

ELIE WAS, as usual, waiting for Stépan in front of the Saponite advertisement on the platform of the Strasbourg–St.-Denis Métro station. He let one train go by and took the next. Though it was rare, they did sometimes miss each other.

As he passed the Auvergnat's café he saw Barsky, Nussbaum, Novack and Gromoff at the bar. Barsky was gesturing broadly and everyone was laughing. Knowing what Barsky was like at that hour, Elie had no wish to be trapped. He hurried by.

He also hurried on entering the building. He was fond of Félix; he didn't mind a little discussion with him in the compnay of Stépan on Sundays, before lunch and after returning from the public baths. But during the week, all alone, after work and before dinner, he didn't care for it at all.

The elections were getting close. It was still only December and they weren't scheduled until April, but at both Mercier Frères and in the loge on rue de la Mare the campaign was in full swing.

The cousin from Lot, Cousin Martial, the Socialist deputy who had years before speeded the naturalization of the Guttman and Roginski families, had showed up at Mercier Frères, and Paul Mercier reminded his cousin of this episode as he introduced Elie. "Our Lilyich," he had specified, tapping Elie, whom he generally called Guttman, on the shoulder. Martial Mercier remembered—remembered so well, as a matter of fact, that he had asked for news of the boys: they must have grown quite a bit since . . . Elie blushed, admitted that they had indeed grown, but that actually there was a Guttman boy and a Roginski girl. His correction was lost in the general hubbub caused by the appearance in the workshop of a cask of Cahors wine, which the parliamentarian had escorted to the capital to mark his visit there. Everyone had toasted the victory of the workers, and more particularly, the victory of the Socialist Party. It had been like a little celebration, and after his third glass Meunier had sung *"La Butte rouge,"* then announced that he himself never voted but that he was ready to take Monsieur Martial's "Popol" to the circus . . . since he was making one of his rare visits to Paris.

This anecdote, marking back to rue de la Mare, had not made Félix laugh. "Demagogy with the help of red wine . . . *Chez nous,* we take things seriously," he had remarked, shaking his head gravely.

The *"chez nous,"* or "in our place," a phrase Félix made frequent use of, could take on different meanings, and over the years Elie and Stépan were often perplexed until the theme of the discourse would definitively set them on the right track. *"Chez nous"* could mean Savoy or the concierge's loge or the family, or the Post Office, or even the Party cell, or the entire Party—in other words, the international Party.

For some time, Félix's *"chez nous"* had been serving exclusively to point up what was being done badly *"chez eux"*—"in their place"— among the Socialists. And only the Socialists. All the others were very rarely evoked and always in the aggregate, under a common label. Félix simply called all the others "the others," without violence but with implacable contempt.

Félix's constant use of *"chez nous"* had, also for some time, been designed to help the light dawn on Elie. The Mercier brothers and cousins, good bosses, prime examples of *"chez eux,"* were to his way of thinking much more harmful than anyone who was just a boss in the camp of "the others."

And that was why, again also for some time, Elie would walk faster as he drew near the glazed door of the loge.

He hurried now, racing up the stairs. He was about to get out his keys, but hadn't the time. Sonia was already opening the door, and Olga was behind her.

They had removed their work smocks; Sonia was wearing her pretty apron with the blue flowers, and Olga her tartan coverall. He was surprised to find them already there, and they were surprised to find him without Stépan.

They looked so strange that Elie wondered if he hadn't forgotten somebody's birthday.

He went into the kitchen, where they served him his vodka with all the devoted attention of geishas.

Obviously they had something to say, and even more obviously they would wait for Stépan's arrival before saying it. He knew them well, Elie did. He therefore asked no questions and drank his glass in small sips while they smiled and served themselves their half glasses.

"What's keeping Stépan?" asked Olga, just to say something.

"I finished a little earlier today," lied Elie, who, knowing what he already knew and what they still didn't know, was beginning to regret not having waited for Stépan under the Saponite ad.

: :

THERE WERE plenty of things Stépan didn't tell them on rue de la Mare, many worries he left at rue d'Aboukir with his white smock when he took it off in the evening before placing it in the steel locker and going to meet his friend on the platform of the Strasbourg–St.-Denis station. And those he hadn't managed to leave in his locker were confided to Elie on the way back, so he could be free of them before entering the house.

Although the stories about the Mercier brothers and their cousin had excited all the doctrinal severity of the very serious Félix, they had flooded Stépan's heart with envy.

They neither sang nor laughed nor drank toasts on rue d'Aboukir.

Toasts? There had never been any, for anything or anybody on rue d'Aboukir; some laughing and some soft singing at times, yes, but that was all over. For a while now there had been whispering, arguing and shouting on rue d'Aboukir, just as there was everywhere in France at the end of 1935. With one difference, however, and a big one: on rue d'Aboukir, they were afraid. And it was because they were afraid that they shouted at one another more than usual.

And because no one in the fur workshop except Stépan and two old cutters possessed that inestimable and inaccessible treasure, a Voter's Registration Card, the voices raised in Yiddish during the loudest shouting matches were voices that were lost to the ballot boxes already being dusted off in the French *Mairies*.

A real waste! Because they might have made a difference, these voices, even though they didn't all express the same interests. Discordant and useless as far as the elections were concerned, they weren't useless to everyone. Especially not to those who orchestrated their discord.

If there were a lot of shouting matches in the rue d'Aboukir since the rediscovery of fear, it was because they read a lot of newspapers there. Newspapers that had begun to appear just when fear had reappeared. They were all printed in the same Yiddish, but they didn't all say the same things. Reading them brought about discord. And the discord led to the shouting matches.

The shouting was always on the same subject—the one that had brought back scandal, unhappiness and fear.

They'd been brought back in the bundles of the most recent arrivals: the Germans—these unknowns, never encountered on the routes of exodus, more German than Jew, it was said, but whose very presence had led to fashioning the infamous old formula for contemporary tastes. The formula the old immigrants had refused to submit to in the old countries—refused, and fled to find a new country where it was inoperative.

Since their arrival, these Jews from Germany had never been called anything but German Jews, never Jewish Germans.

And the newspapers that circulated on rue d'Aboukir spoke only of them to the other Jews, who, though they hadn't become French citizens, weren't in the least eager to become Polish Jews, Romanian Jews or Slovakian Jews again—and yet that is what certain articles suggested in the name of an international Judaism, the rituals and goals of which escaped them. Though not all of them.

Meanwhile, in other newspapers that were also circulated on rue d'Aboukir and in which they also spoke of German Jews, it was suggested to the same Poles, Romanians or Slovaks of Jewish faith that they regroup in the name of an international proletariat about whose rites they also knew nothing, but whose goals did not completely escape them. Not all of them, anyway.

But whatever it was suggested they do, it was always suggested they do it in groups—in Jewish groups. And all these papers were openly passed from hand to hand every morning on rue d'Aboukir.

Or rather they had been, because for some time now they'd been kept out of sight. They'd been kept out of sight ever since the day Monsieur Jean had come across an issue of *Naïe Presse* in which, to stimulate Jewish immigrant workers to organize for the defense of their rights and their wages, examples of such organization in certain other establishments were cited. And *Naïe Presse* gave a list of the men's garment factories in which, since October, there had already been strikes.

These factories were known; all of them were in the neighborhood. It was also known there had been strikes there. There had already been talk and arguments about the strikes among their neighbors. But now it was in the paper. It was no longer just neighborhood gossip.

And so there had been more shouting. And since it had made a lot of racket, Monsieur Jean had come down alone. You never saw Monsieur Ziegler when there was shouting in Yiddish.

That morning, Stépan had read *Naïe Presse* and its list, as had the others. He had returned it without comment. He understood very well what it meant, but felt only partly involved. He had been an alien Jewish worker. He was still a worker and Jewish, but he was no longer an alien. He was French. And it was as a French worker that he wanted to organize with other workers, whether or not they were Jews, whether or not they were immigrants. But it was difficult to explain in all this noise. And that's why he had returned the *Naïe Presse* without comment.

However, when, from a distance, he had seen Janek pick up the newspaper, read it calmly, refold it carefully and place it back on the table without a word, then look at all of them in turn, and at Stépan a little longer than the others, it was the image of himself as a very young man—capped and leather-booted, jumping from the still-moving train—he had seen again. Because that was the image he read in Janek's cold glance.

He had met that glance, and then, while Monsieur Jean was crossing the now heavily silent workshop to go back up to the office, he had once again been astonished: his brother now walked the way their father used to walk. Like that aging father Janek had never seen—because he had never seen his father again.

: :

IT WAS ELIE, during their trip home, whom he had told about that day. Not Olga or Zaza.

And it was also Elie, the next day, he had told about a typed notice posted on the workshop walls; headed WARNING, it was short but precise:

> READING IS STRICTLY FORBIDDEN DURING WORKING HOURS,
> AND INFRACTIONS WILL BE FOLLOWED BY IMMEDIATE DIS-
> MISSAL.
>
> SIGNED: ILLEGIBLE.

This had really made Elie laugh, because, at Mercier Frères, the Socialist newspaper *Le Populaire* was posted on the wall every morning, with articles outlined in red by Monsieur Paul himself. That was how Elie had come to read all the details of the law closing French borders to new immigrants. "Good thing you came to us early, Lilyich! You couldn't get in now," Meunier had joked. But no one in the shop had said anything about it again, so neither had Elie; and like the others, he had laughed on discovering that some wise guy had gotten into the habit of posting *Le Miroir des Sports* and the Micky Mouse comic strip alongside *Le Populaire* just to get a rise out of Monsieur Paul, who actually laughed as much as the others did.

Just as Stépan had laughed about it in the Métro for a minute or so. But he hadn't said anything to Olga and Zaza about that either, because he would have had to start with the beginning, with *Naïe Presse* and even earlier . . .

In fact, he would have had to tell them about the fear. The fear he didn't want to bring home with him. And Elie thought he'd been right. Especially since he was wrong to be afraid, he would add every evening as they traveled home together. Which reassured Stépan, even though he could see in Elie's eyes and smile that he was saying it to reassure himself.

Stépan saw this clearly, but he didn't say anything to Elie. And as soon as they were in sight of the house—in other words, on the last step up from Les Pyrénées station—they would begin to talk of other things. Of their wives, of the weather, of the Auvergnat, of the kids, of what they'd like to have for dinner. They were going home, down their own street, neighbors of their neighbors. They were going home after work, like every other French citizen. And they liked that.

That's why they hated missing each other at the Strasbourg-St.–Denis station.

: :

STEPAN RAN down onto the platform. He already knew he wouldn't find Elie. A quarter of an hour late was too late, according to their established conventions. But he had run all the same, just in case. And he was really depressed as he got into the crowded car.

Depressed and upset after what had just happened, what had made him late and what he couldn't tell anyone.

Since yesterday, it had been known throughout Fémina-Prestige that the bosses were absent because of a death in the Ziegler family. The newspapers had come out of hiding, causing the tone of the discussion to escalate, and at the same time there had been a vaguely mischievous breeze of unruliness. Not because of the death—they weren't even sure who had been struck down—but because of the absence of those who'd been momentarily called away from the upper floor. Some of the fear had evaporated, and like everyone else in the shop, Stépan had been very aware of it. He'd even said so to Elie on the way home the day before.

Then this morning there had been the leaflet.

Hundreds of copies had shown up, as though by magic, in the entryways, on the stairways and on the tables of all the garment manufacturers in the neighborhood. It wasn't mimeographed, but printed in large black type on yellow paper, and it was obviously meant for wide distribution, since the Yiddish text on the front had been reproduced in French on the back—unless it was the other way around. Nothing in the contents indicated clearly to which of the two cultures it originally belonged. Nothing about its makeup either. It was totally anonymous. This is what it said:

GERMAN JEWISH WORKERS!

COME OUT OF THE SHADOWS! REFUSE TO WORK ILLEGALLY!

NO LONGER WORK ALL NIGHT IN YOUR FURNISHED ROOMS FOR A PITTANCE, WHILE YOUR COMRADES ARE STRUGGLING DURING THE DAY IN THEIR SHOPS TO WRING DECENT WAGES AND HOURS FROM THEIR JEWISH BOSSES!

THE JEWISH BOSSES EXPLOITING YOU ARE THE ALLIES OF HITLER, WHO HAS DRIVEN YOU INTO EXILE.

JUST LOOK AT GALERIES LAFAYETTE, WHOSE JEWISH MANAGEMENT CONTINUES TO DO BUSINESS WITH THE NAZI BOSSES.

THE JEWISH BOSSES EXPLOITING YOU ARE SUPPLIERS OF GALERIES LAFAYETTE.

JEWISH WORKERS WHO ARE NATURALIZED FRENCHMEN, ALIENS OR STATELESS! IT'S UP TO YOU TO STOP THIS SCANDAL!

IT'S YOUR RIGHT AND YOUR DUTY.

REGROUP!

MAKE YOURSELVES HEARD!

YOU TOO MUST COME OUT OF THE SHADOWS!

THE TIME FOR GHETTOS HAS RETURNED

?

The final question mark was printed in a type size much larger than that used for the most emphasized words—if it can be said that anybody or anything was being emphasized in this strange appeal for general mobilization. It was rare to find a question mark that fulfilled its functions and occupied such a space so well. By itself, it monopolized a quarter of both the front and back sides. And whether you turned to the French text or the Yiddish, it was the question mark you saw first, even before you bent down to pick up the yellow and black paper that looked more like a fortuneteller's handout than a protest manifesto. At first glance.

It was a question mark that was both an attention-getter and a conclusion. A conclusion and a signature. In short, a questioning of everything.

Placed as it was, it not only punctuated the last sentence—which could be taken for a boldly optimistic affirmation—with a grave doubt, but above all it multiplied the ambiguities of a text that could, at the very least, be said to supply "food for thought," as Félix, who often said this, would have put it.

Since he said it often, and often when Stépan was present, the latter had taken a liking to this expression and was about to use it with his fellow workers, having read the leaflet on the Fémina-Prestige stairway before going into the furriery.

He kept it to himself. The image seemed too inadequate. You don't eat dynamite.

The bomb had not yet exploded, but the fuse was lit. Its sputtering could already be heard.

The noise, having a tendency to amplify as it rose, could be heard so well that the sound reached the upper floor clearly enough to make Mademoiselle Anita come down. And it was she, timid and frail, who appeared in the shop as a stand-in for the bosses, who still had not reappeared two days after they had disappeared.

Mademoiselle Anita had neither the authority nor the air nor the voice of Monsieur Jean. Nevertheless, her appearance imposed silence. Another kind of silence.

"Look at this, Mademoiselle Anita," Jiri Koustov, the Slovak, said to her, holding out the tract.

"The bastards!" murmured Mademoiselle Anita in her very soft voice, after having read the French text.

It was the first time she had been heard to use a vulgarity. There were several embarrassed laughs.

"Who are the bastards?" asked a voice that rose above the laughter.

"The Germans, who work for peanuts, or the Galeries Lafayette, who work for the other Germans?"

"The people who put together this leaflet," replied Mademoiselle Anita.

"But we, here, we're working for Galeries Lafayette, aren't we?" said the same voice.

It was still Jiri the Slovak, who had given her the leaflet.

Mademoiselle Anita hesitated, and didn't answer.

"But you must surely know, Mademoiselle Anita, if we are or aren't working for Galeries Lafayette?"

"For some things, yes, we do a little work for the Galeries," said Mademoiselle Anita, blushing slightly.

"And the Boches without work permits—do the bosses give them a little work for Fémina-Prestige instead of paying us overtime?"

Jiri, again.

"It's happened," Mademoiselle Anita admitted. "When we've been behind in filling orders."

"So the leaflet is telling the truth!" exclaimed Jiri, pleased with the success of his demonstration.

"No!" said Stépan, who had been standing silently at the rear of the workshop ever since the beginning of the discussion.

Everyone turned round.

"It's Mademoiselle Anita who's right. There are also Italians, Greeks and Armenians, a lot of foreign refugees, who don't have permits and who work, and a lot of others who do have permits and who work legally, for Galeries Lafayette and for other bosses too, and yet no leaflets in Italian, Greek or Armenian are sent to them."

"But it's not the same thing where they're concerned," said Jiri, as if that were obvious.

"Why?" asked Mademoiselle Anita.

No one answered. Such incomprehension could only make you sigh.

"It's just what I said—they're bastards, but very astute bastards, the people who wrote this!" Mademoiselle Anita repeated, calmly folding the yellow paper and slipping it into the sleeve of her gray sweater, under the wrist, like a precious handkerchief she didn't want to lose.

The word *astute* was totally unknown on rue d'Aboukir, so Mademoiselle Anita had to search for equivalents in order to be better understood.

Franz Kafka was also unknown: unknown on rue d'Aboukir, unknown everywhere in the world, and especially unknown in the world of Mademoiselle Anita. Still, it seemed almost as though it was he who inspired her from beyond the grave in which he had been laid to rest twelve long years ago, so finely did Mademoiselle Anita seem to analyze both the logic of those who had launched this tract and the chemistry that made it a bomb.

It appeared to be very complicated, but actually it couldn't have been more simple—even if crafty. Here's how Mademoiselle Anita understood things:

The traditional Scapegoats are gathered together. For the sake of these traditional Scapegoats, a selection of other Scapegoats are fed to them. It's a new experience, but by having taken care to select the new Scapegoats from the heart of their very own flock and to leave them in the very same pen, they create a mass of Scapegoats who turn on one another. And who inevitably make a lot of noise. And since they make a lot of noise, they eventually draw attention to themselves. "We've been hearing them a lot!" those who had temporarily forgotten them because nothing had been heard from them begin to murmur. "We've been hearing nothing but them, you mean!" those who have never forgotten them, even when they were silent, are free to proclaim. "And not only do we hear nothing but them, but look how they gobble one another up! As well as collectively and simultaneously gobbling up the good grass on our pastures or the good wool on the backs of our sheep . . . " as those who had never forgotten them are pleased to say, those who are keeping their wandering flock of Scapegoats in reserve—the herd they've finally managed to regroup into a large flock of Black Sheep.

The bomb is almost ready.

All that has to be done is to denounce the enclosure. And that's when they'll have to be astute.

They'll denounce the enclosure by deploring its existence but noting that the Black Sheep aren't unhappy to be in it. That way they won't have to point out those who outlined its boundaries, retain its key and are in a position to padlock it. They'll be able to unlock it if they find it convenient to bring on parades of Black Sheep which will be so much in the public eye, so noisy, that everyone will say the enclosure wasn't such a bad idea after all.

The time had come to launch the leaflet.

Mademoiselle Anita didn't make use of such pastoral allegories to defuse the work of these bomb-makers. As Stépan had done with his "food for thought," she kept them to herself, especially since the evocation of all these bearded, horned and cloven-hoofed animals wasn't all that pleasant and would have required hours of translation.

But Mademoiselle Anita had other resources. Unknowingly inspired by Franz Kafka, about whom she knew nothing, she was also inspired by Captain Dreyfus, about whom she knew everything, and who, unlike Kafka, had just recently died. He had died the previous July 12, and his death had moved Mademoiselle Anita, the daughter of a passionate Dreyfusard from the Dordogne whose childhood had been punctuated by the developments of the Affair, which she knew as well as other little girls knew their catechism. Last July 12, with the death of the hero for whom her father had fought so loyally, a part of that childhood had died—one might almost say been extinguished.

It was therefore of the two of them—her father and Captain Dreyfus —she had thought on that morning of July 12 as she turned into rue d'Aboukir, which was already decorated with lights in anticipation of the coming Bastille Day celebrations. And she had been a little sad and thoughtful when she started work.

Since neither Monsieur Ziegler now Monsieur Jean nor anyone else at Fémina-Prestige had mentioned the famous death, she'd copied their behavior and kept her thoughts to herself. Until Monsieur Jean had asked for the Jaspard schedule . . .

Though for many years the word "schedule," or *bordereau,* had been spoken at least twenty times a day in the Fémina-Prestige offices, that morning, for the first time, it had sounded so strange in Mademoiselle Anita's ears, reminded her so sharply of the infamous *bordereau* that had been used to convict Captain Dreyfus, that she was upset, and had enormous trouble laying her hands on this innocent accounting memorandum. She was looking for it among the others in the room next door when Monsieur Jean called out impatiently:

"What the devil are you doing with that *bordereau*! . . . Are you forging it, Mademoiselle Anita?"

"No, Monsieur, it's been a long time since that sort of thing was done —or since anyone has been sent to Devil's Island . . . " Mademoiselle Anita had been unable to keep herself from saying to her boss as she placed the Jaspard *bordereau* on his desk.

But Monsieur Jean hadn't answered, and Mademoiselle Anita had wondered if Monsieur Jean had heard her remark, and, if he had understood it, why he hadn't replied. In any case, the day had passed without any reference to Captain Dreyfus, and from then on, Mademoiselle Anita had jumped every time the word *bordereau* was mentioned. In other words, often.

It bordered on an obsession, and had remained so well after July 12.

And it was in thinking about the word *bordereau* that Mademoiselle

Anita took the yellow paper from her sleeve to illustrate what she meant by the adjective "astute," which, insofar as she was concerned, was hard to disassociate from the noun "bastard" and the verb "to forge."

So she removed the yellow paper and, going back to Stépan's comments, asked him if the Yiddish text, which she didn't understand, was really a faithful translation of the French text, which she understood only too well.

It was only then discovered that no one in the shop had thought it worthwhile to read the French version closely. And Mademoiselle Anita decided that they would proceed with a comparative reading.

Time passed; no one did any work, either in the fur department or in the ladies' and girls' coats department. Everyone held on to his sheet of paper, just as he used to do in school. Small differences were soon discovered. So soon that they began with the second line.

They were little nothings, nuances that might have been attributed to poetic license if the author were to present himself with a lyre strung across his chest and the disarming candor of a troubadour intent on singing in the *langue d'oïl* of the north what had been written in the *langue d'oc* of the south.

Thus *"Come out of the shadows! Refuse to work illegally"* was the transposition of *"Do not remain under the cover of the night, alone, hidden from all."* *"No longer work all night"* had been transposed from *"Don't stay up until dawn,"* just as "FOR A PITTANCE" replaced "FOR LESS THAN THE GOING RATE," and *"your furnished rooms"* *"rooms under the eaves."*

Once the two texts had been compared, Mademoiselle Anita was set: she had her *bordereau!*

One of the two texts was a forgery. It remained to be seen which one, which translated which—or, better still, which traduced which. Was it the Yiddish, by metamorphosing the criminal shadows into the obliteration of night? or the French, by transforming imposed misery into a willingly accepted cut rate and a chanteuse's garret into a room rented by the hour?

Mademoiselle Anita had her *bordereau,* and with it she had her clear definition of the word "astute."

She clapped her hands. It seemed more and more like being in school. A good quarter of an hour had been spent in linguistic discussions, everyone wanting to make his own contribution to the search for the truth.

The word *night,* for example, on the surface so simple, had inspired a cascade of possible interpretations, depending on whether night was considered as the end of a day, of a hope or of a life, as the Kingdom of Darkness or of Ignorance—to say nothing of the Night of Time. But they had agreed on the fact that in no case could it be substituted for the word *shadow*. Whether it belonged to a tree, a wall or a hat, a shadow couldn't exist without the sun, and since the sun is always down when it's night . . . In short, at least five minutes were lost finding fault with the word *night*. Another eight were lost with "the room under the eaves," which, according to where one came from, could be situated under thatch, slate, tile, or even cow dung; its attic window, its fanlight, or its bull's-eye opening onto snowy plains, suburban streets, the Black Sea, the Carpathians, or Lake Balaton . . .

At this point, Mademoiselle Anita had clapped her hands to announce the end of the philological re-creation and to call for silence, which she obtained and which Jiri the Slovak immediately filled.

"It's true that it's disgusting to change words that way! It puts a black cloak over the backs of the Boches and all the other 'clandestine Jews,' as the French call them. All that's true! But it doesn't change the rest of it, not about Galeries Lafayette, nor about the bosses, nor about our overtime!"

"Yes, it does change things!" said Stépan, who was still in the rear of the shop. "It changes everything! We don't know if it was the anti-Semites who did the Yiddish translation, or the Jews who have been translated by the anti-Semites! They go after everybody in that leaflet of theirs, you, me . . . "

"No, they say that we're fighting for justice in our shops!"

"Not at all," Stépan answered. "They don't say that in French. They do in Yiddish—in Yiddish they say: 'Your racial brothers are fighting in their shops,' but in French it says, 'Your comrades are fighting in their shops' . . . Not 'your Jewish comrades' . . . "

Everyone looked at their leaflets again.

Mademoiselle Anita was going to make the most of this and take over once more, but Jiri stole the floor from her a second time.

"They forgot to put 'Jewish' next to 'comrades,' but that doesn't change a thing," he grumbled in Yiddish.

"It does, it changes everything, because they didn't forget to put 'Jewish' next to 'bosses.' The comrades aren't Jewish, but the bosses are all Jewish in their French text," replied Stépan, also speaking in Yiddish. "Isn't that so, Mademoiselle Anita?"

Mademoiselle Anita was about to say that she hadn't understood his last words, but Stépan didn't give her the chance. It was the first time he had spoken at such length and so loudly in public, and he added in French, "They're going after me, you, those without permits, the bosses and the Galeries; they're all mixed together in this filth. We should find out who they are."

"I know who they are," interrupted a voice, laughing coarsely. "It's the Samaritaine department store—they've had it translated in a way that would make trouble for their competitors, the Galeries Lafayette!"

There was a lot of laughter, which calmed down when Jiri spoke up again.

"That doesn't change anything. You can make jokes about it if you want, but it doesn't change anything. I don't give a damn who they are, even if it's the ghost of Petliura"—a loud *Oh!* rose from his listeners—" or even the ghost of Herzl who wrote it. I don't give a damn! They're right about the Galeries, and they're right about the bosses. In any case, Ziegler isn't a Jew, and he's my boss nevertheless. Come to think of it, where are the bosses, Mademoiselle Anita?"

"Monsieur Ziegler is still out of town. Monsieur Jean must have come home last night, but I don't think he'll be in today," replied Mademoiselle Anita.

"Well, if he's not going to work, neither am I," declared Jiri, sitting down at his table with folded arms. "In any case, I'm not going to work for Galeries Lafayette, and you can tell him that on the telephone, Mademoiselle Anita. Maybe that'll make him come running!" added the Slovak with a broad, stubborn smile that he passed around with nods of his head by way of encouragement to all those who watched him in silent consternation.

Mademoiselle Anita, feeling that at this point the word "astute" had been sufficiently demonstrated and required no further explanation from her, looked at her watch and announced that after all it was almost ten-thirty.

"So what? It doesn't change a thing," interrupted Jiri. "I'm not working, but I'm not keeping anybody else from working. Get on with it, boys, hurry and get busy!" he said, pointing to their work tools. "And so I won't be in your way, I'll just move over there."

He got up, left the table, planted his chair in the middle of the shop, sat down and folded his arms.

There was some murmuring in Yiddish, and Mademoiselle Anita got the idea that she was in the way.

"I'll leave you to decide among yourselves," she said, moving toward the door.

"Among ourselves? But just who are *we*, Mademoiselle Anita? We the Jews, or we the Fémina-Prestige workers?" said Jiri, as if he were setting a riddle.

Mademoiselle Anita couldn't immediately come up with a good answer to this good question.

"You too, you can decide for yourself: you're not a foreigner, not Jewish, not a worker, but you too work for Roginski-Ziegler, who work for Galeries Lafayette, who work for . . . "

"We know all that, stop it, Koustov!" shouted Stépan, who generally called him by his first name.

"I'll stop if I want to, Roginski!" Jiri parried. "I've already stopped working, I can also stop talking . . . but I'm the one who decides, and at least *I* don't have to account to my family!"

Jiri had lowered his head as he fired this last shot. He was looking at his shoes.

The others were looking at Stépan.

Stépan was looking at Mademoiselle Anita. And this time it was in Mademoiselle Anita's eyes that he again saw himself jumping from the still-moving train under the glass enclosure of the Gare de l'Est.

"You're not being fair, Monsieur Koustov, and you know that very well," Mademoiselle Anita said.

Jiri obstinately continued to look at his shoes.

The others were now looking at Jiri, waiting for him to say something.

And Stépan continued to look at Mademoiselle Anita.

And Mademoiselle Anita looked at Jiri, waiting for him to reply. The yellow sheet trembled almost imperceptibly in her right hand.

"I didn't mean what I said, Stépan," said Jiri finally, his head still lowered. Then he raised it and looked straight into Stépan's eyes. "But still, you have to tell your brother to come. Until he does, I won't work."

"You know very well that I never talk to my brother," Stépan replied, shrugging. "But he should come, if only to tell us if this business about the Galeries is true. Because if it's true, I'll stop working too. But not before he comes. And now, Jiri, you can do whatever you want"—and Stépan went to his metal locker and took out his white smock, which he hadn't yet had time to put on.

"I'm going to telephone Monsieur Jean," said Mademoiselle Anita. "But I think his wife is ill, and . . . "

"My wife's not well, either. She broke her leg skiing!" Jiri called after her as she returned to the second floor.

Everyone laughed, even Stépan. The men from the ladies' and girls' coat department went back to their own place, and work slowly got under way as they waited.

As they waited for the boss.

Mademoiselle Anita came back to say that the Neuilly line was still busy.

At twelve-thirty, everyone got out his lunch pail—except Jiri. He finally left his entry post, from which he'd continuously rattled off old jokes to which everyone had shouted the punch line before he could, because they were such old chestnuts and because he invariably began with, "And do you know this one? . . . " It was his way of laughing at himself. It was also his way of getting through a period that was surely more painful for him than for the others, who still hadn't joined him in his solitary decision.

"If Monsieur Jean comes in, ask him to wait," he declared, putting on his coat. "I've got a business lunch, but I'll be back in an hour." He left.

An hour later he was back. They were still waiting for the boss. Work had started up even more slowly, and Jiri returned to his chair. Up above, they could hear Mademoiselle Anita moving around. They could also occasionally hear the telephone. They could hear it because they were listening harder than ever. It was more like being on sentry duty. And, so as to be better sentries, they kept quiet.

In the early part of the afternoon, Mademoiselle Anita, somewhat embarrassed, came to say that she hadn't been able to speak to Monsieur Jean in person, but that she had left a message with his maid for him "to come to rue d'Aboukir as soon as possible."

"And did the maid say anything to explain why her boss couldn't come to the phone?" asked Jiri.

"I didn't ask her, Monsieur Koustov. I had spoken to Monsieur Jean on the telephone very early this morning, and I knew that Madame Jean was not well, as I explained a little while ago . . . "

"Yes, but very early this morning we hadn't read this! We hadn't, you hadn't and Monsieur Jean certainly hadn't. Because *this* wasn't distributed in the streets around Neuilly!" exclaimed Jiri, brandishing the leaflet. "They spread it around rue d'Aboukir because it's on rue d'Aboukir that Monsieur Jean makes his money! Not in Neuilly. That's what you should have told his maid."

"If he isn't here in an hour, I'll telephone again," said Mademoiselle Anita, who was getting ready to go back upstairs. She hesitated a second, then added: "We can even call together, if you like."

And she went back up to the second floor.

Jiri said nothing, and looked at Stépan.

Everyone was looking at Stépan.

"It's true that he should really come now," they chorused, looking at Stépan.

"It's true," the chorus heard Stépan Roginski say.

Because with that little comment made a while ago—since then disowned, but spoken nevertheless—Jiri had erased the years of daily companionship, and in a way that struck Stépan as irreparable. He looked at Jiri and shook his head sadly. He told himself Jiri had no doubt always seen in him the hated boss's brother—and he hoped more than ever that Janek would come. That he would come quickly, before he made him, Stépan, into the brother of a complete bastard.

But the hour passed, and Monsieur Jean still wasn't there.

And Mademoiselle Anita hadn't come down. And the telephone had rung twice.

She was very red in the face when she finally entered the shop.

"Monsieur Jean will not be coming," she said. "He doesn't want to speak to anyone from the shop. He'll be here tomorrow morning."

"Did you tell him about me and the Galeries and the leaflet?" asked Jiri.

"I told him everything, Monsieur Koustov." Mademoiselle Anita paused.

"Well?" asked Jiri.

"Well, I think that tomorrow he'll be better able to tell you himself what he just told me. . . . Actually, I asked him to do so," said Mademoiselle Anita, with an odd smile.

"It really must be something, if you can't bring yourself to repeat it. Right, Mademoiselle Anita?"

Mademoiselle Anita didn't answer. There was a silence.

"Monsieur Stépan, would you please come upstairs to my office for a moment?"

" 'bsolutely not, Mademoiselle Anita," Stépan replied, with a shake of his head. "Why me? You have nothing to say to me that you can't say in front of the others. Especially if it's a message from the boss."

Stépan didn't so much as look at Jiri or the others. He just looked at Mademoiselle Anita.

"Go ahead, Mademoiselle Anita, what do you want to tell us?"

Mademoiselle Anita took a deep breath.

"I've inquired of our colleagues. The leaflet was distributed there as well. They almost all agree with me that this leaflet is an anti-Semitic provocation, but they've all confirmed that it's true what it says about Galeries Lafayette, whose management has refused to join with a group of other businessmen who are boycotting Germany since the

Nuremberg Laws have denied your German coreligionists the right to work. Some of our colleagues have in turn decided to boycott the Galeries . . . "

Mademoiselle Anita had regained control of herself, and she was less flushed. She had begun the first part of her speech with lowered eyes, and having now raised her head, she saw that the men from the ladies' and girls' department had silently slipped into the rear of the furriery. She faced a real audience, and for a fraction of a second had a fleeting vision of her father as she had so often seen him in the back room of the Café Benoît in Blassac, patiently explaining the machinery at work behind the acquittal of Esterhazy or the condemnations of Zola to a group of unbelieving but attentive farmers. She continued in a more assured tone, looking at all of them.

"Some of our colleagues who have decided to boycott Galeries Lafayette are Jews, others are not. Some have done so under pressure from their workers, others voluntarily. I can already tell you that Fémina-Prestige will not be one of those. The firm will continue to fill orders, whether we like it or not."

"You said 'we like it,' Mademoisella Anita? Does that mean you don't like it either?" asked Jiri, suddenly rising from his chair and extending his arm toward Mademoiselle Anita to interrupt her speech.

Mademoiselle Anita blushed again.

"Did I say *we?* I meant to say *you,* since you're the ones who work on the orders, all of you. As for me, I don't count. I can be replaced . . . "

"I can be replaced, too," said Jiri.

"Yes, you too can be replaced, Monsieur Koustov, if you're the only one to stop working, as you have been today," Mademoiselle Anita replied gravely. "And that's what I didn't want to tell you when you questioned me a little while ago. I would rather that Monsieur Jean himself tell you . . . "

"And why did you want to tell me what you didn't dare tell Koustov, Mademoiselle Anita?" Stépan demanded.

Mademoiselle Anita made no reply.

"Why, Mademoiselle Anita?" repeated Stépan.

"Because I had been asked to, Monsieur Stépan," she said, as though making a confession.

"*Who* asked you, Mademoiselle Anita?"

"Monsieur Jean himself, so you could warn your comrades. If work stops, there will be layoffs at Fémina-Prestige."

"Not me. . . . They won't lay me off," said Stépan.

"Of course they won't!" snickered Jiri in Yiddish.

"Shut the hell up, Koustov!" Stépan called out, also in Yiddish, without looking at Jiri. Speaking just to Mademoiselle Anita, he continued in French. "They won't lay me off because I'm laying myself off. I'm not going on strike, I'm just going. That's all there is to it, Mademoiselle Anita."

He had spoken slowly, calmly. He got up, began to unbutton his smock and moved toward his locker.

"If you beat it, it won't help me any!" Jiri called out in Yiddish.

"I'm not doing this to help you, Jiri, I'm doing it for myself, just for myself," Stépan replied in Yiddish. He bent down and picked up a copy of the leaflet that had fallen off a table. He rolled it into a ball and tossed it away. "This thing is shit, but without this shit I might never have understood what I understand now," he muttered to himself, still in Yiddish, as he opened his locker.

"What did you say, Monsieur Stépan?" asked Mademoiselle Anita, who seemed completely lost.

"Nothing. It's too complicated," said Stépan, his back to her.

He took a towel from the shelf of his locker, and placed in it a small piece of soap and a comb. He rolled up the towel and slipped it into his satchel alongside his lunch pail. Then he removed his smock, carefully folded it, took his coat from the hanger, closed the locker and finally turned around.

The others were looking at him. Stépan was looking at Mademoiselle Anita.

"You can't do this, Monsieur Stépan. At least wait until tomorrow, like everyone else," she said, calling on "everyone else" as witnesses.

"If I were to be run over as I leave, you wouldn't see me tomorrow. . . . It's the same thing, isn't it," said Stépan, buckling the satchel, into which he'd put his smock.

With his jacket on, his coat over his arm and his satchel in hand he looked as if he were just visiting.

"It can't be. . . . You must've already got a job somewhere else, if you're going off like that!" Jiri hinted slyly at this point.

Stépan didn't answer. He was putting on his coat.

"It wouldn't by any chance be at the other branch?"

"What do you mean, Monsieur Koustov? Fémina-Prestige doesn't have any other branch," said Mademoiselle Anita, blushing again, but this time with anger.

"And what do you call the place where his wife is a dressmaker and his sister-in-law the boss? Isn't that a branch?"

"Masques and Bergamasques no longer has any connection with

Fémina-Prestige, Monsieur Koustov. That's a recent development, and I've only just heard about it myself. If I haven't said anything, it's because it doesn't concern you. In any case, not you personally, Monsieur Koustov."

For once, Jiri had no answer.

Nor did Stépan. And for good reason.

"That was all part of what I wanted to say to you in private, Monsieur Stépan," Mademoiselle Anita added gently. "I'm truly sorry . . . " She made a small gesture with her outspread hands.

"I understand, Mademoiselle Anita, I understand, but it doesn't change a thing," said Stépan, with a gentle but somewhat strained smile.

He moved toward the door, his eyes on the ground. About a yard from the door, he raised his head and looked at all of them.

"Well, goodbye everybody!" he said, switching his satchel to his left hand so as to give his right to Mademoiselle Anita.

"All I can see is that you're letting us down!" Jiri exclaimed in Yiddish.

"No, I'm freeing you," Stépan answered also in Yiddish. Then, in French, "Goodbye, Mademoiselle Anita. Send whatever they owe me to 58 rue de la Mare, Paris XX, please. Thank you." And he left without looking back.

: :

THERE WERE still a few yellow spots on the asphalt of rue d'Aboukir, but you had to know the leaflet to be able to recognize it. Thousands of shoes had walked over it since morning.

He saw the time on the large boulevard clock and began to run, but he already knew he had missed Elie.

As he got into the train, the idea that he was going to have to make the trip alone hurt him tremendously. He had so many, many things to tell Elie! Then, little by little, he calmed down. After all, it wasn't so bad to be left alone to think.

To think without being under the strain of needing to spill his heart out quickly before reaching home. For once he'd wait until he'd arrived before spilling it. For the first time in a long time, and for the last time and forever. Even if he didn't do it as completely as he would have done that very moment with Elie at his side. He already knew that he'd wait until he was alone with his friend to talk about the leaflet and the fear.

But as for the rest! The most important thing, actually the only important thing! How good it would feel to come home and announce to Olga, in front of Zaza and Sonia, and to Maurice and the Cléments, and tomorrow in the Auvergnat's café, and to the whole street if it cared to know, that he was no longer and would never again be Monsieur Stépan of Roginski-Ziegler, but Stépan Roginski, a good furrier, very temporarily unemployed for reasons of self-respect! The idea made him smile with joy and impatience.

He could imagine Janek's expression the next day. The expression he may have already been wearing at the other end of the city, in the heart of Neuilly, where Stépan himself had never set foot, seated in a salon in which Zaza had never been offered a cup of chocolate, listening to the unbelievable news communicated by Mademoiselle Anita, repeating it to his wife stretched out on a sofa in a lace peignoir, a young ladies' maid busy at her side.

And it was only then that he thought again of this "branch" business.

: :

SINCE THE WOMEN had moved down to the first floor, he and Elie had gotten into the habit of being totally dissociated from all their wives' fancy-dress business. They'd even reached the point of almost totally forgetting that Masques and Bergamasques was also Roginski-Ziegler. To tell the truth, the women encouraged this. Sonia and Olga never spoke of anyone but Alex.

It had taken that son-of-a-bitch Koustov to remind him of this other affiliation going on under his very nose, and Mademoiselle Anita to inform him that it was over. Ended only recently.

The terrible hurt returned. And Stépan, climbing the steps of Les Pyrénées station, wondered if his return home would be that of a man who was voluntarily unemployed or that of the husband of a woman who was unemployed despite herself.

Then, as soon as he reached his street, the hurt faded again.

He saw Nussbaum and Gromoff, and the back of Barsky—who was on the phone—through the windows of the Auvergnat's. Gromoff signaled him to come in. For a moment Stépan was tempted, but Elie wasn't with them. He waved "No, thanks" with the hand that held his satchel.

His abnormally swollen satchel. Deliciously swollen, because of the smock he was bringing home.

And he climbed the stairs like a schoolboy in July. He thought he saw something written on the door of "the Bonnet place," but Olga's voice made him turn his head toward the second-floor landing.

"We were beginning to worry."

"I'm here, I'm here," said Stépan, extending his arms to his wife. He hugged and kissed her as he hadn't done in a very long time.

$\mathscr{M}$AURICE, Robert and Sami once more listened to one another recite Ohm's Law, the formula for calculating the volume of a cone, and the important dates of Napoleon's Hundred Days.

"That way, even if we screw up the rest, at least we'll manage with the things you have to know by heart!" said Sami, shutting his books. "Well, I'm going home. Get some sleep, you guys!"

He crossed the shop in the dark and slammed the door of "the Bonnets'." Maurice picked up the three cups and the coffee maker and took them over to the sink.

"They mustn't notice we've been siphoning off his coffee," he said, doing the dishes while Robert replaced the package of ground Corcelet on the shelf, alongside their textbooks.

"A lot he'd care if we drank his coffee the night before the pre-bac exams," Robert answered.

"He wouldn't—but my mother would!" said Maurice.

They began to laugh.

"They weren't much fun upstairs this evening. I never even got to explain to them just what the pre-bac is. Papa asked me, and before I could answer, Zaza's father came home. That turned everything upside down. He's left his shop, and they all began talking at once. And anyway I didn't really listen because I was reciting *Tityre, tu patulae recubans* in my head. . . . Do you think they're going to slip us some Virgil tomorrow?"

"What do you mean he's left his shop? Zaza ate downstairs with us, and she didn't say a word about it. I thought the big news of the day was that your mother and Zaza's mother had become some kind of kolkhozniks!"

"Yes, there's that, too." Maurice smiled. "But I understood it better! This Coop business looks good, doesn't it? How did you hear about it? From Zaza?"

"Not from Zaza, not from Josette and not from my mother. From my father! He lectured us on collectivism all through dinner, and even if I hadn't been listening, the word "Cooperative" is written in big letters on the door of our dormitory, so the news that we're entering an era of social change could hardly have escaped me!" said Robert, with pretended gravity.

"And you don't think that's good?" asked Maurice, vaguely uneasy.

"Not good, great. Great! Especially since from now on we'll be able to make free use of this Italian coffee maker and this Brazilian Corcelet coffee, which, since it doesn't belong to anyone in particular, belongs to everyone, and consequently you as well as me. . . . That is, if I understood my father, to whom incidentally I also wasn't able to explain just what a pre-bac is, even though he'd expressed great interest in it before settling down to his pumpkin soup. So you see, they weren't much fun downstairs either, this evening . . . "

Robert looked at his watch.

"It's ten o'clock, and we can read some of *Man's Fate* for a half hour or so. It's my turn:

" *. . . Katov looked at him without focusing his eyes on him, sadly—it struck him once more how few and awkward the expressions of manly affection are:*

" *'You must understand without my saying anything,' he said. 'There is nothing to say.'*

" *Hemmelrich raised his hand, let it fall again heavily, as though he had to choose only between the distress and the absurdity of his life. But he remained standing before Katov, deeply moved.*

" *'Soon I shall be able to leave and continue looking for Ch'en,' Katov was thinking."*

" . . . To be continued! Now let's get some shut-eye," said Robert, fixing the clamp of the little mushroom lamp on the page he had just finished. "Look, we're more than halfway through," he said, placing the book on the chair between the two couches.

He turned off the light.

"We'll have to start reading more slowly, so it'll last longer." Maurice's voice came out of the dark.

"We can always start over once we've finished," suggested Robert.

"It wouldn't be the same thing. We'd know what was going to happen."

"Well, we already do know they'll never get Chiang Kai-shek. There was even a picture of him in yesterday's paper!" Robert snickered.

"Yes, but we still don't know why or how they failed to get him. That's what's so exciting, and it'll never be as exciting again, even if we reread it ten times," said Maurice.

"That's true. Come on, let's go to sleep," mumbled Robert from the depths of his pillow.

They could hear voices overhead, then outbursts of laughter.

"It's not going to be all that easy to go to sleep!" sighed Robert. "They may not have been much fun during dinner, but they don't sound unhappy now, up at your place . . . "

"No," said Maurice, who himself felt like laughing when he recognized his father's laugh above that of the three others. "It's a long time since I heard all four of them having such fun together!"

He searched his memory, but the image had vanished.

"Listen, now Zaza's father is going at it. If this keeps up, I'm going to complain to the concierge!" sniggered Robert.

And that made Maurice snigger, too.

"Poor Uncle Stépan. He hardly ever laughs. They must have had a shot or two after dinner."

"To celebrate the kolkhoze?"

Maurice didn't answer.

The laughter had died down. For the moment, all they could hear was talk.

"How old do you think Katov is?" asked Maurice in a low voice.

"I don't know. Why?" Robert yawned.

"Because he's a Ukrainian, and that makes me think of Papa. Can't you just see me being born in Shanghai if he'd gone off in the other direction?"

"If he'd gone off in the other direction, you'd never have been born, you ass! Katov's a revolutionary, and revolutionaries don't have children. They don't have time," declared Robert.

"I really like that Katov," said Maurice, after a short silence.

Robert mumbled a vague "Me, too . . . but let's get some sleep," and Maurice heard him turn toward the wall.

"Do you know why you like Katov?"

"No," said Maurice, happy that Robert had not yet abandoned him.

"Why you like him more than the others? It's because Katov can't say 'absolutely' . . . he says *'bsolutely,* like your father and mother."

" *'bsolutely!*" exclaimed Maurice. "How did you figure that out, my dear Clappique?"

"Elementary, my dear Ch'en . . . But if you open your yap once more, I'm going to knife you right through your mosquito netting. Good night, comrade."

"Good night," said Maurice, as he too turned to his wall.

: :

THEY HAD JUST invented a game, a game that they still didn't know they would be playing for a long time—a game whose improvised rules would become a secret code for everything and just about anything: laughter, emotion, indignation and gibberish.

Maurice listened to Robert's regular breathing.

Upstairs, things were breaking up. The chairs scraped across the floor. The Roginskis were going back to their apartment, and the Guttmans were about to go into the bedroom.

By listening carefully, Maurice could hear their whispering. His parents had never got over the habit of whispering in their bedroom, as if they were still afraid they would wake him.

That low Mass being celebrated upstairs was probably in honor of the great changes that had come about in the day that was just ending.

Poor ridiculous changes, thought Maurice, with affectionate compassion and a vague remorse at having been unable to participate more fully in their collective joy. Then Sonia's light, slippered footsteps stopped, and so did the whispering. Rue de la Mare was going to sleep.

Maurice sank into Malraux's Shanghai night, pregnant with all possible upheavals, all kinds of courage, cowardice, doubts and loves.

Valérie's ecstasies, May's full flat mouth and the taxi dancers at the Black Cat gave him as much to dream about as Gisor's opium-drugged silences.

He still didn't know that in a few days, in the hundred and fifty pages that remained to be read, there would be deaths. He also didn't know that they'd want to cry, that they wouldn't want to show it and that to hide it better they'd make use of their code.

Before closing his eyes for good, Maurice looked across at the chair.

A feeble ray of moonlight filtered through the orange curtains and was reflected on the yellow mushroom of the lamp.

"It gives Malraux a Chinese hat," he said to himself.

Then he gave one final thought to the next day, to the Hundred Days, to Virgil and to the formula for the volume of a cone.

Iri Koustov had been wrong. The yellow leaflet had indeed been scattered around Neuilly-sur-Seine. It wasn't lying on the carpeting of the stairway at rue Charles-Laffitte, but it had been dropped here and there, then picked up and read at various places in that elegant suburb.

These spots hadn't been chosen haphazardly; they were extremely well populated, including Place du Marché on avenue Neuilly, or Carrefour Inkermann, where the paths of the faithful of the church of Saint-Pierre and the pupils of the Lycée Pasteur crossed, or rue Jacques-Dulud.

Not many people passed along rue Jacques-Dulud, but on it was Etablissements Saoutchik, Deluxe Automobiles, whose high white wall was near the front of a small synagogue. A graffiti artist had even taken the time to carve into the wall's soft stone an arrow pointing to the temple and two words: "same proprietor."

Rue Jacques-Dulud lies parallel to rue Charles-Laffitte. The blue glass of the Saoutchik workshops could be seen from Armelle's kitchen window. But Nicole never walked on rue Jacques-Dulud.

In any case, Nicole hadn't walked anywhere that particular morning. She was sleeping. Finally.

She had fallen asleep at dawn, exhausted by hours of tears, voiceless, and drugged by half a bottle of Passiflorine, which Janek had administered in teaspoonfuls, as though to a baby.

She had fallen asleep in the crook of her husband's left arm, her head resting on his chest. But instead of turning to her own side, as she usually did after a while, she had remained that way, inert and heavy. It was a cramping spasm that had half wakened Janek.

A cramp, or piano scales. They were already at the piano on the floor below.

Haggard and furious, Janek had tried to move his wife. She clung to him like a drowning woman. "I'll be right back," he'd murmured, freeing himself and slipping out of bed.

Lurching, his pajamas wrinkled and spotted with mascara at heart level, he'd gone into the kitchen; Armelle was entrenched there, waiting for them to ring for her.

"Go down to the second floor and knock. Ask them not to play the piano. Tell them somebody's sick up here," he'd grumbled.

"They don't understand French," Armelle had objected.

"Then tell them in sign language," Janek had replied, going toward the salon, where he grabbed the phone.

He had called Anita at home to tell her he wouldn't be coming to rue d'Aboukir.

Then he had called Troyes, to tell them about Maddy.

Finally, he had called Dubâteau-Ripoix, to tell him about Maddy and Nicole.

The piano had stopped. Janek had been very brief on the phone, speaking in a hushed voice as if to avoid waking himself up completely. To Armelle, who was awaiting orders as well as compliments on the successful completion of her mission to the floor below, he had grumbled: "Don't wake us," then had gone back to the bedroom to rejoin his unconscious, warm and disarmed wife, against whom he snuggled with a sensuality that overwhelmed him. And it was in her, who had scarcely moved, that he finally fell asleep for good.

There was no way to know that the yellow leaflet fluttering everywhere would force its way into the citadel of shared sorrow, love and sleep that this large, dark bedroom, cut off from the world, had become.

Yet that—in the form of a sealed envelope from Maître Dubâteau-Ripoix, which had to be handed over to Monsieur Jean personally— is exactly what happened. It was Hubert, the gloved chauffeur, who delivered the envelope. Poor Armelle refused to wake Monsieur.

"There's been trouble . . . " she started to explain.

"We know all that," Hubert interrupted curtly. He hated familiarity and indiscretion, except in his relations with his employer, who sometimes willingly *tutoyed* his chauffeur and told him everything about everything as soon as he got into the car.

Hubert therefore knew "all" about the troubles: Maddy, the rest and a lot more besides. He eyed the Breton girl up and down.

"I'm counting on you, Mademoiselle, to see to it that your employer knows that mine will be here at seven o'clock. It's imperative you give him this envelope before that late hour. Do you understand?"

"I'll hand over your message along with the others, because even though I stuffed a rag into the telephone bell, it's kept on ringing, and I've had other messages since this morning. It's already three o'clock, and Madame still hasn't buzzed. But don't worry, I'll hand over your message with their tea," Armelle declared, with the calm assurance of those who obviously know their job, and she had closed the door.

"What a house, what servants!" Hubert had said to himself as he went down the stairs. He was reminded of Lucas, whose enforced company during the Troyes escapade he'd found truly intolerable.

: :

THE LEAFLET, folded in four, fell onto the wrinkled sheets when Janek opened the envelope. Nicole had unthinkingly picked it up, without either unfolding or looking at it, while Janek read aloud the missive from Maître Dubâteau-Ripoix:

Friend,
  I've tried in vain to get you on the phone, but the young Druid who answered at your end did not strike me as the best interlocutress. I have therefore fallen back on my personal Hermes.
  There is a new development at Chateaubriand. Our young man has just left me. He has some confusing plans.
  I'm rushing to the Palais to plead for poor Gentiane de B., who's had an unfortunate hunting accident. I will therefore be *incommunicado* for the next few hours. But I will be at your apartment at seven to talk this over and to kiss Victoria's hand.

                                        Yours,
                                        Jean-Gaétan

P.S. I've just been handed this nasty bit of paper, which is all over town today. Your colleague Lévy, from "Lady-Couture," also one of my clients, sent it to me. Study both the front and the back. You're in a better position than Roger Ziegler or myself to understand all the terms.

Until later,
J.-G.

Janek refolded the letter and looked at Nicole. She remained silent; her eyelids were so swollen her eyes were completely hidden. He gently took the little yellow rectangle from her hands and began to read it to himself.

"What kind of shit is this!" he murmured in Yiddish after having read the first few words of the French version. He turned the sheet over, continued reading in Yiddish until he got to the question mark, then turned it over again to the French version and reread everything.

"I could feel it coming . . . well, that's it, there we are!" he said in an expressionless voice, and once again he looked at Nicole.

In a whisper, she said something he didn't understand. He was still holding the yellow paper. He bent toward his wife, who covered her face with both hands, and he heard, "Don't look at me . . . don't talk to me yet. . . . Give me time to recover."

Janek put the leaflet in front of her and got up.

"It's already five o'clock. Don't forget that Dubâteau will be here in two hours," he said.

And he left the bedroom.

She leaned her head against the pillow and, with her fingertips, took inventory of the swellings that disfigured her. She hadn't looked into a mirror since yesterday, but she knew.

She could hear the shower running in the bathroom. Then the sound of the telephone. Armelle's voice, followed by a long silence, and finally Janek's voice, low at first, then shouting. The noise he was making, the few words she caught, forced her to emerge from the torpor to which she would have liked to abandon herself a while longer, and she decided to read the leaflet.

First she merely glanced through it, stopping only to reread the sentences with the word "JEWISH," the capital letters of which drew her like magnets. She counted six uses, including one as a feminine adjective that struck her more than the others. . . . It was as though the JEWISH management of Galeries Lafayette was a big fat woman sitting on a throne.

She also counted six uses in Yiddish.

And she could understand the meaning of Dubâteau-Ripoix's postscript, to which she'd paid so little attention earlier. It was the first time the lawyer was openly dissociating Janek Roginski from his very Catholic clients and friends, the Ziegler-Leblancs.

Nicole told herself it was the end of something that had only just begun. And she got out of bed.

She ran a hot bath, washed her hair and then for a long time rinsed herself first in tepid, then in cold and then in icy water. Without looking in the mirror, she rubbed her abundant hair with a towel, then took a bottle and a package of absorbent cotton from a cabinet. The liquid was bluish, and on the label of the Number 120 Lotion, Maddy had written: "To erase the signs of bad vodka hangovers." She prepared two big compresses and, draped in her robe, stretched out flat on the floor of the bedroom. She put the two compresses on her face and placed the bottle within easy reach. She knew she would have to renew the coolness of the compresses if they were to perform their miracle. Having spared herself the fright of seeing herself as she was now, in half an hour she'd look at herself in the mirror and find herself as she had been.

And she forced herself to think about nothing but that.

Under the cotton pads, the struggle began. It tickled; the blood was pulsing with a dull, heavy reverberation. Maddy had never wanted to tell her just what was in the mixture. . . . She'd have to have it analyzed to get a new supply, since Maddy would never again be there to give her any.

A warm, liquid stream trickled from beneath the compress. Nicole pressed her fingers on the cotton and groped for the bottle. She poured a few cold drops on her eyelids, as though to kill the tears.

"If I'm going to begin bawling again, there's no point in this," she said to herself. She repeated the sentence, to test her voice. Nothing happened. It made her want to laugh. And her laugh came out like a fit of whooping cough. "I'll need some honey, some honey drops," she thought.

She wanted to ring for Armelle and send her for some, but she would have had to get up to reach the bell, and remove the compresses, which would interrupt their work and make her lose time. She had no time to lose. There were so many things to be done before seven o'clock: make up her new-found face, braid or not braid her hair, depending on the dress she would choose to wear—something that wouldn't make her look like a member of the vanquished receiving someone she already considered her enemy.

She heard Janek speaking on the telephone. He was no longer shouting, he was talking, and it wasn't with rue d'Aboukir. Could it be with Lévy-Couture, as she called those four brothers she disliked?

There was a ring at the front door, which she heard Armelle open and close almost immediately. Then someone started pounding out four-hand piano exercises on the floor below.

And Nicole thought about the Le Gentils.

About Joëlle's restful vacuousness, about the blue eyes of her mad cousin, about the silver foxes and the smell of fur and the Palais de l'Hermine. And about the smell of apples, lemons, and the vetiver used on the furs at the Palais de l'Hermine, and the little shop window that had shattered when those young men with sticks had passed when she was still very young, about her fear, about her father's reassuring smile and her mother's terror—her mother, who kept shaking her head and saying: "It's beginning again, it's beginning again," her mother whom no one ever answered. Her mother, Anna . . . Who was it who had recently used the word "Polack"? Somebody had laughed and said "Polack." She had to remember, otherwise she'd go on about it for hours, and she had no time to lose . . . It was just recently, very recently . . . with a laugh. And it was the laugh that she recognized.

But she mustn't think about Maddy.

And she mustn't think about Joëlle either, because when she thought about Joëlle, she thought about that little bouquet Maddy had left on the doormat, with that chatty little paper-lace frill around it that was to decide everything. For nine years of their lives. For everyone.

There would be no tenth year. The thread had been broken. But there would be all the other years, and it was about them that she had to think now.

And Nicole forced herself to really think. And it was the leaflet that she thought about, about what it really meant to say.

The cotton was almost dry. That was a good sign. The muscles under her skin had absorbed the precious liqueur. She gave them another shot and gave herself another quarter of an hour of extra reflection and total immobility on the floor.

Downstairs, the two pianos were still going. But the music had become pleasant. The warm-up hour was over.

Nicole wasn't listening, but she heard. And it was against a background of Schumann that she began to dream of departures.

When the sonata was over, the two compresses were dry and Nicole had come to a decision.

"We'll sell out and go," she told herself, getting up. She wanted to call Janek, but she remembered that she still had no voice. So, barefoot, naked under her white robe, her face fresh and smelling of restorative plants, her hair still damp and tumbling over her shoulders, she ran to the salon to repeat her sentence into Janek's ear.

"Go where?" asked Janek, doubly amazed by her recovered beauty and her mad suggestion.

"Far from the ghettos," she said in Yiddish.

And she went into the kitchen to send Armelle for some honey drops.

She passed through the salon again. Janek was so absorbed that he didn't even raise his head. He was busy scribbling on the back of an envelope. She left him and returned to the bedroom.

Seating herself before the mirror of her dressing table, she smiled widely at herself. Her mad little sentence had taken root: Janek was doing his figuring. They were selling out.

They would leave.

She pulled back her hair with a headband and began to put on her makeup.

: :

IT WAS JUST about seven o'clock and Nicole was almost ready when the telephone rang. Uneasy, she went to the door to listen. No, it wasn't that imbecile Dubâteau-Ripoix calling everything off. Janek was using his Aboukir voice. Reassured, she concentrated on the last three of the sixteen marcasite buttons that closed her at-home dress. It was long black velvet, set off at the neck and wrists with champagne-colored Valenciennes lace, a sumptuous, dramatic, old-fashioned affair. And for good reason: borrowed for an evening the month before, the Anna Karenina costume (No. 92) had never been returned to stock.

She was about to coil the serpent bracelet around her left wrist when Janek came into the bedroom.

"My brother has taken off," he said, dropping on the bed without looking at Nicole.

"What do you mean, taken off?" asked Nicole, replacing the bracelet on the bureau.

"Beat it, quit the shop . . . won't come back . . leaving me to cope with all those fucking shitheads by myself . . . " Janek thought for a fraction of a second, then added, still without looking at Nicole, " . . . and that stupid bitch!"

"What stupid bitch?" Nicole asked softly.

"Anita . . . She wanted me to come over . . . Maybe I should have . . . "
He finally looked at Nicole.

"What for? To get back your brother, whom you got out of the
shtetl?. . . Or to settle things for Galeries Lafayette, who'll settle them
soon enough behind your back with the Ziegler-Leblancs? Because
those Ziegler-Leblancs, they're not bothered by what's going on in
Germany!"

"There was a time when it didn't bother you, either. Remember the
fight we had because of that bastard downstairs and his story about Jews
down on all fours . . . "

Nicole placed her hand over his mouth, knelt in front of him and
looked into his eyes.

"There was a time when nothing bothered me. . . . We were happy,
it was summer, we fucked in the Bois de Boulogne, I had Masques and
we had Maddy. Now what do we have? Those Berlin piano-thumpers
who've settled in downstairs and brought all *that* with them!"

She grabbed the leaflet, which was lying on the bed, and waved the
big question mark under Janek's nose. He took the leaflet from her
hands, refolded it and put it in his pocket.

"You're very unhappy, aren't you?" he said gently, holding her face
between his hands.

Eyes closed, she nodded yes.

"Because you've lost Maddy . . . or because you've lost Masques?"

"Both," she said, her eyes still closed. "And now I'm afraid . . . " She
reopened her eyes. "Let's leave, darling, before we're too old."

He kissed her mouth, helped her to her feet and stood up.

Nicole went back to her dressing table, put on her bracelet, placed
her hand on her throat and took a honey drop.

There was a ring at the door.

"Don't mention the leaflet, let him do it . . . " she murmured, her
mouth full, as Janek went to meet Dubâteau-Ripoix, to whom Armelle
was already opening the door.

: :

"MONSIEUR HAS no doubt dined?" asked Hubert, opening the car
door for Maître Dubâteau-Ripoix when the latter appeared at the
downstairs door at about nine o'clock.

"Alas no, old chap, they weren't in the mood for love feasts upstairs.
Let's go home," he said, getting into the back.

They drove along in silence for a time.

"And how is Madame Victoria Jean after all this . . . if I may ask?" Hubert inquired respectfully.

"A ghost, my poor Hubert—I've seen a ghost with disheveled hair, but troublingly beautiful in her disarray."

"This has certainly been quite a week!" Hubert allowed himself to sigh.

"Definitely," agreed Maître Dubâteau-Ripoix, who for once was not in the mood for confidences.

On avenue de la Grande-Armée, Hubert slowed noticeably as they entered rue Pergolèse.

"Is there any news of Monsieur Leblanc's condition?" he asked, turning slightly toward the rear seat.

"Stable . . . condition stable," mumbled Maître Dubâteau-Ripoix, glancing to his right, toward the corner at which he had so often dropped Augustin, who always claimed that he wanted to stretch his legs a little.

Hubert accelerated and said no more. Neither did Maître Dubâteau-Ripoix. He was thinking.

He was thinking and calculating.

He was calculating the total of his fees, for which he had worked hard all that long day, and he was thinking about how to divide them up.

It struck him as impossible. He decided he would have to present two bills for his services. One to his Roginski clients, for having suggested to them the idea of unloading their shares in the Ziegler-Leblanc business, the fate of which struck him as very chancy, given the temper of the times. The other bill would be for his clients and friends the Ziegler-Leblancs, for having definitively rid them of the Roginski couple, whose origins no longer seemed compatible with the temper of the coming times.

"You have to know when to turn the page," he would say to each of them when, thanks to his care, everything had been settled.

Thanks to that little bitch from rue Pergolèse, too, he had to admit. God knows what damage she'd done, that one! But by removing herself from the scene as she had, she'd certainly helped put everything back in place. And none too soon.

They had almost reached the Etoile. Under the Arc, the Champs-Elysées glittered all the way to the Obelisk. Dubâteau turned around. Through the rear window, the long, gaslit ribbon stretched out as far as La Défense.

"This never-ending avenue is so dreary, don't you think, Hubert?" he said, in a tone that suggested he had finished his personal reflections.

"I've noticed that Monsieur always says that to me when we pass this way," said Hubert, delighted to renew the conversation.

"When we used to pass this way, my dear Hubert! *Used to pass!* . . . We'll hardly have any reason to do so in the future. Unless we need new headlights or bumpers, of course, since this sinister avenue de la Grande-Armée is also the motorist's cure-all."

"Monsieur frightened me . . . I thought we were going to leave Paris!" said Hubert, with a laugh.

"No, not us!" exclaimed Maître Dubâteau-Ripoix, laughing in his turn.

He thought again of the Roginskis. He wouldn't bill them for the Chateaubriand business. He'd had no trouble at all in convincing them. He'd hardly begun to transmit that madman's plans when Victoria Jean had stopped him. Rising above her sorrow and her voicelessness, she had produced a kind of staccato whisper that was meant to be a snicker: all that was over and could be forgotten. The Punch-and-Judy Cooperative would have to do without her.

As for the leaflet, since they'd said nothing, he'd kept quiet, as Ziegler had actually asked him to do during the telephone call he'd made from Troyes, where the same leaflet had also been seen. The said leaflet had also helped, too. It had obviously made them want to leave.

" . . . No, not us!" repeated Maître Dubâteau-Ripoix. "We're staying where we belong. My glass may be small, but from it I drink the wine of my own country."

"And that's where one is most comfortable," said Hubert approvingly, as he silently parked the big Panhard on avenue Mac-Mahon.

Hubert opened the back door.

"Have a good evening, Monsieur. I see Monsieur has company . . . "

Maître Dubâteau-Ripoix looked up. Four windows were lit on the third floor.

"I hope my wife's bridge players have left me a bite to eat and that they haven't invaded my office, because my day isn't over, my good man. Tomorrow at ten. Good evening, Hubert," he said, in an exaggeratedly exhausted voice as he moved toward the large wrought-iron door.

He still had to call Troyes. Before the others did.

It would be careless to let them be the first to announce a decision he himself had masterminded.

They were pulling out; they might even clear out. He hadn't been dreaming: as she had seen him to the door, the redhead had spoken of the Americas. Or had he been the first to mention it?

In any case, it would be preferable if he were the first to mention it to the Zieglers. That was the wise thing to do. But he'd have to be quick. And since the elevator was slow in coming down from the third floor, he raced up the stairs.

No one saw him come in except the majordomo, whom he ordered in a low voice to bring a plate of canapés and a whiskey to his office.

In the large salon, the small salon and the boudoir, only the sound of bidding broke the dignified silence.

*T*HE NEXT DAY, very early in the morning, Roger Ziegler left La Bonne Chanson to go to the railway station. It was snowing in Troyes, and he preferred the certainty of traveling by train in order to settle his affairs in Paris.

At the Lycée Voltaire, in a would-be Sorbonne atmosphere, Maurice, Robert and Sami, contrary to all predictions—which only the evening before had favored Virgil—were translating Cicero.

At rue d'Aboukir, they were waiting. For the bosses or for a boss. No one knew for sure. They were waiting because Mademoiselle Anita had said to wait, and Jiri still had not put on his smock.

At rue de la Marc, in the Roginski kitchen, Zaza was having breakfast with her father on a weekday for the first time in her life. Just as though it were Sunday.

: :

ROGER ZIEGLER arrived in the afternoon to announce to the assembled personnel of rue d'Aboukir that, for reasons of health, his partner, Monsieur Roginski, was retiring. Fémina-Prestige, deprived of the exceptional skills of an exceptional professional, therefore had no choice but to close the furriery and content itself with its original vocation, which was the making of trimmed brushed woollens and imitation-fur brushed woollens for ladies and girls. Those furriers interested in learning to work with imitation materials were of course welcome to stay on. However, he would completely understand that as workers used to "noble" materials they might feel reluctant to place their skills at the service of the ersatz, which would in addition not assure them the wages such skills deserved.

All this had been written out in the form of notes on a slip of paper Monsieur Ziegler consulted furtively between sentences.

He concluded by explaining that current orders would have to be finished, but that they would be the last. He said that he was sorry, that he would miss those who were going to leave, but that life was like that and you had to know when to turn the page. Then, amid total silence, he left.

"Well, friends, I leave you to your teddy-bear plush!" Jiri said in French after a moment. And he began to laugh, an enormous belly laugh that no one took up. "They're fantastic!" he then added in Yiddish. "They don't answer our questions, they don't force us, they don't fire us, they don't do us the least harm . . . they simply cut off our hands and our balls. They'd never have dared if Stépan had been here."

"It was because of you that Stépan left. Why don't you shut your mouth, Jiri?" said the oldest cutter.

"How come you didn't say that to me yesterday?" replied Jiri.

"Because yesterday we were waiting for Roginski. Today there's only Ziegler, and Ziegler doesn't give a damn about our Jewish complications!" said the old cutter.

"The hell he doesn't! That's all he's thinking about, and that's why he's getting rid of us."

"He's not getting rid of us," corrected the old cutter.

"You're right, Serge, he's not getting rid of us—he's politely telling us to go fuck ourselves and to thank him for the opportunity!" exclaimed Jiri.

"Let's finish our work. We'll talk about it this evening," concluded Serge.

: :

AT ABOUT the same time, a dozen or so noisy young people invaded Le Bigoudin, a *café-tabac* about two hundred yards from the Lycée Voltaire. Despite the hour—after-school snack time—and the aroma of frothy chocolate, they all ordered beers, took their math scratch sheets out of their schoolbags and began to compare notes.

The Sami method had paid off. The memorized geometry had saved Maurice, who had gotten his algebra problem totally balled up.

"Thanks to that dumb cone formula, you'll get a decent grade," said Sami, "and with your perfect Cicero, you've got it made."

They took a turn at the electric crane, failed to pick up the wristwatch, which fell at the last minute, and shared the green candies, which they found disgusting.

"Your green candies are inedible, but your beer is excellent," said Robert to the proprietor, who'd seen it all before—especially school kids entering a café for the first time in their lives.

: :

AT THE END of the afternoon, Stépan was on the platform of the Strasbourg–St.-Denis station, under the Saponite ad, as usual.

After sleeping late and having his breakfast with Zaza, he'd felt a little intimidated. Olga had gone downstairs to join Sonia at "the Bonnet place," and he hadn't dared go with her when she'd suggested it. She hadn't insisted.

He'd washed the cups, made the bed, shaved and dressed slowly, then left to look for work.

The evening before, Elie had suggested the Society of Fur Craftsmen, on faubourg Poissonnière.

At the Society, they'd asked for his references. He had then phoned Mademoiselle Anita from a café: she shouldn't forget to have a certificate signed for his thirteen years of work on rue d'Aboukir, and she should attach it to the money due him. Mademoiselle Anita had been very kind: no, she wouldn't forget, he would have it all tomorrow . . . "And Jiri? . . . " Stépan had asked, after a brief silence. "I can't tell you anything about that," Mademoiselle Anita had said, and hung up. Stépan had eaten a hard-boiled egg at the bar, drunk a small white wine and left the café.

He thought of going home, but it struck him as an odd time to be returning. He'd only just left.

Tomorrow would be different. Tomorrow, once he had his references, he could leave, return home, leave again—it would be different. For a brief moment he thought of going straight to rue d'Aboukir, getting his papers immediately and then going right back to the Society. But he decided against it. What would it make him look like? He should have thought of the certificate yesterday. He was angry with himself. And he was a little angry with Mademoiselle Anita, who knew all about those things. She was used to them. He wondered if it would be Janek who signed the certificate or if it would be signed "Illegible," like everything else that came out of the second-floor offices.

He'd been walking quite a while, and he still hadn't made up his mind where to go. There was, of course, Le Nabab on rue Barbès, and though he had never set foot in it, he'd often heard the men in the shop discuss it: it was where the bosses went to pick up unemployed furriers, who hung around all day. "Like whores . . . all furriers get down to the salon!" Jiri would say when there was talk of Le Nabab.

He wasn't far from Mercier Frères. He was tempted to surprise Elie and his co-workers, whom he had already met twice: once when he'd gone to thank Monsieur Paul for the naturalization papers, and again when he'd joined them for that march on February 12, 1934. Then he told himself that turning up that way would make him really look too much at loose ends.

And again he thought of Jiri.

And that made him think of Galeries Lafayette, and he decided to go see what was happening there.

Even though it was still daylight, the Christmas windows were already lit up and the mechanical toys were putting on their little pantomimes for those hurrying by.

Inside, he was struck by the slightly damp warmth and by the dull buzz of voices. Some women were choosing celluloid animals from a pile on a display stand near the entrance. "For the very young, everything at three francs," said the sign. Stépan picked up a pretty little swan with a charmingly graceful neck and turned it over; then he turned over a goldfish, a whale, a duck, a crocodile and a frog: all had made the same trip; all were *Made in Germany.*

"I won't buy any of that," said a voice. "Celluloid is inflammable, and with my salamander stove . . . "

He began to amble through the different departments on the ground floor. He neither touched nor turned over any of the articles. But, as though playing a game, he counted his "Made in Germany" points every time his instinct guided him toward a new article on sale. Based on the color and the shape, he made little bets with himself.

At the end of an hour he had spotted mauve hot-water bottles made of ersatz rubber, iron-gray felt shoe-skates with red borders, brown saucerless coffee cups, curling irons, chamois leathers, bouquets of artificial flowers . . .

He took the elevator. On the upper floors he might find what he had really come to look for between the walls of the immense building: the crack, the signs of collapse.

He found it in the "Ladies' Ready-to-Wear" department.

As though they were in a soup kitchen, some unhappy women were extending imploring hands toward a frock-coated section manager. "Be patient, ladies, be patient . . . Some of our personnel has left us, so wait your turn, please," he repeated mechanically, parsimoniously handing out little numbered discs. Clutching them like soup bowls, the women joined a waiting line that snaked between papier-mâché mannequins whose gracefully extended arms seemed to bless them.

At more or less regular intervals, a buzz ran through the line. It saluted the return of one of the three middle-aged saleswomen who, all on their own, were trying to see to the smooth functioning of the severely handicapped section. They grabbed the numbered discs with an aggressive indifference.

Stépan remained immobile, treading water. He was watching.

He thought he recognized one of his squirrel collars on a mannequin. But he wasn't sure. He touched it, and as he did so, his eyes met those of the section manager. He too had been watching, probably for quite a while, this unaccompanied man who wasn't buying, spoke to no one and stroked fur.

Stépan moved toward the stairway.

It was dark outside. Dark and very cold. In front of the windows, the passers-by had become spectators. There were many children up front, and the very small ones sat on their fathers' shoulders. A muzzled, life-size brown bear was dancing in front of a Little Red Riding Hood, a Mother Goose and a Cinderella, who were applauding. "The bear seems so sad," one little boy said. "We won't ask Santa Claus to bring him, he looks too sad," his mother replied. "She's getting off easy," thought Stépan, who retroactively congratulated himself on never having taken Zaza to see these unattainable toys. And he thought again of the pretty little three-franc swan. He took a last look at the bear, and asked himself in what Bavarian shop someone had sewn on such hopeless eyes.

He walked rapidly toward the Métro. He had suddenly decided to go and meet Jiri near Fémina-Prestige. Not to patch things up, simply to tell him he'd been right about the Galeries. Just that.

He didn't have long to wait. Jiri was the first to come out, and he was alone. He showed no surprise when he heard Stépan whistle from the shadows, about fifty yards from the street door of Fémina-Prestige.

"So there you are! Wait till you hear what's going on!" he said, and they entered a bistro they didn't ordinarily go to.

: :

TIRED, WRY and a bit mean, Jiri had told him the news. Everything, including Ziegler's little talk, translated into Yiddish in a hushed voice. Stépan hadn't said a word. His own little speech about the Galeries seemed uninteresting after what he'd just learned.

"If you'd been there, they wouldn't have dared! I know, I know, you left because of me—they told me that often enough today. And I already apologized to you yesterday. You found a job?"

"No, I'm waiting for my certificate."

"Me, I've got mine," said Jiri, tapping his pocket. "I'm not crazy," he added, snickering.

"No, you're not crazy . . . " said Stépan gravely.

"You're still pissed at me, right?"

"I think I'll be angry with you the rest of my life," murmured Stépan. "But it won't keep me from working with you again. If I ever find anything good, I'll let you know."

Jiri didn't answer; he drank half his beer, then: "So you just came to find out what's going on? You're not going to try to make me believe that your brother didn't tell you he was clearing out . . . "

"You can see for yourself there's no way we can ever get along," said Stépan.

"And I suppose you don't know anything about Anita, either, do you? Even though you're pals, the two of you."

"What about Anita?"

"She's leaving, too. As soon as she's got things in order for Ziegler and the teddy-bear makers . . . "

"Where's she going?"

"She didn't say. She simply said that, like me, she was leaving . . . "

"And like me," protested Stépan softly.

"Yes, but it's not the same with you."

"Listen, Koustov! I came to say you were right about Galeries Lafayette. I've just come from there. You were right. That's it! But as for the rest, fuck you!"

Stépan got up, paid for the drinks at the bar and left the bistro, slamming the door behind him.

Once on the boulevard, he checked the time. He didn't have to run. He was sure not to miss Elie.

AT LES PYRÉNÉES, the ground was almost completely white. The light Paris snowfalls had always made Stépan and Elie laugh a lot. It also sometimes made them hum the songs of their childhood. Stépan wondered if it was also snowing in Neuilly.

"Let's buy a quiche to celebrate Maurice's trial-run bac," said Elie. They made a little detour and entered Au Blé d'or de Quimper.

*A*s ALEX told Rodriguez that very evening, the pretty little Allée Chateaubriand garden had lost none of its charm, nor the beveled mirrors any of their brilliance.

The Costumers' Cooperative was legally born on January 3, 1936, but backstage and in the dressing rooms, appointments were still made to meet "at Masques." For a while, the old-time actors were surprised by the disappearance of Maddy and the prolonged absence of Victoria Jean; then, too preoccupied with themselves and their reflections, they forgot to be surprised. They even forgot to notice the bouquet of immortelles, which under its cover, henceforth replaced the illustrious imperial gift: the Fabergé egg was no longer a part of the firm.

Nor was Lucas.

It was Lucas who had been sent by Madame to reclaim the egg that had belonged to Madame's father.

He had taken the egg, but he had returned the Citroën, his chauffeur's uniform, the cap and the leggings.

The Coop didn't appeal to him. He and Gildaise were going to run a café. Gildaise and him, and maybe they'd take Armelle on as a dishwasher. They were going to run the bar-café near the factory he used to work in. The old owner was retiring and had no family: you couldn't turn down an offer that included a place to live and everything. When you're next to a factory, whether or not there's trouble, people are always thirsty when they leave. So, as for the Coop, thanks but no thanks! And as for being a part owner, two owners were better than twenty-five . . .

Ginette assigned Number 224a to the chauffeur's uniform and put it into stock.

She almost called Lucas back to ask him for Number 92, the "Anna Karenina," which had never been returned. But she didn't: someday, she told herself, Victoria would stop by, and she could ask her about it then.

: 224 :

GINETTE NEVER wore the sable cape. It hung in the cold-storage area, undistinguishable from the other furs in their long, black-ticking garment bags. But now, when the door to the storeroom was opened, it smelled the way it used to in the tiny little dressing room at the Capucines.

No number was printed on the bronze-taffeta lining, still in perfect condition. Ginette didn't care to rent it. She didn't care to say why, either. But when pushed, she'd reply, "Sable is like opals or carnations . . . unlucky."

Nevertheless, after a while, the sable did get a number like the others. Whether it brought bad or good luck, it went to work with a will. There were just too many calls for it. The comfortable daily routine of Masques was over. The Coop was picking up again.

It had come about without advertising or fuss, simply by word of mouth—perhaps because of the musical sound of "cooperative" as the name passed around among the young people whom the preciosity of "Masques and Bergamasques" had, until then, kept from venturing into this elegant neighborhood.

But now they were starting to show up, these corduroy-clad youngsters who weren't rich enough to treat themselves to designer clothes but who raided the stock for the avant-garde performances they put on, also as "cooperative" ventures.

Alex was delighted. They amused Ginette, left Mademoiselle Agnès cold and astonished Mademoiselle Anita, who was astonished by just about everything since she had moved into the boudoir-office that had belonged to Victoria Jean and Maddy Varga.

They astonished her and they sometimes gave her trouble. The amusing "cooperator-artists" had a tendency to forget to pay their bills to these obscure "cooperator-costumers." When that happened she became very firm and demanded payment in her soft little voice—then everything would be on the right track again.

Everything *was* all right. Everything was going so well, what with the flow of new clients and the faithful old ones, that Mademoiselle Anita suggested taking on a new member. A specialist: a furrier.

Alex was ashamed not to have thought of it himself. But it was he who transmitted the proposition to Stépan at "the Bonnets' " the very next afternoon.

: :

BECAUSE Stépan would now often stop in at "the Bonnets' " when he returned after an unsuccessful search for work.

His references in his pocket, he had been job-hunting for quite some time. It wasn't that there weren't plenty of places to try. There was a demand for furriers. The demand was actually pretty heavy. But, each time, he noticed that the demand for new personnel generally corresponded with defections about which the bosses were evasive, not to say completely silent. It was clear that furriers were needed, but "scab" furriers. The Galeries Lafayette themselves put out an S.O.S. urgently asking for finishers!

He'd even been to Le Nabab, but he hadn't gone in. He'd caught a glimpse of Jiri through the window.

Then, one morning, alone in the apartment and without telling anybody, he'd written a short letter, in his own words, to Mademoiselle Anita, addressed to her home, 15 Square Montsouris. He remembered having once heard her give the address—and thinking that it suited the mousy little woman very well. In his note, he'd asked her if she mightn't have some work for him, since he had learned that she too had left Fémina-Prestige. He didn't tell her that he'd heard the news from Jiri.

But when he'd found out that Mademoiselle Anita was part of Olga and Sonia's cooperative, he regretted having written to her: it made him sound too much like a beggar, even like a pimp, he thought, and he was angry with himself for having written his letter without discussing it first with Elie.

But it had become difficult to find a moment in which to speak to Elie alone, now that they were no longer taking their daily Métro trips together.

Mademoiselle Anita hadn't replied, and Stépan was almost glad.

After all, there was no reason to think she was still at the same address, or that she had received his letter. In any case, he had once run into Alex, and Alex didn't seem to know about it. Nor about the fact that Stépan was unemployed. Olga certainly hadn't said anything. She didn't like to talk about what had happened at Fémina-Prestige with anyone but Sonia. His leaving rue d'Aboukir had made her happy, very happy even, but she was beginning to get uneasy and it was obvious; that's why he'd stop off at "the Bonnets'" after his long wanderings across Paris. It reassured her to see that he was really looking, that he wasn't discouraged and that he wasn't spending his days in the Auvergnat's café.

First he'd make sure there was no one in the dressing room, and then he would go in. The women would make tea for him, and he'd make them laugh by imitating the bosses he himself had dismissed and who couldn't get over the fact that he'd asked for their own references, their stand on the boycott.

It did make them laugh. But Olga's laugh was a little strained. And that also was obvious. So he'd change the subject and tease Zaza, Josette and Myriam, whom Sonia and Olga had set to basting hems in order to teach them the trade, and because they were overwhelmed with work.

He'd sip his tea in the kitchen, under the shelf that held Maurice and Robert's schoolbooks, and sometimes he'd timidly leaf through them, then put them back, respectfully.

Eventually he'd say:

"See you soon, I'm going home."

"You're not *going home*, Papa, since you're already here! You're *going upstairs* to the apartment," Zaza had corrected him with a smile the first time he'd said this.

"I say what I know!" he'd replied, and after that he would always use the same expression. And each time, as he climbed the stairs, he'd tell himself that it wasn't normal, this idea of working at home: a typical woman's idea! . . . And a woman's shop *'bsolutely* wasn't like a man's shop.

: :

THE TWO MEN had gone up to the second floor to discuss Alex's proposition, which had suited Sonia and Olga just fine. Caught between their joy—which they expressed—at learning that Stépan was perhaps going to find work, and their panic—which they kept to themselves—at the idea that he might be working there, at one of their tables, beneath their eyes, underfoot and on their backs, they had shown signs of dismay of a kind Alex knew very well. And he was the one who had suggested a little man-to-man shot of vodka in the Roginski kitchen.

Upstairs, having seated Alex in the dining room and closed the door carefully, Stépan fetched the bottle and the small glasses from the kitchen, then sat down. Alex watched him, intrigued by this ceremony, which had taken place in complete silence, waiting for him to speak. Apparently what he had to say was delicate. After another few seconds of silence, Stépan began.

"Here's how things stand . . . " he said, spreading out the fingers of his left hand and pressing down the little finger with the index finger of his right hand. Alex recognized the gesture, the same one to which Olga and Sonia often had recourse when the time came to enumerate the long list of their complaints, wishes or projects. Before meeting them, he'd never seen anybody who used the smallest and the last of his five fingers to underline the priority of a suggestion. Among the people he knew, the thumb was used for that purpose. On rue de la Mare, it was the little finger. Alex therefore recognized the gesture used by the women, and the formula used by himself: Stépan's "Here's how things stand" was Alex's personal contribution to the uses and customs of rue de la Mare. He smiled, and Stépan continued.

Of course there was no reason for Alex to believe him; after all, even though they'd met often, they didn't really know each other. But Stépan was ready to swear to him on Zaza's head that if there were two women in the world to whom he never wanted to cause the least bit of pain it was those two women downstairs. The one because she was his wife, the other because she was the wife of his friend, a second mother to his child, and almost like his own sister. He'd give millions, if he had them, millions, to never cause them grief. And nevertheless . . .

Stépan had released his little finger and passed to the ring finger.

. . . Nevertheless, those same millions that he'd give to spare them grief, he'd also give to be able to begin working tomorrow, this evening, right now. It was important that Alex understand this and not begin thinking that he, Stépan, turned up his nose at work. . . . But what he was going to tell him now he could tell *only* to him now, or to Elie this evening. He could never tell them. Never. Not Olga any more than Sonia, because they wouldn't understand and they'd only be grieved, the very grief he couldn't bring himself to inflict on them. Well then, here's how things stand . . .

He grabbed his middle finger, and the pressure was so intense that his entire left hand was jolted by it.

. . . Not even for millions of millions of billions could he see how he could work even one short day in the company of these women whom he adored being with when he got home but wouldn't be able to bear working alongside from morning to evening in the same shop. A shop which, in addition to being their personal fiefdom, was unfortunately so situated that in going down to work there he'd feel like a refugee being charitably sheltered under his own roof. And that was why, under the circumstances . . .

"That works out just fine," interrupted Alex, who saw Stépan attacking his left index finger to begin on the fourth point in his demonstration. "Just fine! We want you to work at Allée Chateaubriand, off the Champs-Elysées, Monsieur Roginski!"

"The Champs-Elysées?!" exclaimed Stépan, the way he might have said "New York!"

: :

THE NEXT morning he left rue de la Mare for the Champs-Elysées with his satchel and with Elie, just like in the old days.

Olga went to the dining-room window to watch them leave, and when they got to the Auvergnat's Stépan turned to wave at her.

"He looks just like Maurice going off for his first day at the lycée," said Sonia, who had joined her.

"Let's hope things work out all right over there," murmured Olga as she closed the window, and it was with an only slightly clouded conscience that they went back down to their domain—from which, without daring to say as much to Stépan or even admitting it to themselves, they had quite simply driven him away.

Stépan and Elie separated at Châtelet, and Stépan emerged from the George V station to a Champs-Elysées that was deserted under the pale winter sun.

He turned down rue Balzac, as Alex had told him to. He checked himself over in the reflection of a still-barred window, to see that the collar of his white shirt hadn't been wrinkled during the trip, and then walked a hundred yards or so before spotting the little garden and its bare bushes.

He'd got there, and now came the hardest part: a new profession, in a new shop, where his coworkers would all be women.

He thought of Olga and Sonia. Then for a moment he thought of Jiri, of Mademoiselle Anita. That helped him pass through the handsome old door and climb the polished steps leading to a completely new universe.

IV

NEWS
OF VOLODYA

T WASN'T New York, but it wouldn't be long before it became Hollywood-on the-Seine . . .

Stépan never suspected this when he became the twenty-sixth member of the Costumers' Cooperative. Nor did Sonia and Olga. Only Barsky had foreseen it, though it would happen without him.

Barsky had never again been able to lay hands on the Verdon brothers, nor put a name to their faces, seen for only a moment between Féfé and Tata Boubou at the bar run by Adrienne, who had totally forgotten his message. He was therefore obliged to announce at "the Bonnets' " that his filmmaking friends had suddenly taken off for the Indies.

"It's not important, Isidore, we'll wait for them," said Alex, who had dined with them at La Coupole the evening before. "We'll wait for them, but we'll have bread on our plates while we're waiting."

Alex had been right. And the bread they'd earn would come from the Movies. It hadn't been delivered yet, but it was on its way.

It wouldn't always be of the quality Alex had dreamed of when he had dreamed of the breathtaking young bride in *L'Atalante*. But it would arrive every day, and in such abundance that the little family of Cooperators would consider it cake.

A cake with a curse on it, Rodriguez would sneer later one evening at Chéramy's, when Alex, in his own inimitable way, had told him the plots of certain films that would henceforth assure both the success of the Coop and surprising prosperity for those who shared its much-discussed benefits—benefits they had never really believed in, despite the flourish of Anita Bourgoin's signature on the Cooperative agreement. But months had passed, the sparrows were already chirping and the trees were beginning to bud in the pretty Chateaubriand garden—as they were everywhere else. In other words, spring was in the air, as it was each year at this time. However, this was the spring of 1936, and one might have shared Rodriguez's astonishment at what it seemed to inspire in some authors. They must have been writing behind such heavily padded doors, such carefully curtained windows, that nothing happening in the outside world could keep them from accomplishing the historic tasks that had devolved upon them.

For example, the task of recounting the ups and downs of *Rasputin's Only Love* or the adventures of an illegitimate daughter of Napoleon III and a Normandy milkmaid to a nation in which half the population was yelling "A forty-hour week!" and the other half "France for the French!", while the country was preparing for a historic vote which, like spring, was imminent.

Cake with a curse on it, maybe . . . But *Rasputin's Only Love* had its ups and downs among crowds of people who were nobly elegant and necessarily dressed in costly animal skins because of the rigor of their native climate. As for the illegitimate daughter of Emperor Napoleon III, since she was followed from her first cry under Normandy foliage to her last sigh under the canopy of a Castilian bed, and since between these two major events she was seen traveling, making love, dancing, singing, running great risks and finding true happiness without ever, ever, ever putting on the same dress twice . . . "You can see for yourself how much that adds up to!" Alex said, by way of explanation.

"And you're not ashamed?" Rodriguez exclaimed jokingly.

" 'bsolutely not! . . . The Coop is only a little family, but like the Big Families, we also have our charities. Ask them, amigo!" Alex said, pointing to a nearby table occupied by the charming pretend cooperators of *The Crime of Monsieur Lange*, who were these days parading through Allée Chateaubriand to have themselves costumed as proles: for Jean Renoir, for *La Vie est à nous* and for not so much as a sou.

"And does your little family enjoy being charitable?" asked Rodriguez.

"In the beginning, not as much as I had hoped, my good sir. Then a miracle took place . . . "

"That's life for you!" said Rodriguez, in Spanish.

BUT IT WAS NOT so much of a miracle as of a woman touched by a miracle Alex was thinking that evening at Chéramy's on rue Jacob, so far from the Champs-Elysées and rue de la Mare.

He should have spoken of Mademoiselle Agnès. Mademoiselle Agnès had initially done a great deal of hesitating before becoming a "cooperator," a great deal of sighing over the memory of Maddy and a great deal of talking about returning to Lanvin, where her sister was still working. Then, faced with the prospect of once again finding herself kneeling in front of society women to verify the hang of dresses that were often no longer right for their age, she had chosen to remain among the "show people," whom she still despised as much as ever but who could "carry off" costumes that suited them marvelously. Given the fact that she would no longer have to undergo the humiliating comedy of the mauve chalk corrections, she had finally agreed. Not in writing, but by a condescending, rather sad smile that could be taken for resignation, indifference and even generosity.

It was she, however, who had very quickly insisted on their hiring an accountant in addition to the accountant-cooperator, Monsieur Anselmo, who was still at his post, invisible, behind the fur storage room. Invisible, but efficient and extremely meticulous, he was responsible for all the Masques and Bergamasques accounts, including the long column of "management entertainment expenses." The furniture in his little nook was shoved back and a folding table added for a second accountant—himself not a cooperator—appointed by the cooperators, who came at the end of every week to verify the distribution of the shares in which he did not share. Monsieur Anselmo found it a little vexing, but, as Ginette had put it, "good accounts make good friends," and he had resigned himself—though he doubted he would ever become Mademoiselle Agnès's friend—she, in fact, was not interested in becoming anyone's friend: everyone had known that for quite some time.

There was thus no reason for her to become friends with the costume borrowers, who showed up in increasing numbers, being sent by Monsieur Jean Renoir, or Jean Grémillon or Alberto Cavalcanti, and about whom she knew nothing except that they were probably poor, possibly friends of Alex's, but in any case and without doubt people who profited from the labor of others. She had complained, but, like Monsieur Anselmo, she too had had to resign herself and, in the name of an artistic solidarity completely foreign to her, agree to supervise the fittings of several modest little flower-print dresses that Alex himself had designed for some obscure beginners to whom she never said "hello" when they arrived, breathless with gratitude, or "goodbye" when they left, still grateful but paralyzed by her silences.

There was also no reason why she should have taken a particular liking to the newcomer, the furrier, a defector from rue d'Aboukir and one of Mademoiselle Anita's protégés. And it was therefore with every sign of indifference that she prepared to welcome Stépan into the bosom of her shop, where she'd arranged a "fur" corner for him.

He'd come in on a February morning behind Mademoiselle Anita and Ginette, who'd introduced him. He was pale, and had smiled gravely on shaking hands. She thought he was quite handsome.

So had the four girls in the shop, who'd shown it by poking each other in the ribs like the schoolchildren they were.

Mademoiselle Agnès had shown nothing at all. She was almost forty-five, and the emotion she'd felt when the newcomer entered was of a very special kind. Much of it was due to Stépan's resemblance to Janek, of whom she'd caught a fleeting glimpse at Allée Chateaubriand once or twice, but of whom she had often thought, and in a very precise fashion. Precise, disturbing, delicious and inadmissible.

It was impossible to spend entire days near Victoria Jean without fantasizing a little about her nights. Not that she said anything about them, but because her whole bearing—her languidly happy yawns, her puffy eyes, the way she touched her breasts, her distant smiles, her late arrivals on some mornings—conveyed much more than any lewd confidence could. Lucas made the lewd comments his department, and Mademoiselle Agnès always pretended not to hear him.

On the other hand, she used to listen to Maddy. Especially when Maddy was unhappy. And when Maddy was unhappy (Mademoiselle Agnès knew that she had been happy only with Alex), she would always make some comment about Victoria's happiness. She envied them tenderly and without bitterness, with perhaps just a shade of regret that she shared nothing more than the accounts that Victoria occasionally confided to her and only to her, but which Maddy in turn shared with Mademoiselle Agnès. She censored them a little, but this didn't at all weaken their evocative power for a woman as imaginative and lonely as Mademoiselle Agnès. The latter never asked any questions; she listened to poor Maddy's amazement at the fact that her friend not only had been lucky enough to find the usual pleasures, but also some quite extraordinary ones in the bed of the same man, and for such a long time.

"It's as if she had ten lovers. He's constantly inventing," she'd say.

"But that's what Slavs are like. Once you've known one, you evidently can't do without them," she'd add, with a fatalistic smile.

"You mustn't think about all that anymore," Mademoiselle Agnès would say. She herself had known only two men—and she could have done very well without them. Though it was true they weren't Slavs.

And so on days when she'd see the mauve chalk tremble in Victoria Jean's beautiful weary hand, she too would begin to daydream about the Caucasus, the Volga or the Vistula just the way other women dream of Venice.

It was therefore as the inheritor of a long tradition, as the hero of exquisite and untellable tales and legends, that Mademoiselle Agnès had received Janek's brother.

She was careful not to show him her emotion, which increased when Stépan opened his mouth to say his first words in a voice so deep that she thought she recognized the accents—and the accent—of Chaliapin.

These geographic errors and ethnic confusions greatly amused Alex, Ginette and especially Mademoiselle Anita, who had been quick to spot Mademoiselle Agnès's dark and secret passion.

It had escaped Stépan completely. Mademoiselle Agnès wasn't a woman to throw herself at a man, and for a long time he was unaware of the reasons for the astonishing solicitude she lavished on him as she explained his first duties. He naïvely attributed it to the spirit of the Cooperative. He was the only one to do so, but the girls were delighted to find that Mademoiselle Agnès could be other than cantankerous, mute and surly. It was something new, and very agreeable for everyone.

Particularly for Stépan, who, never having known her to be cantankerous, mute and surly, thought she was very kind for a woman so competent and no longer all that young. As competent as Olga and Sonia must be, but less pretty, less cheerful, more serious—especially in the midst of all those young girls who, like Zaza, were bursting with good humor.

At the end of that first day, during which he had made up a big otter muff trimmed with real mink tails, he had revised all his opinions, lost all his *a priori* judgments about a costumer's job and about female coworkers. He discussed this quite openly when he returned to rue de la Mare with two bouquets of violets in his hand.

He had bought them at the entrance to the George V Métro, amidst the bustle of an elegant crowd, the almost golden dazzle of the lights, the din of automobile horns and the intermission bells from movie theaters in which films were shown in English. He had bought them to be forgiven for having deserted, for having fled so far from "the Bonnets'," for being happy elsewhere.

From the graceful way Olga and Sonia had accepted his violets, Stépan understood they had forgiven him.

Life was beautiful!

: :

IF ONLY IT LASTS, everyone said, at "the Bonnets' " as well as at Chateaubriand.

And it lasted.

The buds had burst open; the bushes in the little garden were flowering. The apprentices were singing in the shop. Mademoiselle Agnès had once even gone over a refrain of *Roses of Picardy* with them because they had the words all wrong. Most of the time she followed the rhythm without parting her lips. But even that was wonderful, and nothing like it had ever happened before.

Before what? Mystery . . .

The woman touched by a miracle was discreet. Mademoiselle Agnès's passion was neither exuberant nor devouring. She lived it in solitude and fed it in solitude, on the smallest trivialities. But they were trivialities she collected, and which she didn't let escape her. Getting up in the morning, she knew she would find them waiting for her. Except on Sundays, during which she'd languish, thinking about Monday and about the nape of Stépan's neck as he bent over his table, about his voice, about all the happy accidents of work in common that permitted the touch of their fingers in the depths of the furs. Especially during fittings.

She loved these moments so much that she forgot to ask about the accounting problems. The men and women who wore the furs became no more than mannequins with living bodies on which her hand made rendezvous with Stépan's hand. Whether the mannequins were rich or poor was now a matter of total indifference to her.

This was the miracle Alex had spoken of at Chéramy's.

Stépan also enjoyed these fittings on live mannequins. After so many years of never knowing around what faces his assembly-line-produced collars would be wrapped he took great pleasure in suiting them to the look of a particular man—or woman. He didn't recognize the actors and actresses he turned into trappers of the Far North or grand duchesses, but he thought they were handsome and beautiful; he'd ask them their names and carry them back home, where Zaza would supply explanations.

Mademoiselle Agnès had had new smocks cut for him to wear during the fittings that took place in front of the large beveled mirrors, and she had tailored them herself. White, raglan-sleeved, with a pleat in the back and a half belt, they gave him the look of a dentist. He had a set of three, which he rotated, and now he no longer had to bring home his dirty clothes.

Nor an empty lunch pail: at noon, or maybe at one or two, depending on the work to be finished, the Coop would meet at the other end of the garden, on rue Washington, at "Raymonde and André, Home Cooking," where it had its own table in the rear. The first day, Stépan had eaten the lunch he'd brought, but the next day he'd gone along with the rest, just to see . . . The prices were modest, the daily special good, the waitress pleasant.

And so it was that henceforth he would leave in the mornings with Elie, hands in his pockets, without his satchel. On some mornings he could have left a little later, as a matter of fact, but he never did.

: :

JEANNETTE CLÉMENT would see the two of them pass in front of her glazed door and respond to their "good mornings," but she rarely came to the threshold. She was pleased Stépan had found work, but since neither Olga nor Sonia had thought it necessary to explain to her why he had been unemployed for some time, any more than Stépan himself had explained to Félix—whose advice to unionize he had not followed, though he had ended up by finding work anyway—she was merely satisfied, no more than that. She thought it best to remain reserved.

She said very little about it to Félix, who was racing from meeting to meeting (the elections were set for April), and nothing at all to Robert, whose bac exam was set for June: for all practical purposes, he, Maurice and Sami struck her as invisible, inseparable and barely polite.

That left Zaza and Josette, whose studies gave them so little trouble that they were always available. You could talk to them. You could talk about the waistline of Danièle (Parola), Jean-Pierre (Aumont)'s dimple or the heart-shaped lips of Danielle (Darrieux).

Jeannette didn't take it very seriously, but she felt a vague regret that these people never showed up in flesh and blood at the Coop in the XXth arrondissement, though they were apparently always to be found in the one on the Champs-Elysées.

She had proof of that: Stépan had brought home two large photos of Pierre Richard-Willm dressed as a legionnaire, one of them dedicated "to Mademoiselle Elsa Roginski, a friendly souvenir from P. Richard-Willm," and the other, the same shot, "for Josette Clément, cordially, P. Richard-Willm." The differences between the dedication for Josette and the one for Zaza were self-explanatory. But you had to think about it.

Zaza, who was four months older, had a right to the "Mademoiselle." Besides, as the daughter of a man with whom the great artist met frequently, she also had a right to his friendly souvenir. To compensate, Josette was treated with a flattering familiarity proper to her age, a familiarity summed up in that "cordially," which was both fraternal and unequivocal.

Pierre Richard had been tacked up over the folding beds on the ground floor and on the second floor.

Félix hadn't really liked this homage to the Foreign Legion, but Jeannette had reminded him how she herself had cried over *The House on the Dunes,* and Josette had announced that Pierre Richard would soon be Frédéric Chopin on the screen. So the photo of the legionnaire had remained tacked up, but Félix had delivered a brief analysis of the fickleness, the heedlessness and the lust for lucre—in a word, the lack of principle—of movie stars who were willing to portray characters as contradictory as a colonial mercenary and an anti-czarist revolutionary.

"That's true enough," admitted Jeannette, who until then had known nothing about Chopin except his love affair with George Sand and the "Valse d'Adieu."

But she'd thought about Félix's analysis and she wondered, seeing Stépan go by, if frequenting people so lacking in responsibility wouldn't eventually rub off on this man of whom they were so fond, but who had already changed his habits. He now often came home late, ate in restaurants and had his laundry done outside. Jeannette didn't think that was very nice for Olga. Out of discretion, however, she never mentioned this to her.

: :

OLGA DID VERY WELL without the bother of the lunch pail.

Olga found it very convenient not to have to wash Stépan's smocks anymore.

Olga preferred to wait for Stépan before eating, rather than to have him wait for his dinner.

And above all Olga loved to open the door in the evening to a Stépan who was happy, relaxed and full of stories.

Stories about the Coop that he could share with her and Sonia, and discuss with Elie, often in Zaza's presence. Like the story about Pierre Richard-Willm and Frédéric Chopin, for example.

"How about a few lessons in Polish so I can play my Frédéric," the actor had said amiably at the end of a fitting.

"I don't think that would be a good idea, Monsieur Willm, because with an accent like mine, your Frédéric would never have been able to get out of the shtetl and go off to learn to play the piano!" Stépan had replied, laughing.

"You're too modest, Monsieur Roginski," Mademoiselle Agnès had murmured, while Pierre Richard-Willm had himself begun laughing and given Stépan a big thump on the back.

"Excuse me, my friend! So much for me! Well then, *mazel tov* and *shalom*, Monsieur Roginski, until tomorrow . . . " And he had left as Mademoiselle Agnès looked after him admiringly and summed it all up.

"It's fantastic how well he already does . . . in Polish!"

Obviously, Stépan could never have brought stories like that back from rue d'Aboukir. Yet they were a lot like those Jiri used to tell. But Jiri would take them from folklore; Stépan was talking about real life. It was a hundred times funnier, and Zaza had to wait until the laughter calmed down, a good long while after the punch line, to make the request that had been trembling on her lips ever since she'd heard the dazzling names of Chopin and Richard-Willm. She'd gotten no further than these names: she hadn't listened to the rest, and she now felt everyone was making her lose a lot of time by laughing about things she hadn't paid any attention to.

"Papa, do you think you could get a photo for Josette and me?" she managed, in a relatively quiet moment.

"I'll try," answered Stépan, who had forgotten to inquire about the real meaning of the expression *So much for me*, which he had taken to mean "just like me"; but on rue de la Mare this misinterpretation hadn't done any harm to anyone. Certainly not to Pierre Richard-Willm, in whom Olga had found a vague family resemblance to a relative in Galicia when Stépan had brought the photo home.

The legionnaire's costume had aroused no criticism. Olga and Sonia had studied the drape of the long white scarf that fell in such handsome folds. As for Stépan and Elie, it reminded them of men they had known, men who were not mean, not violent, a little drunk sometimes, who, after waiting for papers that never came, living among people whose language they didn't understand, experiencing loneliness and homesickness, had one evening ended up joining the Foreign Legion.

Not everyone had been as lucky as the two of them. But they didn't speak of their own luck or of the misfortune of others until the next morning. It was between the house and the Place de la République that they returned to serious things.

Or else they'd wait until Sunday.

But that was when they really had things to talk about: about themselves, about others, about France and the world—the whole world, but obviously and especially that part of the world they knew so well, which they had left for the France they knew so badly.

France had, however, made Frenchmen of them. Frenchmen who were going to vote for the first time in their lives.

They attached great importance to the gesture they would have to make in a few weeks. They wanted it to benefit all those who had adopted them and whom for the last two years they had seen marching, though they themselves had been little involved in their marches, since they were neither factory workers, nor civil servants, nor veterans, nor unemployed, nor militants nor even union members, and they had never been either deprived or betrayed for the simple reason that they had been promised nothing—in any case, nothing that the thousands of marchers were demanding to the sound of familiar music that was unfamiliar to them, to improvised words they didn't always understand.

They wished all the marchers well. Before they fell into the ballot boxes, their two ballots, which seemed so light, would weigh heavily in their hands because they were charged with the weight of their scruples and their gratitude. And with their past as well.

Inevitably they spoke of their past. Of the Poland and the Ukraine of yesterday and even of today.

Stépan didn't like to talk about the infrequent letters he received from Poland. They were always so terribly sad. Frédéric Chopin had died almost a hundred years ago, but the latest news made it clear that Jews were still trembling every bit as much in the former kingdom of Poland. He had never been able to speak of this with Janek during all those years at Fémina-Prestige. He had got out of the habit of discussing it with Olga, whom such discussions made unhappy. He spoke of it only with Elie. And less and less frequently, since things had been going so well at Allée Chateaubriand.

As for the latest news from the Ukraine, it was neither sad nor happy, good nor bad: it was nonexistent. Not that the content was humdrum, futile or vague. There simply were no letters.

So Elie couldn't possibly know if the Jews had completely stopped trembling in the young Soviet Republic of the Ukraine. That had been true in the beginning, and he had received proof. But nine years had passed since then . . .

And so, inevitably, one Sunday they had talked about Volodya.

N order to speak of that old story again without being disturbed, the next Sunday, even before going to the public baths, Elie and Stépan had walked along rue des Pyrénées toward Place Gambetta. It wasn't the kind of conversation to have at the Auvergnat's café. Still less at home.

The only person in the neighborhood with whom or before whom they would have been able to speak about Volodya freely and without restraint was Monsieur Florian. But old Monsieur Florian was never in the neighborhood on Sunday.

There had been one Sunday, however, when he had taken the trouble to come and knock at the Guttmans' door. It had even happened twice, on both occasions after lunch, so as not to be in the way.

Each time, Maurice had been sent out to play in the street, having first been reassured that no, his teacher hadn't come to complain about him. He'd come to talk to Papa and Mama about things that didn't concern children.

All this went back a long way. Because to talk about Volodya, it was first necessary to talk once more about Simon Petliura and Samuel Schwarzbard. And therefore about Monsieur Florian's second visit, the one in 1927, at the time of the trial.

When he had come to knock at the door of the Guttman apartment that Sunday, Monsieur Florian hadn't come just to talk. He had come to bring something—two things, in fact.

First a newspaper clipping, which he gave to Elie. Elie returned it and asked if he might fetch his neighbors, Monsieur and Madame Roginski, who would surely also be interested, especially if Monsieur Florian agreed to read it to them. It would be easier for the women, who didn't read the newspapers.

Elie and Stépan had seen several newspapers since the beginning of the trial, in other words since the previous Wednesday. At rue d'Aboukir, they were snatched up, and there was talk of nothing else; there was no shouting because of Monsieur Jean, but even though everyone spoke in a low voice, they all spoke at once and it was impossible to form an opinion about anything. At Mercier Frères they were also snatched up, but for other reasons: talk in the shop was only about Coste and Le Brix. Because on the same day and pretty much at the same time (taking into account differences in time zones) the assassin Schwarzbard landed in the dock in the Court of Assizes of the Department of the Seine, the two French Naval Air Force aces were landing triumphantly on the arid runway of a South American airport. So except for Monsieur Paul, who had given Elie an optimistic and knowing wink, the other leather craftsman had shown no interest in the fate of the Russki. On the other hand, they had told Lilyich everything about the French aviators Védrine and Santos-Dumont, Guynemer, Blériot and Assolant, Nungesser and Coli.

Elie brought in Stépan and Olga. Sonia made some tea, Zaza was sent off to play with Maurice and the Clément children and Monsieur Florian, speaking in the voice that during the week was reserved for his dictations, began his reading to an audience that was as attentive as it was respectful.

The article was entitled: "I DO SO SWEAR":

All during the week the prosecution has paraded before us an elegant cohort of extremely polite people who have come to tell us of the esteem in which they held their leader, whom they insist on calling the first President of the Ukrainian Republic. We have seen them remove their gloves from their white and manicured hands to bear false witness. There were thirty of them.

This coming week we shall see the true witnesses. There will be eighty of them. And these will tell us of the true Petliura, leader of a band of torturers and killers.

And we will listen to and watch these survivors. They have traveled from the four corners of the globe and have just arrived. To tell us of the horrors they have lived through, to show us the mutilations, cuts and scars that these horrors have left on their bodies and in their memories.

They will speak to us of their dead, of those thousands of corpses that have for so long fertilized the soil of the Ukraine and of Poland.

They will not look as attractive or speak as well as the accomplices of the murderer of their brothers, their fathers, their sisters and their children.

They will be weary, because they are coming from a long way off and recovering from incidents that took place even a longer way off. They will speak our language badly. We will have to pay close attention. They won't have to take a glove off their right hand to say "I do so swear," because some of them will have lost that hand, but from their shattered faces we will hear the truth.

In all truth, I do so swear.

It was signed "Le Bihan, legal columnist." And Monsieur Florian explained that he had clipped the article from a weekly publication called *l'Instit.* It wasn't available on the newsstands, and that's why he had brought it.

In the Guttman dining room, everyone was silent. The two men had understood almost all the words that Monsieur Florian had spoken so carefully. Olga and Sonia had lost many of them, but they had retained the fact that there were eighty survivors. Timidly, Sonia was about to ask a question when Monsieur Florian began to speak again.

"That isn't all," he said. "I also found this, which I think may interest you, Monsieur and Madame Guttman. I cut it out of a very bad newspaper, but that doesn't matter!" And he took from his wallet a small photograph headlined *The Bolsheviks in Paris* and began to reread the caption quickly to himself:

Sparing no effort, the defense has spent money to have Soviet citizens come here from the Ukraine, and beginning next week they will fly to the aid of the murderer of President Petliura. Here is one of them who was surprised by our reporter yesterday as he arrived at the Gare de l'Est. From his smile, we would bet that the "witness" Vladimir Guttman has suffered no more from the voyage than from the "pogroms" that have obviously left him in perfect health.

Monsieur Florian carefully folded back the headline and the caption. "Look at this," he said.

And slowly, almost solemnly, he placed the photograph on the table in front of Sonia and Elie.

They bent over it together, and what was heard then couldn't be called a scream. They didn't scream—they seemed to breathe a long groan in which the two voices mingled. And when they raised their heads, their expressions showed fear, incredulousness and an almost mad joy.

Despite the saber slash that striped half the face, Elie and Sonia had just recognized Volodya in the photograph.

Volodya—friend, cousin, almost brother. The man they had thought dead because he had been seen dead in Zhitomir during the great pogrom. The last one. Or, rather, the last one in the lives of Sonia and Elie Guttman.

The handsome and kindhearted Volodya was alive. So alive, that in the photo he could be seen extending his hand toward the camera as though to protect himself from it. He had no doubt made the gesture too late, and since he was smiling, he seemed rather to be protecting himself from the rays of the sun. The sun of Paris.

And Sonia collapsed tearfully in the arms of Elie, who patted her shoulder and looked at Monsieur Florian, smiling and nodding his head, as if to excuse the way his wife had let herself go in front of a stranger.

A stranger—despite everything, that was the right word. Monsieur Florian was as moved as he was embarrassed; he felt a little like a voyeur at a spectacle he himself had brought about.

He got up.

Sonia was now laughing in Elie's arms; she kept repeating "Volodya . . . Volodya . . . ", and it was Olga who began to cry silently, her face buried in her hands, and Stépan who was patting her shoulder and saying "I know . . . I know . . . "; and, to excuse his wife, he explained the situation to Monsieur Florian.

Olga was crying because back in the old country, in Poland, not everyone was as lucky. The dead were completely dead; they didn't return. They knew that from the letters they had received.

"Volodya couldn't write us because everybody thought he was dead . . . " Sonia had objected with a shrug of her shoulders, the way you might reply to someone who had just said something extremely foolish.

Monsieur Florian had in turn almost added that those who had been resuscitated weren't obliged to pretend to be dead so as to remain true to their reputation as dead men, but he'd kept the remark to himself. Just as he'd kept his question to himself. His stranger's question, which he hadn't dared ask because it was too French: "Why have you received letters from Poland and not from the Ukraine?" And if he hadn't asked it, it was because he was afraid he already knew the answer, and he no more wanted to make them say it than to say it to himself.

He was about to leave, but everyone was upset. How could Volodya be found on Sunday in a Paris that was almost as unknown to the four of them as it must be to the ghost from the Ukraine?

Monsieur Florian gave them little hope for that Sunday. But he promised to look into it. And he had an idea. If it worked, he'd let them know through Maurice. Tomorrow.

"No, not through Maurice, Monsieur Florian, please," Sonia had asked, almost as if she were pleading.

"All right, not through Maurice. I'll send you a note," Monsieur Florian had agreed.

"I'd rather come to meet you when school gets out," Sonia had suggested.

"If you like, Madame Guttman," said Monsieur Florian, who had just realized that Sonia didn't know how to read.

He had shaken their hands and left the dining room. Elie had accompanied him downstairs. The street was deserted, and the children could be heard laughing in the alleyway. Elie had taken Monsieur Florian's hand into both his own, and, shaking his head, had thanked him three times; then he'd given him the telephone number of the Mercier shop. Monsieur Mercier was very kind, and, if necessary, he would even let him go early should Monsieur Florian ever have news of Volodya.

In the meantime, Sonia had gone with Olga into the Roginski dining room: she wanted to put Volodya into The Family Picture Frame even before she'd really seen him again. And especially before the children returned.

In October, it grew dark early; they'd soon return for their after-school snack, and Sonia wasn't ready to answer their questions. There were always questions, whenever The Family Picture Frame was taken down. For once, the reply would be alive. Tomorrow, Volodya would answer them himself. Or rather, he would tell them how come Uncle Volodya was visiting Paris. No more than that. They'd see to it.

Tomorrow . . . but after all, why not this very evening?

Monsieur Florian had said that Paris was too big and that it was Sunday. But since, among these thousands of streets, in these millions of houses, behind these billions of doors, there was one street, one house, one door, sheltering a man whom they had thought dead in another city but who was alive right here in Paris, it proved that in life anything could happen. Even on a Sunday.

And, on rue de la Mare, they began to wait for Volodya.

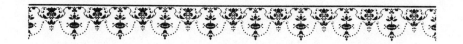

*T*HE LAWYER defending Samuel Schwarzbard was named Henry Torrès. Elie never knew how much audacity it had taken for an obscure schoolteacher to disturb France's most prestigious and sought-after lawyer in his own home as night fell on that Sunday in October 1927. Nevertheless, that is exactly what Monsieur Florian had done. Instead of returning home, he went to consult the phonebook in a café on rue des Pyrénées, thought for a moment of telephoning and then decided that if he was going to put anyone to any trouble, he might as well begin with himself.

Maître Henry Torrès was as known for his generosity and his courage as he was for his talent as a lawyer. Like all courageous people, he would be able to recognize the courage of Monsieur Florian, who, without an appointment, without introductions, dared to present himself on avenue Hoche at the door of such a famous man, whose only free day was Sunday. As was true for Monsieur Florian himself. Of course he also had Thursday as well, but he was afraid that Thursday might be too long to wait before getting the information he needed.

This was how, before crossing the threshold, he had excused and explained himself on the landing in front of the door that Maître Henry Torrès, wearing a somewhat baggy smoking jacket, had opened in person.

Monsieur Florian didn't want to be taken for one of those shady characters who, having just done something—and sometimes even just before doing it—came to bring a retainer to the lawyer whom they had already decided upon for their defense should they be caught.

Monsieur Florian had heard talk of such things. So had Maître Henry Torrès.

"People like that don't come to me. They prefer certain of my colleagues. Come in, Monsieur," he'd said with a smile, and he had led his visitor to a large office, so encumbered that you had to step over piles of dossiers. He had asked him to sit down and had listened to him attentively.

Unfortunately, he couldn't give him a Paris address for the witness Vladimir Guttman, he said, having consulted a long list of names among his piles of papers.

The witness Guttman was a Ukrainian from the Ukraine. Not a Pole. There were Paris addresses for the Poles from Poland. They had come in a group, with a rabbi, and almost all of them were living on rue Vieille-du-Temple in a small hotel that had given them a good rate. A few of them, however, had preferred to stay with relatives. This complicated things a little when you wanted them all at the same place at the same time.

There was no such trouble with the Ukrainians from the Ukraine. They too had come in a group, without a rabbi but with two interpreters, even though there were only five witnesses in all—and none of them had expressed the desire to be on their own. In any case, they were always together and didn't seem to have any personal connections with anyone in Paris. Nor did they seem interested in establishing new friendships with the other Ukrainian witnesses who had come from elsewhere: from all the countries in Europe as well as from America, where those working on the defense had gone to look for them during the seventeen months of the preliminary inquiry.

The latter, the Ukrainians from elsewhere, had come separately, without a rabbi and without an interpreter, and they were a little undependable about schedules. They lived just about everywhere, but he did have addresses for them.

But about the Ukrainians from the Ukraine like Monsieur Vladimir Guttman, nothing was known. They had been there since the first day, in other words since Tuesday, October 18. Like the others, they had responded when their names were read out in court. And since that time they had shown up punctually every day before the opening session, remained in the witnesses' waiting room, left after the session was over and, unlike the others, never complained about having been made to wait for nothing, or asked when they would be called to testify.

There was no need to go looking for them. They were always there.

As for where they came from or were brought back to, one might as well look for answers in an inkwell. The older of the interpreters, the one to whom the summonses were given, had spoken of a "nice little place in the country," which Maître Torrès's young assistant translated as meaning a "house in the suburbs." But was it to the north, south, east or west of Paris? Impossible to know. The chauffeur of the little van that brought them spoke no French.

"I had a lot of trouble getting them permission to come. I had to argue for months. They're here. I'm not about to make a fuss to find out if they sleep in Argenteuil or in Bécon-les-Bruyères. I won't be able to get their address, my dear sir, because they won't give it to me. They are the survivors of the massacres of Berditchev, Proskurov and Zhitomir. I wouldn't wish to be responsible for their disappearance here in the Seine-et-Oise."

Maître Henry Torrès had spoken with a melancholy humor. It was obvious he was tired. Monsieur Florian again apologized for having disturbed his only day of rest during this battle he was fighting. All for a simple address.

"Don't apologize, Monsieur. You were right to come. The world is full of people who wouldn't lift a little finger to try and find the address of a cousin who isn't even theirs. . . . They are the same people who lock their doors when they hear cries for help on the floor below, and who prefer to call Schwarzbard "the Assassin" rather than "the Avenger." So I actually find it reassuring to meet a man like you after the week we, my client and I, have just spent, and before the week that lies in store for us! I hope there will be people like you among the members of the jury, who have been lied to since last Tuesday and who will have to come to a decision next Thursday. I hope so for the sake of Samuel Schwarzbard, who claims the honor of being guilty under the law. I hope so for the honor of us all, despite what my colleague Campinchi says, and despite the real grief of his client, the widow of the "victim," who is also the widow of the only true assassin in this affair of bloody crimes. I say *crimes* in the plural, and I mean the rivers of blood, not the splash that stained the sidewalk of rue Racine in Paris for a few hours . . . "

Monsieur Florian had never heard a case being pleaded. He was fascinated. Maître Henry Torrès noticed this.

"Don't think that I'm rehearsing, my dear sir. I am expressing my indignation, expressing it for myself alone, and perhaps that is why I am able to express it before the entire world," he said, smiling.

"Very likely," said Monsieur Florian, smiling in his turn.

"But let's get back to your friends and to my witness from the Ukraine. Is it possible to reach you by phone in the afternoon, and if so at what number? I'll have my young assistant call—perhaps he'll figure out some way to arrange a meeting in the vicinity of the Palais. In principle, my poor survivors are scheduled to address the court on Tuesday or Wednesday at the latest."

Monsieur Florian gave the number at the school. Blushing slightly, like one of his pupils, he also specified the times of recess and dismissal.

"I promise not to forget you," said Maître Torrès, as he accompanied him to the door.

"Nor will I forget you, Maître. I'll never forget you," murmured Monsieur Florian.

He was about to go down the stairs when the lawyer called him back.

"Tell me . . . Do you speak of all this to your pupils? Do they ask questions, the grandchildren of the men and women who died?"

Monsieur Florian came back up two steps. He shook his head.

"Their parents don't wish to share that memory with them, and they place their children in my care so that I can teach them to remember France, and know her history . . . "

"Well, then, let's say that if we save Samuel Schwarzbard, it may make a nice little chapter in the history of France for some later date!"

"Yes, for these children's children. But I'll no longer be there to conduct the class," said Monsieur Florian, leaving for good this time, with a little wave of his hand toward the softly closing door.

: :

OF COURSE it was impossible, it was insane, but even so it would have been wonderful if Volodya had suddenly knocked at the door before Sunday was over.

Up until very late that evening Sonia had vaguely believed he would, and it wasn't until Barsky grumbled and coughed as he passed the door that she gave up the idea that this slow and hesitating step might belong to Volodya, lost on an unfamiliar stairway.

Then, getting ready for bed, she admitted that maybe it was better that way. It left more time to get organized, get everything ready. Food, drink, flowers and—why not—a place to sleep.

Mightn't Volodya like to sleep there? They'd take Maurice into the big bed, between the two of them. Or they'd put him in Zaza's folding bed, with his head in one direction, and hers in the other. And even if Volodya didn't want to sleep there, they'd have to roll Maurice's cot into the bedroom so that they could spend the night talking, all night if they wanted to. Anyway, they'd see tomorrow.

They'd also see about the finishers' material tomorrow. She'd put her own garment bag with Olga's in the Roginski dining room. That way her dining room would look like a real salon.

She also mustn't forget to put The Family Picture Frame on her own mantelpiece. Volodya wouldn't understand if his photo were kept in the neighbors' apartment. Even if they were their family in France, still they weren't real family.

They'd order a quiche Lorraine. So he could get a taste of French cooking.

And they wouldn't say anything to the others in the building. Especially not to old Madame Lowenthal. Nor to the Cléments, either. Volodya was really only their concern. Theirs, the Roginskis' and—of course—Monsieur Florian's.

Before putting out the light, Elie finally confessed to Sonia that he had written several letters to the village and to Zhitomir giving his address in Paris. It was strange that Volodya had never given them a sign of life.

Sonia didn't answer because she had already done so in front of Monsieur Florian.

She said that it was indeed strange, but Volodya would certainly explain. Tomorrow.

T WAS ON Wednesday, October 26 at about four-thirty that Monsieur Paul Mercier came looking for Elie in the shop.

He was expected at the café-restaurant Les Trois Marches, on Place Dauphine in front of the Palais de Justice, on family business. He was to be there between five and five-fifteen at the latest and without fail.

: :

ON RUE DE LA MARE, there had been no need to roll Maurice's folding cot into the bedroom. Monsieur Florian had sent word on Monday that as for the address, it was a little complicated—they'd have to wait and be patient.

So they had waited. And Monday had gone by.

On Tuesday, one of the three red roses had already lost two petals. The hothouse mimosa was still all right, but it was less velvety and a golden dust made a halo around the vase in the center of the dining-room table. That evening, after dinner, they had ended by eating the quiche for dessert in the Roginski kitchen, since Tuesday had also gone by.

Once back in her apartment, Sonia had wept. If Volodya didn't come, maybe it was simply because he didn't want to see them. Didn't want to see them any more than he had wanted to write to them, not even to say that he had nothing to say to them.

And Sonia questioned Elie: was there something he once might have said or done to Volodya that he, Elie, might have forgotten, but that Volodya hadn't?

Elie told her she was crazy, that she was the one who was losing her memory. The evening before the big pogrom they had all three eaten together in Volodya's father's house. They had laughed all the time and had parted with an embrace, saying they'd see each other the next day . . .

"Yes, but the next day we escaped . . . Maybe that's what he hasn't forgiven us—for not having died with him," Sonia had said; then she caught herself: "I mean, for not being half dead, like him . . . "

This made Elie smile.

No, as he, Elie, saw it, Volodya was very busy. A trial is like a war, like being in the army. You had to get permission to obtain leave. The witnesses remain mobilized until the war is over. This one was in the process of winding up. The day before, three men had already testified for Schwarzbard; he'd read about it in the paper. Tomorrow it would be Volodya's turn, and that of all the others, the eighty of them. Afterwards, Volodya would be free, free to go wherever he wanted. He wouldn't be mobilized anymore. He'd leave the barracks.

And maybe Schwarzbard would leave his prison.

Elie realized that this was the first time since Sunday that he was speaking of Schwarzbard with Sonia. Or rather that he was speaking of Schwarzbard to Sonia, who couldn't think about anything but Volodya. Mobilized or not, he hadn't found either the time or the means to jump over the wall and come embrace them: that was all she could see.

She didn't say that to Elie. But on Wednesday morning she threw the faded bouquet into the garbage can and untied the garment bag in her own dining room. As usual. If Volodya decided to come, he'd find them as he'd find them, her and her dining room. She in her finisher's smock and the dining room set up as a combined workshop-children's room. If only to show him that they were no longer really expecting him.

She said as much to Elie before he left. Elie said she was wrong to feel that way, but at the same time he thought she had some reason to. As he told Stépan during their Métro ride.

Stépan wasn't sure what to say. He and Olga had shared the surprise and the wait; they were beginning to share the insult. But, after all, they weren't the ones who were being insulted. In the final analysis, Volodya wasn't their cousin . . . So Stépan just said he found the whole thing rather strange.

They were still at the bottom of the steps of the Strasbourg-St. Denis

Métro exit when they heard the hoarse voice of a newspaper vendor: "DRAMATIC INCIDENT AT THE CHOUASSEBARRE TRIAL . . . THE WITNESSES FROM THE UKRAINE AND POLAND GO HOME . . . DRAMATIC INCIDENT AT THE COURT OF ASSIZES . . . "

Elie and Stépan each bought a paper. Elie read his in the street before reaching the Mercier shop.

The vendor had told the essential facts. In the article, which took up three columns of the front page, it was explained that after the depositions of Messieurs Goldstein (Tolstoy's former lawyer), Siliosberg and Tiomkine (former members of the Ukrainian Assembly under Kerenski)—depositions that were true indictments against the hetman Petliura—the cause of the accused Schwarzbard had been so well understood (the jury had wept) that Maître Henry Torrès had decided against calling his eighty witnesses, who had come from abroad at his personal request. He had announced this in court, pointing to the door behind which these survivors of Petliura's hell had been waiting for days, in anguish at having to relive their calvary so as to better describe it, in anguish also at having to exhibit their wounds and infirmities so as to be sure of being believed.

He had only to say a word and they would come in. But after what had been heard from the three witnesses who had testified the day before, he now wondered if it was really necessary to violate decent feelings once again—theirs as well as those of the jury, the judges and the public, all of whom seemed saturated with horror.

Maître Henry Torrès also thanked Assistant Public Prosecutor Raynaud for having called on Messieurs Goldstein, Siliosberg and Tiomkine. These three honorable men were not witnesses for the defense but for the prosecution.

Maître Henry Torrès then spoke of another witness, called by the plaintiff. And Maître Campinchi had for a second time to sit through the reading of a declaration of the Ukrainian Colonel Butakov, who, the previous week, had called the Proskurov pogrom led by Petliura a "work of divine inspiration." The lawyer then asked Maître Campinchi if he wanted to see two of the beneficiaries of the "divine" inspiration proclaimed by his witness Butakov: "They are there. Only a few feet away, my dear colleague. Two citizens of Proskurov. One of them will show you his remaining leg, the other won't dare show you anything at all. He was emasculated in Proskurov on the night of February 13–14, 1919 . . . "

And the reporter concluded with a description of the unbearable emotion aroused by the eloquence of Maître Henry Torrès, who was so sure of his client's cause that he was giving up his right to call on the eighty foreign witnesses he had taken such trouble to find in every corner of the world. The article called the event "a dramatic *coup de théâtre*," and held out for the next day the prospect of a plea that would be more moving than any made by a defense counsel in this century, and the possibility—now very likely—of the pure and simple acquittal of a murderer promoted to the rank of avenger.

Of all that, written with a lyricism in which the reporter tried to compete with that of Maître Henry Torrès, Elie remembered only one thing: Volodya was leaving.

Volodya, come for nothing, was about to disappear without having accomplished the only thing that would have given this long journey real meaning.

And Elie was almost angry with Monsieur Florian.

Without him, they would have known nothing—not about Volodya's resurrection, nor about his presence in Paris. And Sonia and he would have continued to remember a dead man and weep over him in their hearts—a dead man who had now been brusquely transformed into an invisible and unfindable living person. Unfindable even by Monsieur Florian, who had nevertheless undertaken to find him.

If it hadn't been for Monsieur Florian, he would have been able to rejoice for Samuel Schwarzbard without thinking of anything but Samuel Schwarzbard.

But it was of Volodya that he was thinking as he entered the shop, where his worried and unhappy look surprised his coworkers, who for once had kept up with the news.

"Lilyich, don't show us that sour face now it looks like our famous mouthpiece Torrès is about to win an acquittal for your Russki!" Meunier had exclaimed.

Elie had smiled. And Monsieur Paul had come in with another newspaper that told just about the same story as the one Elie had bought. At noon, they had drunk to the coming liberation of Samuel and of France, the land of welcome and of the Rights of Man—to say nothing of the Ladies of rue Blondel, Meunier had added, as an ending to Monsieur Paul's toast.

Elie had laughed with everyone else. But he was thinking of Volodya, of Sonia's unhappiness and of the bouquet that had been thrown away before it was completely faded.

But then, right in the middle of the afternoon, he had received the unbelievable message. "Palais de Justice . . . family business . . ." That could only be Volodya!

Volodya had looked for him, Volodya had found him, Volodya was waiting for him. It was fantastic!

He left the shop so quickly he forget to take along his satchel and his empty lunch pail.

It was fantastic—but when he got home it was soon going to be even more fantastic. He would knock at the door, and when Sonia opened it, he'd push Volodya ahead of him and say casually, "I ran into Volodya, and I brought him home for dinner . . . "

He got off at Châtelet, as he had in the past, when he and Stépan, before they were naturalized, would go to the Préfecture to have their alien registration papers stamped.

In the past . . . It was only a year and a half ago, but it already seemed so far away. How quickly you get used to tranquillity, he told himself as he strode along the almost deserted Quai de l'Horloge. It was the first time he had walked on this side: in fact, he had just discovered that the Police and Justice departments were sheltered under the same roof, shared the same palais. And in discovering Place Dauphine, he also discovered that the doors of the Justice department opened majestically onto the most peaceful of small provincial squares.

It even had its own café-bar. It was called Les Trois Marches, because you had to climb three steps before crossing the threshold.

He climbed them one by one.

He was in a sweat.

: :

IT WAS MONSIEUR FLORIAN rather than Elie who was to retain a clear memory of the strange and brief reunion of the Guttman cousins.

Informed by Maître Henry Torrès's young assistant that the Ukrainians were leaving that very evening for the Ukraine but that they would be at Les Trois Marches for a light snack before taking their train, he had phoned the Mercier shop. But uneasy lest the small part of his mission he had been able to carry out come to nothing, he too had crossed Paris and gone to Les Trois Marches.

The lawyer's young assistant was waiting for him at the bar, his black robe with its white collar slung over his arm like a raincoat. He had pointed out a rear table around which seven men were sitting and talking. They had been served sandwiches and tea.

Monsieur Florian immediately recognized Volodya because of the scar. Like the others, he was well dressed in brand-new clothes. He had curly dark hair and he was smiling. He was smiling so much that

Monsieur Florian was reminded of the deliberately disfigured hero of Victor Hugo's *The Man Who Laughs*.

"They didn't want to stay another day. They're not even waiting to hear my boss sum up, or for the verdict . . . And I must tell you, Monsieur, that I'm not sure if the interpreter translated my request to the witness named Guttman, about his family . . . He smiled when I asked him to do so the day before yesterday, but he, too, smiles all the time, even though his face hasn't been slashed," the young assistant said in a low voice. "We'll see what happens when your friend gets here . . ."

"Here he is," said Monsieur Florian, spotting Elie's silhouette behind the glass panel of the bistro door.

"Let me handle this," said the young man, heading for the table.

He said something into the ear of one of the men. The latter turned around to watch as Elie came in, then said something to Volodya, who also turned around, just as Elie was extending a hand to Monsieur Florian, who couldn't take his eyes off Volodya.

Volodya, who was looking at Elie.

And what happened in that second, when a look of panic and of intense, sad joy spread over that face condemned to a perpetual smile, was seen only by Monsieur Florian.

Volodya had gotten to his feet, and so had the interpreter; and because Monsieur Florian wasn't looking at him, Elie also turned toward the group, which he hadn't yet noticed. Volodya came forward. And it was without a cry, in total silence, that the two men embraced. Head against head, eyes closed, they swayed together so violently and for so long that they stumbled dizzily and had to cling to each other lest they collapse like drunkards on the tiled café floor.

The interpreter had remained standing at the table, where the five other men were watching the scene in silence.

"Do come and sit with the rest of us, please, gentlemen," he said in a loud voice. The invitation included Monsieur Florian, the young lawyer and Elie, who let go of Volodya but kept his eyes fixed on him.

One of the other men now rose and, without asking the proprietor, pulled up another table and three more chairs so they could all sit together.

"What will you have?" the interpreter amiably asked Monsieur Florian, who was coming closer; the lawyer, who was sitting down; and Elie, who remained standing where he was, his eyes on Volodya's, his two hands resting on Volodya's shoulders. He had not as yet said a single word to him. "Come, my friend, we must hurry," the interpreter said. He added something in Russian, and Volodya gently pushed Elie toward the table.

As he sat down, Elie shook hands with everyone and murmured a few words Monsieur Florian recognized as being Yiddish.

No one really replied.

"Would you like some tea or a liqueur?" asked the interpreter.

"Tea," Monsieur Florian, the lawyer and Elie replied together.

"Please . . . three additional teas!" ordered the interpreter, turning his head toward the bar. Then, calling on Monsieur Florian to bear witness, he addressed the young lawyer. "And so we see it's all worked out well, Lawyer . . . The trial ends in our favor . . . "

"Almost, Interpreter, almost," said the young lawyer, smiling. "It's a pity you're not staying for the real end, the acquittal."

"Very sadly a pity that we are completely obliged to return home, very great pity," repeated Dmitri, the interpreter, shaking his head fatalistically.

"But when are they leaving?" asked Elie, who had just noticed the small pile of suitcases carefully stacked in a corner of the café.

"This very evening," specified Dmitri, with a grieved expression and consulting his watch.

"That's impossible!" exclaimed Elie, looking at Monsieur Florian. "Not already!"

He put his arm around Volodya's shoulder and asked him something in Yiddish, to which Volodya started to reply something in Russian and which Dmitri took it upon himself to translate simultaneously into French:

"No . . . impossible to stay a few days longer in Paris, too much work now back home . . . good work . . . you must come and visit us . . . And Sonia? How is Sonia? . . . Have you made a family? . . . "

Yes, Sonia was fine, and they had a little boy, Maurice, Elie mechanically replied in French.

"How old is he?" Dmitri asked, for his own information.

"Eight," answered Elie, spreading his left hand and three fingers of his right hand.

"Eight years old . . . " repeated Volodya, probably in Russian and smilingly shaking his head.

"If you had been patient, Monsieur Guttman, you would have waited with Sonia until we got rid of the counterrevolutionary pogromist Petliura and you would have made a family in our country, and today little Maurice, who is eight years old, would be a very good little pioneer in the Ukraine . . . "

Dmitri immediately translated his declaration for his compatriots, who all agreed and smiled, so that for a brief moment they all resembled Volodya.

"But little Maurice is a very good little French schoolboy," said Monsieur Florian, looking at Elie.

"Well, then, everything's fine," admitted Dmitri, who didn't think it necessary to translate either the intruder's comment or his own reply.

The proprietor brought three teas.

Despite the rattling of the heavy cups and the teaspoons, Monsieur Florian heard Elie's voice apparently asking Volodya a new question, for which the latter was apparently having difficulty finding an immediate reply.

"That's because he no longer lives in Zhitomir," said Dmitri. "We all of us have new cities and new lives. We also give you new addresses, Monsieur Guttman, and you give us Paris address for next time. Or maybe you come visit us with Sonia, little Maurice and new little sister . . . No?"

Elie blushed, smiled and took the piece of square-ruled paper held out by Dmitri. It was a sheet torn from a red notebook he had taken from an inside pocket.

Monsieur Florian was already holding out his fountain pen when Dmitri, with a magician's flourish, produced a mechanical pencil, the silver clip of which embellished his outside pocket. Taking it, Elie was surprised at its weight and by the solid-gold monster that had to be worked to produce the lead.

"A battlefield souvenir, Monsieur Guttman . . . You know, many of our men died, many of theirs too. But ours had empty pockets full of holes—the Whites had full pockets, and we made some holes in them . . . "

Bursting into laughter, Dmitri immediately translated himself, and once again everyone resembled Volodya, but this time looking considerably more cheerful.

Monsieur Florian kept looking at Volodya as Elie was applying himself to half of the square-ruled sheet. In large block letters, he wrote his name, his wife's name, his son's name and the number of his house on a street of this city that Volodya was going to leave without having known either the street or the house in which was growing the child that he didn't know, born to a woman he might not have recognized.

Behind the smile tattooed by the scar, Monsieur Florian could read in Volodya's despairing eyes that the large block letters printed on the square-ruled paper stood for no more than the absurdity of a missed appointment. Missed because it had never been made, in a place about which he knew nothing and of which he would never be able to think either happily or sadly when he would later recopy those letters on an envelope, if he ever wrote. It was too stupid and too sad, Monsieur Florian told himself.

"What time does your train leave?" he asked Dmitri suddenly.

"Why?" answered the interpreter, who was signaling for the check.

"I thought we might take Monsieur Vladimir Guttman to his cousin's house, just for a moment, and then bring him back to you at the railway station," suggested Monsieur Florian, too softly for Elie to overhear. Elie was now leaning over Volodya's shoulder, watching him in his turn write on the other half of the square-ruled paper.

"Too bad . . . definitely too late . . . yesterday very possible . . . really too bad . . . " Dmitri sincerely regretted, rising and leaning over the back of Volodya's chair in a posture that was both severe and paternal, exactly the one that Monsieur Florian adopted every day in order to keep an eye on those of his pupils who were too inclined to let their attention wander.

Elie read aloud the words being written in Cyrillic as Volodya traced the name of a village, of a city followed by that of a district and of several numbers preceded by a capital letter. The city was no longer Zhitomir, it was Poltava; and the name of the village, like that of the district, meant nothing to him—no more than the undecipherable code of ciphers. Still, it was as if Volodya was drawing him a large postcard made up of colors, smells, noises and sounds so familiar he himself could have drawn it from memory.

Volodya had finished. But he kept his hand on the paper and the silver mechanical pencil between his fingers, and he was looking at Elie, whose face was very close to his. He again bent over the paper and put a black dot on it, as if to begin a word that he didn't begin. He abandoned the black dot, on the left of the square-ruled paper, and on the right he drew a heart in which he wrote "Sonia, Maurice, Elie, Volodya," in Cyrillic.

Dmitri leaned over his shoulder, took the pencil from his hand, clipped it onto his outside pocket and picked up the square-ruled sheet. He folded one half over the other, crushed the fold between his fingers, ran his nail down it and with a sharp gesture tore the sheet in half. He gave Volodya's address to Elie, and Elie's address to Volodya.

The others were talking among themselves; Dmitri remained standing; the lawyer got up and insisted on paying the proprietor, who had come over with the check, for the teas and sandwiches. He moved toward the bar, the white collar of his robe dragging on the tiled floor.

A man dressed in a long gray smock and wearing a cap came in.

"We must go now," said Dmitri in French, before repeating it, probably in Russian. Everyone got up.

It was only then that Monsieur Florian noticed that the man near him had a wooden leg which ended in a thick disc of black rubber, and that his neighbor's neighbor's right sleeve was empty. It was he who handed a cane to the one-legged man, who had left it on the pile of suitcases the man in the gray smock had picked up with all the ease of a porter in a big hotel.

Then everything happened very quickly. Dmitri shook hands with Monsieur Florian, the only one to remain seated. Elie had got up at the same time as Volodya, whose hand he was holding as one might hold the hand of a woman or a child; he had to let go of it to shake the hand Dmitri held out to him. Dmitri indicated that Volodya was to go ahead of him, and held him by the shoulder while he shook the hand of the young lawyer, who was still at the bar. The others had already left.

On the threshold of the open door, Dmitri stopped. He was now holding Volodya by the arm.

"And so we're really expecting you in our country now that you've rediscovered family there, Monsieur Guttman . . . "

A big smile lit up his smooth, handsome face.

Elie stepped forward, took Volodya's head between his hands, kissed him on the mouth, and with his thumb did what he had probably not dared do until that moment. It was a gesture he might have dared to make at home, after Maurice had fallen asleep and the three of them—Sonia, Volodya and he—were alone.

With his thumb, Elie gently caressed the entire length of the scar, which started at the base of Volodya's neck and lost itself in the roots of his hair. It had carved out a wild zigzag, sparing in its passage only the superb blue-green-mauve-gold pupils in which Monsieur Florian suddenly saw a glint of humor. . . . And for the first time, Volodya said something in Yiddish.

For the first and the last time. Dragged along by Dmitri, he descended the three steps and, without turning around, climbed into the back of a small, tarpaulin-covered truck, whose motor was already running.

The truck started off immediately.

Standing in the doorway, Elie started to wave goodbye, then let his hand fall. "With that tarpaulin, it's not much use . . . " he said to

Monsieur Florian, who had joined him. He waited until the truck had disappeared before turning to the schoolmaster.

"What did he say to you just before leaving?" asked Monsieur Florian.

Elie smiled.

"He said: 'Don't worry about me. Girls like scars . . . ' That's what he said, Monsieur Florian. And I never even asked him if he was married, or if he had children or what kind of work he did—nothing, nothing, nothing. I know nothing!"

And the sentence begun with a smile ended in despair. And Monsieur Florian could think of nothing to say.

After taking leave of the young lawyer, who was still at the bar, they in turn descended the three steps. They walked in silence for a moment, then Monsieur Florian stopped and looked up at the four stories of the very old building above the café-bar called Les Trois Marches.

"Jean de La Fontaine lived in this very place, Monsieur Guttman . . . This evening, you'll be able to tell Maurice that you've been in La Fontaine's house . . . " he added, with a friendly smile.

"Is that right?" said Elie, who no longer really remembered just who La Fontaine was, despite the fact that he loved to hear Maurice recite the fable of "The Wolf and the Lamb." Maurice, to whom he already knew he would say nothing of this heartbreaking meeting, of which nothing remained.

Less than nothing. More like an intolerable feeling of abandonment, though he couldn't say just who had abandoned whom: he, Elie, by allowing Volodya to get into the tarpaulin-covered truck that was taking him back to the Ukraine; or Volodya, by leaving Elie in the doorway of a Paris bistro that had once been the home of someone called La Fontaine, who for all he knew might have been a general, a prince, a poet or an alchemist from days buried in a History of France he had never learned.

They walked toward the Métro.

"My cousin Volodya was really well dressed. Much better than in the old days . . . " he said suddenly.

"Yes, very well dressed. Actually, they all were," said Monsieur Florian.

"He must have thought I looked funny in my old leather jacket. If I'd known, I'd have gotten dressed up, too, this morning, in my suit . . . "

"You were fine, Monsieur Guttman."

"No, I looked *poor*," insisted Elie.

Monsieur Florian said nothing. Especially not that the double-breasted suits worn by the Ukrainians were much too similar and much too new not to have been distributed to them as they were leaving. Nor that he had seen the one-legged man empty the sugar bowl of Les Trois Marches into the depths of the very new pocket of his international traveler's outfit.

As they were going down the steps at the Châtelet Métro, Elie remembered he had forgotten his satchel and his lunch pail at the Mercier shop.

"Sonia will give me hell!" he said, laughing.

Sonia . . . What would he tell Sonia, and what would she think when he told her that Volodya had left without ever having really come, that he hadn't done it on purpose, that it wasn't his fault, nor his, Elie's, fault, but that everything was fine and they were going to write to each other . . .

He was right to be worried.

: :

SONIA HAD taken things very badly.

She had accepted them as true, but had judged them to be unacceptable.

As did Stépan and Olga, but they had merely said it was "strange," so as not to add to Sonia's bitterness.

And Elie had waited until he was in the darkness of the bedroom before giving way to a real grief that had little by little transformed itself into vague allusions to possible returns to the vast plains, to the birch forests in which the new men were building new cities for new lives, lives undreamed of by the people in France.

Sonia listened. And even in the dark, she could see what he was getting at.

She listened to him at the same time as she listened to the silence of her street, the familiar creaking of her house.

And she touched the rosewood of their bed, which matched that of the mirrored armoire and the two chairs—bought on the installment plan at Le Bucheron and finally paid for. She touched wood so as to guard against the DANGER sign she imagined poised over their heads.

And she, who was never vulgar, had summed things up so coarsely that she was herself as astonished as Elie. What it came down to was this: Whites, Reds, Greens or Yellows; Jews or non-Jews; Ukrainians and especially that pig Volodya could all go fuck themselves! And Elie Guttman could join them if he missed them so much. For her part, she was staying home, right there in France, with her son, the little French-man. And now she was going to get some sleep, and since he had forgotten his lunch pail, tomorrow he could just make himself a sandwich or go to a bistro.

Elie hadn't said another word about a return, or even about a trip as visitors. He hadn't said another word about anything, and he had finally fallen asleep facing the wall, since his wife had turned her back to him.

: :

THE NEXT MORNING the news vendors at Les Pyrénées were already anouncing Samuel Schwarzbard's acquittal.

Elie and Stépan were so happy that this was the only thing they could make out from the cacophony of the different headlines being shouted. And during the Métro ride, Elie scarcely thought about Volodya, who must still have been rolling between snow-covered tracks, unaware that in Paris, right opposite Les Trois Marches, during the night, twelve French citizens had established the innocence of this unknown brother who had avenged him, him and his own. In the name of his own who weren't even any longer his own.

And Elie was feeling very proud of the Ukrainian-born naturalized Frenchman Samuel Schwarzbard as he opened the door to the Mercier Frères shop, very proud of the French-born Henry Torrès and very proud of the honest French jurors and of France in general. He really wanted to say as much to his co-workers.

Unfortunately, reality had again decided differently. At Mercier Frères, the news of the day that day was something else—something neither he nor Stépan had heard among the vendors' shouts.

During the night, off the coast of Bahia, in Brazil, the *Principessa Mafalda*, an Italian steamer, had sunk with thirteen hundred people on board . . . So instead of talking about the living man whose head had been saved, they preferred to talk about the dead whose bodies had not been recovered. And about all those other dead whose bodies had never been found: those on the *Titanic* and the *Lusitania*, those on the *Medusa* and its raft, and about the sharks, and the swordfish and the cabin boys who were so young and tender that the others hadn't even waited for the sharks but had drawn straws for them, like black cannibals, and speaking of blacks . . . the newspaper had been wrong last week, it was in Rio de Janeiro and not in Buenos Aires that the aviators Coste and Le Brix had landed after their flight from Paris. It's the same general

area, but even so, they should be more careful and get things right
. . . Sometimes it might be serious . . .

"Are you sure they didn't make a mistake with that Russki of yours?"
Meunier suddenly asked Elie, struck by the fact that Lilyich seemed
quiet and abstracted.

"No, they didn't make a mistake, and at noon I'm standing everybody a drink at the bistro," Elie had said with a smile.

And as he smiled, he thought that Sonia had certainly been right.
This was where they belonged.

$\mathcal{O}$ONIA HAD NEVER again spoken of Volodya. Except to Olga, when she congratulated herself on not having ever mentioned the matter to Madame Lowenthal, who would have made a fuss, nor to the Cléments, whom they still didn't know well enough. She hadn't, however, taken Volodya's photo out of The Family Picture Frame. Little by little it had been covered over, first about half of it, then, after the addition of Maddy, completely.

She had even agreed to pose with Elie and Maurice for a photo Stépan had taken in front of the house, a photo that Elie slipped into the first of the letters he sent to B-7, the new village near the old city of Poltava, in the new P-8 district.

In his second letter, he complained of not having received an answer to his first, but he had nevertheless included a drawing Maurice had made of his school.

In his third letter, which he'd made very short, he was really angry.

There had been no fourth letter.

And Stépan never mentioned Volodya again either. In any case, never in front of Sonia.

Which didn't mean he never thought about him. But when he did, it wasn't deliberately and it wasn't so much about Volodya as about the Ukraine, or rather about what everyone called either Russia, the Bolsheviks or the Soviet Union, depending on what they thought and said about it.

Like Félix, for example, who thought about it and spoke about it more and more positively as the years went by.

Elie was quite willing to believe Félix, whom he liked and respected, but he would have preferred to have more direct information. And why not in the form of answers to the three letters he'd sent, letters that seemed to have gone astray, since they'd never been returned to the sender even though his name had been clearly legible on the back of the envelope? And because Félix, after all, was in a position to know, he had one day taken up the topic of the Post Office with him.

Félix had admitted that the question of mail delivery left a lot to be desired over there, but that things weren't so easy in such a vast country, where people were beginning to learn to read at the same time they were discovering they could replace rag wrappings with shoes and boots for marching in the snow . . . "They're a hundred years behind, my poor Guttman—you know what that means?"

Oh yes, oh yes, Elie knew quite well what it meant, and he knew there were good reasons for it. Especially when it came to boots. He had made boots when he was there, and he knew that it wasn't poor people who wore them . . . Nevertheless, he wouldn't have thought they'd choose illiterates to take care of delivering letters . . . And he'd jokingly said so to Félix.

Félix hadn't really laughed that day. Then he'd said that everywhere in the world people failed to answer letters that had been sent them. He ought to know. Everywhere in the world there were people who were careless or indifferent. Maybe fewer of them over there than elsewhere . . . But over there, there was so much work to do that maybe they didn't have time to write. Especially to those who weren't taking part in the work that still had to be done . . .

Félix hadn't said it nastily, but Elie had thought he heard a slight reprimand which, for the space of a second, had reminded him of the interpreter Dmitri. Minus the accent, of course.

Immediately after, to close the "correspondence" discussion on an optimistic note, Félix had called out in a joyously prophetic voice, "Don't worry about it . . . As we say *chez nous*, no news is good news!"

And that was the day when for the first time Elie had asked himself exactly where these *chez nous* of Félix's were, since in the future the various uses of the expression were to puzzle him, Stépan and their wives.

He'd hesitated between locating it in Savoy, in the Post Office or just in France. He had opted finally for France, and adopted this optimistic philosophy as his own. To "no news is good news" he'd grafted "out of sight, out of mind," another much-used *chez nous* expression he'd picked up at Mercier Frères. Placed end to end, they made good answers to the questions he'd ask himself whenever he happened to think of Volodya. Of whom he never spoke.

: :

YEARS HAD PASSED. It had taken Bonnet's departure and his alarming farewell discourse—in fact, it had taken Alexandre Stavisky, Adolf Hitler, Léon Daudet, Joseph Stalin, Maurice Thorez, Jacques Doriot, André Gide and Félix Clément to make him speak of Volodya again. It was on an evening when he thought that he'd be alone with Stépan, and Maurice had come in just as they had begun to ask themselves real questions about "no news from the Ukraine is good news"—reassuring when you compared it to "bad news from Poland and worse news from Germany," so bad that Elie was comforted by his certainty that at least in the Ukraine you *'bsolutely* didn't have to worry about being Jewish.

"But maybe you still have to worry about being Ukrainian?" Stépan had suggested.

It was a funny thing to say. It's true that Stépan had drunk two glasses of Julien Damoy champagne at the Bonnets'.

"Or maybe nobody in the Ukraine is worried for the simple reason that everybody is dead . . . without letting us know, like Volodya, who is always dying and never writes!"

Elie had been about to tell Stépan that the mixture of champagne and vodka had really gotten to him when Maurice had come in with his story about wanting a room of his own.

Needless to say, they had changed the subject.

And the next morning, as they rode to work, Stépan had admitted that he no longer remembered what he had said the night before.

Then months had passed. And they had gone into a nasty period. A period when, on rue d'Aboukir, you again worried about being Jewish and still Polish, Bulgarian, Slovak, Hungarian or Ukrainian even though you were in Paris. So as for Volodya and the silences from the Ukraine . . .

Then Stépan had shaken off the Aboukir nightmare and been admitted to the delightful Chateaubriand garden, where no one worried, had worried or would ever worry about anything except the possible whims of a difficult actress or the bad dye job on a piece of lace that didn't go well with a rabbit-chinchilla trimming. Of course, that didn't keep him from thinking about all those who were afraid elsewhere. Even if he had tried to forget them, he wouldn't have been able to, since it took only a Pierre Richard-Willm to remind him of them.

But all the same it was more agreeable to exchange pleasantries with Pierre Richard-Willm than to argue with Jiri, and it was more amusing to imagine Frédéric Chopin humming in Yiddish as he sat at his piano than to have to submit, every day at the same hour, to the reading of three contradictory editorials from the *Kadimah*, the *Pariser Haint*, and the *Naïe Presse*

It was also a lot more educational. After two months at the Coop, he'd caught up on his French. Now he spoke almost as well as Elie did.

"You're becoming a *goy*, a real *goy*," Elie had said to him one morning, laughing and speaking in Yiddish (in Yiddish only because it wouldn't have sounded funny in French).

Because unless they had something very serious to say to each other, they spoke French together in the Métro. That dated from the time the "Germans" had begun pouring in: they didn't want to be taken for what they weren't. They didn't want to be called dirty Huns, as had happened once just as they were getting off the train.

: :

BUT ON THAT particular Sunday, on the sun-flooded terrace of the rue des Pyrénées café they had chosen because they knew no one there and no one there knew them, it was in Yiddish that they had once again spoken of Volodya. In Yiddish and in low voices. And from the strange way that Elie had announced he had finally received some news, Stépan had understood it wasn't good.

To say that the news was recent was only a manner of speaking and of referring to the postmark—March 17, 1936—on the envelope Elie had taken from his pocket.

The news didn't come from the Ukraine, but from Zurich. The letter Elie handed to Stépan was typed in French on white paper so thin it was almost transparent. Stépan had to spread it on the marble café table and bend down to read it. He began, and immediately raised his head to look at Elie, who signaled him to go on.

This is what that letter, which had neither letterhead nor address, said:

Monsieur,

I regret to inform you of the death of Monsieur Vladimir Guttman in March 1929 in the Irkutsk region.

Only just back from a business trip to the USSR, I hasten to carry out this painful mission confided to me over there by a "work" companion of Monsieur Vladimir Guttman, who for reasons you will no doubt understand was for many years unable to send you this sad news himself.

This gentleman, who is now back in Moscow, urgently asked that I let you know that for the almost two years they spent next to each other, Monsieur Vladimir Guttman often spoke of you, and that his last thoughts before dying were of his cousins in Paris.

The gentleman gave me the enclosed paper, thanks to which I was able to do what he requested.

Please accept my respects and sincere condolences.

It was signed Duchaud, or Duchard or Duchand—impossible to say which: the writer or his secretary had forgotten to type the name under his businessman's signature.

"And here's the paper," said Elie, taking from his wallet something grayish and about the size of a sugar cube.

Once unfolded, the half of the square-ruled page torn from Dmitri's red notebook was impeccably clean on the inside, the printed letters drawn by Elie perfectly legible. Except that they were broken at the folds.

"What was he doing in Irkutsk?" asked Stépan, after having checked the word in the letter from Monsieur Duchaud, or Duchard or Duchand . . . "And where is Irkutsk?"

"I don't know . . . I don't know anything," Elie replied, replacing in his wallet the small dirty square that automatically refolded itself. "Maybe it's a new city . . . "

"So when you wrote to him at Poltava, he probably wasn't there anymore?"

"Yes, probably . . . "

"He might have sent you his new address!"

"That's just what Sonia said last night, when I told her that Volodya was dead."

"And why couldn't his friend write himself to tell you that Volodya was dead?"

"They still don't know how to read or write over there," said Elie after a brief silence.

"That's not the only place!" Stépan concluded.

This made Elie laugh. He wasn't despairing, only sad.

Only sad because the so-recent news was too old to grieve over. Volodya was dead. That meant they'd never again have to wait for news of Volodya.

It was almost like a weight taken off his shoulders. Not that it had weighed all that heavily during the nine years in which "no news is good news" had worked very well.

Now that they knew, they'd realize that "no news" didn't always mean "good news," just as they'd realize that "out of sight" didn't always mean "out of mind."

They'd know that in these old folk sayings used *chez nous*, there was often, as Félix used to say, "food for thought."

What they didn't know and would never know was what Volodya had gone to do in Irkutsk right after his return from Paris—at least if the dates indicated by Monsieur D. were correct. It was mostly of this that they spoke as they walked to the public baths.

When they came out, they felt so fresh and clean that they talked about other things. Even about the two girls who rode by on their bicycles, their skirts billowing. It was spring on rue des Pyrénées. And on rue de la Mare, the Auvergnat had put out his three chairs.

They drank an Amer-Picon with Gromoff, who was sunning himself as he waited for Barsky and read *Paris-Longchamps*.

V

LIFE IS
BEAUTIFUL!

I T COULDN'T be called a procession, nor could it be called a demonstration. It was a Sea. An Ocean.

They dived into it together: the Cléments, the Guttmans, the Roginskis, the Nussbaums, the Auvergnat and even Monsieur Katz and the Sterns, who hadn't voted since they weren't French citizens. Even Gromoff and Barsky, who'd forgotten to vote. And all the children who weren't old enough to vote.

Only the Lowenthals were missing, but they'd probably voted wrong. In other words, Madame Lowenthal had made her husband vote wrong.

All rue de la Mare was on Place Gambetta that Sunday evening after the run-off vote. And all rue de la Mare loved one another, hugged one another and sang to celebrate their victory. Elie and Stépan looked at each other with tears in their eyes and pounded each other on the back when the election results tumbled triumphantly from the loudspeaker installed on the second floor in the *Mairie* of the XXth.

"This is the happiest day of my life!" Elie shouted suddenly in Yiddish.

"This is the happiest day of my life!" was also heard in Italian. This from Monsieur Benedetti, who was nearby.

It was no accident that each proclaimed his joy in his native tongue: it was, as one says, a cry from the heart. It was what they used to celebrate the victory of what they had every right to call *their* France, since it was the France they had picked for themselves.

And they sang "The Internationale" like everyone else, for once without being afraid of getting the words all wrong. When they blundered, no one looked at them strangely. They had the right to do anything, since that evening they were brothers.

And that's what they kept saying to themselves at the Auvergnat's café until late in the night, while the owner stood the men drinks.

The women and children had returned to their apartments. The Sterns had returned to theirs. And Maurice, Robert and Sami to the Bonnets'.

: :

"YES, I KNOW it's a celebration . . . Congratulations, Papa! But since neither Blum nor Thorez is going to take my bac exam for me, I'm leaving!" Sami had said to Monsieur Nussbaum after an hour or so spent with the family on Place Gambetta. And he had sounded.

And had been heard. Even in the middle of an angry or delirious crowd, even in the uproar of a turbulent classroom, in the silence of a study hall or the din of the Métro—when clearly whistled, the first eight notes of the Laurel and Hardy theme never failed.

They'd finished their reviewing and were now talking and drinking Phoscao.

They'd started drinking Phoscao several weeks earlier. First, because Sonia had made a scene one morning when she'd gone to make Alex's coffee and found the package of Corcelet three-quarters empty. Second, because Phoscao contained phosphorus, and because phosphorus is good for the brain and the memory.

They were talking about *Man's Fate*, which Sami had now discovered, and it was he who was doing most of the talking. He was still at the beginning of the book and thought May was "pretty sharp and very sexy, but a bit of a slut just the same, for having slept with Langlen and especially for having gone and told Kyo, who got all cut up about it at a time that really wasn't the right time . . . "

"Just wait . . . " Maurice and Robert had said simultaneously. "Just wait! That's not what the book's about, you'll see!" And they'd looked at each other like accomplices who are in on the same secrets. They too had taken the same route, at the end of which they'd been dazzled and bruised by the life and death of heroes their friend had not yet met. They'd almost envied him for being just at the beginning of the journey.

"Just wait, you'll see . . . And the antiquarian's shop, and the train whistles . . . " said Maurice.

"And the cyanide . . . " said Robert.

"Shut up!" said Sami, who'd plugged his ears. "Don't tell me . . . "

"You talk too much, my dear Ch'en! You're annoying our friend, who still doesn't understand the Shanghai dialect," snickered Robert, when Sami had taken his hands from his ears.

"Assholes!" Sami laughed. He too had just discovered the game, but he still didn't have enough of the clues to play it properly. "Goodnight, you two, I'm going to bed. See you tomorrow," he said, loading his books under his arm. And as usual, he slammed the door of "the Bonnets'."

It was too late to read. Now it was Jack London's *Martin Eden* that was on the chair between the two beds and wore the little yellow Chinese hat.

An accordion could be heard in the distance.

They were almost asleep when they also heard the men return home from the Auvergnat's.

"It sounds like the old boys have slugged down a few to celebrate their taking the Bastille!" said Robert.

"They couldn't be happier," replied Maurice. "I've never seen mine like that. He made me want to bawl . . . "

"Wait until the evening after the bac—we'll need bedsheets to mop up the floor after they've finished crying around here . . . " said Robert, going him one better. "Especially if we flunk it!"

"Fathead!" Maurice yelled out, doubling over with laughter as he touched the rosewood of the chair.

"You're not only vulgar but superstitious, Guttman! Well, I've often threatened to, but this time I'm really going to do it . . . "

"I know, you're finally going to complain to the concierge, right, Clément?"

" 'bsolutely, Guttman, and things may go pretty high up, pretty high up . . . as high up as the third floor, for example. Or maybe even higher. Can't you guess, Guttman? Afraid to answer, Guttman? What could be higher than the third floor? Come on, Guttman, think a little . . . An eye, a smashed eye that looks down at you from the sky . . . "

"You don't mean the Doctor's eye?"

"Dr. Pierre! Exactly, Guttman! But we won't go any further this evening . . . Please, let's get a little sleep."

"Oh, it feels good to laugh, but it *hurts*, " complained Maurice when he could finally speak.

"When I'm around, things are never boring—someday you'll realize that. But it'll probably be too late, comrade!"

"Do you think Sami and Jeannot have as much fun at night in their place as we do here?"

"Nobody has as much fun as we do, especially not Jeannot, who never has any fun. He doesn't even want to read with Sami. He says books are dumb. You can imagine how he feels about the bac."

There was a short silence.

"I mustn't flunk, I mustn't flunk. It would make my father look bad at the Merciers'," said Maurice.

"And what about mine? You think it'd make him look good at the Post Office?"

"And then there's Florian. He'd be really miserable if we mucked it up."

"Right. It'd be awful for him."

"He'd look bad, too. Well, old buddy, that certainly makes a lot of people who'd look bad!" sighed Maurice.

"Especially if you add the two of us. Because if we don't make it, we're the ones who'll look worst of all!" mumbled Robert, with a long yawn that announced the definitive end of their discussion.

The end for that evening, at least—though they weren't fooled. They knew that one way or another they'd begin again the next day, and the day after that, too, and every evening until the very last one: the one that would come before the night that would come before the morning when they'd get out of bed and say, "This is it—the time has come."

For months, every evening as they fell asleep they'd been thinking only of that morning. The morning of the execution. And they still didn't know if they'd greet it with a strut or with a stumble.

The history books they'd been leafing through since childhood were filled with pictures of condemned men either strutting or stumbling in front of gallows, execution squads or guillotines.

"The question is whether we'll be Marshal Ney or Madame Du Barry," Robert would say when Maurice kept repeating that they'd have the jitters when they woke up on the morning of June 22.

In exactly forty-nine days.

No, forty-eight now. It must have struck midnight, and firecrackers were being set off in the distance. They exploded between the arpeggios of the accordion playing a *pasodoble*.

THERE WAS NO accordionist on the platform at Les Pyrénées, nor in the Métro car Stepan and Elie took to work the next morning, but it felt like it. The celebration was still going on, as could be seen from the faces of the passengers and even of the ticket-punchers.

It was also going on at Mercier Frères, where things were even more cheerful because Monsieur Julien had just come home from a trip.

"Right in time to vote so that I wouldn't catch hell from Paul. Apparently it's because I wasn't there for the first round that we needed a recount. So I jumped on the first available boat, got here and saved the situation. Thank me, my friends, and let's raise a glass!"

Considering the hour at which they were beginning, it was clear that a lot of glasses were going to be raised at Mercier Frères.

Monsieur's Julien's little speech inspired one from Meunier. He too had taken a boat yesterday, but it was to go fishing, since he wasn't voting. But he'd be glad to raise his glass with Monsieur Julien anyway, if Monsieur Paul would guarantee him that the wretched of the earth would all buy crocodile bags and peccary dressing cases before going off on their paid vacations . . .

Inevitably, he sang *"La Butte Rouge,"* and the others sang along with him because it was certainly the day for it and because no one really believed he had gone fishing.

Nor that "cro-cro" would no longer sell. All you had to do was see what Monsieur Julien had brought back from Africa: it certainly wasn't the sort of thing you could sell in an inexpensive store like the Samaritaine.

They were cheerful in the Allée Chateaubriand, but then they were rarely sad there, anyway, for things had been going very well and Mademoiselle Agnès was no longer acting like an old dragon.

So the first day of Year I of the Popular Front caused hardly any upheavals in the atmosphere of the firm, except possibly that the young girls in the shop seemed a little more tired than on other Mondays because they'd danced late into the night with their boyfriends, their brothers and, for once, their papas.

Mademoiselle Agnès hadn't danced with anyone. She was cheerful because it was Monday. Her Sunday had gone by as slowly as all her other Sundays. To come back to a Stépan who seemed so happy made her even more cheerful than on other Mondays. And so that no one would know, she voiced her joy at the risk of betraying her oldest convictions: "I'm laughing because I'm thinking of the expressions on the faces of customers at Lanvin this morning . . . " This wasn't very kind to her sister, whom she had almost rejoined on the faubourg Saint-Honoré before opting for the Cooperative.

Mademoiselle Anita was pleased because she was thinking about her father, who would have been pleased if he had lived long enough to see all this. From a distance she greeted Stépan, and the smile he returned from a distance told her the extent to which they were both thinking of the same thing. Of the joy they shared that morning in being elsewhere than on the first and second floors of rue d'Aboukir, where, if people were pleased, they probably had to hide before they could say so.

Ginette was radiant, but her reasons were also personal: Renoir's assistant—the handsome (they were all handsome, but he was the most handsome) Italian, Luchino—had returned to borrow some coats and blouses for the filming of *La Vie est à nous*, and on leaving, he'd said: "Thank you, *cara*, you're the prettiest of the lot . . . " and had kissed her hand. She *was* pretty, and though she'd received compliments of all sorts—some more subtle than others—this was the first in a long time that had so affected her.

"In Italy, they like their goddesses to be plump," Alex had commented guardedly; he had no desire to destroy her illusions. He was in too good a humor for that.

As inventor, promoter and creator of the Coop, Alex felt like a pioneer on that particular morning. He even had a tender thought for old Madame Leblanc, and felt a scrap of sorrow and regret for Maddy.

As for Monsieur Anselmo, the little nook in which he worked behind the fur storage was so separated from everything else that no one knew if he was pleased or not.

At noon, the Coop shared a drink during dessert at Raymonde and André's with the waitress and Madame Raymonde, but without Alex, who was lunching at Fouquet's. The waitress was in seventh heaven, but Stépan thought Madame Raymonde looked a little worried. Could it be because of Monsieur André? He hadn't come out of his kitchen to join in the loving cup.

"I'm not about to begin loafing today, even if it seems to be the new fashion!" they'd heard through a great clatter of pots and pans, despite the fact that the rush hour had been over for a long time.

For so long that Mademoiselle Anita looked at her watch and gave the signal to leave.

"Didn't your boss come to work today?" said the waitress in a low voice as she gathered up the empty glasses.

"Monsieur Alex isn't our boss. We don't have a boss. *We're* the bosses of the Coop!" said the girls, getting up with a loud scraping of chairs.

"Isn't that something!" said the waitress, who had finally understood that *Coopé* wasn't an abbreviation for *Coppélia* as she'd always thought, because of all the talk about tulle, mousseline and tarlatan she'd overheard while passing plates at their table.

The bossless ones crossed rue Washington two by two the way they do at boarding schools, and entered the peaceful little Allée at the end of which the most amusing, the least dirtying, the least degrading and the most inoffensive of daily tasks awaited them.

It was so beautiful outside that they worked with the windows open. They could hear the sparrows chirping in the flowering bushes.

: :

TOWARD SIX O'CLOCK that afternoon the bucolic chirping began to be overpowered by waves of distant rumbling. By leaning out the window the cooperators could place them: they came from the Champs-Elysées.

The excitement that reigned near the George V Métro station when Stépan tried to get near it half an hour later had nothing in common with the excitement that had transformed Place Gambetta into a carnival the night before.

Here, too, one could speak of the Sea. Of the Ocean. In fact, the words that particularly came to mind again were "demonstration" and "procession." Now it was a martial procession that made it so difficult to get to the Métro entrance.

Stépan, blocked as he was at the corner of rue Balzac, watched the marchers go up the Champs-Elysées, flowers in their arms and on their lips a "Marseillaise" sung in a way that made him feel he was hearing it for the first time.

He had heard the "Marseillaise" sung many times in his short life as a naturalized Frenchman, but generally only in bits and pieces, as part of the noisy confrontations of the last few months and always in the neighborhood of Place de la République or Place de la Nation—never on the Champs-Elysées, and never in its entirety. And never sung with one voice by so many people.

He found it impressive.

A true connoisseur, an expert in the "Marseillaise," would have gone well beyond this innocent appreciation. The scholar studying the interpretation given it that May 4, 1936, between six-thirty and eight o'clock on the Champs-Elysées, could not have failed to observe that this was the most striking manifestation of what was already being called in certain enlightened circles (well before the formula reached the streets) the spontaneous phenomenon of a *rereading* of the work of Claude-Joseph Rouget de Lisle. This rereading became obvious in the well-known passage about *sang impur,* "impure blood," which the marchers shouted out as one word, *sanguimpur.* The fact was that other singers of the "Marseillaise," bogged down no doubt in the routine of flag-waving commemorations, persisted in always placing the accent on the fact that these howling enemies, fierce and ready to murder French sons and sweethearts, were soldiers, soldiers of a foreign army whose streaming hordes were endangering the Republic. The virtue of these particular singers was that they shook up the routine: it was no longer those who wore the uniform of some army or other who were being denounced, but the impurity of the blood running in the veins of an enemy who was not specified as military but who was, according to all the signs, endangering France. This impure blood no longer circulated under tunics and military medals, and, if it came from abroad, it was not with flashing sabers it had forced France's borders. And it was to make this blood flow, because it was impure, that the singers called for arms. It was so that they could become soldiers themselves. Soldiers of an army without uniforms, but one in whose veins streamed the purest of bloods.

Such would have been the conclusions of our scholar when faced with this revolutionary interpretation, which—without changing a line of the original text—threw a new light on intentions that until then had been badly understood.

Stépan was not that scholar. He found this "Marseillaise" impressive because he was impressed by those who were singing it. By their fervor, their determination and, above all, their number.

But the new light brought by this rereading of the theme of *sanguim-pur* illuminated nothing for him. The enigma remained. And as he tried to work his way toward the entrance to his Métro station, he once more wondered about the meaning of those three mysterious syllables, which on that particular evening were being howled in a louder voice than usual.

He had never dared to ask that they be explained to him. He had eventually contrived an explanation of his own, but it seemed so shaky he'd never discussed it with anyone. As he tried to construct the syllables, they seemed to spell *sans-guimpures,* and it occurred to him that maybe these sans-guimpures were a peasant version of the Revolutionary *sans-culottes* who were assigned by their fellow citizens to cultivate the land, which was so poor at the time. They didn't even *have guim-pures* to wear, but nevertheless they watered the land for the good of everyone. Could this be it?

Anyway, it would have to do by way of explanation, at least for the few times he heard the "Marseillaise."

There were many other expressions which neither he nor Elie really understood, but he didn't want to ask the children to explain lest they laugh at him, the way they had the time it was raining so hard and he'd said it was "raining Katzen dogs" . . . Even yesterday, on Place Gambetta, he'd again wondered how they could "join hands" when they were brandishing clenched fists.

He managed to get his train after having elbowed his way down the stairs and onto the platform. He backed into an already crowded car and remained pressed against the door. He could see the passengers reflected in the glass. They didn't look anything like those who'd got on in the morning at Les Pyrénées. They seemed indifferent rather than pleased, and unaware of what was happening up there above their indifferent heads. The rhythmic steps of the marchers didn't reach below ground; their voices carried no further than the Unknown Soldier's tomb, which they were going to bedeck with flowers.

These passengers came from too far away to have heard the marchers, some of them even from Pont de Neuilly. And for just a second Stépan once more thought of Janek, as he did every evening, because of the board displaying the map of the stops on the Vincennes-Neuilly line.

Where was Janek this evening, and what was he thinking about?

Someone behind him said, "Excuse me, Monsieur," just as the train was coming into the Concorde station. Stépan got off to let two women out. In their buttonholes they wore a charming assortment of royal blue, ivory white, and poppy-red satin ribbons. They murmured "Thank you, Monsieur," and Stépan got back on the train.

It occurred to him that they were going to be caught up in the crush of the demonstration when they got out at Place de la Concorde. Then it occurred to him that maybe they were going to meet their husbands and join the march, just as, yesterday, Olga, Sonia and all the wives of the men on rue de la Mare had followed their husbands to Place Gambetta.

And he thought again of that crowd up there, which had awakened this morning in a France that was no longer what it had been yesterday, and certainly not what they had wanted for the future. There hadn't been enough of those people, and they had lost. Stépan belonged with those who had won. Not against the crowd up above, but for and with the others.

As for those others, the losers, he didn't know them. He'd really just met them for the first time in his life, and the way they preferred—as a group and on their own ground. They didn't seem at all defeated to look at them, Stépan told himself, thinking he was probably the only one on rue de la Mare to have run into them that day.

He was in a hurry to get to Châtelet and change from the Vincennes-Neuilly line. Especially since at Palais-Royal an old woman wearing a lot of makeup had got on, preceded by two enormous breasts between which she too had pinned a blue-white-and-red bouquet, but this time it was made of artificial flowers that unhappily reminded Stépan of the ground floor of Galeries Lafayette.

As he was changing trains, he thought of Jiri. Not that he suddenly felt kindly toward him, but he told himself that Jiri couldn't vote, and that wasn't fair. He also wondered if Jiri had found work.

Finally he got "home," where the celebration was still going on. There were even fire eaters and mandolin players at the top of the steps at Les Pyrénées.

: :

THE CELEBRATION went on and on in the weeks that followed, in the hearts and in the streets of the quarter, which was decked out like a bride with an interminable train of turkey-red cotton and a wreath of red roses and carnations. And to keep the train and the flowers fresh, something had to be celebrated every day, and every day they found something to celebrate.

The glorious past of the people of Paris and of the whole of France was rich, and it could be drawn upon endlessly. From it they also learned about impatience and strikes. But the gendarmes fired neither on the strikers nor on the sidewalk performers who came to amuse them on the site.

During the week, as on Sundays, the nights were streaked with lights over the XXth arrondissement. But the play of light was nothing more than will-o'-the-wisps, Catherine wheels or Bengal lights from the subprefecture in comparison with the fireworks display that took place one evening on rue de la Mare, and whose finale lit up the entire Parisian sky with its streaming multicolored showers.

A few hours before the celebration, a quasi-biblical scene had greeted the homecoming of the newly graduated son (baccalaureate, first part, section A).

"This is the happiest day of my life!" the Father had exclaimed to the Son.

"Again! . . . But that's the second happiest day of your life in six weeks! You're going to have to make up your mind, Papa!" the Son had said to the Father.

"No, this one is my first happiest day! The other belonged to everyone, this one is mine. Mine and your mother's!"

And the Father had taken the Mother and the Son into his open arms. And the tears had flowed.

This scene took place in the Guttman dining room, but the same scene, or a very similar one, was being enacted at that very moment in the Clément loge and, a little farther away, in the Nussbaum apartment. Maurice, Robert and Sami were the first in the whole cluster of houses to pass the first part of the baccalaureate (section A).

The forty-eight-day countdown separating the two happiest days in Elie Guttman's life had become more and more agonizing for the Guttman, Clément and Nussbaum sons. To give themselves courage, Maurice and Robert, before falling asleep, had indulged in dialogues whose childishness increased as the day when they would have to prove their maturity and the depth of their knowledge drew closer.

"It's not Phoscao we need, it's Blédine—the stuff they fed us when we were babies!"

"We'll end up going *gurgle-gurgle,* and that'll really be a joke!" Robert had said one evening.

It was June 19, three nights before the fatal dawn.

They'd laughed like madmen.

Then, on June 22, they had woken up strangely calm. And from that moment on, everything had happened not as though in a dream, not even as in a nightmare, but exactly the way things happen when you have your feet firmly planted on the ground and a secure head on your shoulders, full of things you know to a T because you've learned them thoroughly and understood them well.

For them, the Adventure wasn't in the written or oral questions, which they were able to answer, but in the voyage to the heart of the Citadel of Learning.

The Adventure was the Sorbonne, its statues and its ushers, the Capoulade and the Dupont-Latin cafés, with their *céleri rémoulade*s and their waiters.

The student snake dances and the student rah-rah boys . . .

Especially one roisterer who sported a beret and must have passed his bac in 1922, if he had ever passed it, and whose "Form the snake, form the snake, form the snake"—to the rhythm of stamping feet as he twirled a knobbed cane—rapidly became "Popular Front, Fuckular Front, we'll kick your asses," without any musical accompaniment at all. It was then that the Adventure had ended for Maurice and Robert, and they had left the ranks of Gentlemen Scholars, which the eternal student's cane was now directing toward the Chamber of Deputies.

They'd reached the corner of the boulevard Saint-Michel and the quai des Grands-Augustins. Great: there was a Métro entrance just in front of them.

: :

VERY SHORTLY after their return home, the news had spread that the heroes were back. And what happened then was to remain in the memories of the neighborhood for a long time.

It was something like the "garden party" and the "open house" that the special Hollywood correspondents of *Pour Vous* and *Cinémonde* liked to write about in the weekly reports Zaza and Josette would gobble up greedily. It was from them—rather than from the solid basis provided by reading *Alice's Family*—that they absorbed the rudiments of their Anglo-Saxon culture.

Alice's Family was part of the syllabus taught by Mademoiselle Delacroix. It gave a detailed account of the daily life of a young English girl and her family in a nice house in a nice London suburb, and the only thing that seemed to spice the tranquil monotony of the happy days lived by Alice, Tom (her young brother) and Mr. and Mrs. Smith (their parents) was the incredible number of irregular verbs used by the members of this family to express the simplest things. The "garden" of the Smith home was too small for "parties," and the single door of the "cottage" was too narrow to open to anything or anyone but the immediate neighbors, who were called the Simpsons and who visited the Smiths only two Saturdays out of four, the other two being reserved for "Grannie" Smith, who lived in London itself. Visits to "Grannie" Smith furnished the occasion for interesting discoveries: Trafalgar Square, Hyde Park, and the "Bloody Tower"—as well as, needless to say, new meetings with new irregular verbs.

In *Pour Vous* and *Cinémonde*, the "gardens" were "parks" with innumerable paths, and the "cottages" were "mansions" or "bungalows" with doorways that were so numerous and so wide that they were open to everyone on the evenings of "garden parties," during which the eminent correspondents of the two magazines always seemed to be in friendly and privileged conversation with the man or woman in whose honor the "party" was being given. And their accounts always ended with the complete list of those lucky guests with whom they had "gossiped" informally or even, on occasion, danced, thanks to the orchestra hidden among the palms, the cedars and the sycamores.

"*Yes! Everybody in town was there,* or if you prefer, All-Hollywood was present, including, of course, yours truly, who now says, '*See you next week!*' " Such was the magic formula with which the author would generally conclude his prestigious reports, dropping English words here and there.

Well, it would have to be said that on that evening "all rue de la Mare was there." And number 58 held "open house," from the ground floor to the third, with doors and windows wide open and the street itself like the Main Walk of a "park" in which strolled those who had not yet been able to enter—or those who were coming out of—the Bonnets', where there was a "party" that was about to turn into a "surprise party," the guests who had invited themselves bringing food and drink. And music to dance by.

For several weeks they had been in the habit of celebrating, celebrating and re-celebrating, and they had spontaneously decided to celebrate one more time, but for once without commemorating anything.

People came to the Bonnets' to embrace, to touch and to compliment three boys who were very much alive and who might one day do honor to the nation, but who were for the time being doing honor to their parents, their friends, their teacher and their neighborhood. And it was this that they had all come to say, even those who no longer lived in the neighborhood, even those who had never lived there.

Like the Novacks, who now lived in the XIth. Or Bruno and Gino Benedetti, who were mechanics in Joinville and whom no one ever saw anymore. Or Alex, who had driven Stépan home in the Coop Citroën, which he was using for the first time.

He had brought a new phonograph and a stack of records of Jean Sablon, Mireille, Duke Ellington, Red Nichols, Fats Waller, Louis Armstrong, Georgius, Jean Tranchant, Gilles and Julien, Ray Ventura, Charlie Kuntz, and Charles and Johnny.

People were dancing to every kind of music, whether or not they knew how. Robert, Maurice and Sami scarcely knew how. But the Benedettis knew, and so did Jeannot Nussbaum—it was the nonreaders' revenge.

Zaza, Josette and their friends from the Intermediate Course were spinning around and around; it was their first ball. Myriam didn't spin at all: as soon as she'd seen the phonograph brought in, she'd raced home and taped an adhesive bandage around her ankle for a sprain she didn't have, which, she explained, she had just gotten while racing home. She preferred to talk to Sami, to look at Sami and to suffer when she saw him trying to dance with Zaza, who was dancing with everyone, even with Alex when he could spare a moment.

Because Alex had a lot to do. Like all "masters of ceremonies," as "See-you-next-week" would say.

It was he who'd been able to transform the workroom into a community-center hall. First he'd seen to the safety of the mannequins, the materials and everything that could be damaged; and to avoid the stairs, he'd stowed it all in the Stern apartment. Only afterward had the sewing machine been pushed into the kitchen and the work tables set in front of the fireplace. In the eyes of Sonia and Olga, who were watching all this happen, the room looked almost as it had at the time of the Bonnet farewell.

Little by little, on a sheet that served as a tablecloth, the offerings piled up as people began to arrive.

The small, buttered rolls, the pieces of cold chicken, the slices of roast beef, the cornichons, two tarts, goat cheeses, sugared almonds, cherries, potato-tomato salad, herrings, raspberry ices, chocolates and LU brand petit-beurres were spread out on unmatched dishes among which you could recognize platters, plates and bowls spirited from the kitchens of the Cléments, the Guttmans, the Roginskis, the Nussbaums, the Sterns and even the Lowenthals—and the glasses, too, including those the

Auvergnat had contributed, along with a small cask of white wine from his native village that stood in a place of honor amid the bottles of champagne, sparkling wines, Cinzano, Byrrh, Dubonnet, cider, vodka and pretty little bottles of fruit juices Alex had wheedled from the manager of the Pam-Pam on the corner of rue Lincoln before leaving the Champs-Elysées.

Alex was coming, going, dancing a little, opening bottles, changing records and rinsing glasses as though he had been doing it all his life. Actually, it was because he had done a lot of it that he did it so well and so happily. It made him feel ten years younger.

From time to time he'd go up to the second floor, where little by little the parents—having timidly experimented with dancing—had taken refuge and were now talking to one another of the joys and hopes their respective children had brought them, whether they were manually or intellectually inclined—a conversation that gave pleasure to all and pain to none.

Alex brought news of the children, reassured the mothers of the girls and the fathers of the boys, then went back down to keep an eye on how the drinks were being mixed.

Madame Lowenthal had stuck her head into the Bonnets'—where she had left Monsieur Lowenthal, who enjoyed winding up the phonograph and watching the young people spin around—and then had gone to stick her head into the Guttman apartment. Since she'd lent her large salad bowl, she couldn't be completely excluded from the festivities.

It was her first return to the heart of a community in which there wasn't really much for her to do. She hadn't known the joys of maternity and had just learned the bitterness of defeat. As a matter of fact, it had taken the salad bowl to renew the contact, which had been broken off since the elections. No one that evening had been unkind enough to ask her if it was his association with diamond manufacturers, for whom he did polishing work, that had led Monsieur Lowenthal to be such an unlucky voter. Yet that was what was said in the building, especially on the ground floor.

But since, during a silence, Madame Lowenthal had sighed, "How proud Madame Lutz would be of her little Maurice this evening . . . " another truth put in an appearance in the Guttman dining room, like an angel from the past.

It wasn't the diamonds, then, but the Cléments themselves—those unpardonable and inexcusable replacements for Madame Lutz—who had incited Monsieur Lowenthal to vote as he had.

"And wouldn't Madame Lutz have been proud of my Sami and of Robert?" asked Monsieur Nussbaum slyly.

"Come to think of it, what's happened to the Bonnet twins?" Jeannette Clément added, just as slyly.

"As of last month they were doing very well indeed," shot back Madame Lowenthal, rising and adding that there was no hurry about the salad bowl: tomorrow would do, assuming the little savages hadn't broken it. And she'd gone back upstairs.

Now they knew the real truth: Monsieur Lowenthal had voted like Monsieur Bonnet simply because Madame Lowenthal had never recovered from the cranial trauma Monsieur Bonnet had suffered two years ago, on February 6.

And since the rightist riots of February 6 had been mentioned, Félix inevitably mentioned the twelfth, the only one of all those February days that really mattered: the one that had sealed the sacred union against political corruption with a call for a general strike.

And naturally Félix brought up the elections again.

And the ladies moved to the Roginski dining room. Even Jeannette.

They wanted to go on talking about their children and about the radiant future opening to those who could be heard laughing and singing on the floor below, even louder than Ray Ventura and His Collegians.

: :

MAURICE WAS the first to notice Monsieur Florian. He was leaning against the doorway, not quite inside the room. He was watching and smiling, but he didn't come in.

Maurice felt himself blush and began to move toward the phonograph, but Monsieur Florian signaled to him that he was only passing by, that Maurice shouldn't stop the music but should instead come and join him on the landing.

Maurice then whistled the first notes of the Laurel and Hardy theme; Robert and Sami looked at him and, discovering Monsieur Florian in their turn, left the girls with whom they had been dancing awkwardly and went to join Maurice at Monsieur Florian's side.

Giving them each a manly shake of the hand, Monsieur Florian probably had to fight back the desire to embrace them like the sons he had never had.

"We wanted to come see you tomorrow, Monsieur," said Maurice a little loudly, because *"Tout va très bien, Madame la Marquise"* was playing on the phonograph.

"Yes, that's right, sir, we wanted to come see you," Robert and Sami confirmed.

"Won't you come in and . . . " Maurice didn't quite dare say, " . . . and have a drink?"

"No, boys, it's just chance that I'm still in the neighborhood so late in the evening. I must get home," said Monsieur Florian, with a last glance inside the room. "Aren't those the Benedettis I see jiggling up and down so sportively in the rear of the room?" he asked.

"Yes, sir," answered Maurice. "And the Novacks are here too. Shall I go get them?"

"No, my boy," Monsieur Florian said, after a slight hesitation.

"Won't you go up to my parents' apartment? I know they'd be happy to see you," Maurice suggested feebly.

"Some other time, my boy, some other time."

He bent down and picked up a package from the third step of the stairway.

"Here, you can pass these books around among yourselves during your school vacation. Because let me remind you that you're not finished: don't forget that you've only half your bac! Don't forget, because soon I'll no longer be around to remind you. I'm going to retire to my native village. Well, I must be going."

Monsieur Florian handed them the package. It was Maurice who took it.

"Thank you very much, Monsieur," they said in chorus as their former teacher started down the stairs.

: :

"MAYBE WE SHOULD have insisted," murmured Maurice.

"Oh, he didn't really want to come in," Robert said hypocritically.

"It would certainly have put a damper on things, and we couldn't have had any more fun."

"And if he'd gone upstairs, it would have put a damper on our folks. It's better this way," Maurice concluded. "We'll go to see him, to say thanks and goodbye, since he's taking off for the country."

He felt the package.

"It's books," he said.

The two others had already gone back to their partners, and Maurice opened the bedroom door to put away the parcel, which he hadn't unwrapped. On his couch, Jeannot and a girl from the intermediate course whose name he didn't even know were kissing by the light of Robert's little mushroom lamp.

"Sorry," said Maurice, tossing the package onto Robert's couch and hurrying out.

He looked around for Zaza.

She was standing in front of the buffet talking to Alex, who seemed to be listening. On coming closer, Maurice discovered that Zaza was wearing lipstick. It was badly put on—she must have done it in a hurry after her parents left. He looked among the other girls there to see if he could discover who had lent Zaza the tube of dark, cherry-red lipstick.

Actually, he didn't have to look: he knew. It was the Auvergnat's niece. She'd come with her uncle when he'd brought the barrel of wine, and had stayed on. Nobody had ever seen her around the neighborhood. She was at least eighteen or nineteen, had very black hair and eyes, big breasts under a lemon-yellow dress, orange-painted fingernails, rather thick legs, white shoes with thin straps and high heels, no stockings, and silver-painted toenails.

And her big mouth was almost black.

And right off the bat she'd danced with Jeannot Nussbaum, then a lot with Gino Benedetti, and now she was at the buffet, a glass of Cinzano in her hand, her little finger in the air, and she was watching Alex, who was watching her while pretending to be listening to Zaza.

"Want to dance?" asked Maurice, as if it had been the easiest thing to ask.

She put her glass down on the table.

"You'll be able to recognize it by your lipstick marks," said Maurice, as if it had been the easiest thing to say.

She smiled.

And as if it had been the easiest thing to do, Maurice gently placed his right hand against the lemon-yellow back, without pressing it, with just the thumb a little firm, as he had seen Gino do, and, his left arm riveted to his body, took her right wrist in his left hand, without clasping it too tightly.

The phonograph was playing a potpourri of foxtrots by Charlie Kuntz, and the Auvergnat's niece hummed all the tunes, her eyes half closed.

From time to time she'd open them and look toward Alex.

Maurice tortured himself in an effort to find something to say to her.

He had begun well enough with his allusion to the red marks left on the rim of her glass. He didn't want to descend to commonplaces. He didn't want to be pedantic, but he also didn't want to seem dopey. He felt too warm. She was wearing too much perfume. It reminded him of the mixtures that would make him and Robert snicker when the dressing room became their bedroom again. He told himself that it was more exciting to imagine things when the air was heavy with "the smell of dames" than to have a dame in your hands but have to be careful about what your feet were doing at the same time.

Robert brushed against the silent couple and whistled the first four notes of their theme. Maurice made sure the Auvergnat's niece was lost in her own dreams, turned his head toward Robert and raised his eyes to heaven: as the label promised, the "Charlie Kuntz Medley" seemed to go on forever . . .

And just then they stopped hearing it and began listening to the sound of a guitar, a banjo and singing voices coming from the stairway. It was Gromoff, Barsky and an unknown man. And everyone took up the song, because it was a tune that everyone knew, that for several weeks had been sung everywhere.

It was *"Allons au-devant la vie"*—"Let's Meet Life Head On"—but the three newcomers were singing it in Russian. Because it was a Russian song.

It drew the old-timers out onto the landing of the second floor.

It was after ten o'clock, but it was still very early and the celebration got its second wind.

T ABOUT NOON the next day, while looking for his other shoe, Maurice found Monsieur Florian's package under the bed where Robert was still sleeping.

He also found that the workshop had been put in impeccable order and looked as though nothing had happened there the previous evening.

The mothers must have been very careful not to wake the sons while setting things to rights. And the sons must have been very tired to have slept so long.

They must also have done a fair amount of tippling, since they had no memory of when or how they'd finally gotten to bed. The last thing Maurice could remember was Barsky, Gromoff and the banjo player singing *"Je sais que vous êtes jolie,"* and his father and mother dancing . . .

The rustling of the paper woke Robert.

The first of the books was Joseph Conrad's *Typhoon;* the second was Emile Zola's *The Fortune of the Rougons* and the third was André Malraux's *Man's Fate.*

"We won't tell him—we'll just exchange it without saying anything," said Maurice, carefully refolding the bookstore wrapping.

"I've got a hangover," groaned Robert, who had just understood the true sense of the expression so often encountered while reading books very unlike those their old teacher had just given them. "Who went off with the big one in lemon yellow?" he asked.

"I don't know. But is she ever dumb!" exclaimed Maurice.

Robert didn't answer, but turned his head so Maurice wouldn't see he'd noticed his blush.

"That Jeannot really knows how to come on with the girls," said Maurice.

"He should—he's got nothing else to do!" remarked Robert. "That and the flea market with old Nussbaum and Manolo . . . he must have lots of opportunities!"

"So will we," hazarded Maurice. "We won't have a damn thing else to do for the next three months."

Robert laughed, and said nothing.

: :

IT WAS THEIR mothers who had put them both to bed at about two in the morning. Contrary to what they thought—with more than a touch of vanity—they weren't as drunk as they liked to keep saying all the following day. They were intoxicated with their emotions and with accumulated exhaustion. They weren't drunk.

Actually, no one had really been drunk that evening. Not even Barsky. And Alex had definitely not been drunk when at about midnight he had very seriously suggested to Gromoff and Barsky that they temporarily work for the Coop. He had only needed to see the two of them just as they were bending over a plate of LU cookies.

This association of ideas might seem surprising, but it wouldn't have surprised either Ginette or Mademoiselle Anita. Gromoff and Barsky were exactly the men they had needed for almost a week: a driver and a prospector/middleman for the two big jobs, pieces of cake that the firm had under way.

In recent days they had done a lot of lending: not only to Jean Renoir, Grémillon, and Cavalcanti and the customers of the Chéramy and La Coupole, but also to the little groups of militant amateurs that had entertained the sit-down strikers with old songs and spoken choruses—which were not always enthusiastically received. It was more than time to think about bringing in some bread, some paying projects. And it was to find them that Alex sometimes lunched at Fouquet's, because that's where they were to be found.

He had brought back two big slices. One of them was called *The Volga Boatman*. Paradoxically, that wasn't the film Alex had been thinking of when he turned to Gromoff and Barsky; it was the other one— the one whose title he had been reluctant to tell Rodriguez before going into considerable detail about how the Coop would probably donate its services to the costuming of Renoir's *La Marseillaise,* as soon as it finished working on . . . *Grégoire, Get Your Gun!*

The Nantes biscuit manufacturer, author of *Grégoire, Get Your Gun!,* was also its sole backer. He had paid a considerable advance just before the elections, and for a time the people in charge of the cash register at Allée Chateaubriand had been afraid he was going to give up his project and ask to be reimbursed under the force majeure provisions of the agreement after May 3, and especially after May 20, when the strike had become general, even in the movies.

But Monsieur Le Goff clung to his project. He had been clinging to it for ten years, and no minor social upheaval was going to make him give up the idea of telling the epic saga of an ancestor—a baker—who had abandoned his fiancée and his oven to grab his gun, his ivory Virgin and his drinking gourd and join, at the risk of his life, in the counter-revolutionary Vendée insurrection under Monsieur de Charette.

The story ended well for Grégoire—in any case, better than for Monsieur de Charette, whom he did not accompany to his final calvary. Slightly wounded, saved, in fact, from ambush by a soldier of the Republic, he had rejoined and married his fiancée, relit his oven and become a kind of founding father of the Nantes biscuit industry, whose Pomponnette biscuits had forever after enchanted the taste buds of young and old in all of France under all her governments.

Encouraged by a friend who owned a movie theater in Vannes, Monsieur Le Goff had therefore written this family history, which he considered a keystone in the building of French regional reconciliation.

To his great astonishment, in the letters sent to Monsieur Le Goff acknowledging the receipt of this work—read, of course, with great interest—every film director had made it clear that he wouldn't be free for years to come.

Once more spurred on by his friend who owned the theater in Vannes, where the weekly programs encouraged the comforting notion that "it wasn't all that difficult to make a movie," Monsieur Le Goff had decided to produce the film himself.

As chance would have it, Madame Le Goff had an old boarding-school friend, Madame Charlotte Verdon, with two grown sons living in Paris, both of whom were "in the movies."

The Verdon brothers, discouraged by not being able to make their own film—that nice little film which took place in forty-eight hours, a little in the street, a little in a bicycle factory, at the edge of the sea and in a bed where two contemporary adolescents made love—found themselves promoted to the rank of "technical advisors" to a millionaire biscuit manufacturer on whose beach they had built sand castles in their childhood and who would never have agreed to put even a sou into their own project, but who was going to have to cough up millions for the preparation of his own, a film about which they were already prophesying that though it might very well someday see the light of day, it would surely never see the artificial light of movie theaters.

Out of honesty, they had at first tried to dissuade Monsieur Le Goff from plunging into this adventure, but, faced with his fierce stubbornness, they had resigned themselves to take the money that would otherwise have found its way into the pockets of some swindler who probably would not have been generous enough to allow his friends to share in the opportunity.

Hired as advisors, they advised. And among the first bits of advice offered after they began getting their weekly checks was the advice to give priority to costuming. The actors could be dealt with later. The important thing was the costumes. As they had explained to Monsieur Le Goff, it was easier to remake a Breton costume to fit this or that actor than to remake the physique of an actor who had been chosen in advance and who, it would be realized only too late—after having hired him, or in other words, paid him a little something—didn't look at all believable under a round hat.

Like Raimu, for example, whom Monsieur Le Goff had briefly considered for the role of Grégoire and who, his friend who owned the Vannes movie theater assured him, could do any kind of accent. Luckily, the Verdon brothers had arrived in the nick of time. As advisors, they strongly advised against Raimu. An excellent actor, agreed, and maybe a good baker, but absolutely impossible as a Breton baker. You couldn't go around throwing money out the window.

No, it was better to do as they advised. The costumes first, the actors afterward. And as for the costumes, there was only one place to go: the Costumers' Cooperative. They had friends there, and Monsieur Le Goff would be satisfied.

Monsieur Le Goff was delighted, and the Verdons had rarely laughed so much since the year when their little low-budget film, directed by those enthusiastic young cineastes, had been rejected over and over again.

The bargain was sealed at the bar in Fouquet's, where at the request of Alex, who now knew the place very well, Laurent Verdon had for once consented to appear wearing a tie. On pocketing the big check from this major competitor of Petit-Beurre LU, the founder of the

Costumers' Cooperative had felt a little ashamed. But he had also pock-
eted his pride, then listened without laughing as Laurent spoke of
beginning to shoot early in September.

"Will we be prepared?" Monsieur Le Goff had asked.

"Always prepared, Monsieur Le Goff," Laurent had replied, giving
him a Boy Scout salute.

"Fine, fine," Monsieur Le Goff had said. "And when are you and
your brother sailing?"

"Tomorrow at dawn, Monsieur Le Goff."

"You're going to Brittany by boat?" asked Alex, who at this point
was ready for anything and everything.

Laurent Verdon had shrugged his shoulders pityingly and raised his
wonderful green eyes to Fouquet's ceiling.

"To Wales, Scotland and Ireland, my dear sir . . . A little research
. . . How can we approach this work without returning to the sources
of our Celtic heritage?"

"Of course," Alex had admitted, plunging into the remains of his
port flip.

"These two young rascals are sparing no effort," said Monsieur Le
Goff, who was overjoyed to see things going so well.

He had paid the bar bill and returned to Nantes.

Alex had returned to the Coop, placed the check on Monsieur Anselmo's table and decided with Ginette that they'd send someone to go
through the attics and convents of Brittany in search of costumes that
had scarcely changed since the time of the Chouan uprising. Even if
Grégoire, Get Your Gun! never went before the cameras, despite Laurent Verdon's promise to the Nantes Baden-Powell, it was a good
opportunity to replenish the stock, which was a bit weak in the historic
folklore dress so much in demand during these days of celebration.

They'd agreed they would have to find someone, then hadn't done
anything about it. They hadn't done anything about it because they
were busy with *The Volga Boatman,* a film for which they had also been
paid—and which was really being shot—and in August at that. No one
had been sent to empty the attics on the shores of the Volga, but the
research and manufacture of the costumes had been so absorbing that
no one had been available to go prospecting in Brittany, either.

And Ginette had spoken more and more often of that someone they
would never find if they didn't look for him, and of Monsieur Le
Go-Go, who would one day telephone from Nantes.

She had brought the matter up again just that evening, when Alex
had decided to use the Citroën to transport the phonograph, the records

and the bottles of fruit juice. The Citroën had been rusting in the garage ever since Lucas had left. And Ginette had also spoken again of the need for a chauffeur.

So because of Ginette, the petit-beurre from Nantes, the one-way streets that had given him so much trouble between the Champs-Elysées and rue de la Mare, because of the Verdons, whom Barsky had lost all hope of one day identifying, Alex suddenly had the blinding revelation that Gromoff should abandon his taxi and drive the Citroën across the gorse, with, at his side, the man who would be best equipped to drink with the Breton men and convince the Breton women to open their most tightly locked armoires. After all, buying up secondhand merchandise had been Isidore's first profession—before he had fallen in love with the movies.

Only Zaza had heard them come to an agreement.

She hadn't been drunk at all, either.

Forty-eight hours later, in the early morning, the Citroën's motor had started up on rue de la Mare. An old studded leather valise covered with stickers bearing witness to luxurious stays in luxurious hotels, a new pasteboard valise, a guitar case and two knapsacks—so stuffed and rounded that they looked like balls for a giant game of soccer—were securely stowed away on the car's roof rack.

Up front was the chauffeur-prince, driving with the cineaste Isidore at his side. Piled in the rear, on the seat and on the carpeted floor, were the three owners of half a bac—Clément, Nussbaum and Guttman—and the two young girls from rue de la Mare.

On the sidewalk, the fathers and mothers said goodbye to their children, and Myriam Goldberg to her friends.

It was summer 1936, and they too were going to discover the sea.

: :

AT THAT very hour, the steamship *Champlain,* belonging to the Compagnie Générale Transatlantique, was already on the high seas. The sun had not yet risen.

The evening before, from the deck, the passengers had watched the land recede. But since they had no one to wave their handkerchiefs to, Janek and Nicole Roginski had gone down to their first-class cabin even before the cliffs of Europe had disappeared from sight.

$\mathcal{T}$HE UNKNOWN man who had played the banjo to accompany Gromoff on the guitar during the celebration, and who hadn't said a word all evening long, wasn't completely unknown to Alex; he'd already seen him someplace, though he didn't know where.

He found out a few days later, when he saw him again where he'd seen him the first time: at the Coop. Seated silently in the vestibule under the portrait of Lucien Guitry, he was waiting.

He was waiting for his friend Valeri Inkijinoff, on whom Mademoiselle Agnès was fitting the boatman's rags for *The Volga Boatman*, in which he was going to play a small part.

Alex had been moved to tears when he had welcomed Valeri Inkijinoff the first time he had appeared in the frame of the door which Alex himself had opened, so eagerly had he been awaiting him. The others hadn't understood, couldn't understand. You had to be a friend of Rodriguez to know the source of the unusual respect with which the very casual Alex Grandi had led this foreign actor through the upholstered salons.

No one had ever seen Alex behave like that, not for Pierre Richard-Willm, nor for Véra Korène, Pierre Blanchar, or Charles Vanel, who had come the previous day to have their measurements taken and who were the stars of *The Volga Boatman*.

No one had ever seen Alex behave like that. But then no one had ever seen Valéri Inkijinoff in *Storm Over Asia*. Perhaps they'd seen him in *The Head of a Man*, in *Amok*, or in *The Battle*—or in that other thing about the Volga, *The Volga on Fire* or *in Flames,* no one was quite sure which. He hadn't been bad, he was a character, a special type, an exotic! But there was no reason to fuss about him as though he were the Duchess of Uzès! said Mademoiselle Agnès, who for her part thought he looked more Chinese than Russian and, consequently, completely lacked all the attractions and mysteries that she so passionately cherished in Slavs.

More Chinese than Slav and more Asiatic than Chinese, the Siberian Inkijinoff had a special way of being silent, of smiling, of nodding his thanks and wrinkling his fur-trapper's eyes to express astonishment or amusement; and Alex, dazzled, stared at the descendant of Genghis Khan just as he and Rodriguez had stared at him again and again when they'd been very young and films were still silent.

As silent and mysterious as Inkijinoff, who didn't say a word about anything. Not about Meyerhold, nor Pudovkin, nor the dead poet Sergei Esenin, nor that other dead poet Mayakovsky.

Not a word about *before.* Nor a word about why there had been a before 1930, nor about why since then there had been that *after.*

An *after* that was now bringing him to try on the rags for the unimportant role of Kyro, only given a name to make it easier to classify the costumes that would soon be leaving, heaped up in baskets labeled "Minor roles and extras: *Boatman.* "

That first time, Alex had studied Inkijinoff while Mademoiselle Agnès was pinning his costume. He might perhaps have caught a glimpse of the friend with the banjo, but he'd hardly looked at him. Seeing him under the portrait of Lucien Guitry, he'd said hello to him as to a friend. Because of the celebration. And he'd told Stépan that the banjo player of the other evening was outside. And Stépan, who was working on the collar of a colonel's fur cape—there weren't just poor people in *The Volga Boatman*—had gone out to say hello to this friend of Gromoff's: after all that, and after a lot of grinding of teeth, he'd ended by letting Zaza leave with Gromoff at the wheel . . .

Valeri Inkijinoff's friend wasn't a close friend of Gromoff's, only someone he knew from the race track. But he really was the friend of Valeri Inkijinoff.

A childhood friend who came from the same region: from Irkutsk.

The coincidence struck Stépan as being so extraordinary that he repeated the name:

"Irkutsk? . . . That's funny!"

"Do you know it?" asked Inkijinoff's friend.

"No, but I know someone who died near Irkutsk. A Ukrainian . . . But that was a long time ago, in 1929," Stépan explained.

"In 1929? Well, that saved your convict friend from dying of starvation in the Ukraine," said Inkijinoff's friend, with a bitter smile.

"Just where is Irkutsk?"

"Why, in Siberia, Monsieur," answered Inkijinoff's friend, as if stating the obvious.

Stépan didn't say anything. Merely that he had work to do. He went back to the colonel's collar. And he thought about the evening to come.

They were going to talk about Volodya again on the second floor, very sadly this time.

And since for once they wouldn't have to hide from the children, they'd probably talk about him for hours.

And Elie would probably also take out the letter from Monsieur D. in Zurich again, so they could read it more intelligently now that they knew where Irkutsk was.

And Sonia would probably say that Volodya must have done something very bad to have died in prison.

And she and Elie would probably argue, since they wouldn't have to hide from the children.

And since no one, no one in the world, would ever come to say what Volodya had done that was so bad, they'd be no further ahead.

And there'd be this story of the famine, which no one, no one in the world, had ever heard of.

And Elie would be quite capable of going down to the Cléments' loge to ask Félix if he knew anything about it.

And Félix would probably say that it was just another one of those tall tales from Mercier Frères . . .

Then Stépan would be obliged to say that it had come from the banjo player who'd been there the other evening with Gromoff, and Félix would say that that didn't surprise him. Because he was very nice, Gromoff, but after all he was what he was . . .

. . . And probably Félix would scold Jeannette for having gotten him to agree to let the kids go off with a Russian prince and a clown from Odessa, who was also very nice, but who did and said just about anything and who drank too much.

Not that it wasn't true, but they already knew all that.

They had talked about it enough, discussed it enough; they had lectured the kids, Gromoff and Barsky often enough before giving in and letting them go.

So what would be the use of talking about it all again, since what was done was done? No use, except perhaps to almost certainly ruin an evening that already promised to be bad enough.

Very bad, even, as it was every time poor Volodya was discussed or even mentioned.

It was unfortunate but true that they'd never be finished with Volodya.

And Stépan, bent over the otter skins and the braided black silk that decorated the colonel's collar in *The Volga Boatman*, began to ask himself if it was really so urgent and so necessary to bring home the news that evening that Irkutsk was a city in Siberia. Or that several years ago people had died of hunger in what was commonly called the breadbasket of Europe.

In one way or another, they'd learn someday that Irkutsk was in Siberia, and the later the better. Especially for the reputation of Cousin Volodya.

As for the famine in the Ukraine, they'd hear about that too, if it was true. Things like that were like pogroms. They're hidden from the world, then one day they're talked about. All you had to do was wait.

There was no reason why he, Stépan, had to be a bearer of bad tidings. On this beautiful summer evening when for once the children weren't there, and they could do things they never did when the children were there. Eat out, for example. In a brasserie, in the open air, on the terrace, like foreign tourists. Or maybe in the little pavilion-restaurant in front of the pond at the Buttes-Chaumont, where the Guttmans had taken them, Olga and him, when Maurice was still in his stroller and Zaza in Olga's belly.

Yes, that's what they were going to do that evening. And instead of rehashing the long-gone past, they'd talk about recent events. After all, the restaurant on the Buttes was also the past, since Zaza was now fourteen.

They could even take advantage of the occasion to talk about Zaza's future. Maurice's seemed assured, since he loved school. But Zaza? What were they going to do about Zaza?

That was a lot more important than all the Cousin Volodyas from the Ukraine, Poland or Germany—or even from Palestine, like the Sterns' cousin.

Zaza was from here.

She was going to have to decide to do something with her head or her hands. Smearing on lipstick and going off to fish for shrimp weren't going to help her prepare for the future that awaited her.

ᴢᴀᴢᴀ ʜᴀᴅɴ'ᴛ gone off to fish for shrimp. Nor to discover the sea, the iodine and mists of which were so beneficial to the lungs of city children, as she had insisted when presenting her travel plans the day after the celebration.

She'd just as soon have gone off to the mining communities of Le Creusot or Hénin-Liétard to search for the dresses and aprons worn by coal sorters if Alex had been commissioned to costume *Germinal.*

Zaza had left so that she might be taken seriously by Alex.

And it was because she wanted to be taken even more seriously that she'd thought it a good idea to borrow the lipstick belonging to the Auvergnat's niece before confiding to Alex that she didn't want to go to school anymore, that she wanted to work and that he had to help her tell this to Olga. He'd listened to her, but she wasn't sure if he'd really heard.

Because there'd been a lot of noise, and also because the Auvergnat's niece had kept looking at him.

And then there'd been Alex's proposition to the two old men, which she'd heard and listened to as closely as possible.

And she'd told Alex that if he trusted those old men who knew nothing, he could just as easily give a chance to a young girl who'd grown up playing at the feet of two dressmakers' mannequins.

But since she knew they'd never let her go off with two old men to fish for Breton costumes, she'd convinced the young people around her that it was time to discover the sea.

Even if it had to be in the company of two old men.

So they'd gone, and Stépan was wrong to worry: Zaza knew exactly what she wanted to do with her hands, her head and her life.

And she was the only one of the passengers in the big car to tell herself she was going off to work.

To work for Alex.

Because she was also the only one who was in love with Alex—and had been since she was ten years old.

: 307 :

THE VERY occasional postcards they took turns scribbling said the weather was fine and that they were having a good time. In fact things were much better than that. The weather was positively glorious, and they were having great fun—fun such as they'd never had in their lives as small children, or even as adolescents.

And the funniest thing about it was that they were having fun with and thanks to people who were older than the old-timers who were their parents.

Older, not as attractive, a little lazy, drinkers, gamblers, ladies' men, seducers who were still seductive—these old-timers had one incontestable superiority in the eyes of the rue de la Mare children: the fact that they weren't *their* old-timers—which was why they could really have a ball with the two grownups, Andrei Alexievitch Gromoff and Isidore Barsky, who were allowed to claim this adult status just so long as their names, written in hotel registers, were followed by the dates and places of birth shown on their French identity cards—said cards having no protective holders and looking like playing cards that had been used for a long time, not always with very clean hands.

Their worn look attested to their age and the carelessness with which their owners treated such irreplaceable documents. The identity cards showing that the Guttman, Roginski and Nussbaum parents were naturalized French citizens were perfectly legible behind the celluloid windows of wallets always kept within easy reach. Gromoff and Barsky would eventually manage to fish theirs out of one pocket or another, but only after a few minutes of searching. Then would come a moment of high emotion brought on by the photos that showed them so young, followed immediately by an explosion of consternation and incredulity at the realities of a life that had turned them into fifty-year-old Frenchmen.

The skit was more or less well received by the hotel concierges, who were always invited to share in these different phases of the operation known as the registering of tourists.

The children had caught the premiere performance at Redon, the first overnight stop of the *Grégoire, Get Your Gun!* expedition. It had made them laugh so much they asked for it to be repeated at each new stop.

These were numerous, and the skit improved from hostelry to hostelry. Sometimes Gromoff and Barsky went so far as to shed tears over their youthful portraits; sometimes one of them would pretend he'd never learned French. Once, Barsky played a blind man and Gromoff a deaf man. Whether at hotels, inns, coachhouses or boardinghouses, the children would always get out of the car first, take up their orchestra seats in front of the counter, and await the arrival of the clowns. They never tired of it.

: :

THEY RETURNED home ten days later, tanned, their hair sticky with salt, smiling but not very talkative. They repeated that the weather had been fine and that they'd had a good time.

The booty of the *Grégoire, Get Your Gun!* expedition was too abundant to fit into the Citroën. It arrived at the Gare Montparnasse in two wicker trunks bought in Vannes.

They were opened at "the Bonnets'" in the presence of Alex.

Alex was more surprised by the quality of what the trunks contained than by the quantity. There were short jackets, dresses, trousers and hats in good condition; and then there were a number of raggedy items. Raggedy items worn by time, but their bits and pieces miraculously held together by panels of velvet, taffeta, moiré, satin and plush embroidered and overembroidered with silk, multicolored beads and gold thread, and buttons of silver, amber, ivory, millefiori, shells and rare wood. There were shredded belts whose brass buckles bore unknown heraldic devices and symbols, and bits of marriage trousseaux bordered with lace, monogrammed and with folds yellowed from lack of use. There were red cotton stockings, widows' shawls and even the straw harnesses used to protect the heads of infants just learning to walk.

The treasures in the trunks showed a subtlety of choice for which Alex congratulated Barsky.

"It's the little girl who chose everything. The two of us just talked to the people, and I did the bargaining," Barsky replied loyally.

So then Alex congratulated Zaza. Zaza blushed and kissed Barsky, which didn't exactly please Olga and Sonia.

After all, Barsky wasn't even a member of the family! There was no reason for him to play Uncle Isidore, just like that, from one day to another.

The women were counting inaccurately, as were all the other rue de la Mare parents. Their children had been been living far away from them for ten whole days. Urged to tell about their trip, they talked about the sea, the rocks, the sand and the salted butter, about *far,* which was a custard with prunes, and about *noa,* a grape that was still unripe but already had a raspberry taste. About the large boats in the Gulf of Morbihan with black hulls and red sails that were called *sinagots.* Synagogues? Yes, sinagots! And about the *crêperies* and the menhirs of Carnac.

But they didn't talk about their real discoveries:

That Gromoff had a wife and a grown son who lived in London, where she was a pianist and he a doctor.

That Barsky could recite Mark Antony's speech in *Julius Caesar* by heart in English and even in Shakespeare! And that he'd spent twelve months in prison in Odessa when he was about sixteen or seventeen year for what he called "agitation." At just about the same time, Gromoff was already running from casino to casino, riding thoroughbreds and driving his first torpedo convertible.

And that both men could rattle off the names of all the stars, because they'd spent a lot of nights roaming around.

That had been when Barsky had had trouble falling asleep, in the days when he had loved a cabaret singer who worked until dawn and who had died—but all that was ancient history.

So ancient that Barsky and Gromoff were both truly stunned by it. And that explained why it was so easy for them to amuse the children by pretending to be stunned when they signed the hotel register in the evening.

How could the others tell about all that without betraying anyone?

How could they tell about the woman who sat alone with her child in the boardinghouse dining room, her eyes on her plate during the whole meal, and who was seen coming out of Barsky's room at six o'clock in the morning? Barsky, who never mentioned it and whom they hadn't had the courage to ask how to go about it . . . But who explained it to them one evening, when the girls were already in bed and asleep in the pretty, cretonne-decorated room in the Hôtel de l'Epée in Vannes. And how it was the kind of real conversation they'd never had with their fathers.

And how could one of the boys tell about the girl who brought his breakfast, or the other about his Scottish lady tourist in the afternoon? And the third, about the camper, two days later, in a tent in the little wood of Port-Louis, without the girls in the group ever noticing?

Without either Barsky or Gromoff asking if it had gone off all right, even though they were dying to tell because they were so pleased, and particularly pleased that the advice they'd been given was good: just look at them insistently, a little out of the corners of your eyes, smile and make them laugh . . .

And how could they tell about how they'd also learned to play poker?

And about the Masses they had pretended to follow with closed eyes so that the parish priest would think well of them and be so convinced of their faith that he would recommend them to his flock, who would never have opened their armoires without his benediction.

And who had opened them wide because it was for a movie about Monsieur de Charette. And because it was certainly the right time.

Because General Hoche and his soldiers of the Republic had killed more Breton women and children in Brittany in 1793 than the Prussians in France had killed in the North in 1870 and 1914. And because the Bretons had never forgotten, even if no one in Paris ever mentioned it.

And why should they tell about how frightened they'd been that day when Josette had almost drowned on the Côte Sauvage, at Penthièvre?

Or about the first time Sami had really tied one on and while they were on the road was given his first dose of salted coffee by Gromoff, who held his head so that he could heave into a ditch at the side of the road?

And what was the good of talking about the ridiculous golfing cap Barsky would sometimes put on so as to look like a filmmaker? And about the two little silver dessert spoons bearing the arms of the Duchess Anne restaurant, swiped so as to teach the proprietor not to be so rude? And better yet, about that evening after dinner at Port-Navalo, when there was some guy with almost white hair, incredibly handsome in his navy-blue turtleneck sweater, drinking all by himself while staring first at Josette and then at Zaza, looking sideways at them with his light-blue eyes and smiling without saying a word . . . And how those two idiots didn't want to leave and go to bed!

Nor did they want to leave Port-Navalo the next morning, arguing that the sister of the lighthouse keeper had promised Zaza to find her great-great-grandmother's wedding dress and bring it to her in the afternoon—to that same café, as a matter of fact, where they had waited for her but she hadn't come.

Nor had the white-haired man, either. And Zaza and Josette had sat in the car and sulked for a good ten miles. And Gromoff and Barsky had sung "My heart is a vi-o-lin on which your bo-w-string plays" and they'd eventually burst out laughing. Nevertheless, Zaza had sighed deeply and said it was a pity, because Alex would have been so happy to have had a real wedding dress . . . "And I suppose you wouldn't be!" Maurice had teased. And she'd said "Shit!" to him!

And how could they have told about the last day? Buying the two wicker hampers, "big enough for four corpses, if you cut them length-wise!" And then rather foolishly buying shell souvenirs for the mothers and for Myriam, and the last crêpes and cider, and the last hotel and the following morning, very early, the last breakfast together before taking the road, knowing they'd no longer make stops, since there was nothing to see that they hadn't already seen on the trip out.

And how could you tell parents you love that it was sad to come home, and at the same time very pleasant for them to have a number of secrets that they'd never share?

AT ALLÉE CHATEAUBRIAND, the Breton lots that were in good condition were cleaned and numbered, and the ragged ones carefully disassembled. The women went into ecstasies over the salvageable treasures discovered among the tattered bits and pieces, and over the flair and talent of the "little girl" who had been able to sniff them out. No one knew for certain who this "little girl" Alex had spoken about was, but they knew she had a gift.

Stépan heard them go into ecstasies. It both pleased and displeased him.

It pleased him that Zaza was good at something, and it displeased him to have been the last to notice it. It especially displeased him to have been faced with a *fait accompli*.

There was no doubt about it—Zaza was like her mother and Sonia. A man leaves his house in the morning and says goodbye to two finishers, and he returns in the evening to find it's now a costume-makers' shop. You're a second-floor tenant, and suddenly you find yourself a first-floor co-tenant. You quit Fémina-Prestige, and by the time you get home, they belong to a cooperative. You send a schoolgirl to the seaside, and she comes back a costumer.

When he heard Ginette and Mademoiselle Agnès talk about how they ought to get her for the shop before she was hired elsewhere, he became panic-stricken and announced that the gifted "little girl" was no other than his daughter. But that she was still going to school, that she'd only done it during her vacation, for fun, they'd just have to see, and maybe later . . .

There was one thing Stépan didn't want and had trouble admitting to himself because he thought it was monstrous, but that's the way it was: he hadn't wanted to work at rue de la Mare in his wife's company any more than he now wanted to work at Allée Chateaubriand under his daughter's eyes. Not after so many years spent working at rue d'Aboukir under his brother's thumb!

What Stépan wanted was to go on tranquilly enjoying what was still so new for him: the little bit of prestige of which he never took unfair advantage, but which he savored, every moment—the prestige of being the only man in a shop of women for whom he had the charms and the charm of a man who was neither their husband nor their lover—and, above all, certainly not their father.

He wanted to go on making them laugh when he made mistakes in French; he wasn't interested in being corrected.

He wanted to go on pretending to be unaware of Mademoiselle Agnès's passion; he didn't want to hear that she was old and ugly.

He wanted to go on being able to compliment the waitress at Raymonde and André on how well she was looking, to sip an after-lunch liqueur, to walk idly down the Champs-Elysées looking at shop windows and even women, and to take his Métro at Marbeuf, if he was in the mood, instead of at George V.

And he wanted to go on taking the Métro as far as République every morning in the company of Elie—but only of Elie.

It wouldn't be easy to say all that when he got home that evening. But actually, if Zaza really wanted to work, she could learn more with her mother and Sonia: at home, at "the Bonnets'."

At least that way they'd always know where she was.

But first this school business would have to be settled. He'd talk it over with Olga. After Zaza had gone to bed.

After all, Zaza was only fourteen.

And Stépan put aside for a moment the astrakhan *chapka* worn by the colonel's aide-de-camp in *The Volga Boatman* and went to admire his daughter's discoveries.

"She's got a good eye—she gets it from you, Monsieur Roginski," said Mademoiselle Agnès, making the light play over the hundreds of tiny turquoise and garnet crystals encasing the bottom of a long black wool skirt elsewhere completely eaten away by moths.

"From me and from her mama . . . " Stépan had the courage to say, but so feebly Mademoiselle Agnès probably didn't hear him, because she neither said anything nor smiled.

"*Oh là là,* it's beginning already!" grumbled Stépan as he returned to his work table.

: :

He was wrong to be worried.

Zaza hadn't the slightest intention of coming to sit and sew alongside her father at Allée Chateaubriand, or of remaining seated at rue de la Mare to sew alongside her mother.

In fact, she hadn't the slightest intention of sewing at all.

She wanted to move around—to climb into attics, to go down into cellars, to fish out and hunt down marvelous treasures, just as she'd proved she could.

But she also wanted more. She wanted to follow these treasures wherever they went, even if they went very far, to be their protectress and guardian. In short, she wanted to work for the Coop, but to work on the outside—in other words, inside the movie industry but in the part that took place in the open air.

And she said as much to Alex, right in front of Olga.

Alex thought it was a good idea and said so, right in front of Olga, who announced it to Stépan when he came home.

After all, Zaza was almost fifteen, and since she no longer wanted to go to school, as Stépan must know . . .

Or to be more exact, as Stépan should have known if Olga, who now apologized, hadn't forgotten to tell him two weeks earlier, when it had been decided.

The evening of the celebration—shortly after midnight.

: :

ZAZA HAD HER baptism as a movie trainee on the banks of the Marne disguised as the Volga.

Not really a dresser, not exactly an assistant, something of a canteen keeper and a gofer, she ran about a great deal and did a lot more sewing than she had thought she'd have to do. She always sewed standing up, making big stitches at top speed, because it was not so much sewing as resewing something that had split just as shooting was about to begin, and it didn't have to last a lifetime.

When she wasn't resewing the costumes, Zaza was distributing them to the nonspeaking boatmen—that is to say, nonspeaking in the scenes, because they had plenty to say between shots and at the canteen. And she wasn't at all embarrassed as she adjusted the brass buckles of Chouan belts to the waists of these Czar Nicholas II convicts—buckles with Celtic inscriptions that from a distance could very well pass for Cyrillic.

Because Ginette, faithful to the tradition that had so long been the fashion at Masques and Bergamasques, had been unable to resist the temptation to do a little *Boatman* business by drawing on the stock for *Grégoire, Get Your Gun!*, which was still awaiting the casting of both speaking and nonspeaking actors.

Meanwhile, first the tatters were put to work, then, little by little, some of the precious gold and bead trimmings were used to set off the very chic outfits of the colonel's wife in *The Volga Boatman*. The treasures remained on the bosom of the colonel's lady only for as long as it took to shoot a scene. Once it was done, they were immediately unsewn, then wrapped in the tissue paper that retained the freshness they had kept for a century and a half in the Breton armoires.

It was Zaza who unsewed them.

It was also Zaza who—as soon as it fell from the shoulders of the colonel's lady—shrouded the sable cape in black ticking, the cape without which that lady's outfits would have been sadly lacking in chic.

: :

ON HER FIRST DAY, Zaza had said that she was sixteen and that her name was Elsa. And since everyone found her amusing and pleasant, they all affectionately called her Zaza.

When she wasn't running around sewing, resewing, unsewing or pinning, when she wasn't opening beer bottles or spreading slabs of bread with pâté and cornichons, when she wasn't boiling water on a sterno stove, when she wasn't moving dress hampers from place to place, Zaza would sometimes sit down and watch.

Not so much the actors—speaking or nonspeaking—as someone who spoke very little but always to the point, whose name was Mireille and whom everybody called Mimi, and without whose advice apparently nothing could be done on the set and for whom all the men seemed to have great respect and a fraternal affection.

It took only a few days for Zaza to realize that she'd probably found her real vocation. She'd try to be a script girl, later.

And she said so to Mimi, who had already grasped as much, since she noticed everything that happened around her.

ZAZA WAS NEVER seen at Allée Chateaubriand. On the other hand, a great deal was seen of Gromoff and Barsky, whose temporary collaboration had been extended. They dealt with Ginette and Mademoiselle Anita, for they had become the liaison men between the banks of the Marne-Volga and the Costumers' Cooperative.

They were the ones who'd pick up and repatriate the costumes rented by the day, especially the precious ones like the Breton treasures, which had to be returned to stock immediately in case Monsieur Le Go-Go's phantom troupe should finally turn up, or like the sable cape, which no one on the set was willing to assume responsibility for when it had finished "acting" on the shoulders of the colonel's lady, who had the irritating habit of leaving it just about everywhere, since it was very hot around Paris that mid-August, even under the shade of a fake birch.

Since Ginette was delighted to have a driver at last, and since Mademoiselle Anita, who knew about prices, had evaluated Barsky's talent for bargaining at its true worth, they were retained at a monthly salary without making them actual Coop members. When the women met them, they both had the vague impression they'd seen them somewhere before, but since neither man refreshed their memories, the women turned to other things.

When she handed over the black-ticking bag to the men for the first time, Ginette had warned them to be extremely careful, and she had given them a short lecture on the value of the sables, which were her personal property. Barsky had smiled at Gromoff, but Ginette had been busy padlocking the door of the fur-storage locker and the smile had escaped her.

The men were often seen at Allée Chateaubriand, but only in passing. Coming or going, they'd make a little sign to Stépan if the door of the shop was open; they never went in, and Stépan preferred it that way. He wasn't thrilled to have rue de la Mare at Allée Chateaubriand, but all the same he was pleased that rue de la Mare saw to it that Zaza got home in the evening.

"That way, at least somebody's got an eye on her," he'd say to Ginette, as if to justify his having agreed to let the girl have a little more fun before going back to school, which he still pretended to believe she'd do.

"It would be a pity for her to go back to school," Ginette would comment. "And as for keeping an eye on her . . . my dear Stépan, if your daughter wants to go off on a spree she'll find a way, whether she's in school or working for the movies. For the moment, from what I hear, she's really serious about it. Look how she takes care of my costumes. She hasn't lost so much as a gaiter button!"

Of course Ginette actually meant a Breton button. But if she had unconsciously evoked the tragedy of Sedan, when the French army was said not to have been missing so much as a gaiter button, it was because she lived in terror of the scandal that threatened them: her frenzied passion for renting out material was now limitless. On days when many extras were required on the *Boatman* set, even the round hats so difficult to place anywhere but in a production based on Lamartine's *Jocelyn* had been put to use. By bashing, feathering and veiling them, she had turned them into the felt hats worn by horsewomen on a wolf hunt in the Moscow forest.

Laurent Verdon liberated her from her anguish and simultaneously liberated the stock "held in reserve": *Grégoire, Get Your Gun!* was not going to go before the cameras. Too absorbed in his artistic reveries, Monsieur Le Goff had so neglected his duties as a biscuit manufacturer that one fine morning he'd found himself standing in front of closed gates behind which were waiting the entire personnel of his Galettes Pomponnette. More than a little surprised, he'd read in the eyes of these men and women the same fierce resolution he'd so hoped to see light up the eyes of the actors of his film—the film he still believed, before his arrival at the doors of the family business, he'd be able to make.

Though they were a bit behind their compatriots, Monsieur Le Goff's employees—who from father to son and from mother to daughter had always kneaded dough for the Le Goff sons, fathers and grandfathers—had just become aware of their new rights. In Saint-Pol-Blazan (Lower Loire) they were on strike.

Everywhere else the strikes had begun right after May 8. Transformed into a general strike on May 20, they had come to a halt on June 1, the day the Matignon Collective Agreements had been signed, bringing into law several radical changes in French labor laws. That had been two months earlier, but the Hôtel Matignon wasn't exactly next door.

Perhaps it was the caravans of people going through the hamlets on tandems and bikes, in cars and on motorcycles and even on foot—people who sang songs never before heard in the mouths of tourists—whatever the explanation, the news eventually spread to Saint-Pol-Blazan. And for the first time in the history of Galettes Pomponnette the bakery workers had repeated the historical gesture of their ancestor Grégoire: they had let the ovens go out.

They had neither pitchforks nor rifles, and the only arm they brandished behind the gate was a copy of the Collective Agreements. Monsieur Le Goff could do no less than read it in his turn. Actually, he had probably already done so, but with so distracted an eye that he had completely forgotten to apply its clauses. It was time he did, if he didn't want to lose the summer season.

Packaged biscuits sell well in the summer. They were likely to sell even better that particular summer. The wrappers left behind by the new camper-vacationers were proof of this. The ovens therefore had to be lit again—and quickly, before the tons of flour bought on credit began to rot and pile up in the Pomponnette warehouses.

Forced to choose between the perishable and the more durable stock, Monsieur Le Goff had made up his mind.

"Our friends at the Costumers' Cooperative will be very unhappy," the two Verdons had sighed when Monsieur Le Goff, sick at heart, had told them of his decision to postpone the production of his epic until some later date. "They've put their best people to work for you and gone to a lot of trouble. You've made the Coop lose valuable time," Laurent had added, with quiet anger.

"I know," Monsieur Le Goff had admitted sadly.

He knew because, while scouring the Breton countryside for him, the Movie Citroën, as it was known, had raised a lot of aspirations, sowed many hopes and left many memories, whose echoes had reached his ears. During the ten days the expedition had lasted, the news of its travels had flown from belfry to belfry: "They're on the way . . . they're here . . . will they come back? . . . " was heard in the country, in the fishing ports and on the heaths.

Well, no, they wouldn't be coming back. The Movie Citroën had passed as caravans pass, just as full of magic and promise as those other Citroëns, the ones belonging to the Asian and African automobile expeditions, which had also passed, never to return yet never forgotten.

"I know," Monsieur Le Goff had repeated even more sadly, because he had just realized he should have hung a Pomponnette sign on the back of the Movie Citroën. "I know . . . I've seen what they've done . . . What can I do to make it up to them?"

"A check," the two Verdon brothers had curtly replied in unison, as if it were obvious.

. . . .

SINCE THEY WERE honest, they had turned the check over to Alex, who had immediately paid it into their kitty—the kitty they'd built up in the twelve weeks during which their invaluable technical advice and their unverifiable expenses had for a time wrenched the Nantes biscuit-maker from the monotony of his life and opened the doors of freedom to them: the freedom, at last, to make their little inexpensive film. In the streets, inside a bicycle factory, within the four walls of a bedroom and on the beach—and as a cooperative venture.

ALEX ANNOUNCED that the Le Go-Go stock could now be used freely.

It was therefore with a light heart and a calm conscience that Ginette could let her Breton costumes be rented out and checked in exactly like her Venetian gondoliers, her Savoyard chimney sweeps and her gypsy dancers.

At the end of this particular summer afternoon, with all the windows open, she was airing out the stock in her large wardrobe closets and doing a little inventory. An empty hanger caught her attention: Number 92, the "Anna Karenina," had never been returned.

Ginette counted on her fingers: it had already been out for eight months.

Eight months since Maddy had died and Victoria had disappeared from all their lives.

She often thought of Maddy, even though she never spoke of her— except sometimes to Alex, and even then with only a word or a smile. She never thought of Victoria.

And even now, faced with the empty hanger, she was thinking more about the 92 swiped by Victoria than about Victoria herself.

"Madame Victoria Jean still hasn't returned the 'Anna Karenina,' " she said to Mademoiselle Agnès, going into the shop.

Stépan hadn't raised his head.

"You ought to send Monsieur Isidore to pick it up from her. After all, she sent Lucas to you for her Easter egg!" replied Mademoiselle Agnès, with a smile reminiscent of the old days.

"Her egg? Why, I saw it last Sunday in the window of an antique shop!" one of the girls announced.

: :

ALEX PAID A LOT of money for it on the faubourg Saint-Honoré, out of his own pocket, not from the Coop's funds. The proprietor of La Vieille Russie had regretfully lifted it from the black velvet pedestal on which it had been sitting in state in his window since July.

"A unique item. I'll miss it," he had said, pressing the little uncut ruby. "A family heirloom . . . very beautiful woman . . . leaving for abroad . . . too fragile to transport . . . "

The Russian voice had whispered the words so as not to drown the harpsichord notes, and the Fabergé egg had opened like an orange.

: :

AND SO THE PEOPLE at Allée Chateaubriand learned that they'd never see Number 92 again, the "Anna Karenina," and Stépan learned he'd probably never see his brother again, either.

He said "brother" in his thoughts, because the picture of Janek disappearing around the bend in the muddy road, his hand raised in a last sign of love for the little eleven-year-old boy who stayed behind, was a memory that almost made him want to cry.

It was true that he'd never see that brother again for the simple reason that he'd never found him again. And a familiar storm of rage and bitterness caught him by the throat, replacing the sobs that had never had the chance to escape.

The old rage against Her! She who had spoiled everything from the beginning. She who had wanted the war between them and had just won it. Without a battle, simply by disappearing with this brother whom She had taken and never returned. If only She'd died. Or even been unfaithful and gone off with another man. Or else become ugly, so that his brother would have begun to detest Her as she deserved. . . . All that might still happen, but Stépan wouldn't be there to see it; it would happen far away.

And Stépan became aware that he had never really stopped waiting for the day when Janek would finally give him the smile he had withheld under the glass shed of the Gare de l'Est. That young man's smile and that friendly wave he couldn't keep himself from dreaming about on certain evenings on the platform of the Neuilly-Vincennes line, when the red first-class car was about to come to a halt in front of him. He would purposely stand there on those evenings, because this was how he'd imagined things: Janek would see him through the window and rush from the first-class car to catch Stépan before he could get into one of the second-class cars, and they'd embrace. Neither of them would say anything. Stépan would bring Janek back to rue de la Mare, and it would all begin as it hadn't begun earlier. Thanks to Her, who would no longer be there.

She, She, She, he thought, unable to give her any of her other names.

All around him, in the shop, they were talking about the return to the firm of the egg that had belonged to Madame Victoria's father, and for the benefit of the young girls who had never heard it, Mademoiselle Agnès was telling the fabulous legend of Piotr, the Rodin of fur, and about how he had been spirited away in a troika one white night in St. Petersburg.

"Isn't that true, Monsieur Roginski?" Mademoiselle Agnès asked, turning toward Stépan, who ought to know, since he was a member of the family.

Stépan said nothing. He was still thinking about Her. He was wondering what She had invented to get his brother, who had come from so far away, to leave and search elsewhere for what he had already found here.

What they had all found here: bread and liberty.

Mademoiselle Agnès repeated her question.

"I don't know," said Stépan, who hadn't really followed the story about Piotr. "And where is this egg?"

"In the vestibule, where it belongs," said Mademoiselle Agnès.

Stépan got up and went into the vestibule to look at the egg under its cover.

He lifted the cover. There must be something more to this egg than its egg shape, he said to himself.

It was only after he'd discovered the little uncut ruby that he remembered the mechanical egg.

Barsky and Gromoff's mechanical egg. The one for which his brother, Janek, had paid as much as he, Stépan, had earned in six months at rue d'Aboukir ten years ago. And Stépan began to laugh heartily.

Less heartily, however, than Barsky and Gromoff did when Alex later confessed to them how much he'd paid the owner of La Vieille Russie for their egg.

"So much for me! You're always someone else's sucker," said Alex, laughing in turn—which made Ginette laugh, too.

"Actually, if things ever get bad, we can always rent it out," she added, touching the wood of the pedestal.

"And why should things get bad? Life has never been so beautiful . . . Right, Stépan?" exclaimed Alex, looking toward the door of the shop, which had remained open.

" 'bsolutely," replied Stépan, nodding his head.

You really had to be as stupid as his brother had become to leave a country where life was so beautiful.

: :

Alex showed no one but Mademoiselle Anita the odd message that had arrived in his mail late in December. Even before it had been opened, the envelope's size, color and texture were enough to make one wonder about it. It was abnormally large, rigorously square, salmon-pink and as grainy as tapioca soup into which someone had poured tomato sauce.

Before inspecting the stamps and the postmarks, Alex turned the envelope around. Engraved in raised purple gothic letters that slanted all across the right side of the flap could be read:

SEVENTEEN ALPINE DRIVE (B.H., CA. U.S.A.)

Alex was so impressed that he slit the envelope with the letter opener he never otherwise used, and his whistle, first of astonishment and then of mockery, was so sharp that it brought Mademoiselle Anita out from her little office-reception room.

On the first page—white, smooth, thick as a blotter—of what could have been an announcement or a catalogue, were four facing miniatures. They were framed in old gold, in the fashion of the *Très Riches Heures du Duc de Berry,* and arranged like portraits in a gallery. Joan of Arc was easily recognizable in armor and on horseback, Lafayette with drawn sword and wearing a plumed hat, Louis Pasteur studiously bent over his microscope and Napoleon seen from the rear as he contemplated Moscow in flames.

Alex had already understood and was beginning to laugh to himself. But it was not until he had opened the "catalogue" that he gave free rein to a roar of laughter.

In the very center of the right-hand page, a *Merry Christmas and a Very Happy New Year 1937* burst forth in relief, in purple, in gothic and not at all on a slant, but in very big letters. Underneath, still in relief, in purple, but in such a free-flowing Italian hand that it seemed to have been written with a quill pen, could be read: *From Jack and Vicky Rogin.*

On the left-hand page, Nicole had written a few lines in a handwriting that did honor to the elementary school on rue Saint-Ferdinand:

My dear Alex,
Everything passes, everything perishes, everything palls, even the great deceptions and the small betrayals. Only sorrow remains, but life goes on.
Note our address; one never knows.

Love,
V.

P.S. You might like to know that Janek is the exclusive representative, for all of California, of an association of Canadian fur trappers, and I am now the historical consultant for period films taking place in Europe and especially in France. Hollywood is fascinating, and Beverly Hills as divine as Neuilly-sur-Seine. Humming-birds flutter around the sycamore in my garden.
P.S. I haven't found any mauve chalk here—but I make do with red.

"That Vicky! . . . " Alex said, handing the document to Mademoiselle Anita, who also found it amusing—less than he had, however.

They agreed not to tell the others about those purple, gothic and Anglo-Saxon wishes, which were obviously meant for Alex alone.

As it was, after the egg returned to the firm, there'd been enough trouble between Ginette and Mademoiselle Agnès about the missing Number 92. Suddenly the Mademoiselle Agnès of the old days was back. With clenched teeth, she'd finally agreed to recut a new Number 92. She didn't care for the velvet, the lace or the buttons. She carried on rather as if she were Michelangelo being asked to reproduce a design from the Sistine Chapel ceiling, but without anyone having had the decency to make available to him the first-class materials with which the original had been created.

For a few days everyone in the shop had been made to suffer, and now that the younger version of Anna Karenina hung peacefully in the stock alongside Number 93, Vronsky, they weren't about to stir up old memories.

Especially not at Christmastime.

And besides, Mademoiselle Anita had added, there was really no need for Stépan Roginski to discover that, in discovering America, his brother had chosen to amputate a syllable from a family name that was also his own.

And Mademoiselle Anita Bourgoin replaced the catalogue in its envelope. She carefully cut off the Lincoln and Roosevelt stamps for her little neighbor on Square Montsouris and filed the large tomato-tapioca square in the folder labeled "Masques."

Alex was briefly tempted to steal it from her and take it to rue de la Mare, just long enough to make Olga and Sonia laugh, but after thinking it over he abandoned the idea. Olga had been calm ever since she knew that her "enemies" were gone for good. She'd spoken of them only once—and even then the comment had slipped out accidentally —one day when Alex had complimented her on her relaxed air.

"It's because I breathe better now. If someone knocks on my door and I'm not expecting anyone, it might be the devil himself, but it won't ever, ever, be *Them*. . . . I know that, and I sleep better because of it. So does Stépan."

Alex had smiled and been careful not to ask her what made her so sure about her husband's serenity. Sometimes he would watch Stépan from a distance during the day, and he was occasionally surprised by his pensive look. And Mademoiselle Anita had told Alex that one evening, when she and Stépan had taken the Métro together, he'd asked her if anyone knew where his brother had gone.

But Stépan probably left his preoccupations at the door of his apartment—and he was right to do so.

" . . . Zaza also sleeps well, but she goes to bed very late these days," Olga had said, still thinking about sleep.

"I'm sure she does, but learning what she's learning to do makes it all worthwhile," Alex had replied.

"Who's this Vaqué and this Jacques she's always following around?"

"Wakhé is a designer whose name is Wakhevitch, and Jacques is an assistant director whose name is Becker . . . "

"A Frenchman, then?"

"Becker is. Wakhé is a Russian, and if she follows them around, it's because she's helped them find what they need to make beautiful costumes for a beautiful film called *La Marseillaise*, " said Alex.

"Then that's all right. They're respectable."

"They're young, handsome and completely respectable," Alex had confirmed. "And Zaza knows what she's doing."

"Then that's all right," Olga had repeated, proud of Zaza.

Smiling calmly, she went to make him another cup of coffee, and Alex followed her into the kitchen.

There were fewer books on the shelf: they were thicker, but less varied.

"The boys know what they're doing, too!" he'd murmured, putting a fat textbook back in its place.

"They'll be men of learning," Sonia had said, thinking proudly of Maurice as she started her sewing machine.

Before leaving them that day, he'd glanced over toward the mantelpiece. Maddy had regained her old spot. As in the past, she'd again covered up several other occupants of The Family Picture Frame.

Alex was careful not to ask them when and why they'd come to this decision. After all, since they thought the Enemy would never, ever come knocking at their door, they were perfectly free to accept as their own the beloved child of their conquered foe.

It was only fair.

: 326 :

IN THE STREET, he had run into Josette and Myriam returning from school. They were hardly ever seen at the Bonnets' since Zaza had gone to work. He'd found them changed, but still terribly schoolgirlish compared to Zaza.

Zaza . . . He'd spoken the truth a little while ago: she knew what she was doing, and, insofar as he knew, the young and handsome men she was with all day long, and often until late in the evening, were "respectable."

And this whole little society was admirable.

He ought to know.

It had happened—or rather hadn't happened—two or two-and-a-half months ago, at his place on rue Campagne-Première. He didn't remember the exact date, but it wasn't winter yet, since Zaza was still wearing ankle socks.

He was working alone at his drawing board, which was illuminated by a single light. It was still raining heavily outside, after a big storm, when, at about five o'clock, someone had rung the bell. It was Zaza, soaked from head to foot, who wanted to show him a selection of minor period jewelry about which she pretended she needed his advice immediately, before she bought them . . .

The six silver earrings and the cheap ornamental chain she took from the pocket of her raincoat were so lacking in interest that he should have asked her why she had come all this way in the rain for his expert opinion. But he hadn't asked her.

He'd said, "You're dripping all over my floor . . . Go into the bathroom and dry your hair with a towel, then slip this on. The collar of your blouse is soaking wet." He'd tossed her his black turtleneck sweater, which had been thrown over the back of a chair, and went back to his drawing without looking at her.

He hadn't lifted his head until he'd heard the bathroom door open.

On Zaza, the far-too-long sweater became a far-too-short black dress that stopped at midthigh and had far-too-long sleeves. The hem of her pleated white skirt peaked out like a slip. She had taken off her shoes and rolled down her socks. She was standing in the doorway watching him. The light from the bathroom was behind her, and she was drying her hair with a white towel, not saying anything and watching him watching her.

He hadn't budged from his drawing board. He *was* watching her.

She was lazily rubbing her head; her hands seemed like black mittens against the whiteness of the towel, and her breasts moved under the cashmere with her every gesture.

"¡*Cuidado . . . Cuidado!*" Alex told himself, just as Rodriguez would always say to him whenever there was any danger. And he'd looked quickly away from the blue eyes fixed on his own through the tangle of blond curls that were still damp but already transparent.

"Put your shoes on and let me get back to work. As for the old lady's gewgaws, okay, buy them from her," he'd grumbled, bending over his drawing. "Keep the sweater; you can give it to your mother."

When Zaza was already on the way downstairs, he'd called to her from the doorway.

"Listen, Zaza, I think you're still too young and already too old to make afternoon visits to gentlemen who live alone . . . Know what I mean?" And he'd smiled at her gently.

Zaza had looked him straight in the face without smiling, slowly drilled her right index finger against her right temple, shrugged her shoulders and raced down the stairs.

A few days later, Olga had returned his sweater, mended at the elbow and newly washed with soapbark. He'd been vaguely sorry about all this, but he didn't let it show.

Zaza had never again gone back to rue Campagne-Première alone.

: :

A LITTLE while ago, up in her apartment, Olga had asked if this Wakhé and this Jacques, whom Zaza was constantly following about, were "respectable" . . . She hadn't mentioned any Laurent. Therefore, if Zaza hadn't spoken of Laurent at home, it must mean that she hadn't yet looked at him. Therefore, that she hadn't yet seen him. Because on the day she saw him, she'd be sure to take a really good look. Or she'd be the only girl not to, Alex said to himself with a smile.

It remained to be seen if, sometime soon, one of the three famous Shetland-wool sweaters belonging to Laurent Verdon—either the bottle-green-mottled-with-turquoise-blue, the moss-green-mottled-with-tobacco or the light-green-mottled-with-blue—would be taking its turn soaking in the hand basin full of soapy water that was so good at washing away tender little memories . . .

: :

ALEX HAD reached rue des Pyrénées. About a hundred yards from the Métro, a sign raised above a crowd of people said: "Christmas Fund for Spanish Republicans." In the center of the crowd a man was talking, and at his feet was a big copper cauldron containing a few coins. Alex put in a ten-franc note, and without listening to the speech, went on to the Métro.

That evening, at La Coupole, Rodriguez would again say that though he didn't feel in the least bit like doing it, he was nevertheless going to have to go to Spain and fight his idiotic civil war.

And the funny thing was that Rodriguez was very likely to do just that: Rodriguez, who wouldn't hurt a fly, protected ladybugs, loved only painting, women—somewhat fat, not too young and not too beautiful—his friends, the bistro, the silent cinema (except when Prévert made it talk) and who held his fork as though it were a paintbrush . . . What was he really going to be able to do with a rifle in his hands in a country he'd left ten years earlier so that he could paint in peace?

"I'll do what Goya did—I'll paint 'The Disasters of War,' " Rodriguez had replied the other evening, when he was a little drunk.

"If that's your motive, you don't really have to go all the way to Spain to do it," Alex had told him, unaware just how prophetic his comment would turn out to be.

Six months later, without having to change a word of his December prophecy, he would indulge himself by repeating it to Rodriguez, who was still talking about leaving but who was still in Paris.

"You see," he would say to him at the Spanish Republican Pavilion of the International Exposition, "You see: he did that from rue des Grands Augustins, Paris, VI. Do you think anyone could have done better by being there?"

Rodriguez would shake his head. They would both tear themselves away from "Guernica" and toss some change into the mercury fountain, the only other attraction offered visitors to the small, whitewashed pavilion.

: :

AT ABOUT the same time, Maurice, Robert and Sami also took in the Expo, between the written and oral parts of their second bac exam—philo for Maurice and Robert, math for Sami.

Félix had prepared their itinerary: after the USSR Pavilion, which they were to see first, they were to be sure to go throw their contribution into the mercury fountain in the center of the Spanish Republican pavilion. As for the picture everyone was talking about, he'd let them judge for themselves: he thought Josette could easily have done as well when she'd been four years old . . . But after all, the important thing was that this Picasso got people to visit the pavilion.

More preoccupied by their approaching bac than by these windows on the world, they just wandered around eating ice cream, going from Mexico to Switzerland, from Hungary to Egypt, without paying any attention to Félix's program. They weren't as hard on Picasso as he was; they found that the picture wasn't easy to take, but after all, they didn't know anything about painting, and they very ceremoniously deposited their coins on the shiny surface of the quicksilver that had so fascinated them as children.

From the exterior, the modesty and sparseness of the little white pavilion was a permanent insult to the two giants in close competition only a couple of steps away, for they had chosen to confront each other face to face under the Parisian sky. The two flags fluttered to the same rhythm under the spring breeze, but in their folds the black swastika circled in white stood out more clearly on the red flag of Germany than did the golden hammer and sickle on the red flag of the Union of Soviet Socialist Republics. On the other hand, the Communists' building was taller than the Nazis'.

"That unpleasant bird is going to get the girl's sickle and the young man's hammer right in the teeth if it doesn't fly away in time!" Robert had remarked shrewdly, tilting his head toward the tops of the buildings. Up above, the Prussian eagle—caught by the artist-sculptor in its favorite position of poised and intense vigilance—was indeed within the firing line of the robust peasant girl and the muscled worker whom another artist-sculptor had caught at the very moment they were going forward to meet life, brandishing on high, "with two joined hands" (as Stépan would have put it), the humble tools of their daily labor.

There was such a long waiting line in front of the two skyscrapers, star attractions of Expo 37, that Saturday afternoon that the boys had to give up the idea of visiting either. They returned to their own neighborhood and went to study under the tall trees of the Buttes. And also to talk about plans for the summer.

The year before, they had discovered the sea by smuggling time from their work. This year, they'd get to know the mountains. Quite legitimately, all together—including Jeannot and Myriam—and under the guidance of Robert and Josette, who'd rediscover them with the others and for the others.

The tent, already bought secondhand, came from a batch of Post Office supplies. It was khaki-colored, so large and so tall that it made them think of the headquarters of Generals Lee and Grant during the American Civil War.

Though the notion of sleeping under scraps of cloth at the foot of the eternal snows had given rise to laughter or anxiety in the Guttman, Roginski, Nussbaum and Goldberg households, it had enchanted Félix and Jeannette Clément. Finally the people on rue de la Mare would know what this *chez nous* of the Savoyards was like!

Under the trees of the Buttes, Maurice, Robert and Sami completed their lists: lists of books they wanted to take along no matter what. As for the other stuff, Jeannot and the girls could take care of it.

In mid-July, their bacs passed, the boys led the camping expedition. With Coindreau's translations of Hemingway, Dos Passos, Faulkner and Caldwell in their knapsacks, they were assured of the new spiritual nourishment they were entitled to. The troops followed with the pots and pans, the thermos, the sterno stove and the most recent issue of

Cinémonde. The H.Q. was registered as baggage along with the sleeping bags.

They took the night train from the Gare de Lyon and got off at Grenoble, where they started up the mountain. First by bus, then on foot.

: :

ZAZA WAS the first to return to Paris to go back to work, right after August 15.

Glowing with health, she brought back astonishing news: having gone off like a vagabond, she was returning a landowner. Or, more exactly, a co-owner, with her friends, of a parcel of land on which stood whatever remained of the stones that two centuries earlier had been the pious retreat of Italian nuns.

Zaza had told her fabulous story to Olga, Sonia and Myriam's grandmother—hired by the hour to do some hemming, since there was so much work coming in.

The Post Office tent, which had been planted in a pine wood at the top of a hill, had torn loose from its old ropes one stormy night, forcing the occupants to go down into a little valley and shelter under a real roof. They had found it: and not only a roof but the thick walls that supported it, in an almost abandoned hamlet belonging to a Monsieur Dupuis, mayor of the community, owner of a sawmill, master mason and the proprietor of seventy surrounding hectares . . .

At this point in her story, Zaza had taken a snapshot from her knapsack. The women recognized Josette, Zaza and Myriam seated on the ground in the front of the picture; behind them, looking both happy and serious, were Maurice, Robert, Sami and Jeannot, holding large shovels, their backs to an immense stone fireplace surmounted by a Christ carved in the same stone. On the left, a pile of plaster looking like a pile of snow masked the beginning of a stairway that seemed to lead to a lordly upper story.

"The mayor took the photo the day he made us a gift of the Convent on condition that we repair it," Zaza explained soberly.

"Gave you? Just gave it to you?"

"Gave it to us: a gift for life!"

"And for the lives of your children as well?"

Zaza had shrugged and said they were a long way from that.

When he was consulted, Félix had delivered an objective analysis of the affair and drawn the following conclusions: first of all, when you own seventy hectares of land that really belong to everyone, the least you can do is give a few square meters to some people who have nothing; he noted, however, not unhappily, that it was a Savoyard mayor who had done this. Second, the repair or renovation of a holy place could be considered an obligation owed to the glorious heritage of the past. As for the trashy tent, its rottenness showed the contempt in which the security of Post Office workers had been held for years before new supplies were finally issued.

At the Auvergnat's, Monsieur Nussbaum made quite a stir when he announced that his two sons, Jacob and Samuel, had retired to a convent. Monsieur Lowenthal repeated the news to Madame Lowenthal, who was only slightly surprised by it: raised without a religion of any sort, the children of rue de la Mare had found one of their own. It was another kind of kibbutz—the kibbutz of the converts! Things had been bad enough when boys and girls had been allowed to go off and sleep together under the stars . . . but now all this collaborating was going on within the nonjudgmental shadow of a Catholic church—well, that was just too much!

The convent dwellers, male and female, returned at the end of September, announcing immediately upon their arrival that they'd go back up there for Christmas—for all the Christmases, Easters, Trinities, Pentecosts and summers that would make up the rest of their lives.

The three scholars brought back in their knapsacks the uncut pages of their Hemingway, Dos Passos, Caldwell and Faulkner. And their hands were callused.

At the Bonnets', Maurice and Robert had to make their way between the wicker hampers that reminded them of the ones they'd bought "for four corpses, if you cut them lengthwise" the year before. "That was a long time ago," they told each other. The labels stuck on the baskets read "Coolies, *Pirates du Rail,*" "Equestrians, *Gens du Voyage,*" "Mother, grandmother and servant, *Partie de Campagne.*" They gathered that the Coop was doing quite well in the movies.

"Forgive us, but we have to brush our teeth, Monsieur Gisors," said Robert, kissing the empty sleeve of a sumptuous midnight-blue mandarin tunic made of heavy silk embroidered with silver.

"Do you think they might make a movie of our *Man's Fate?*" asked Maurice.

"I'd just as soon they didn't. No one has the right to make Malraux's characters look like anything but the way I saw in my head . . . "

" . . . And me in mine," added Maurice.

AS FOR the hampers, the boys hadn't been wrong: things were going very well for the Coop because things were going very well for French cinema.

"It's the beginning of the Golden Age!" Alex would say. "You, you were right not to leave. And you, you were very right to have come . . . "

The first sentence was addressed to Rodriguez, the second to a woman sitting between Rodriguez and Alex at a table in a somewhat austere café on the corner of boulevard Saint-Germain and the very provincial rue Saint-Benoît.

" . . . Very right!" repeated Alex, looking at the woman gravely.

She must have been about thirty, very pale, with extremely wide gray eyes bordered with lashes lightly brushed with dark-blue mascara; she was smiling, and her large well-shaped lips were free of makeup. She had a slim neck and very black hair. She wore its waves combed back without a center part; she had gathered the heavy mass in one hand and it looked as if it were knotted into a loose chignon a little above her nape. Her name was Angelina Crespi, and she had an American mother and a Hungarian father; there was something of the princess about her; she spoke unaccented French and came from Austria, where she had until then done painting and design work for the Vienna Opera—for which, she was saying, she would never paint or design again.

In the afternoon, even though he was overwhelmed with work, Alex had taken Angelina Crespi to the little white Spanish Republican pavilion to see the Picasso again, this time with her. The Expo was still open. The mercury was still gushing in the fountain, and the charitable contributions were still pouring in.

The war in Spain went on. It was being fought without Rodriguez, and Alex was very glad of this.

So glad that when Rodriguez had introduced Angelina Crespi to him the day before, he hadn't even heard his friend say, after announcing her name, "*Cuidado, cuidado* . . . "; it had been lost in the hubbub of La Coupole and the bursts of laughter from Laurent Verdon.

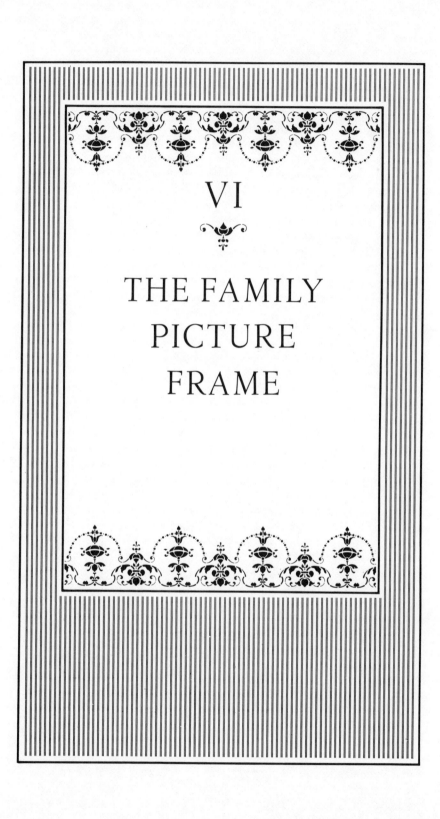

VI

THE FAMILY
PICTURE
FRAME

*M*AURICE SPOONED up the sugary brown paste re-
maining in the bottom of his coffee cup and ate it like candy before he
told Robert, "I swear . . . I almost said to you: 'I know him!' "

There were no more customers in the little restaurant on rue Bonaparte. It was almost three o'clock in the afternoon. They'd eaten at a
table for six. The other four were regulars who knew the waitress
well—for that matter, so did all the other customers. During the meal,
they had spoken loudly about things that Maurice and Robert knew
nothing about: forms and formats, colors and coloring, matter and
materials. They held their glasses in paint-stained hands, sometimes
using them to outline a point in a space of which they alone knew the
ideal limits.

Maurice and Robert faced each other at one end of the table. They
didn't want to listen, but they couldn't *not* hear, and it made all real
conversation between them impossible. They'd smiled while they
waited for it all to be over, and they'd even laughed at the loud jokes
the others had wanted them to share. And suddenly the bistro had
emptied, as swiftly as a schoolyard after recess.

"They were funny . . . they could be living on another planet,"
Robert said after the stampede, when they found themselves alone and
eating their caramel custards.

"They're lucky," Maurice sighed, pushing aside the red-and-white
checked curtain to watch them cross rue Bonaparte and enter the

Beaux-Arts courtyard. "We should have become painters or sculptors," he added, letting the curtain fall back.

"Bad news from Earth always eventually reaches Mars. The poor bastards will soon find that out," said Robert.

This was their own way of going back to the conversation they had let drop on entering this restaurant neither of them knew and which they had particularly chosen so they could be undisturbed.

It was November. To be precise, it was November 10, 1938, and Monsieur Ernst von Rath had just died.

Monsieur Ernst von Rath was the Third Secretary at the German Embassy in Paris. And he had died during the night of November 9–10 because a young man had put two revolver bullets into him on the morning of the seventh.

This young man's name was Herschel Grynszpan; he was of Polish nationality, of Jewish faith, and he was seventeen years old.

And it was this extraordinary news item that Maurice and Robert were getting ready to discuss again while ordering their coffees from a waitress already turning chairs upside down on the other deserted tables.

"Come to think of it," Robert said suddenly, "didn't something like this happen when we were younger? A Jew who had assassinated some kind of Russian general . . . We were just kids at the time . . . "

Maurice looked at Robert and said nothing.

"Don't tell me you don't remember . . . You even thought you saw the killer on the empty lot! It was the day we discovered . . . "

"It was the day we discovered Dr. Pierre's glass eye!" Maurice confirmed quietly.

"So why are you pretending not to know what I'm talking about?"

"I'm not pretending anything. I just didn't think you remembered."

"So what was his name?"

"Petliura," replied Maurice.

"The murderer?"

"No, the man who was murdered. I don't know the other one's name. I never did."

And Maurice told Robert about "Pouett-Pouett," because "Pouett-Pouett" went back to the days of Madame Lutz.

And when he'd finished, he scooped up the sugar in the bottom of his cup and said, "That morning, on rue des Pyrénées, when I read his name, I swear I almost said, 'I know him.' "

"And why didn't you tell me?"

"Probably because it was too complicated . . . "

"What year was that? Before or after Lindbergh?"

"It must have been before, because when we used to play at being Lindbergh we couldn't use the empty lot anymore, they'd begun to build on it . . . We'd go to the alley to play Lindbergh . . . "

"Then it was in twenty-six," said Robert. "The weather was great, and we hadn't been in Paris very long . . . "

"You came during the Easter vacation."

"In that case it was April or May of twenty-six . . . How stupid—now we'll never know. Stupid and irritating."

"So stupid and irritating that we've got to settle it," said Maurice. "Come on, let's pay up and get out of here . . . We're going to find out!"

They didn't go to the National Library or the National Archives or the *Gazette des Tribunaux*. They went only a couple of steps away: Maurice had just remembered old Moreau d'Argy, the madman of rue Séguier.

But even if Moreau d'Argy had been the madman of the Batignolles, they would have gone to him. They had all the time they needed. All day, just as when they were children.

It was a Thursday, the day before Armistice Day.

Robert had come from Le Havre that morning; he'd been a teacher's assistant there since the fall. He'd met Maurice at the Carrefour Danton *tabac*. Maurice had come from across the way, from the Villeneuve University Bookstore on rue de Seine, where he'd been working and living since August.

Maurice was preparing his philo and Robert his history-geo after an unforgettable final school year together at the Lycée Louis-le-Grand in a class that was preparing them for entrance into the Ecole Normale Supérieure. During that time, they had finally come to know the Latin Quarter from something other than the songs bawled out by the beret-wearers at the time of their first bac. Then, after four weeks of school-boy vacation out in the country, they had separated for the first time in their lives.

They were no longer lycée students, though they were able to meet that November 10, after several weeks of separation, thanks to school vacations that made a long weekend possible for teachers, their students and their booksellers.

"Don't be afraid," Maurice said to Robert as he pushed him under a porte-cochère on rue Séguier. "He's nuts, but he's got it all. He's the King of Bloody Crime."

NOT A DROP of blood justly or unjustly shed on French soil during the last twenty years had escaped the disturbing collector's talent of Joseph Moreau d'Argy.

Starting with the principle that wholesale legal slaughter had died a natural death on November 11, 1918, Joseph Moreau had been intent on proving, first to himself and then to a very select clientele, that the modest flowing of blood on a small scale was only the consequence of bad habits contracted during the exercise of what he called "industrial-scale assembly-line killing."

This had all begun right after his demobilization, when he had read a newspaper item about a particularly horrible slaughter on a farm in Creuse, the sad protagonist of which had been a hero at the battle of Chemin des Dames.

The idea of a book had immediately sprouted in his head. He promised himself he would write it and had even decided on the title. It would be called *The War College of Crime.* And to shore up his work with concrete examples, he had subscribed to all the Paris and regional newspapers.

But the abundance of newsprint that arrived every day, the time spent removing subscription bands, which often stuck to the paper like a bandage to a pus-filled wound, the care he took in pressing the pages with a warm iron so as to erase the creases that made reading difficult, the cutting and pasting of material that could be used to swell his files for *The War College of Crime,* had forced him to postpone the writing of the first chapter.

In any case, the scarcity of army veterans who were also killers soon made itself felt, and Joseph Moreau indulged himself with desultory reading that led him astray from his self-imposed path, inducing him to cut and paste stories in which the plentiful blood that flowed wasn't necessarily the work of some valiant *poilu* (or even of a man: Joseph Moreau also discovered crimes committed by women).

The owner of a handsome house on rue Séguier, he had had a shed built at the rear of the courtyard, to which he moved all the dossiers that encumbered the third-floor apartment he shared with his mother. Little by little the shed had changed from a storehouse to a study, then from a study to a public reading room. Joseph Moreau had made ivy grow over the walls of the shed, and planted a potted wisteria, the clusters of which curved gracefully over the windows of the entrance in summer. No one could have suspected that this sunny pavilion sheltered the best collection of crimes—crimes that were often unimaginable and yet had in fact been imagined by those who had perpetrated them, and whose names were carefully stored on the polished shelves of what Madame Moreau d'Argy, his mother, called "Joseph's Little National Library" and his clients called the "House of Crime."

Joseph Moreau never used that word when discussing his clients; he called them his "consulting habitués." People "visited Moreau's": they didn't "buy." They consulted and paid. They paid by the quarter of an hour. The consulting habitués were of two kinds: criminologists and criminophiles.

The criminophiles visited and revisited, buying quarters of an hour that they would sometimes prolong into half a day. They could be recognized by the fact that they took no notes and asked for the same volumes time and time again, a little like passionate music lovers who play the same record over and over.

The criminologists rarely went past the allotted time, and noted dates, places, names, ages of witnesses and verdicts.

Maurice had made his first visit to the "House of Crime" for a professor who frequented the Villeneuve bookstore. "Good day, my young customer!" had been the greeting of a fifty-year-old with carefully tended hands and a double chin whose folds rested on the silk of a loosely tied, navy-blue, white-polka-dotted bow.

"We'll look under incest," Joseph Moreau had replied when Maurice had asked him to verify a detail of the Violette Nozière trial.

And thus it was that Maurice had discovered the unusual classifications of the Moreau method.

Unable to complete the work he had in earlier days dreamed of devoting to a special type of crime, Joseph Moreau had nevertheless not abandoned his respect for genres in general. He rejected the idea of mixing everything together under the vulgar pretext of a chronological classification: his system was based on a subjective judgment of newspaper items.

"I don't mix dishtowels and napkins. Everything in its place," he was in the habit of saying when explaining his method.

So the victims and victimizers were arranged in families and family groups. Each set of shelves had its own, and each volume in each set of shelves bore the number of a year in gilt letters. The volumes began in 1919 and ended in 1937, the current year being at the bindery.

There were eight sets of shelves, each bearing an identification panel on which the initials indicating the classification Moreau had decided to attribute to it were inscribed:

C.D. for CRIMES OF DEBAUCHERY

M.P. for MURDERS OF PASSION

H.M.P. for HOMOSEXUAL MURDERS OF PASSION

H.C. for HOMOSEXUAL CRIMES

S.C. for SADISTIC CRIMES

I.M. for INCESTUOUS MURDERS

P.EX. for POLITICAL EXECUTIONS

G.A. for GRATUITOUS ACTS

He was obviously very careful about nuances. And since he also had his moods, he would sometimes show to the door some impertinent habitué who would want, for example, to move to the shelves devoted to toughs (H.C.) some young, sentimental and unlucky invert whose unfortunate blow with an eighteenth-century Castilian dagger to the heart of an unsympathetic antiquarian had incited Joseph Moreau to bury him—after capital punishment had been carried out—in the H.M.P. section, 1932.

"Welcome, young customers! Gracious friends!" Joseph Moreau had exclaimed when he noticed Robert following behind Maurice. "Is this young Viking your brother?"

"Not really, but he might as well be, Monsieur Moreau. I'd like a quarter of an hour from you," Maurice said, placing a five-franc note on the little table around which Joseph Moreau sat eating pastries with his old mother and Sylvestre Bondy, the secretary-landscape painter who shared their family life.

"Do I have to take you by the hand, or do you know where you want to go?" asked Moreau.

"Thank you, but we know, Monsieur Moreau. We're going straight to P.EX.," answered Maurice, digging out the year 1926 and placing it on the big oak table in front of which Robert had taken a seat. He sat down next to him, while Joseph Moreau started the timer so familiar to chess players and to habitués of the "House of Crime," and it was to the rhythm of this discreet tick-tock that they began leafing through the book.

Flipping through the first three months of the year 1926, after April 16, Maurice slowed down as he came to the large stiff pages on which were pasted those press clippings Joseph Moreau had judged worthy of notice.

"Here we are," they both said softly and simultaneously when they got to the end of May.

Three different headlines had been selected, and each one took up a full page, dated in red:

WEDNESDAY, MAY 26

"A POLITICAL CRIME"
PETLIURA,
FORMER DICTATOR OF THE UKRAINE,
ASSASSINATED IN PARIS BY
ONE OF HIS COMPATRIOTS

was the one from *l'Echo de Paris*;

PETLIURA, COUNTERREVOLUTIONARY
GANG LEADER WHO RAVAGED THE UKRAINE,
ASSASSINATED IN PARIS BY A
RUSSIAN JEW

was the one from *L'Humanité*;

POLITICAL HATRED!
GENERAL PETLIURA,
FORMER PRESIDENT OF THE
REPUBLIC OF THE UKRAINE,
IS ASSASSINATED ON RUE RACINE
BY A RUSSIAN EMIGRANT

was the one from *Le Matin*.

"Here's the one I saw!" said Maurice, putting a finger on *Le Matin*. "Funny—the way I remember it, 'Petliura' was spread across the whole top of the page, but it really only takes up two columns."

"Yes, but they've got pictures of both of them," said Robert. "And a spelling mistake. Look at the other guy—they spell his name 'Schwarzbar.' They left out his final *d*!"

Maurice studied the two faces he'd caught a glimpse of so long ago. Petliura's emerged—delicate, aristocratic and indifferent—from an officer's collar decked with gold braid, and there was the suggestion of a leather bandolier on his left shoulder. Schwarzbard's face looked like one of those rare photos of Chaplin when he wasn't playing the Little Tramp.

"Read it to me," said Robert.

And Maurice read out this document, the one he'd so hoped to find where he'd left it, at the top of the Métro steps, the evening he'd gone to wait for Elie at Les Pyrénées station. His voice was a little hoarse.

"POLITICAL HATRED!
General Petliura,
former President of the
Republic of the Ukraine,
is assassinated on rue Racine
by a Russian emigrant.
"His murderer, a naturalized Frenchman, is arrested.

"The drama that occurred yesterday afternoon on rue Racine lacked the banal motive of jealousy that characterizes so many Parisian dramas of today. If he is to be believed, when the murderer gunned down his victim with seven pistol bullets he was intent on satisfying a hatred that had its origins in both politics and religion.

"Samuel Schwarzbar, the murderer—a Jew from Smolensk (Russia), where he was born in 1888, and a naturalized French citizen who fought in the French army during the Great War—had for several years owned a small watch-repair shop at 82 Boulevard de Ménilmontant. Anyone seeing this short, blond, forty-year-old, dressed in a white smock and usually leaning over his worktable from morning to night, his loupe in his eye, would not have recognized him yesterday on rue Racine, bareheaded but still in his smock, as he bent, pistol in hand, to fire into the body of his dying victim.

"At approximately 2 P.M., a passer-by, aged about forty and with a clean-shaven, prosperous face, was leaving a restaurant on rue Racine, about to turn into boulevard Saint-Michel. He heard his name called: 'Hey, Pan Petliura!' (In Slavic languages, Pan means 'Lord,' or 'Royal Highness').

"The passer-by, whose name was indeed Petliura, turned to face a man in a white smock who was brandishing a high-caliber pistol.

" 'Scum, defend your hide!' he shouted, at the same time firing three shots into Petliura's chest. Before the witnesses had time to intervene, the murderer bent over the dying man and fired his weapon three more times.

"He was about to fire his last bullet when the pistol jammed.

"Samuel Schwarzbar stood up and waited calmly.

"He handed his revolver to a policeman who arrived at top speed and who, with the help of his colleagues, had considerable trouble protecting the murderer from the fury of the crowd as he was being taken to the Odéon police station.

"The victim was quickly identified. M. Simon Petliura was born May 10,

1879, in Kiev (Ukraine) and was currently living at 7 rue Thénard in the Vth arrondissement.

"The watchmaker Schwarzbar's bloody act was a political crime, as he himself explained in a report to Police-Commissioner Mollard of the Odéon quarter.

" 'In 1917 I was part of a French military mission to Petrograd and Odessa. At that time I heard detailed accounts of the Jewish massacres in the Ukraine, where Petliura was leader of the provisional government. He was driven out by the Soviets, but his hatred of the Jewish race made him pursue them through Poland and Czechoslovakia. From then on, I was determined to avenge my brothers and kill this man. Two weeks ago I finally met my enemy. He was leaving a restaurant, but was with a woman and a young girl. I did not want to fire at him then, lest I injure the women. Today, I made up for lost time. I killed him, and good riddance!'

"Petliura's Past

"Simon Petliura lived with his wife and twelve-year-old daughter in a small furnished apartment at 7 rue Thénard.

"A friend of the deceased informed this correspondent that from the autumn of 1917 Simon Petliura headed the Ukrainian Nationalist Movement. He was the Ukrainian government's war minister following the separation of the Ukraine and Bolshevist Russia. Then, after the Skoropadski coup d'état, was elected president of the governing council of the Ukrainian Democratic Republic. He was forced in early 1921 to withdraw into Poland with the army, and remained there until autumn 1924, when he came to France.

"Although an ardent nationalist who led the struggle against Bolshevism, it is incorrect to assume Petliura was the inspiration for the anti-Jewish pogroms.

"Later that afternoon, Police Commissioner Mollard, accompanied by the murderer, went to search Schwarzbar's home at 82 boulevard de Ménilmontant. All information collected concerning Schwarzbar appeared favorable.

"Schwarzbar had fought in a French infantry unit during the war, was seriously wounded in March 1916 and earned a brilliant citation as well as a Croix de Guerre.

" 'I knew nothing about his plans,' declared the weeping Mme. Schwarzbar."

Maurice turned to the next page.

In its May 27 issue, *Le Matin* published a letter sent express from Schwarzbar (who still hadn't recovered his *d*) to his wife.

My dear wife, I am going to do my duty and avenge my poor country, in which thousands were massacred, raped, robbed and oppressed. Petliura is responsible for this. I beg you to remain calm, and I accept total responsibility for my act of vengeance. Goodbye. Samuel.

"Can you imagine! Still wearing his smock, he stopped on the way, between boulevard de Ménilmontant, right near our neighborhood, and here in rue Racine, to mail an express letter to his wife!" said Maurice, turning the page.

In their May 29 issue, *L'Echo de Paris* announced: "Petliura was assassinated by the hand of Moscow," and *L'Humanité* retraced the "career" (in quotes) of the "adventurer Petliura," but made no mention of Schwarzbard.

"We'll never know if *L'Echo* ever gave him back his *d*," said Robert.

They found the epilogue of the affair in a half page from *Le Petit Parisien*. It was a photographic report on the funeral of "General Petliura" at the Montparnasse cemetery. Three large pictures: the widow and the orphan, a portrait of the deceased and a kneeling crowd made up of the fifteen hundred Ukrainians in Paris who had come to say goodbye to their venerated leader.

"Come to think of it, May 26 was a Wednesday! Why weren't we in school?" Maurice said suddenly.

"Because we hadn't had any school either Tuesday or Wednesday," replied Robert. "But I can't remember why."

"Hold it—wasn't there croup or meningitis in the neighborhood?"

"Croup! You're right: that's why your mother kept you in bed for twenty-four hours."

"Not twenty-four hours, because the next day you told me that he would have killed all of us . . . "

"No! The next day was Thursday, and there was no school, so you slept all day!"

"You're sure?"

"You bet! I went up to your place three times."

"You're kidding! But I could have sworn . . . "

"The fragility of human testimony!" said Joseph Moreau, who hadn't missed a word of their discussion. "Should I stop my timer, young customers? Your quarter of an hour is about to expire . . . "

"Just another minute," said Maurice. "I want to glance at the trial, and then we'll be finished . . . "

"Since I know the affair you're interested in, I can assure you that a glance won't do. The epilogue, as collated by me, is extremely copious, my young friend. Come back again some day," said Moreau, his hand on the timer.

Maurice contented himself with opening the voluminous dossier of the trial at random and had only time enough to read that it had begun on October 8, 1927, and to see the photo of a man who, with his hand toward the camera, was trying to hide his smiling and scarred face.

He was about to close the book when he stopped and looked again.

The hand, the smile and the scar were as familiar to him as the rue de la Mare's flowered wallpaper, Sonia's laugh, Zaza's whims and his father's footsteps on the stairs. Yet he couldn't begin to understand why and for how long that image had been so intimate a part of his life.

He closed the album.

"You can cut your motor, Monsieur Moreau," he said.

He was looking at Robert. "I can't go into this 'I know him' routine with him again," he told himself. "I'll have to figure it out by myself." And he tried to get rid of his sense of *déjà vu*. He even began to wonder if it wasn't due to "false recognition," otherwise known as "memories of the present," whose effects as described by Bergson he was just then studying at the Sorbonne and in the Villeneuve bookstore.

"That was time well spent!" Robert exclaimed. "Now we know that it was a Wednesday at 2 P.M. on a May 26, and in 1926 . . . "

"When will your bindery return the current year, Monsieur Moreau?" asked Maurice, replacing the 1926 volume in the P.EX. section.

"When the year has expired, poor thing!" said Moreau.

"Let's hope he hasn't skimped on the leather spine and that he's been generous with the casing, because as of the day before yesterday you've got two new important inmates," declared Maurice, calling on Robert for confirmation.

"Funny you should mention that! Mother, Sylvestre and I were talking about it just this morning," said Moreau, munching on a cream puff. "It's difficult to know where we're going to put those two. . . . Delicate, very delicate!"

"Why? Doesn't 'Political Execution' strike you as the place?" suggested Robert.

"If you take a closer look at their pictures, you begin to wonder," said Moreau, turning for approval to Sylvestre Bondy, who gave it with a sad smile. "Who can say what bonds united these two young men to the point of disuniting them in so deadly a fashion?"

"Do you mean to say that if I come back in January 1 may find Monsieur von Rath, Nazi, and Monsieur Grynszpan, Polish Jew, in the section devoted to Homosexual Crimes of Passion? Come now, Monsieur Moreau, don't give us that backwards García Lorca business again! After all, it was Franco's Fascist militia that executed the Republican Lorca, not his jealous lover, as some people have written!"

"I've got so much to do keeping up with France that these Spanish upheavals don't interest me," said Moreau.

"In other words, it's all sombreros and mantillas as far as you're concerned, right?" said Maurice, suddenly becoming very pale and snapping his fingers like castanets.

"Come on, let's beat it," Robert called to him as he walked toward the exit.

"Until next time, young customers," said Joseph Moreau.

They didn't answer, but went out through the door he was holding open.

: :

"THAT FELLOW of yours isn't crazy—he's a dangerous son of a bitch," commented Robert when they were out in rue Séguier.

They walked on a moment in silence. They were both thinking the same thing, and Robert was the first to voice it.

"How are the Nussbaums taking it?"

"It's awful," said Maurice. "It's been two months since they first found out. At least old man Nussbaum goes to Clignancourt, so he has to move around a little, but no one sees Madame Nussbaum outside anymore. She just sits in her kitchen crying. Myriam does her shopping and the cooking . . . She's forbidden Manolo to enter the apartment because of his Spanish accent . . . "

"And Sami?"

"Sami? It's all his fault."

"How come it's all his fault?"

"His fault for everything. His fault because he's the living brother of a dead brother, his fault for having let him go, for studying medicine, for having had a fight with Jeannot three days before Jeannot left to join the Brigades, for having been one of Florian's best students, for liking to read and discuss and fool around, for liking Fred Astaire, Charles Trénet, the Marx Brothers, Django Reinhardt, and his fault for having chased off the Committee mourners who wanted to hold a reception in front of Jeannot's crepe-draped picture while a funeral march was being played, his fault for having seen the humor of it and telling me, his fault for seeing the sun come up in the morning . . . his fault, period!"

"In other words, like us," said Robert.

"Like us . . . if you want to put it that way . . . "

They were on rue de Seine.

"Do you see my room? It's the window at the end, on the fourth floor," Maurice pointed out when they reached the Villeneuve bookstore, whose iron grill was down. "Want to come up? I'll make you a good cup of Phoscao!"

They crossed the street, and before entering the handsome Louis XIII house Robert glanced at the bookstore window through the grill-work. There were just a few books, but they were carefully displayed —works of philosophy, contemporary history and sociology. Beyond the window, the shop seemed to go back a long way.

A simple iron railing ran along the stone flights of stairs. On the landings two doors painted dark green faced each other. On the third floor there was only one door, on the left; on the right, a wooden stairway led to a landing on the low-ceilinged fourth floor. Maurice's room was at the end of the hallway, right above the third-floor apartment.

"Look at this: I've got two entrances—or exits, if you prefer," Maurice pointed out.

He raised a trapdoor in the middle of the room. Below it was a spiral stairway that led to a waxed wooden floor.

"Do you use it?" asked Robert.

"Of course," replied Maurice, closing the trap. "Whenever the Villeneuves invite me down, or when they're out. They have three kids —seven, nine and twelve. When the Villeneuves go out and I'm home, I open my trapdoor and play Nanny. What I mean is, I listen to them sleep . . . "

"In other words, just like me," said Robert, laughing. "But I've got to listen to thirty of them sleeping, and not only don't they sleep, but I haven't got a trapdoor I can close when I want a little peace. . . . All I've got is a thin curtain at the end of the dormitory. . . . "

Robert had sat down on the bed. It was a real mahogany bed, shaped like a boat. He looked at the worktable loaded with books and newspapers and placed in front of a window overlooking the dome of the Institute, at the pretty walnut chair in front of the table, at the small black marble mantelpiece, and at the toile-de-Jouy-covered screen behind which Maurice was running the water.

"If I were to go in for the nineteenth century, it would be something in the style of Daudet's *Petit Chose* . . . But you—you've obviously drawn on Balzac, Flaubert and Stendhal . . . By the way, how old is this Madame Villeneuve?"

"Idiot!" exclaimed Maurice, setting two glasses and a pitcher of water down on the table. "The Villeneuves are fantastic people."

He opened a cupboard and took out a half-full bottle of whiskey, which he set down beside the pitcher.

"Fantastic in what way?" asked Robert as he poured a few fingers of whiskey into a glass.

Maurice thought for a moment.

"Let's put it this way. If we're young nineteenth-century characters, then the Villeneuves could be called eighteenth-century humanists, if you see what I mean . . . "

"Well then, to their health!" Robert sang out, lifting his glass. "They must have their work cut out for them in times like these."

"Evidently no more than usual. If you talk to them and to the people who come to their apartment, or to the bookstore downstairs, you begin to realize that the world has always been a mess. And people like them have always worked at trying to make it better, at trying to help those who were in trouble. The people you meet downstairs are almost all survivors of old battles that are still going on, battles you and I have never heard about . . .

"Don't tell me they've got Chouans downstairs?"

Maurice burst out laughing.

"I haven't seen any yet, but then I still haven't met everyone. On the other hand, I've already met Tonkinese, Arabs and Madagascans who've spoken to me about struggles against their own General Hoches, and Irishmen who've spoken of theirs, and a few North Americans who've told me about the chivalrous South in which Negroes are hanged from sycamores, and a few South Americans who've told me things about the Spanish and Portuguese conquests they never taught us in school. And I've listened to the talk of Italian Socialists, Polish Bundists, Russian Trotskyites, Hungarian Communists, Armenian Nationalists, old Turkish militants who were Young Turks, Greek anarchists, Baltic barons, Germans . . . "

"And all these people don't go for each other's throats?"

" 'bsolutely not. . . . They discuss and they compare."

"What?"

"For one thing, they compare their prisons, because almost all of them have been in one. In their own countries, and often for opposite reasons. But their prisons are very much alike, and they themselves end up being very much alike too . . . Funny, isn't it?" said Maurice, pouring himself a small shot of whiskey and a lot of water.

"Side-splitting!" said Robert, going him one better.

Robert was standing in front of the small marble mantelpiece, with his back to Maurice. He looked at some photographs slipped between the tarnished gilt frame and the narrow spotted mirror. There was a very big one in the middle.

"How did you do this?" asked Robert.

"A friend of Zaza's, a movie photographer, had it blown up for me," said Maurice.

As on a press photo, Maurice had written along the bottom edge: *The Convent, August 1937.*

Zaza, Josette and Myriam were seated on the ground. Robert, Maurice, Sami and Jeannot were standing behind them, and all seven were smiling in front of an immense fireplace dominated by a Christ cut into the stone. The boys held large shovels, and on the left of the photo, at the bottom of a stairway, a huge pile of plaster made a white spot, like a pile of snow.

"That's the one the mayor took . . . I've got the other one," said Robert, searching through his wallet.

It was smaller but exactly the same, except for the fact that where Jeannot had been there was a tall man wearing a black felt hat of the type worn by mountain men.

"When we began fixing up the convent," said Robert, "Jeannot wasn't talking about going to Spain."

"No," replied Maurice, while Robert inspected the other photos. "No, we were the ones who did the talking about it—Sami, you and I. And we never stopped . . . "

"We never stopped talking about going, and we never went. He went, and now he's dead," murmured Robert as he continued to examine the snapshots. "You and I aren't Katovs or Ch'ens. No more than our papas are . . . " he added, with a laugh. "My papa also talked a lot about leaving. Well, he did eventually leave, but for the Allier. It's not exactly Catalonia . . . "

"That's a rotten thing to say!" said Maurice, who couldn't keep himself from laughing. "You know, I saw him down there . . . "

"Who, my papa?"

"No, Malraux. He's a friend of Villeneuve's. He blew in and out late one evening. He was leaving for the frontier that night . . . "

"Apparently he never set foot in China!"

"Yes, I know, but I don't give a damn. It doesn't change a thing for me. What I mean is that it doesn't change what I got out of *Man's Fate.*"

"For me either, and even less for *him*," said Robert, placing his index finger on Jeannot's smiling face. "Since he never read the book . . . "

He had slid his finger from Jeannot's face to the stone Christ, then to the pile of plaster.

"Have the Villeneuves ever seen this picture?"

"Yes," replied Maurice.

"They must've thought we were some kind of church group!"

"No, I told them all about it—camping in the mountains, the storm, the tent that blew away, the ruin where we took shelter, and rebuilding the ruin . . . "

"And did you tell them that the ruin is ours now?"

"I told them everything, and they thought it was very funny and very moral. They even asked me if we couldn't take their oldest with us the next time we go up there."

"But not next Christmas. There's still too much work to do on the first floor now that we've finished down below. You'll be surprised how much we got done after you left. It's more like Versailles now, not the public baths on rue des Pyrénées!" said Robert, still looking at the photos.

"We're talking like real landlords!"

"No, comrade, like kolkhozniks! Kolkhozniks who are the curators and preservers of the glorious heritage of the Savoyard past, as my father has explained on numerous occasions . . . And who's this?"

Robert had put his finger on the only unknown face among those adorning the tarnished mirror frame. It was a little Fotomat snapshot.

"A girl . . . an English girl."

"Jesus, Guttman, all you need is a few months of freedom and you . . . "

"Don't be an ass!" said Maurice, a little curtly. "She's gone back to her own country, and I loved her very much."

"Was it this summer?"

"Yes, when I began working in the bookstore."

"And?"

"And in September there was Munich and she went home."

"So it wasn't that long ago . . . "

"No, not that long ago."

Robert turned from the mantelpiece and came back to sit on the bed.

"Does anyone sleep at the Bonnets' these days?" he asked, playing with the switch on the yellow mushroom lamp he'd just found clipped to the head of Maurice's bed.

"Yes, Zaza does."

"Did she choose my bed or yours?"

"She chose a davenport. Manolo took away all the folding beds in the house, including Josette's, when your folks left the loge. Your mother told mine that there were four rooms plus a bathroom in the 'professional accommodations' in Neuilly-le-Réal. It wasn't all that easy explaining to my mother just what 'professional accommodations' meant! But she did understand about the four rooms and a bathroom. As for Neuilly—Réal or not—the very word made Zaza's mother die laughing . . . In short, the folding beds have disappeared, along with all our dreams as children of rue de la Mare, and now Zaza does her dreaming on a soft couch with a telephone at the head of it. That was your father's farewell gift. Before going off to take up his job as chief postmaster of the main Post Office in Neuilly-Whatever, he sent his pals from the XXth to make an emergency installation in the costumers' kolkhoze. PYR 23-89 is what they've been known as since October. Please note that they stuffed a rag in the bell so that Madame Lowenthal won't find out, and now whenever I call I have to let it ring at least ten times before they finally hear it!"

"How about another shot of Phoscao?" asked Robert, holding his glass out to Maurice, who poured him a little whiskey, then poured himself even less, drowned in a lot of water. "In other words, you phone them but you never go there?" he continued, after a brief silence.

"I go there once or twice a week, but between the Sorbonne and the bookstore I have a lot of work to do, you know . . . "

"Actually, you're just like me: there's a gap. Yours is between the VIth and the XXth, and mine between the Lower Seine and the Allier, but it's the same thing. You're doing philo and I'm doing history— we're not leather-working or dispatching postal orders. That's the way it is. We've got to face it and not be ashamed."

"I'm not ashamed, but sometimes it makes me a little unhappy. Especially when I don't feel like going and I just telephone."

"You should have come along and been a *pion* with me in Le Havre. That way you would have had all the excuses you needed."

"No, there I would really have felt as if I were abandoning them."

"I abandoned mine all right, plus a very young sister!"

"Yes, but yours are called Clément, not Guttman or Roginski," said Maurice.

"I don't see . . . "

"Yes you do. You see very well!"

"Your bookstore customers are beginning to get to you with their obsessions," said Robert, shrugging his shoulders.

"I don't need them—nor does Zaza. I was about to tell you before, but we got off on the folding beds. Whenever Zaza doesn't sleep at the Bonnets' it's because she's 'on location,' as the movie people put it. She was supposed to leave last week as assistant to a script girl, a very nice girl called Mimi . . . "

"Doesn't she do costumes anymore?"

"Yes, she does, but at the same time she's learning about scripts. As I was saying, she was supposed to leave with a French crew, for a French film, with French actors, for location shots in Germany. At the last moment, they left her behind. They noticed that she was maybe a little Jewish, but they told her that she was a little young . . . At home, she told them she wasn't going because they thought she was too young, but she told me the truth, which she'd learned from Mimi . . . "

"And why didn't she tell the truth at home?"

"She didn't want them to be frightened. Or rather, she didn't want them to be frightened again . . . "

"They never struck me as being afraid!" Robert exclaimed.

"Nor Zaza or me, either, because they must have kept it hidden from us. They were still almost children when they had us—children who had always been afraid. And so they wanted to have children who wouldn't be afraid. Zaza and I didn't realize this until recently. We had to move out of the house before we began to remember little things . . . little things that made us laugh at the time."

"Things that I knew about?"

"Of course! The assassination of Paul Doumer by Gorguloff, for example—you remember that, don't you? We must have been about thirteen or fourteen years old. Well, the first question my mother asked that day was 'Gorguloff? At least it's not Jewish, is it?' . . . No, it wasn't Jewish. Oof! And only then were we free to weep for the dead president, for his poor wife and for his poor children, several of whom had given their lives for France. We were free to weep with a clear conscience in the second-floor kitchens, just as the Bonnet twins were weeping in the first-floor kitchen, and to quietly curse the foreign assassin—'bsolutely not Jewish—of the great French president . . . "

"No one was weeping in the ground-floor kitchen that evening!" Robert noted with a smile. "We were discussing things, because there was a problem. We had *two* villains to get our teeth into—the victim and the murderer. The victim was a dirty colonialist, and the murderer a dirty counterrevolutionary. Papa had a lot of trouble deciding how he felt about it! But what made you think about this Gorguloff business?"

"Because of Weidmann and his six innocent victims. My mother had exactly the same tone in her voice: 'Weidmann . . . Six corpses, how terrible! But tell me—Weidmann isn't Jewish, is he?'—'No, simply a German, like Hitler,' Zaza told her."

"And so?"

"So nothing. My mother looked at Olga, and then she began to talk about something else, the way they did when we were children. They don't want to talk about Hitler when we're around. Hitler is far away, Hitler is in Germany. Just as Petliura was in the Ukraine. Here, we're in France, and we don't talk about such things. . . . Just think, it took Old Lady Lowenthal's damned goulash before the name Petliura was spoken at home—where by the way, I've also never heard the name Schwarzbard . . . You've got to admit it's odd!"

"On the other hand, we did talk about it downstairs," said Robert. "But today I understand why . . . "

"So do I. It's because you weren't Jews, but especially because Petliura was anti-Bolshevist!"

"Exactly."

"It's funny that old Florian never spoke to us about it at that time either, seeing he always talked to us about everything."

"Maybe he thought it was none of his business. He was teaching us the History of France, since we were little Frenchmen." Then Robert added, "Besides, you and Zaza do the same thing. Zaza tells them she's too young so that she won't frighten them, and you let her do it . . . And Madame Mimi, what does she do?"

"What about Mimi?"

"She's going to Germany anyway, even though she knows they're not taking Zaza because she's Jewish?"

"I think so."

"Well, then, you see? No one ever tells anyone anything," Robert concluded, getting up.

He put his glass on the table.

"You're right," said Maurice. "Though you have to admit I said quite a bit to you today . . . More than you've said to me, in any case."

"That's because I don't have much to say," replied Robert.

He had moved around the table and gone to stand in front of the window. The light was failing.

"I don't have anything to do with the cosmopolitan intelligentsia, and from the window of the classroom where I keep an eye on things, I don't see the sun go down over the French Academy. I keep one eye on the kids, and with the other I study my history from mimeographed sheets. If I keep my nose to the grindstone, one day I'll have a license to teach history, and in the cells they'll say, 'Remember that his mother was a concierge in Paris and that his father was a city postman, after having been a country postman in weather so foul that he had to . . .' What did he have to do, Guttman?"

"He had to

> *Be ever ever on the alert*
> *Serve the Post Office till it hurt*
> *Put on big long wooden skis*
> *Just like wild and woolly Russkis*
> *And slaughter hungry wolves somehow*
> *Just as in wild and frozen Moscow.*
>
> *In Paris it was to Barksy*
> *And not bespectacled Trotsky*
> *To whom he valiantly brought mail*
> *Oh, brave Félix, hail, all hail!*
> *No, no postman was ever faster*
> *Than this brand-new postmaster*
> *Of the Popular Front.*"

Maurice had joined in after the first few words, and together they declaimed this "Ode to Félix," especially composed not long ago to celebrate the great news, which had spread unofficially that morning when Jeannette had opened the letter from the minister confirming Félix's nomination as postmaster, an appointment he had justifiably solicited for a long time. Robert and Maurice had thrown together this bit of doggerel on a corner of a desk at the Lycée Louis-le-Grand, and they'd brought the still-warm "Ode" back to rue de la Mare and recited it to Félix in the loge, where for once a little celebration was being held.

That was last June. They'd never recited the "Ode to Félix" since then, and they complimented themselves on their memory: it had been five months ago.

"It was the last celebration before the 'diaspora,'" said Robert.

"How come you're swiping words from my folklore patrimony?" Maurice asked, smiling.

"It's still the best way there is for talking about occasions lacking in gaiety. That little celebration wasn't exactly joyful, what with your mother, my sister and Zaza's mother outdoing one another weeping, Josette sobbing and my father accepting congratulations by repeating over and over, 'We'll come back. We'll come back.' And yet we all knew that something was finished, didn't we?"

Robert turned to the window again. Maurice said nothing.

"As I was saying, I don't have much to tell except that some day I'll be a university professor, that I don't see the dome of the French Academy from my window, that I don't rub elbows with the cosmopolitan intelligentsia and that as often as my schedule will allow I fuck the bursar's sister, whose photo I don't carry around but who's from Le Havre and well stacked. The only beautiful foreign women I see are those I watch from a distance as they embark on the big steamships, while I sit on the terrace of The Old Seadog—a Le Havre bistro which, like the Le Havre girl, I've also taken to visiting—before returning to my little nonpoliticized *pion*'s cell at the end of a dormitory that doesn't have a secret exit. I wouldn't exactly say that I'm having a great time, but it's very healthy for someone who's got a lot of work to do. And that's that. Shall we take a walk in the neighborhood?"

"Which neighborhood?"

"Ours. I'd like to make sure that the staircases are being kept clean so I can report back to my mother . . . Do you think yours could give me a bite to eat before I take my train?"

"What time's your train?"

"About nine."

"And when are you going back to Le Havre?"

"Sunday evening . . . Do you really want to know why I'm going to spend November eleventh with the family?"

"Because you love them, asshole!"

"That, too . . . but I'm going mostly to catch my father's performance as a local dignitary, wrapped in the tricolor and singing the 'Marseillaise' in front of the war memorial in Neuilly-le-Réal near Moulins. I wouldn't miss it for the world!"

Robert gave a short snicker, then, looking at Maurice, said, "Shall we go?"

"Let's," said Maurice, moving toward the door.

On his way out, Robert stopped in front of the mantelpiece again.

"Your little museum looks messy. I'll have to buy you an album, or a big picture frame . . . "

"That's it! I've got it!" exclaimed Maurice, striking his forehead with his open palm. "Ever since we left that old idiot Moreau's place I've been trying to remember. Now I know where I've seen that guy before . . . "

"What guy?"

"The one in the photo . . . I'll explain. Now we're going to beat it to rue de la Mare as fast as we can!" he said to Robert, grabbing at his sleeve.

: :

"AND YOU never told this story to my father, Monsieur Guttman?" asked Robert, in a hushed voice.

"No, my boy. You see, it was a family story," said Elie.

He had just refolded the grubby little square of paper and set it alongside the square-ruled rectangle of clean paper on which the Poltava address was written in Cyrillic letters between a small black dot and a heart filled with first names. He replaced them both in his wallet. The letter from Monsieur D. in Zurich remained open on the table, next to the disassembled Family Picture Frame.

"A family story you never told the family either, Papa!" said Maurice, his voice so choked it could barely be heard.

He was holding Volodya's photo in his hands.

Elie nodded.

"It was too sad, too complicated for someone your age," he explained without raising his eyes.

"But my father was old enough to be told," said Robert.

"You know, my boy, sometimes it was difficult to talk to your father . . . Your father didn't like the Merciers because of Léon Blum . . . So when I spoke to him about how no news came from the Ukraine, for example, I could see that he thought my employers were *stuffing my leg* . . . "

"Pulling my leg, or stuffing my head, Papa! You've got to choose one or the other, not both!" Maurice corrected rather sharply.

"You say it your way, I'll say it mine, my son," said Elie.

"But Papa, your cousin Volodya was a Jew, a Ukrainian and a Communist, wasn't he? If he hadn't been a Communist they'd never have let him come to Paris to testify against Petliura, would they?"

"Of course not . . . And so?" replied Elie.

Robert looked at Maurice. He pointed to the letter from Monsieur D. in Zurich.

"Monsieur Guttman, you know where Irkutsk is, don't you?"

Elie shook his head.

"It's in Siberia, Monsieur Guttman. And what the letter from this gentleman in Zurich is trying to tell you is that your cousin Volodya —a Jew, a Ukrainian and a Communist—was sent to Siberia soon after he'd seen you in Paris. And that he died there. You should have shown this letter to my father, Monsieur Guttman . . . "

Robert looked desperately unhappy.

"It wouldn't have changed a thing," said Elie. "In any case, it was too late . . . "

"Maybe not too late for my father," Robert murmured.

"And this, Papa, did you read this?" asked Maurice, who had just discovered the caption Monsieur Florian had once carefully folded back so that it was hidden under Volodya's photo.

"Put it all back for me before your mother comes upstairs," said Elie, taking the picture from Maurice's hands. "She'll be furious if she notices that you took her Family Picture Frame from the Bonnets'. Hurry . . . "

"Papa, I'm almost nineteen years old!" Maurice exclaimed, looking Elie directly in the eyes.

There was a brief silence, broken by Robert.

"I have to catch my train . . . "

"I'll go with you," Maurice said, as he rose to his feet.

"Say hello to your parents and Josette, my boy," said Elie, shaking Robert's hand. "Well, it looks as if I'll have to put this all back myself," he added, shaking his head.

And he put the little brass fasteners into The Family Picture Frame.

"Goodbye, Papa!" said Maurice.

"Is your shop closed tomorrow?"

"Yes, Papa, the bookstore is closed . . . " he confirmed, raising his eyes heavenward.

"A bookstore is a shop, isn't it? . . . Well then, come and see us. Nobody in the family is working tomorrow, not even Zaza."

"I know, Papa. In any case, I'll phone. . . . "

"Do that," said Elie without lifting his head.

Robert and Maurice were already on the landing.

They hesitated in front of the door to the Bonnets', but when they heard the loud laughter of both men and women, they decided against ringing.

"They're still working," said Maurice. "I'll say goodbye for you. Let's go."

They had already passed the Auvergnat's café, toward which neither of them had turned, when Maurice finally said something.

"What with all this business, you've had nothing to eat . . . "

"I'll grab a sandwich at the station. I'm not really late, you know . . . And actually, I'm not really hungry either."

"I know," said Maurice, and stopped.

He went up to a wall, leaned heavily against it and, burying his head in his forearms, began to weep.

Robert waited without either moving or looking at him. A few minutes passed, then Maurice rejoined him.

"I'm being dumb, right? But I've been holding it back for an hour . . . I feel better now," he said, forcing a smile.

They began to walk toward rue des Pyrénées again.

"Let's treat ourselves to a taxi for once. I don't feel like looking at all those ugly faces in the Métro," said Robert.

The driver was very talkative, very patriotic, very happy about the flags that were flying all along the route, very happy that Blum had been forced out and very happy about Munich, which had made this beautiful November 11 possible. That would show them . . .

"Asshole," murmured Robert, as they got out of the taxi. "Great, I've got plenty of time," he said, consulting the clock face on the square tower of the Gare de Lyon.

A news vendor passed with a *Paris-Soir* extra. The names von Rath and Grynszpan could be seen on the front page in large letters.

"Grynszpan! . . . Herschel Grynszpan? . . . That's not a Jewish name, is it? . . . " Maurice asked Robert, mimicking Sonia's voice.

"You're gross!" said Robert, bursting into laughter.

"It's just as well I kid around during the time we have left together. You've seen what happens when I don't!"

While Robert was buying his ticket for Moulins and a platform ticket, Maurice went to get him a sandwich from the buffet. They stopped for a moment at the bookstall.

"How about my treating you to a copy of *Nausea*?" Maurice suggested.

"You're just like old Florian. . . . You've got trouble keeping up with the newest literary developments. I read that at least two months ago. And in its real setting, too. The Bouville in his book is Le Havre. Sartre was a philo prof in my school, and it's too bad he quit before I got there . . . "

They left the kiosk. Robert said:

"What did we exchange Florian's copy of *Man's Fate* for?"

"We didn't. Like bastards, we got the bookstore to give us a re-fund! And like bastards, we also never went to see Florian. The poor old guy—when I think of all the trouble he went to in order to find Vladimir . . . "

"Why do you call him Vladimir?"

"Because that was his name. In our family, when we like Vladimirs we call them Volodyas," Maurice replied.

"I'm going to get on here," said Robert, stopping in front of a third-class car. "Well, *shalom,* you Ukrainian Jew!" He placed his hand on Maurice's curly black hair and gave his head three taps.

"*Kénavo!*" replied Maurice, watching him get into the train.

The eight notes of the Laurel and Hardy theme made him move toward the fourth window of the car, from which Robert stuck his head as the train slowly began to move. The locomotive gave a long blast on its whistle.

"It's my last bit of cyanide, don't lose it!" called Robert, laughing and grabbing the hand Maurice was holding out to him.

"I've got it!" called Maurice, responding to their old code as he let go of his hand and pretended to shove something into his mouth.

Robert gave him a final nod and withdrew his head into the compartment.

: :

BEFORE LEAVING the railway station, Maurice bought a late edition of *Paris-Soir.*

Below the article describing Third Secretary von Rath's last minutes, surrounded by his helpless parents and Adolf Hitler's personal physician, alongside a brief summary of the circumstances of the assassination and of the identity of the murderer, Herschel Grynszpan, a young seventeen-year-old "Polish Jew," there was a mention of the fact that the latter's defense would be handled by Maître Henry Torrès.

Maurice found what he was looking for: a last-minute dispatch reporting that, contrary to what had been thought the day before, the fire that had swept through the synagogue of the little German town of Helsdorf had not been an accident.

Since the confirmation of Monsieur von Rath's death, nine synagogues in various corners of Germany had been set on fire during the night of November 9–10, and at the same time the shop windows of all businesses owned by German citizens of Jewish faith had been systematically smashed:

As we go to press—in other words, a few hours before November 11—the noise of shattering windows is such that passers-by on the streets of both large and small cities of the Reich have trouble hearing what their companions are saying. After walking over the debris of windows, Germans have baptized this night's "spontaneous" convulsions of wrath with a name of their own. They are already calling it *die Krystall Nacht.*" This translates as "Night of Crystal." As can be seen, poetry still has a place in the land that gave birth to Goethe . . .

Maurice refolded the newspaper, which he'd read outside, standing under the station overhang. He was about to toss it away, changed his mind, ripped out the dispatch, shoved it into his pocket, then crumpled up the rest and threw it into the gutter.

As he went down the Métro steps, he still hadn't decided where he was going. He was halfway between Les Pyrénées and Odéon.

He badly wanted to go back to rue de la Mare, just to run in for a moment, simply to give his father and mother a big hug and say something stupid like: "I love you, don't be afraid, I'm here . . ." Then he told himself he'd panic them by returning so soon. It would make more sense to go tomorrow. He might say something stupid this evening. Tomorrow, Zaza would be there . . . and it was Zaza he had to see. He had to find her, right away.

And he decided to head for Odéon.

At this hour, she must still be eating with her movie friends. He saw her back through the window of Chéramy's. The man sitting alongside her had his arm around the back of her chair. Facing them, Alex was talking to a woman Maurice didn't know.

Alex was the first to see him when he came through the door.

"You've eaten?" asked Zaza.

Maurice shook his head. He gave Zaza's closed lips a closed-lipped kiss, and shook hands with Alex, who introduced Angelina Crespi and Laurent Verdon.

"Maurice Guttman," he said, as he sat on the banquette in the place made for him on one side by the neighboring customers and on the other side by Angelina Crespi, who moved closer to Alex. "Have you seen the papers?" Maurice asked the others.

"We've done better than that," replied Zaza. "Mimi telephoned me last night from Berlin. She put the receiver up to her hotel window, and for three minutes I listened to an international communication. Then Mimi got back on and said, 'Did you hear?' I said, 'Yes.' Then she said, 'A big hug from me, darling, and I'm glad you're not here to see what I'm seeing.' "

Laurent Verdon took Zaza's wrist and kissed the hollow of her hand.

Chéramy brought over a plate of sausages and lentils, the day's special chalked up on a slate near the bar.

"A small carafe of wine?" he asked.

"Yes," said Maurice, then, turning to Zaza: "Did you mention Mimi's phone call at the house this morning?"

"Of course not!"

"And she was right not to," approved Alex. "It took me years to reassure your mothers. You were still babies when I began teaching them to laugh . . . You're not going to destroy my work now that you're grown up!"

"We're not the ones destroying it, Alex. In any case, I must tell you that it's all about to collapse," replied Maurice, as he began to eat.

Everyone waited for him to say more.

"Tell me, Zaza," he continued, "A guy, smiling and trying to hide his scarred face behind his hand . . . "

"That reminds me of something!" said Alex.

"Go on . . . " said Zaza.

"It's a cousin," said Alex, laughing. "But not one of my cousins— a cousin of either you or you—" He had touched first Maurice's and then Zaza's shoulder, the way you do when you're playing counting-out games.

"Monsieur Grandi wins first prize! Mademoiselle Roginski hasn't won anything!" exclaimed Maurice. "Monsieur Guttman hadn't won anything until this afternoon, either! But thanks to Divine Providence —not Urbaine, the other one, the real one!—he's been able to uncover one of the secrets our families thought were protected by a picture frame the children never noticed . . . "

"The Family Picture Frame?" exclaimed Zaza.

"It held many other secrets, your mothers' Family Picture Frame . . . " murmured Alex, with a strange smile.

"Did it?" asked Angelina.

"We all have a past, my pretty," continued Alex, replacing a tortoise-shell hairpin that was working its way out of Angelina's dark, heavy chignon.

"That's true," said Angelina, with a sweet smile on her un-made-up face. She had very wide, light-gray eyes, and a few tiny wrinkles gave the lie to the youthfulness of her expression. She was wearing an oversized black turtleneck sweater, and Maurice remembered that he'd often seen Alex in it.

"So this cousin," said Alex. "Which one of you does he belong to?"

"Me. . . . But his story belongs to both of us," replied Maurice, looking at Zaza.

"As I understand it, it doesn't concern the rest of us, does it?" asked Laurent Verdon.

"It concerns the whole world!" exclaimed Maurice.

And, skipping nothing, from "She went 'Pouett-Pouett' to me" to the absurd death announcement from Monsieur D. in Zurich, Maurice told them the whole Volodya story.

The couple seated at the neighboring table had gradually stopped talking. They were listening to Maurice without looking at him, but they exchanged frequent impatient glances. They got up after the business about the letter from Zurich. At the door, the man made way for the woman, let her go out, then took a step toward the table.

"Let's say that your story is true, which is by no means certain; you're still a son-of-a-bitch to spread it around at a time like this!" he called out to Maurice before leaving, slamming the door behind him.

Maurice got up.

"Don't move," said Alex, getting up in turn.

Maurice was already at the door, reopening it. Alex pushed him away and went out into the street, closing the door behind him.

"Alex is wrong to argue with him," said Chéramy, who'd watched everything from the bar.

"Do you know him?" asked Laurent.

"He's come here two or three times. Each time there's been some sort of fuss. I won't serve him anymore."

Alex returned, a smile on his lips.

"The idiot called me a Fascist!" he said, sitting down again. "Well, not exactly: he said that by telling this story about Volodya you were playing the Fascists' game. And that I was doing the same by listening to you!"

"And then?" asked Angelina Crespi.

"And then his wife said that she was Jewish, that she hated your 'Pouett-Pouett' story, that you were both badly brought-up. Then he told her she was getting everything all mixed up as usual and that that wasn't the problem, and then he talked about Spain, and she began to cry and he said they'd never come to eat here again," Alex summed up, turning toward Chéramy.

"Just as well!" exclaimed the latter.

"And so?" asked Angelina Crespi.

"And so they walked off among the wild autos, and night alone heard their words . . . " recited Alex, parodying Verlaine.

There was a brief silence during which nothing could be heard but the dishtowel squeaking over the glasses Chéramy was wiping.

"It's true, this old story about Volodya comes at a bad time," murmured Maurice, without looking at anyone.

"What's even truer is that poor young Volodya was born into a bad time," said Angelina Crespi.

: :

"SHALL WE WALK a bit more?" asked Maurice.

They were on the boulevard Saint-Germain and Alex had a hand on Maurice's shoulder. They had left the others in front of Chéramy's. Zaza had climbed into Laurent Verdon's car, and Angelina Crespi had walked off by herself. Alex had said, "See you later," and had placed his hand on Maurice's shoulder. They'd been walking along since then, with Alex doing the talking.

He talked of happy, silly, useless things, the way one does in families to quiet a child's terrors before sending him to bed.

It hadn't been easy, and during the first hundred yards of their stroll along the deserted rue Jacob neither of them had said anything. Alex, who knew just how to talk to Sonia, to Olga and now to Zaza, had had to search for words with which to calm this adolescent whom he had seen grow up but to whom he had never really paid any attention, and whose adult preoccupations and masculine troubles made his head spin.

Because they hadn't been his own preoccupations or troubles, nor were they ever likely to be. Not if he lived a hundred years, he thought, walking along.

When they had reached the end of rue Jacob and were standing in front of a fence covered with a newly pasted-up poster, especially well illuminated by a street light, the silence was broken by a great burst of laughter.

Just at eye level, standing against a background of an angry sea, his beard, oilskin slicker and hat dripping with water, a brave Breton fisherman was brandishing a giant biscuit and grinning like the black on the familiar Banania cocoa box. The "IS IT GOOD? THEN IT'S POM-PONNETTE!" slogan had been crossed out with chalk, and playing on the slang meaning of "*pomponnette,*" someone had written diagonally across the poster: "SO, YVES MY BUDDY, BLOW JOBS VERY GOOD?"

Everything had changed after that corner. Alex was so relieved to see and hear Maurice doubled over with laughter that he decided to mine this rich vein. He therefore went into great detail about the seamy underside of the Le Go-Go business—the great merit of which, as he saw it, had been to give the rue de la Mare children a wonderful vacation. And since Maurice had not only continued to laugh but added in his turn certain unknown details about their famous Breton vacation, instead of going down rue de Seine on the left, they'd gone up as far as the boulevard Saint-Germain.

They were at the corner of boulevard Saint-Michel when Maurice suggested they continue for a bit: they crossed the boulevard. He was still laughing. Because after the story of the *Get Your Gun!* expedition, since known as *Get Your Biscuit!*—in other words, get your dough, in the current vocabulary of the Coop—Alex in his own special way had told about life at Allée Chateaubriand: the mute and passionate flutterings of Mademoiselle Agnès, the wild infatuations of Ginette, the young seamstresses, the workshop over which Stépan ruled as king—king bee of a happy and carefree hive . . .

"Let's go to the right," said Maurice, who was still smiling but apparently no longer paying attention to Alex.

"If you want," said Alex as he noted the name of the street.

It was rue Thénard, a very short street that climbed steeply to the majestic steps of the Collège de France.

They walked along for several yards, then Maurice came to a halt.

"He'd really settled in!" Maurice said, looking up at the five stories of a handsome provincial building at number 7, and he showed Alex a small placard marked: "AT HOME, student Hôtel-Pension."

"Who?" asked Alex.

"Pan Pouett-Pouett Petliura!" giggled Maurice.

Alex said nothing.

"He'll be doing a jig in his grave this evening! The echoes of German-Jewish crystal being smashed in Russian fashion must really be loud in the Montparnasse cemetery . . . "

"Is he buried at Montparnasse?" asked Alex, after a brief silence.

A light went on in a third-floor window of the At Home.

" . . . Look! That may be his widow or his orphan," murmured Maurice, pointing toward the light. "Yes . . . at Montparnasse, and tomorrow these two women will take flowers to the man who helped get the anti-Semitic ball rolling . . . "

"Come on, let's go back now," said Alex, giving Maurice a gentle push with the hand he'd still not taken from his shoulder. "It's late. Time we were in bed . . . "

They left rue Thénard.

"Yes, I'm going home to sleep, if I can . . . But not you, Alex. Someone's waiting for you," said Maurice, with a knowing smile.

"Just what are you getting at?" said Alex, giving him a light tap with the flat of his hand.

"Something that's none of my business. But she's going to be angry with me, Angelina is. It's late, as you were saying, and she's waiting for you . . . "

"Angelina understands everything," said Alex, with a tender smile.

They walked along in silence.

"What was the other secret in The Family Picture Frame, besides that of the Ukrainian Scarface?"

So Alex told him about Maddy. Well, not all about Maddy. He told about the Maddy of the days of the beautiful dress, of the paillettes. Paillettes? Those first paillettes? The ones the children found every-where—on the staircase, in the folding beds, even in Josette's hair . . . those paillettes? . . . Oh yes, Maurice remembered that very well. As a matter of fact, everyone in the neighborhood remembered it.

And Maurice started to laugh again. And of course Alex took advan-tage of the paillettes just as he had taken advantage of the Pomponnette Biscuits to keep Maurice laughing, the way you keep a drowning man's head above water. He summoned up all his memories of the first days with Sonia and Olga, and even invented a few—he spoke of four crinolines crowding into the small dining rooms, and had Madame Lowenthal appear and disappear much more often than she actually had. According to Alex's account, the second floor of rue de la Mare became another Marx Brothers' steamship cabin . . .

And as Maurice laughed harder and harder, the ghost of Maddy eventually disappeared from the conversation.

When they got to rue de Seine, Maurice was still laughing. Alex hadn't had time to tell him that the woman who wore the paillettes, the woman he had loved, was dead.

Nor how she had died.

And certainly no time to say that about a hundred yards from the hole in which she lay rose President Petliura's mausoleum, and that even then it was buried under flowers.

Ten years after his death. Scarcely three years before the Night of Crystal.

VII

...OUT
OF MIND

*T*HE SNOW was falling so heavily that Maurice got up to close both casement windows. He did it very quietly, and none of the children awoke. It was then that he remembered the drawing. He could see Zaza take it from her pocket, unfold it and show it to him, but he didn't recall her putting it back in her apron pocket. They must have left it downstairs after their talk.

Instead of lying down again, he sat on his bed, put on his heavy woolen socks, pulled his sweater on over his pyjamas and, by the light of the moon that completely illuminated the large room, walked past the six camp beds from which only the children's slumbering heads stuck out beyond their sleeping bags. He stopped and looked down at Loulou's face. "When she's asleep, she looks more like Sami," he told himself, as he did every time he watched her sleep.

He left the dormitory, quietly shut the door and walked down the marble staircase. It was still quite warm in the vaulted room; the cooking stove hadn't gone out yet.

Groping, he found the switch of the big lamp. The drawing was there, unfolded, its red, yellow and black standing out against the white oilcloth cover of the long trestle table. It was a woman of the sort that all five- or six-year-old children draw: with no nose, but with eyes, a mouth, ears—gigantic ones—and an enormous amount of black hair scribbled around an imperfect circle set above a red rectangle from each side of which two black sticks emerged, extended by two balls bristling like sea urchins; on the bottom were two other sticks so long that there was no more room on the page to draw the shoes. In the middle of the rectangle, a kind of sun almost as big as the head looked like a golden decoration on the woman's blood-red dress. Between the two footless legs, the word MAMMA, in big yellow letters, was scrawled in crayon.

Maurice picked up the drawing and glanced at the small black oak door set into the stone on the right of the fireplace. He listened: nothing stirred. He refolded the paper in four.

Tomorrow morning, they'd try to find out who had drawn the woman Zaza had found in the afternoon while sweeping between Loulou's and Dédée's beds. Maurice thought Loulou was too young to remember. Zaza didn't agree. They'd see. In any case, the drawing mustn't be left on the table like that, especially if they wanted the children to write their letters.

He decided to tuck the drawing into Zaza's bag.

Zaza's bag was at the other end of the large room, lying on the desk, or what they called the desk: an old pantry sideboard, a pitch-pine buffet that helped Zaza maintain a little order among the children's books and notebooks. The buffet-desk, like the double sink anchored upstairs in the tubless bathroom next to the dormitory, had been acquired at an auction sale in Grenoble one day in 1938 when they'd all driven down there in the little van with Marcel, the mayor's workman.

It was the liquidation sale of an old Hôtel Métropole, and in the same lot, for almost nothing, they'd acquired a scuffed old leather club chair and the ugly floor lamp mounted on an imitation wine-press screw thread that was stained walnut and decked with gilt-trimmed imitation parchment. They had tried to trade the lamp right then and there for towels initialed "H.M.," but they hadn't been able to, and Myriam had said that all in all the lamp wasn't that ugly . . . And Robert had told her that she could have it for a wedding present if she ever married Sami. In the meantime, they'd plugged it in. It provided good light.

And since then the lamp had just stayed there.

Since Christmas 1938. Or rather the period between Christmas 1938 and New Year 1939, the last time they'd all been together at the Convent.

Except for Jeannot, of course. But they'd forbidden themselves to speak of Jeannot at the Convent. It drove Sami insane, and they wanted him to be happy. He himself wanted to be happy, and Myriam wanted it for him even more. That's how, in the little bedroom behind the low door, while all the others were sleeping in the dormitory, one night Myriam and Sami had made Loulou, "on Christmas, in a crèche as the snow fell, and with our blessing," Robert had summed up from Le Havre in a letter to Sami about the "Tidings Brought to Myriam Goldberg."

Maurice took a last look at the drawing and closed Zaza's bag.

It was a shoulder bag made of fine peccary leather with exposed handsewn stitches, a model created for Lancel that Elie had given Zaza for her eighteenth birthday. Maurice saw it on the buffet every day. It was covered with a patina now, and Zaza had no other. He saw it every day, but he never touched it. The smoothness and softness of the leather surprised him. He carried it to the lamp and ran his finger over the stippling left in the leather by his father's needle. The white thread, once so elegant, had become invisible under the grime of years and travel.

He listened to the silence: the silence from the outdoors, from the dormitory, from Zaza's bedroom.

He set the bag down on the white oilskin tablecloth and dropped into the club chair, but immediately got up again to fetch a large bottle three-quarters full of a transparent liquid from under the sink, poured some into a bowl, took the bottle with him, placed it next to Zaza's bag, sat down again in the chair, drank a mouthful and examined his hands attentively.

It always began that way when he couldn't sleep or read and would go down into the large room to be alone. But it happened more and more rarely now.

It had become rare for him not to be able to fall asleep: the days began early, the air was sharp, the work endless. But when it did happen, it always began this way: he would sit down, look at his carpenter-mason hands, and take little sips of the local marc. He didn't go downstairs so that he could drink in secret. He drank so that he could think in secret.

It was a habit he'd formed to enable him to survive, ever since that evening when Zaza had told him she no longer wanted to share his "poisonous little madeleines"—she'd also called them "Prague *ku-glach*," which had made Maurice laugh.

It had happened a few months ago. One evening at dinner, when he'd just told the children about Dr. Pierre's glass eye, Zaza had suddenly gotten up from the table, gone to poke furiously at the fire in the cookstove and made that comment, whose affectation, coming from her, was surprising.

Maurice had complimented her on her erudition and asked her when and where she'd had the time to read Proust and Kafka. She'd shrugged her shoulders and screwed her right index finger into her right temple; this had made the children laugh.

But Maurice had got the message. Zaza had just become aware that she was pregnant; he didn't want to upset her. And since then, he had set out alone on his pilgrimages into his memory.

Zaza was wrong to think he was giving in to a morose pleasure; something very different happened when he undertook these dives, which he was now perfectly able to control—like a deep-sea diver who knows where to find the ancient treasures whose exact location he has verified, but which he has no intention of bringing to the surface because such treasure couldn't survive in the open air.

Maurice monitored these descents, and took just enough of the rot-gut Marcel provided for him to make him feel lightheaded and almost happy.

His first joy, when he got to the bottom, was to note that he could still hear the voices of his parents. Not their accents: the sound, the timbre, of their voices. He knew this miracle wouldn't last forever, he feared the moment when he'd no longer be able to bring it off, and he smiled with gratitude and relief when he realized that that moment had not yet come.

Only then would he play with the images, but not haphazardly. He would choose a theme and forbid himself to go beyond its frontiers. For example, it might be the image of all the clothes he had seen his parents wear at all the different stages of his life, from his earliest memory on. He'd count them; then, if he'd forgotten one, he'd begin again from the beginning, because to omit some item of dress was to skip a date. New clothes always went with an important date. Sometimes he'd hesitate, because when it came to the dresses he was no longer sure if it was Sonia or Olga he could see in the flowered blue dress under such-and-such circumstances, since they'd often lent each other their things. When that happened, he'd continue his investigation, like a stubborn detective looking for signs and indications, gathering evidence.

The images were impregnated with the odors of fur and tannin, mixed with the scents of both soap and eau de Cologne, and the smell of stews, soups and cakes, herbal teas, mustard plasters and iodine, polish and strong soap; and with all the noises at each of the doors, the second-floor doors as well as that of the Bonnets'. The sound he could most easily recognize was the latch on the kitchen-pantry door, just his own height when he was small, whereas he had trouble remembering the sound of the latch on the pantry in the Bonnet kitchen, even though he and Robert had used it as a bathroom cabinet every day during those last years.

When something slipped away—like the latch in the Bonnet place—he would persist, would watch himself go through the motions that should have brought back the sounds they were supposed to. When it proved useless, he'd be very disappointed, tell himself they'd come back the next time and pour himself some more brandy.

Because he knew there'd be a next time. Another secret ceremony that, like the others, would end in the Image, the one that was now on its way and from which he couldn't escape.

It was a tremendously happy image: Sonia, Elie, Olga and Stépan were at the window of a second-class sleeping compartment, and they were all four laughing, and the train was about to start. Sonia was wearing a navy-blue straw skimmer with white trimming that matched the white collar of her blouse turned down on her navy-blue suit jacket. Olga had a black velvet beret worn a little bit on a slant, a small lacquered black feather across the front, and the collar of her sky-blue blouse was buttoned under her black suit jacket. Both women wore a touch of makeup, and their crocheted white cotton gloves rested on the top of the lowered compartment window. A very small spot of lipstick looked like a drop of blood on Olga's index finger. From the crook in their arms hung the black box-calf handles of their brand-new handbags. Behind them, Elie and Stépan had their hands on their wives' necks. Elie wore a brown tie, Stépan a blue one with white stripes; their shirts were immaculate, and when they leaned their faces between those of Sonia and Olga, the padding of their double-breasted dark-gray suits rose comically on their shoulders.

"Watch out for that Cahors wine, kids! It can really hit you!" Maurice had called out to them.

It was 8:05 P.M. at the Gare d'Austerlitz, and the Paris-Cerbère that had just started up was due at the Cahors station at 4:33 A.M. The date was March 13, 1939.

After that, there was a hole. The water there was so viscous, the bottom so muddy, that he could see nothing more. And Maurice would begin his slow ascent.

Or else, with a final shot of marc, go over the last image again, then the one just before it. He'd go back to the previous weeks, then to the day, the hour, the minute before the train left. He'd imagine all that might have happened to prevent the train from leaving. Or, if it absolutely had to leave, all that might have happened to prevent them from taking it. When he, Zaza, Alex and even Jeannette Clément, by phone, had really done everything they could to get them to take that train. "Such a beautiful trip, such a wonderful celebration!" Even Félix, though he didn't like the Merciers, had said a few words from Neuilly-le-Réal to overcome Sonia's hesitations: it might be demagogic, but it was a generous gesture; you couldn't say no.

So they'd got themselves ready. Alex had had the pretty suits and hats made for the ladies—and by Mademoiselle Agnès herself—and, like actresses, they'd gone to Allée Chateaubriand for fittings; they were driven there by Gromoff and invited first to dine at Raymonde and André's, sitting at the Coop table, where Stépan had introduced them to everyone—except to Mademoiselle Agnès, who wasn't lunching. Then Stépan had left them. He wanted to use the time to go and buy his handsome suit on the Champs-Elysées. Elie had bought his on the boulevards. And lo and behold! without consulting each other or being aware of it, they'd chosen the same suit! Funny, wasn't it? In any case, it was too late to change.

"Your suits are fine," Maurice had said that Sunday, the Sunday before their departure.

Then his mother had shown him the big box of chocolates for Madame Martial Mercier. If the Marquise de Sévigné wrapping hadn't been so beautifully done up with ribbon, they would have opened the box so he could tell them if the chocolates were good. There were two layers—cream centers and liqueur centers.

"I'm sure the chocolates must be very good," Maurice had said.

Then Elie had wanted to explain to him that Martial Mercier was the much-discussed cousin, the deputy who . . .

"I know, Papa, the one who got us the naturalization papers when we were very young, and I also know the Mercier brothers and their cousin are very nice to invite all four of you to celebrate the centenary of the departure on foot from Cahors of their ancestor Fabien, who rolled his barrel before him, and I know they're paying for your second-class couchettes . . . I know all that, Papa . . . "

"Well, if you know all that, why are you asking questions?" Elie had said with a laugh, and just then Barsky had arrived with the new imitation-leather valise he was lending them for the trip. Sonia hadn't wanted Gromoff's, the one with all those old stickers, because it was really too skinned . . .

"Scuffed, Mama!" Maurice had corrected.

"She says what she knows," Elie had shot back, and then he'd gone into the bedroom to take off his new suit.

Maurice had hung around rue de la Mare another five minutes, had winked at Barsky, who'd had himself served a little vodka as he pretended to listen to Elie, who was beginning the story of the ancestor Fabien again, and then had left, saying he'd see them tomorrow.

"Be on time! The stationmaster won't wait for Monsieur Maurice Guttman to get there before he gives the signal," Elie had warned.

"At seven-thirty on the platform," Maurice had confirmed, as he went down the stairway.

At first, it was Zaza who was supposed to attend to the "Austerlitz Farewell," as they called it between themselves during the four weeks when they'd talked of nothing else. But Zaza had gone off for some location shooting in the Vosges.

From there, she had telephoned Maurice at the Villeneuves'.

"You go for me. I'm afraid they'll panic and get lost along the way . . ."

"Don't worry about it! It's only an overnight trip, and they've already taken a train from much further away . . ."

"Yes, but that was a long time ago," Zaza had said before hanging up.

So he'd done as Zaza had said.

He'd done as Elie had told him to.

He'd been on time, and the Gare d'Austerlitz stationmaster hadn't had to wait for him before blowing the whistle, at exactly 8:05 P.M., for the Number 67 on the Paris–Cerbère line that was to jump the tracks a few hours later, after leaving Châteauroux, at exactly 10:49 P.M.

: :

FOR YEARS he had refused to think of the horrible, absurd and ridiculous ceremony in the cement-paved shed transformed into a funeral chapel.

Those images—the last ones registered before his fall, the black hole into which he had tumbled and remained for months, of which he remembered practically nothing—those particular images didn't belong to the rainbow-colored treasure that his memory cherished, cultivated, colored and no doubt embellished. They were in black and white, as precise, pale and cruelly ugly as a newsreel.

With one spot of color, however: Zaza's red scarf knotted under her chin.

Zaza, arriving late, pushing aside the black curtains draped across the shed entrance just as the prefect was making his speech. Zaza dressed like a boy, as if on the job, with the bright strap of her bag cutting a diagonal across her gray pullover, who looked for him with the eyes of a madwoman, found him, elbowed her way through the crowd in black to get to his side and who held his hand without looking at him.

Like him, she was looking down at the concrete pavement on which stood nineteen boxes of varnished wood, the light from the glass roof streaming down on them, and the golden shimmer of a dozen candles flickering from tall cast-iron candlesticks.

For the sake of symmetry, eighteen coffins had been aligned in three rows of six, and the nineteenth had been placed up front, alone, like the prow of a ship.

The prefect looked down on them, speaking from an improvised pulpit spread with silver-fringed black cloth.

"In which . . . where are they?" asked Zaza.

"I'll tell you later," said Maurice.

The prefect spoke of fate, of misfortune, of France and the Department of Indre, which were in mourning, and of the ox that had escaped from the cattle car and been the cause of everything that had happened. And his voice resonated between the concrete and the metal framework. It was often drowned by the arrivals and departures of locomotives that didn't jump the tracks, but when the silence returned, deep sobs accompanied his mournful sentences.

The other spot of color was provided by the large French flag flying at half-mast behind the prefect, who now descended from the pulpit, to be followed by a representative of the minister of transportation. The latter repeated what the prefect had said about fate, misfortune and the ox, which he called *the bovine*. He spoke of the transportation department, all of which was also in mourning, and (even though this wasn't the proper time for material questions) he wanted to assure the families, who too were in mourning, that they would be properly compensated —but of course nothing could make up for the loss of a loved one.

"Cars of rotting wood . . . disgusting . . . " rang out. But a rustle of indignant "shushes" made the insolent voice fall silent as the perfume of incense announced the arrival of a priest followed by two altar boys, all three in lace.

"Oh no . . . " murmured Zaza with a movement that Maurice arrested.

"Let it alone," he said to her.

They both watched as the priest, who did not ascend the pulpit, said a few words about the equality of God's children in the face of death, then followed with a few words in Latin; with an ample gesture of his arm, he next made the sign of the cross in the direction of the nineteen anonymous dead men and women. They watched him as he went from coffin to coffin, praying with closed eyes and followed by the two children swinging their censers. Finally, they watched all three of them leave as quickly as they had come.

And the prefect came forward with the man from the Ministry. And everyone had his hand shaken.

It was almost as though they were being congratulated, as though they were the children of heroes. You could read it in the stricken looks of the prefect and the assistant-assistant minister: "The men and women who sleep here at our feet were France's best sons and daughters . . . We will never forget them," they seemed to say.

"Now we've become wards of the railway authorities!" Zaza murmured after they'd passed.

Maurice looked at her. She was haggard and she was laughing.

"Come along," he said.

And he took her by the hand.

"Here they are," he said when they got to the first four coffins in the second row.

"You're sure?"

"I saw all four of them before the coffins were sealed . . . They look peaceful . . . They were sleeping when it happened."

He was lying to her. Lying from the bottom of his heart.

It was true that he had seen them, since he'd been asked to identify them early that morning when they'd arrived—Alex, Gromoff, and he —in the Coop Citroën, while Zaza was still speeding across France in Verdon's automobile, only to arrive too late.

Late enough, in any case, to believe him when he repeated that they'd been sleeping. He swore it to her.

In the neighboring shed, he'd also seen what remained of Barsky's valise, which he'd also been asked to identify. And he didn't want Zaza to see that, nor to have her ask where their handbags were. They hadn't been found—neither their handbags, nor their hats, nor anything recognizable.

He also didn't want her to read the numbers on the tags attached to the brass handles. He spoke before she bent to do so. He said: "Mama, Papa, your father, your mother," each time accompanying his words with a movement of his head. He had stood very straight, and so did she, since he held her hand.

"Come on, they're going to give them back to us now"—and he pulled her toward the black door.

Outside, the sun was shining brightly. Now it was she who was pulling him, pulling him toward Laurent, Gromoff and Alex, who were already in front of the shed alongside. He said: "Wait a minute . . . "

That was all. After that, there was nothing more.

: :

LATER, much later, they told him he'd fallen. They told him where and how. But they interrupted one another, made mistakes, contradicted one another. He'd never know if his skull had shattered because he'd fallen, or if it had shattered first from the inside, and so violently that it had made him fall to the white concrete.

He'd always have a big scar above the nape of his neck: he'd always know exactly where, because his hair hadn't ever grown back over those few inches that his fingers could find under the curls that hid them. But he'd never know if they had repaired his skull because it had split open, or if they'd opened his skull to repair what was inside.

But he'd know that for more than a year he hadn't known anything about himself, the others or the world.

He'd know because they would tell him, when they'd finally begun giving him news of himself, of the others and of the world.

Initially in spoonfuls, when he'd finally asked his first questions, and then in great big dollops, so that he could make up for lost time, as they put it.

Finally they told him about the war. They had to, since he wanted to know why the windows of his white room were crisscrossed with strips of khaki-colored adhesive tape.

They told him when and how the war had broken out, and that they had just lost it.

They gave him dates, facts, the names of treaties—just like a historical outline designed for a course about a very old war.

And when he began to want to know more, they'd go into detail with an obvious and happy satisfaction. Because his curiosity was proof that he was on the mend, that he was returning to the world of the living.

And so little by little they told him everything. Since he had asked about everything.

By turns "they" were his doctor, Zaza, the nurses, the aides, Zaza with Myriam and Sami, Zaza with Madame Villeneuve, Laurent Verdon alone, Laurent and Zaza together, and Sami all alone.

It was never Robert. Nor Alex, nor Villeneuve, nor Gromoff, nor Barsky: they'd come, but it was during the war and he was still asleep.

But one day Madame Villeneuve gave him a letter and a postcard.

The card was dated July 1, 1939, and came from London. In a pretty round handwriting it said: "Thinking of our last summer. Love." There were three little x's, and the signature Anny.

The letter had been posted in Marseilles on August 29, 1939. Robert had written it on square-ruled paper, and a photograph had been clipped to the corner:

Dear Brother,

I came to see you, but once again you snubbed me and had your people say that it was too early and you were still asleep. Your loss. I won't be coming to your château door again. Like Clappique, I'm sailing alone, leaving my father Félix to the embarrassment of swallowing and digesting the python-sized insult just served up to him by the compatriots of your cousin Volodya. I'm taking off.

So I'm going to add to Félix's distress as a confused militant the affliction and shame of also being the father of a deserter—which saddens me. But not as much as I'd be saddened by the receipt of military papers ordering me to leave for the war, which is the egg of the python and which will hatch tomorrow, the day after tomorrow, or in a week.

I've therefore decided to heed the call of the open sea before I get my call to the colors.

As a geographer and a historian, I am leaving to perfect, deepen and consolidate my knowledge of history and geography.

There will always be a Monsier D. somewhere to give you news of me, and as you can see from the photo I had made especially for you, the eye of you-know-who will watch over me.

Sleep well for as long as you can.

Robert

The photo showed him, hands in his pockets, at the foot of a high wall, from which the remains of what had once been the sprightly Dr. Pierre were flaking away.

In bulk and in bits and pieces, with no particular chronology, he would learn that no one knew where Robert was, that Villeneuve was a prisoner in Germany, that the bookstore was closed but that he could still have his room, unless he wanted to live with Verdon and Zaza, because Zaza had closed up rue de la Mare a long time ago, just after . . . in other words, shortly before the war, that the Coop was also closed, and that Alex had left for America, for Hollywood, with Angelina Crespi, and that Zaza and Verdon weren't married but that Sami and Myriam had been, at the *Mairie* of the XXth, also before the war, and that Myriam had already been very pregnant and that Loulou was now almost a year old. She was called Louise, like the Socialist heroine Louise Michel, and when Robert had come to see mother and daughter at the hospital he'd said that the child should have been called Josépha-Adolphine, because she'd been born right after the pact. What pact? The pact between Hitler and Stalin, which Maurice had initially refused to believe in. Sami had had to bring him an old photo, cut from *Paris-Soir*, showing Molotov and Ribbentrop shaking hands. It seemed that Félix had cried in Neuilly-le-Réal, where he'd been mobilized immediately after the pact, since the war had broken out in September. Verdon had spent his war in the Army Cinematographic Service. They'd never been able to film a battle because for months there had been none, and when the battles began, things went so quickly that the ACS had to pull back, and they filmed the exodus. The *exodus*? Yes, there had been an exodus. Everyone had left Paris—except Zaza, who had remained behind because that was when Maurice had really begun to wake up, and Myriam, because Sami had been mobilized as a stretcher-bearer at Val-de-Grâce and she wanted to remain near him with Loulou and her grandmother. But all the others had left: Gromoff and Barsky in the taxi, heading toward the Midi; the Lowenthals, the Nussbaums and even the Sterns, who had gone to Brittany in the flea market van. Barsky and Gromoff hadn't returned: the Auvergnat had said something about their being in Monte Carlo. The others had got no farther than Le Mans before coming back. It turned out that Madame Lowenthal, even on a three-day trip, was worse than Big Bertha back in 1914! But when they'd come back, the *others* were already there.

And how were these others? Nobody knew for sure. They seemed polite and calm in a deserted Paris.

One more question remained to be asked. He put it off from day to day, then one lovely afternoon he made up his mind as he and Zaza were strolling through the hospital gardens alone. Just then, the *others* were passing on the boulevard beyond, singing together and singing very well.

Where were their parents? She hadn't put them in Montparnasse, had she? No, they were in Père Lachaise cemetery. Everyone had come: everyone from rue de la Mare, the Novacks, the Benedettis, the Cléments from the Allier, the Mercier brothers, the people in their shops and even Monsieur Bonnet from Saint-Mandé.

One day he was told he was cured and that he'd made up for lost time. He told himself he hadn't lost much of anything during his months of absence. He left the white room, the white bed, the white curtains and all that white silence.

And it was almost with regret that one morning in September 1940 he signed his release form from the Salpetrière hospital.

His discharge from prison, his doctor called it, laughing as the two nurses looked on misty-eyed at the thought of his departure. It was a pretty picture for someone about to reclaim his freedom to carry away with him.

: : : : : : : : : : : : : : : : : : 383 : : : : : : : : : : : : : : : : : : :

MAURICE HAD no need to think about what followed in secret behind Zaza's back. He had only to descend into the depths of his memory with the help of Marcel's booze. What followed was still going on now, three years later. Three years in which he had been constantly on the alert, every minute, every hour, every day.

Actually, more than three years, if he counted carefully. It had been three years, five months, and one week: from October 1940 to now. But out of habit he rounded it out to three years; the five months and the extra week were the additional days that had gone by without either him or Zaza having been afraid for so much as an hour.

That made one hundred and sixty days. It had been that long since the *others* had come up from Grenoble for the last time.

They had never again returned to this village of some fifty souls, where they had never found anything suspicious, especially not in the house of the mason-carpenter whose pregnant wife taught her smiling children at the foot of the large crucified Christ.

They had never again returned because they were too busy elsewhere. On the other side of the mountain, where they were awaited with rifles; in the city, where they were being dynamited into the air; and much, much farther off, to the east of the world, where their young people were dying, buried under snow. Real snow.

The last of them to come up to the village had been very old. Very old and very sad. They never came up again.

A hundred and sixty days of respite subtracted from more than a thousand days of fear—seven hundred of which had been spent in Paris —since that day when the unthinkable, the unbelievable, had begun to settle in, secretly and gently, amid general indifference. First, by a simple registration order.

As orphans with no fixed abode, he and Zaza had disobeyed. They didn't register, and the fear began on that day in October 1940, much stronger in them than in those who had obeyed and who thought they were protected by their obedience.

Those on rue de la Mare, for example, all of whom had obeyed. They knew this from Myriam, who reproached them for their disobedience. On rue de la Mare, they had all put themselves right with the authorities, even the Sterns. Madame Lowenthal had taken them with her to the police station to declare themselves: all of them had had "Jew" stamped on their identity cards, and all of them had got their ration books.

Rebelliously, he and Zaza sank deeper into delinquency: forgery and the use of forged materials. They had to eat, and without an identity card you couldn't get ration books.

Zaza was the one to find the forger. Astonishingly, it was Eugène Bonnet who provided them with a legal means of subsistence by baptizing them Roux, Elsa, and Gauthier, Maurice, born in Saint-Mandé in 1921 and 1919, in a little street that had long been removed from the registry records because it had been demolished.

And then they had known the fear familiar to all those who carry false papers. The fear of being recognized by people who knew their real identity.

Not so much Zaza, who was known in the movie industry only as Zaza, period, and who was sometimes even called Zaza Verdon, for obvious reasons. But at the Sorbonne it wasn't so easy to become Gauthier overnight when for a year you'd been known as Guttman.

The bookstore customers also had their troubles. The store was still shut, but the customers kept coming to the apartment to see Madame Villeneuve. And some of them had changed their names, too, and now they were suspicious of one another; they were suspicious of Maurice, and Maurice was suspicious of them. And Madame Villeneuve was suspicious of everyone. She had had no more news from Germany.

Then one evening Villeneuve came home. He wore a beard and glasses, and he no longer called himself Villeneuve.

And other people began coming to the apartment. And slept there sometimes. Often they were Spaniards. They spoke very loudly.

And given what Maurice knew about them, he was a little more afraid than usual when he closed the trapdoor on those evenings.

Zaza was a little less afraid, since Verdon was reassuring. But not his concierge, who didn't like Zaza because Zaza wasn't Madame Verdon.

Madame Verdon, *mère*, didn't care for Zaza either. But she was very fond of her son's concierge, with whom she would often talk of her other son, Louis, who had lived with her son Laurent before that young woman had come to rue des Saints-Pères.

One day, when he'd come to visit Zaza, Maurice ran into Madame Verdon talking to the concierge. Their silence as he went by the loge had frightened him even more than the loud voices of the Spaniards in the Villeneuve apartment.

Villeneuve was now called Berthou, never went out and hadn't reopened the bookstore. In any case, not on rue de Seine. They had even lowered the metal shutter in front of the window—but they were working behind it. They were doing more writing than reading, and the copying machine put out texts that weren't sold but that nonetheless circulated; a cyclist came to pick them up. Until the day he didn't come. Then the package they had prepared was burned in the basement boiler. And Maurice had been very afraid that day, because there'd been a lot of smoke in the courtyard and the boiler hadn't been used for some time because of the lack of coal. And Villeneuve-Berthou went off on a trip for a few days. And Madame Villeneuve was afraid, but didn't say anything to Maurice, who could see it but who didn't say anything about it to her.

Zaza worked a little, but she'd given up the notion of being a script girl because papers were being checked very carefully. You had to have a professional card stamped by the Propaganda-Staffel. Mimi told her to be careful, to watch out for Tata and Féfé Boubou. Tania boasted that her brother was part of some German service. Zaza went back to looking for costumes, and when she went onto a set she was always afraid of running into the Boulanskys.

She was also afraid to draw on the stocks of the Coop, which was no longer the Coop but had again become Masques and Bergamasques. The Zieglers had bought it back. Mademoiselle Anita had preferred to return to her native Dordogne. Ginette had stayed on. Mademoiselle Agnès too. But she hadn't forgiven Stépan for dying, and still less for having been a Jew in those days when she'd loved him and thought of him as a Slav.

So Zaza would do her looking in the flea market, where Yiddish was spoken only in a low voice, so low that she could say she didn't understand.

And when she got back home, she was afraid of the concierge, but she never said anything to Laurent. Because Laurent was cheerful and strong, had his professional card—he was again working as an assistant —and would tell her that nothing bad would ever happen to her as long as she was with him. So she let him think that she believed him. And he didn't know she was afraid.

Nor did Maurice.

They were always afraid, but they got used to it. The time of terror was still to come.

The terror came in May 1941.

The Sterns were the first to be picked up. Exactly seven months after they had voluntarily made their declaration to the census-takers at the police station of the XXth arrondissement.

They left under the protection of the French police. With them were Monsieur Katz and several others from rue de la Mare. And Madame Lowenthal said that it was because they were aliens. Of course it was sad, but they should have done as she had and become naturalized. Besides, they had been taken in for questioning, not arrested. They would come back.

Since neither Zaza nor Maurice ever went to rue de la Mare anymore, it was Sami and Myriam who came to the Verdon apartment one Sunday to tell them about the departure of the Sterns.

And now it was Myriam who was afraid, because she had seen everything. She had been walking in the street with Loulou when it had happened. It had all been done very smoothly, without brutality. Monsieur Stern held Madame Stern's hand. They were both very carefully dressed. The cops had helped them get into a van at the corner of the alley. When the van was full, they took off. And Madame Stern had smiled and made a little sign of farewell with her hand.

And everyone had waited for them to come back. They didn't come back. The Auvergnat went to see what he could find out at the police station. He was told that they'd been taken to the Japy Stadium. But he was also told that the only reason they were telling him was because he wasn't Jewish. And he'd repeated this to old Nussbaum. Since then, Myriam had been afraid. And Sami would yell at her. And Zaza, Maurice and Laurent would reassure her. It must be some kind of mistake . . .

But none of the three really believed it had been a mistake. And Laurent began to understand. And to be afraid, because Sami would have nothing to do with their pious lies. He openly mocked them: no, there had been no mistake, it was the beginning of the program, that was all—the *zakuskis* before the roast, the trial run before the race. . . . It would be better to recognize it and stop telling yourself stories. It was war—the beginning of another one, or the continuation of the same one. He'd only been a stretcher-bearer in the last, but in this one he'd be a rifleman, a crack shot . . . and this was what he'd come to tell these ladies and gentlemen called Verdon, Roux and Gauthier, who were obviously expected to keep it to themselves!

Since he'd had a bit too much to drink—even though everything was rationed, Laurent always had a few good bottles that he got from the studio prop man—they didn't say anything. But Myriam went to cry in the kitchen, where Zaza followed her.

Sami had told the truth. He had met some men, and they were going to go into action. Armed Jewish action. Like bandits, Jewish bandits.

Zaza said it was insane, and Myriam begged her to tell that to Sami, because Sami never listened to anything that she, Myriam, said. There was only one person Sami did listen to: a Slovak or a Bulgarian, she wasn't sure which, whom Sami had met at a hospital consultation and who had completely roped him in. Just when Sami was lucky enough to be able to continue as a nonresident at the Cochin, where they were asking only one thing of him: don't make trouble.

But before Zaza could tell Sami he was insane, it had already been done. Laurent and Maurice had already told him, and Sami had gotten angry and the Nussbaums had left—Myriam in tears, Sami sneering.

And Laurent said he didn't want them to come anymore because they were too dangerous.

Already delinquents, Zaza and Maurice were afraid of Sami, a potentially greater delinquent.

And Zaza met Myriam outside, never at Laurent's apartment, and Maurice waited for Sami at the exit of the Cochin and asked him not to come to the bookstore anymore either.

Sami bowed with mocking obsequiousness: Monsieur Gauthier could rest easy—Sami Nussbaum would never be seen on rue de Seine. Maurice swallowed hard but said nothing. He watched Sami go off and join a tall fellow who'd obviously been waiting for him some ten yards away.

Maurice just couldn't tell Sami why he mustn't set foot in the Villeneuve place, where tactics had completely changed overnight.

They had changed between the 22 and 23 of June, to be precise. The time necessary to make a decision, just after June 21, the beginning of summer 1941, which was also the beginning of the war between Germany and Russia.

Villeneuve had shaved off his beard and put away his phony glasses. He was no longer Berthou, but once again Villeneuve, formerly a prisoner in Germany and freed thanks to the levy of "volunteer" workers sent to replace him. Living proof of the efficacy of collaboration, he showed himself in the neighborhood and rolled up his iron curtain. The storefront was cleaned, and in the window Bergson was replaced by translations of Nietzsche alongside Gobineau's treatise on the inequality of races.

But the three children and Madame Villeneuve were sent to live with grandparents in Tours. The Spaniards were seen less frequently, and passed through in silence.

The copying machine was taken upstairs, along with reams of new paper, and the trapdoor between Maurice's room and the apartment was always half open, unless someone new was expected. Someone they weren't sure had the right to know that the place had an emergency exit.

There were only two really new new people, but there were ghosts from before the war. Ghosts, or "Revenants," as they were called, who had played dead from the summer of 1939 until the summer of 1941, and who seemed to emerge from a long hibernation, from some solitary retreat made because of a disappointment in love, the betrayal of a beloved. They had the all-forgiving, gentle, indulgent air of men running into an adored mistress after she'd left them for what they'd known all along would be only a passing fancy. There were three of these "Revenants." They were about forty years old.

So were the two new ones. But these people had never hibernated. They didn't love the adored mistress of the "Revenants" and had never felt betrayed, but since they hated the Germans as much as the "Revenants" hated the Nazis, they had no objection to an alliance—in any case, at least not for the moment. The "Revenants" often came off best in discussions because they had their troops, knew where to find them, knew they'd been bursting with impatience—so they assured the others —since September 1939. The new people tried to recruit, but it was more haphazard, and so they accepted the situation. All of them got together often and did an enormous amount of talking.

If Maurice hadn't been so afraid, he'd have been amused, like any private, to listen to the conversations of the general staff. But in the double life he now had to lead, he felt a double fear: fear when he was upstairs, running the copier, and fear when he was downstairs, watching Villeneuve in friendly conversations in German with young soldiers who confused bookstores with stationery stores and came in to buy postcards of Paris. Plus the additional fear that overtook him when civilians really wanted to buy a Gobineau essay on Nordic supremacy, which he fetched for them and which they took and paid for before going off with a conspiratorial smile. And just as much fear of the contemptuous looks of the shoemaker next door and the florist across the way on the morning he'd erased the *Kollabo* inscription scrawled in chalk during the night on the wooden panel of the glass door.

And finally the fear of the face that came regularly to press against the shop window and watch him over the book display, and continued watching him as he moved around the store, until he was paralyzed, unable to make the most ordinary gestures. Then one day he recognized in this obstinate voyeur the man from that couple at Chéramy's: the man alone—without his Jewish wife—who had known that Maurice had finally recognized him and who pointed to the books, nodded his head, applauded with his fingertips, spat on the window and left.

He never came back.

And Maurice told Zaza, but Zaza didn't really remember that evening at Chéramy's. There'd been so many of them, before the war . . . Besides, she had something much more important to tell him, something that had happened that day. And it was very frightening.

: :

LOULOU COULD walk, she could even run, since she was more than two years old. But on some days Myriam still took the stroller. When they got to the paths in the Buttes, Loulou did the pushing. It amused her, and it amused the passers-by. That day, when they had reached a bench, Myriam and Zaza had taken the pail, shovel, rake and molds from the stroller, and Myriam had led Zaza toward the sand pile, where Loulou had already joined two other children. Zaza had wanted to sit on the bench alongside the stroller, but Myriam had insisted. The stroller remained unguarded, and Myriam began to use baby talk: "Aunty Zaza is going to make you a nice sandpie . . . " Then she gave the pail to Zaza. Zaza looked at Myriam and noticed that she was keeping an eye on the bench, which a man had just approached. He sat down right next to the stroller and took a newspaper from his pocket, opening it wide. "He's taking our bench!" exclaimed Zaza. "I'll go," said Myriam. She made a possessive grab at the stroller, pushed it to the other side of the bench, patted down the padding, then sat down. The man folded his paper, got up and left.

Zaza came back to the bench. Myriam's mouth was smiling, but her eyes were terrified, and her hand trembled when she tried to stop Zaza's hand from lifting the corner of the padding to make sure she hadn't been dreaming: she was sure she'd seen the man touch the stroller before Myriam had moved it to the right side of the bench. She hadn't been dreaming: there was something under the padding. It was lumpy, triangular, wrapped in a gray rag. "You're insane . . . " she said to Myriam, collapsing onto the bench. "You're all insane, insane . . . " she repeated. Myriam made a gesture with her head, shoulders and hands that seemed to say simultaneously, "Yes, no, but that's the way it is, it has to be done and I'm doing it."

Two women came to sit on the bench. They thought Loulou was very cute in her red wool snowsuit. Myriam thanked them and asked what time it was. "We've got to go home," she decided. They collected the pail, the shovel, the rake and the molds, still covered with sand, and heaped them into the stroller. Loulou wanted to push, and the women said she was very strong and grown up for her age. Everyone laughed and said goodbye.

While they were walking toward the gate, Myriam asked Zaza not to look so upset. It was nothing, just a transport assignment, the third she had carried out. The pistol must have been used for something, but she didn't know what. Someone had come to return it, and she was carrying it, that was all. But while she was carrying it, she preferred not to have Zaza along.

They said goodbye at the Métro. Before going down the stairs, Zaza turned. Myriam had just placed Loulou in the stroller full of toys. She took her daughter's forearm and made her wave goodbye to Aunt Zaza. Zaza responded. Myriam smiled and, taking hold of the stroller handle, moved off with her cargo.

That's what Zaza told Maurice in the Vert-Galant park, where they met when they didn't want to talk at the Verdon's or in the bookstore, where Zaza didn't like to go.

: :

THAT DAY, they'd both been afraid. And a little ashamed when they agreed that Zaza would no longer go walking with Myriam and Lou-lou. Laurent had been right—they were dangerous.

But Maurice didn't tell Zaza that in the Villeneuve apartment on the third floor, the people who came to visit were all just as dangerous. He kept this from her because he didn't want her to be even more afraid. She thought he was so safe behind the rampart of all those opportunistic books, and safer still because he was an *au pair* man in a family as opportunistic as the books they sold.

If she'd only known.

AND IF MAURICE himself had only known what was awaiting him a few weeks from then, on an evening in March 1942, when he came up from the bookstore at about seven in the evening.

In the apartment, the dining-room door was closed, as it was each time there was a meeting. Before knocking, Maurice listened. The voice speaking was unfamiliar to him, but it was as though he'd been stabbed to the heart. The voice had just said '*bsolutely* in a way he hadn't heard anyone say it for the past three years.

He knocked. "It's me," he said, and entered.

The unknown man who'd been talking was seated between Villeneuve and one of the "Revenants." One of the two new people faced the "Revenant" and the other, sitting with his back to the door and wearing a brown leather jacket, now turned around. It was Sami.

Sami gave no sign that he knew him.

"Samuel . . . Jiri . . . friends," said the "Revenant" quietly.

Maurice nodded hello and sat down next to Villeneuve.

"Go on, Jiri," said the "Revenant."

Jiri spoke. Maurice listened, but he kept watching Sami. Sami had grown thinner, his eyes bigger. He resembled Jeannot a great deal. He looked only at Jiri.

Making many mistakes in his French, Jiri said the same things Sami had said that famous Sunday in the Verdon apartment. But more bluntly. He said that he was a Jew and an alien, that his men were Jews and aliens, and that they'd formed a group because when they'd first started, the French groups hadn't wanted them. And they'd begun well before June 21, 1941—from the moment the Boches had begun to take action against the Jews . . .

"The Nazis," the "Revenant" corrected amicably.

"I say what I know," said Jiri.

And Maurice tried to meet Sami's eyes. He stared at him hard, with desperation. But Sami kept looking at Jiri, who continued.

His men (he said "my" men) were organized, knew what they had to do and did it because they had nothing to lose. Among themselves, each man knew only two others. As for him, Jiri, he knew them all. And there was someone above him who'd sent him here to make contact.

"We know," said the "Revenant."

Apparently the new man didn't know. He said nothing. Neither did Villeneuve. But it was he who seemed most affected by Jiri's logic. The old habits of a cosmopolite, Maurice told himself. In any case, he didn't have the polite, distant attitude of the "Revenant," nor the distant and totally indifferent attitude the new man displayed.

"It's very risky," said the "Revenant."

"For whom? For us or for you?" Sami asked at this point in his impeccable French, still without looking at Maurice.

"But you're not a foreigner, are you?" said the "Revenant," astonished.

"I wasn't, but I've recently become a naturalized foreigner," said Sami, who got up when he saw that Jiri was already standing.

"Come on, let's go. We're frightening these Frenchmen," Jiri said to Sami in Yiddish.

"What's he saying?" asked the "Revenant."

"I said that we're going," answered Jiri.

Sami was already at the door. Jiri went to join him, looked at the beautiful pictures on the wall, and caressed the mahogany of the pretty English chairs. He smiled in a vague sort of way.

"We'll talk. How do we find you?" asked the "Revenant."

"You don't," said Jiri sharply.

And they left.

"They're dangerous," murmured the new man after he'd heard the door slam. "Especially the old one, with that face and that accent. If we have to meet again, it had better be somewhere else."

"You're right," agreed the "Revenant," who never used *tu* with the new man, or with him either.

Villeneuve was silent. He looked at Maurice, who looked at him. He suddenly seemed to remember that Gauthier's real name was Guttman. And Maurice went up to his room. His head hurt a lot. He wept and felt somewhat better.

The next day he went to the Cochin. No one had seen Sami for two months.

So on Sunday he went to rue de la Mare, to Myriam's grandmother, and Zaza went with him.

: :

MAURICE's "Jewish" move wasn't carried out until after Zaza's.

Hers took place on May 31 at about nine in the morning, in front of the Buttes sand pile, when Myriam turned Loulou over to her along with another little girl and four little boys between five and six years old, whom Zaza didn't know. All had schoolbags prepared by their absent mothers.

Myriam was wearing a burgundy cardigan over a gray skirt. Over her heart she'd sewn a brand-new star given to her the day before. She said she had put it on so she wouldn't draw attention to herself on rue de la Mare, but that she was going to unsew it as soon as she'd left the children with Zaza. She embraced Zaza and went off immediately. Loulou didn't even notice that her mother was gone.

Because the move had been well planned, it was Josette Clément, who had made a special trip from the Allier, who led Zaza and the children to a train that took them to Moulins that same day. The unoccupied zone began at Moulins, on the other side of the Allier River.

Laurent drove them all to the Gare de Lyon in a van belonging to the film propman. He helped Josette and Zaza get the children, who were very happy about going on a trip, onto the train, then got back down on the platform. Zaza appeared at the lowered window. She was sobbing. The train started. The move had been made.

It was only a small move, but for Zaza it was gigantic. Laurent called out that he would join her soon. She looked at him the way you look at someone you never expect to see again.

: :

MAURICE carried out his own move a week later. His, also well planned, was bigger in scope.

He had planned it carefully, rehearsed it, timed it. Sami had provided the supplies, but Maurice acted alone. He was the one who had chosen the target. And there'd been nothing haphazard about it. Ideally, to capture the beauty of the gesture, he would have preferred to go into action on May 26, sixteen years to the day after Schwarzbard. But May 26 was a Monday, closing day for the bistro.

It was 10:50 P.M., on June 17, 1942, when a bottle tossed through the open window exploded in the rear room of Le Dragon, the evening gathering place of four Ukrainians members of the Gestapo from the Hôtel Lutétia.

A few seconds later, Maurice went down the staircase of the Sèvres-Babylone Métro. Behind him, flickering lights illuminated the cross-roads, where the noise of broken windows had exploded in crystalline cascades.

Myriam was on the platform at Châtelet, sitting under a poster of the singer Léo Marjane. She'd cut and dyed her hair, and the star had disappeared from her burgundy cardigan. When Maurice came along, she got up and walked ahead of him. He followed her at a distance, and they left the station. The big clock on Place du Châtelet said 11:15 P.M. The Brasserie du Théâtre lowered its metal shutters, the gates to the Métro were closed, Myriam walked toward the quai de Gesvres, and Maurice stopped and vomited against a tree. It was painful because his stomach was empty except for the pill Sami had given him—the tranquilizer he'd swallowed at about 9 P.M. Myriam slowed down. He caught up, and remained about five yards behind her. She was walking quickly now, and he had trouble following her. There were many people taking a walk before curfew, and he was afraid he might lose sight of her. They crossed a bridge—he didn't know which—and he kept following; he was cold: though the night air was mild and he knew it, he was cold. He was irritated with himself for having vomited up the remains of the pill.

Myriam turned into one little street, then into another. There were no more passers-by. She stopped, pushed a door, and left it open for him. In the darkness, she took his hand, closed the door, then pressed the automatic light switch to turn on a small yellowish light.

It was 11:35 P.M. when Myriam left him. She'd gone upstairs and set the Jazz alarm clock for 6 A.M. In an envelope, she'd left a second-class ticket for the Paris-Moulins train leaving at 8:05 A.M.; an identity card in the name of Jean Berthier, salesman, born December 13, 1921, in Algiers; and the money that had been collected from the children's parents. She'd checked the contents of the Boy Scout package she'd prepared for him and from which she'd taken a thermos of tea she told him to leave behind, together with the alarm clock. She'd given him a quick hug: all he'd have to do in the morning was to close the door, but before six-thirty. She'd said she had to get back. She didn't say where to.

Maurice closed the small basement window. Trembling with cold, he took a gulp of the tea, which he immediately threw up into a new, blue enamel pail that still carried its price tag from the Bazar de l'Hôtel de Ville.

He stretched out on the folding bed and wrapped himself in a red-striped khaki blanket. He blew out the candle and closed his eyes.

The footsteps of a woman wearing wooden-soled shoes went rapidly past the window and echoed for a few seconds, then there was the sound of an outside door closing and, in the reestablished silence, the first strokes of midnight. Maurice recognized the bell of Notre-Dame, so close it deafened him.

The explosion must have been heard as far as rue de Seine. If not the explosion itself, then the fire trucks and the emergency police. Above the bookstore, the people on the third floor thought he was asleep. In the morning, Villeneuve would climb up through the trapdoor. Unless he already had.

The note slipped between the tarnished frame and the mirror didn't say much. Merely "Goodbye and thanks."

Nothing had been left in the room. After Sami's visit, he'd torn up all the photos in which they might have recognized Sami and him. But before destroying the shot of the Convent, he'd carefully cut out the heads of Jeannot and Robert. As bright and glossy as paillettes, they were now pasted on the back of the little picture of Anny, which he'd slipped under the mica of his card case along with the pictures of Sonia and Elie as a bridal couple, Robert standing below Dr. Pierre—and Volodya.

The dead, a vagabond and a foreign woman were the only clues Jean Berthier would provide, if he were ever captured.

He relit the candle. Reexamined his new identity card and the ration book that had gone unnoticed when Myriam had given him the envelope. Jiri had been right—his people knew what they had to do, and they did it well. His people, both men and women: cold, calm, determined, as efficient as Myriam, whose air of doing this every day was frightening.

The basement room was also frightening, with its false collection of old things, and its new accessories and its simple wooden latch.

He blew out the candle again.

At about four in the morning, he sank into a half sleep.

: :

AT 1:12 P.M., under a sunny sky, he got out of the train at Moulins just as the German police were getting on to check the passes of travelers who were passing through to the unoccupied zone and who would have an hour's wait stuck in their compartments.

He gave his ticket to the man collecting them and offered his identity card to a German soldier, who gestured to him that it wasn't necessary. Josette was waiting at the exit. She was wearing a red skirt, a white blouse and a knapsack slung across her shoulder. Two bikes were resting against the wall of the station. Josette embraced Maurice, who was rested and cleanshaven.

He'd shaved at about seven-thirty in the station restroom, before the train had left. He was rested because he'd slept almost all the way, having leafed through the morning papers lent him by those who shared his compartment.

He'd found only about ten lines on the last page of *Le Petit Parisien*. They mentioned an explosion due to a gas leak in a Left Bank restaurant. In addition to a great deal of damage, there had been several victims whose identity the police hadn't revealed. They were customers, three people who frequented the establishment. The other voyagers said that accidents of this sort were more frequent since the gas shutoffs. Imagine how many short circuits there would be as a result of the power cuts. Maurice stopped listening. He'd fallen into such a deep sleep that the man next to him had to wake him shortly before they arrived at the Moulins station. "If it hadn't been for me, you'd have found yourself in the unoccupied zone with us, young man," he'd said obligingly, as he took from his pocket and pinned to his lapel a silver battle-axe of Frankish design—the emblem of the Vichy government.

An hour later, Maurice was in the unoccupied zone, about five miles from the railway station.

Whispering, Josette had led him across the frontier that snaked, invisibly, through the heart of a forest of which she seemed to know all the trees, all the copses, every bush. They left their bikes at the edge of the wood, in a little shed to which Josette had the key. After that, she moved about as surely as other people find their way in a city. She took shortcuts, avoided forks in the road and went along paths that became darker and more overgrown with their every step. She often went ahead of him and gave him her hand, the way mountain guides do. She whispered. She said more in a whisper than he'd ever heard her say out loud during his entire childhood. In those days, it had always been Zaza or Robert who did all the talking.

She whispered to tell him what he'd have to do once he was over the line, explaining where to catch the bus after he left the woods and where to take the train when he got off the bus.

She whispered to warn him against going to Neuilly-le-Réal just then. The pro-German militia was keeping an eye on the Post Office, Félix and Jeannette. They had aged, and they were depressed. Robert hadn't sent word to anyone since the summer of 1939. After a horrible scene with his father, he had disappeared without a trace. Maurice didn't say anything about the letter from Marseilles.

She whispered that the other day the hardest thing had been to keep the children from laughing too much while they were crossing the line.

She whispered even more softly to ask him how his head felt now, and she stopped to feel under his curls for the scar, running her fingertips along it. He'd closed his eyes. She started walking again and would never know about the incredibly savage desire for her that had seized him for a moment. Almost sneakily, he let her get a little ahead of him so that he could get a better look at her red cotton skirt, gathered at the waist in a way that made her buttocks waggle from side to side with every step she took. She turned around to wait for him, whispering that they were almost there. She looked at him as though he were an exhausted child. She whispered that Zaza had also been tired after the long trip. He said yes and smiled. He didn't tell her that he had killed some men the night before.

They still had to descend some twenty yards of clinging moss before getting to the bottom of a little ravine into which the sun reached only in irregular, dancing spots. She took his hand, and together they walked along a veritable wall of dwarfed trees, roots, vines, ferns and tangled brambles. She paced off fifteen large steps and came to a halt. "It's here," she murmured, and she took a pair of black leather gloves from her knapsack and slipped them on. With her hands and arms she spread the bunches of long stems bristling with a fresh growth of thorns. The gap appeared. "Go ahead, but be careful. There may be water on the other side," she told him. He kissed her on the cheek and crawled under the barbed vault she made with her arms. When he stood up on the other side, she was already replacing the branches just the way they had been. She waved to him before restoring the last bunch, behind which she completely disappeared from sight. He couldn't even see her red skirt when he heard the eight notes of the Laurel and Hardy theme, which neither she nor Zaza would have dared to use in earlier days.

He replied with a whistle that was more like a breath, waited a second without moving, then decided to cross the pebbly bed where a trickle of water was running. He drank a mouthful from the hollow of his hand. The water had the taste of blood. He had been pricked by a bramble thorn. He wrapped his handkerchief around his left hand and began to climb up the other side of the ravine. For the first time since yesterday he was hungry. It made him walk faster.

At Saint-Pourçain, he bought a loaf of bread with real tickets from his phony ration book. He ate it while he waited for his bus.

At Varennes-sur-Allier, before taking his first train, he bought a Velpeau adhesive bandage. While he was on the bus he'd noticed that his blood-spotted handkerchief made him look suspicious.

At Lyons, his hand neatly bandaged, he bought the latest newspapers, both from the unoccupied zone and from Paris. He glanced through them while waiting for his second and last train. None of them mentioned the attack or the explosion. And in the last edition of *Le Petit Parisien* there was no mention of even the slightest gas leak.

At Grenoble, he barely managed to catch the last bus, which was filled with people who knew one another and were returning up the mountain together just as they had come down together in the morning. It must have been market day in the city; they spoke of the things they had bought for the week, and then they fell silent: the diesel-oil motor made too much noise as soon as they started climbing the mountain. At every stop the bus emptied a little more, and every time the doors were opened the air that rushed in was cooler and cooler. By the end of the trip, there were only four passengers getting off—two women, an old man and himself, and it was positively cold in the little square of the last village.

Maurice hadn't recognized anyone in the bus, and no one had seemed to pay any attention to him. They saw mountain climbers all year long. No one paid any attention to them unless they fell into a crevice. Then they were a lot of trouble for everyone. That was probably the only thing the villagers told themselves when they saw Maurice set his knapsack on his shoulders and slide his thumbs under the straps as he began to walk the five remaining miles. He was alone again for the first time in hours.

As he walked, he thought that at this time yesterday he'd been getting ready to kill, at the same time that he'd been getting ready—maybe—to die. Today, the men he had killed were probably anonymous corpses, and he was unknown and alive. Unlike Samuel Schwarzbard, he wouldn't get his picture into the paper, and the four little Gestapo Petliuras from the Hotel Lutétia wouldn't have their mausoleum in the Montparnasse cemetery. They'd be replaced by others, who would do their drinking elsewhere at the end of the day.

His day was almost finished. He breathed in great gulps of cold air, but he wasn't cold. He stared at the snow above, and, above that, at the sky, so incredibly clear that it was royal-blue—no, more periwinkle—and at the reddish sun, so high that it still would not have set before his arrival. And he asked himself how he would have to think of this day in time to come.

As the day following a murder? As a day of flight? As a clandestine border crossing? Later, all of it would probably be mixed together in his memory—assuming he was allowed to have a later.

It would be all of that, mixed together, but with something else added, something he hadn't stopped thinking about ever since it had happened. That sudden savage and brief desire to make love to Josette.

To make love to her, to toss her on her back, to fuck her on the ground or up against a tree, right then and there, a girl he didn't love but who happened to be there. A girl he didn't love but whom he liked very much—which made it worse.

Worse . . . Thinking about it, he wasn't sure. Little Josette's whisperings in the undergrowth, with her fleeting caress and her scarlet skirt, had in all innocence given him back the hope that had been confiscated in the hospital and that he had little by little resigned himself to renouncing. He had often shed tears of rage about it, alone at night in the pretty little boat bed on rue de Seine once so miraculously too narrow for two. So tenderly too narrow for him and Anny, the little English girl he had loved so much, and who had also whispered. Who would fall asleep whispering, wake up and slip away in the morning with a whisper. He'd wept, and not only for Anny. Wept for the woman camping in the woods at Port-Louis, a woman whose face and voice he didn't even remember, but who, under the tent, had also whispered.

Walking along he told himself that, later, this day would also be remembered as a forest walk during which he had had an erection for the first time in months. To break down more complete the walls of his old modesty, his incorrigible timidity about using the real words the others—Sami and Robert, for example—always used, but which he never did, he said them to himself out loud. All the verbs he knew for saying it, he said aloud, he conjugated, he repeated in cadence; and he blushed and walked faster.

He still had to reach and cut through the large stand of fir trees. It was there that the mayor's seventy hectares began. On the other side, down in the little valley, he'd see the twenty houses of the hamlet, the sawmill and, a little bit to the side and all alone beside its well, what remained of the Convent, where Zaza wasn't expecting him.

No more than were those little strangers whose names he now rehearsed in his head. Yesterday, in the basement, Myriam had repeated them to him twice as she gave him the envelope of money. In addition to Loulou, there was a Markus, a Luis, a Fredo, a Dédée and a Dany. He decided that considering the circumstances his memory was still pretty good.

On the other side of the wood, he saw not only the hamlet but the smoke coming from the Convent chimney.

Ten minutes later, he pushed open the big door, called out, "It's me!" and went inside.

Under the vaults, the children were sitting around the table. Zaza was in front of the stove. She turned and the children giggled and elbowed one another as they watched her rush into the arms of this unknown man with the injured hand.

: :

THE BRAMBLE had left an all but invisible slash. Still, that night, by making the lamplight play over his open left hand, Maurice once more managed to find the somewhat jagged trace, the slight shininess that differentiated this line from the others in his hand. At such times, as though the ridiculous wound had wanted to record a date elsewhere and otherwise than in his memory, the barely perceptible furrow took on the proportions of a true scar.

There were now many others on the inside of his hands, but those had no secrets to tell him. They were the marks of his early awkwardness with hammer, nails, saw and pick. He had since learned to use these tools correctly.

On the table, alongside Zaza's bag, Marcel's bottle was almost empty. He smiled vaguely at his workman's hands, which hadn't opened a book for twenty-two months.

A summer, an autumn, a winter, a spring, another summer, another autumn and another winter had passed, and the children who slept upstairs had had enough to eat every day.

They'd played, fought, made up their quarrels, learned to read and write, rolled in the grass and in the snow. They'd been warm in their house when it was cold outside. As the seasons passed, they had grown as the children grow in the romantic stories of Charles Nodier: without other nocturnal terrors than those inspired by the barking of a dog mistaken for a wolf or the sound of the wind under the door confused with the moaning of a ghost.

Twenty-two months of survival snatched from the children-snatchers who had been preparing to take them away. Snatched from the police, from the informers and the indifferent, from all those who took, ordered the taking of, or permitted the taking of sisters, brothers, parents and grandparents about whom the children perhaps thought in secret since they drew pictures of them but didn't want to write to since they never got an answer.

Volodya had never answered either; he too had left an address.

The one Myriam had left was there, hidden at the bottom of Zaza's bag. But the false name, the number of a real street in a real Paris suburb

—that handwritten address was as deaf, mute, useless and out of date as the other one, written in Cyrillic and carefully folded in Elie's wallet.

Volodya's address had been buried with the corpse of Maurice's father, Elie Guttman, born in Zhitomir and resting peacefully in Père-Lachaise, in Paris, in his neighborhood.

Yes, his father was resting peacefully alongside his mother and near his friends: Maurice was now sure of this.

All four were resting peacefully under stones that bore their real names, their dates of birth and the date of their death, which had come just in time. It had prolonged their sleep and given them a peace they would never have known again if they'd lived a little longer.

Maurice poured out the remains of Marcel's brandy and toasted fate, which had allowed them to die in time to be mourned and honored.

He saw again the prefect in his handsome uniform, the assistant-assistant minister in his cutaway, and told himself that they'd been wrong to complain of an unhappy fate. It was a happy fate that had allowed living people who had lived out their lives before his eyes to die before they became living people who might already be dead for all anyone knew.

He drank to the rest and peace they'd found, according to the promise made them in Latin by the Châteauroux curé at a time when France went into mourning for nineteen of its children, crushed in a train because an ox, terrified at the idea of death, had escaped from a badly padlocked cattle car.

In the days when cattle cars were used only to transport cattle, and buses were for people who could get out at the next stop if they wished.

As for the buses, he and Zaza had known about them for a long time, thanks to an old telegram the Auvergnat had sent to Félix, who'd given it to Josette, who'd seen to it that it got to Zaza. She'd kept it; it too was in her bag, and it said: "Old la Mare friends in serious condition. Stop. Emergency transportation by bus dawn this morning. Stop. Greetings—Boubalou." It was dated July 1942, when thousands of Jews had been rounded up and taken by the busload to the Vel d'Hiver stadium.

As for the cattle cars, he'd only learned of them that day. He still hadn't said anything to Zaza, and he'd end by not saying anything. If it hadn't been for a friend of Marcel, a porter at the Grenoble railway station, he himself wouldn't ever have known. At the Grenoble railway station, everyone knew. It happened in full daylight, on a siding where the empty wagons waited. The trucks came in by way of the freight station. When the cattle cars were full, they'd be padlocked. Only when they were all padlocked were they hooked up to a locomotive. There were no scheduled departures, and no one knew their destination. That depended on *them*—the German stationmaster and the S.S. The trucks were handled by the militia. After the roundup, they went back and forth. Evidently they weren't rounding up only Jews. They were in such a state of panic down there that they jumbled everything and everybody together. In other words, it was a mess!

It was this disorder that had especially astonished Marcel's friend when he'd told them about it before leaving the building site, where he had come to lend a hand.

The building site had also astonished him. He hadn't expected to have to climb so high up the mountain on his day off, nor to find what he had found up there. He'd looked at the tower, whose framework now stretched above the surrounding pines and, shaking his head, had asked Marcel what nut was building a lighthouse up here on the mountain. A Lyons astronomer, Marcel had answered. His friend had shrugged and said that the world was really topsy-turvy and that this whatchamacallit was really a *Mirliflore* mirador—a dandy of a watchtower.

He'd laughed so much over his own joke that he repeated it two or three times, to the rhythm of his hammer. And what had to happen inevitably happened. As dazzling as suns, as sonorous as cymbals, the words Mirador and Mirliflore were picked up by the children playing among the pines.

Maurice did everything he could to metamorphose the watchtower into a Minaret, Donjonnet, Tourmalet, Pigeon House, Tour de Nesle and Eiffel Tower, but nothing worked. It was too late: the abominable Mirador and the marvelous Mirliflore had already revealed their prodigious treasures. They glittered like a Christmas tree in Ali Baba's cave. In earlier days, in the childhood of Maurice and Zaza, it had been at night that the witch Pet-Lura, unnameable under her dirty tatters, under her begging bag, would surge over them like a shadow. Unfindable, immaterial and unbeatable, Mirador and Mirliflore were covered with gold, with miracles and mirages and mirrors, with Miror wax, with toreadors with golden behinds, with dogs named Médor, with sun-ripened mirabelle plums, with musical mirlitons, with millions of mimosas, with millers milling in song and fable, with astrologers in pointed hats, with nonsense that had the charm of alliteration, rhyme, or both . . .

Though the verses of the song were constantly improved on, the refrain remained unchanged. Because the children had immediately found the right music: it was simple and catchy, easy to remember:

Mirador, don't be sad!
Mirliflore is quite mad!

They sang it all day long, and all the way on the road downhill.

Maurice lost his temper trying to get them to keep still when they reached the hamlet. They wanted to know why they couldn't keep singing. To begin with, Maurice told them that there was no such thing as a Mirliflore. That, in addition, the astronomer was a very-very-nice man, that he wasn't mad, that he didn't have a pointed hat, and that if they ran into him in the hamlet while they were singing, his feelings would be hurt. That he liked his tower and that it would be very pretty when it was finished. That it wasn't a mirador. That they mustn't ever say that word. That it was a very nasty word for such a nice high tower, which the astronomer would someday let them climb so he could give them a closer look at the sky, the moon and the stars. Provided they were very good.

They wanted to know when.

When what?

When they could go up to see the sky, the moon and the stars from close up.

When the tower was finished and the astronomer could have big glasses, or rather telescopes, big loupes, something like that, brought up . . .

When would that be?

When they'd have permission.

Why didn't they have permission now?

Because they didn't have permission now, and that was all there was to it.

They didn't have permission to look at the sky, the moon and the stars up close?

No, not for the time being. And no more questions, Markus.

They had stopped singing. Behind his back Maurice could hear their smothered laughter. He turned around in time to see Loulou drill the index finger of her right hand under the hood of her cape. It was snowing again, and Maurice walked faster.

They didn't run into the astronomer as they went through the hamlet.

IT WAS to him, to that city innocent who had acquired the top of a mountain to observe a topsy-turvy world better, that Maurice drank the last few drops in the bottom of his bowl.

He still had something very difficult to do if he didn't want to wake Zaza. But he could do it; he had done it before: to be sure the armchair didn't creak as he got up, wash the bowl and hide the bottle, put out the lamp, walk in the dark to the staircase and go upstairs without stumbling.

This evening, he also had to replace Zaza's bag where it belonged, on the desk on the other side of the room. The distance he had to cover caused him to hesitate a moment; he finally made up his mind, and got there and back without incident.

Proud of himself, before turning out the light he looked one last time toward the oak door, behind which nothing had stirred.

He'd made it: he could go back upstairs to bed.

O N HER ROOM, her eyes wide open, Zaza heard Maurice's somewhat heavy tread as he returned to his bed in the children's dormitory. The footsteps overhead hadn't awakened her. She hadn't been asleep. She was never asleep when Maurice went downstairs to drink by himself, but she always pretended to be.

She heard the footsteps, but she wasn't really listening to them. She was listening to her belly with her hands. She was trying to imagine the light, circular and vaguely painful waves that she always felt resonating and vibrating within her entrails as soon as she lay down.

She had given no name to what was still only barely stirring within her. Before it had stirred, she had never even called it a child. A child, children, meant the others upstairs: Loulou, Markus, Luis, Frédo, Dany and Dédée.

What was inside her she had first called being late, then anguish and finally panic. All the old remedies so complacently enumerated, discussed and compared by the tall naked girls who in earlier days stood around Bruno's laundry basket on rue de la Mare had flooded her memory. She tried boiling milk with pepper, since she had no saffron. And footbaths in very hot water. Which had made the children laugh and had intrigued Maurice. And that was all it had done, other than make her vomit.

So she'd told Maurice she was pregnant. He'd said, "Suffer the little children to come unto me," and glanced up at the Christ above the stove.

She hadn't told Laurent anything. Nor had she written to him. But she knew exactly when her child would be born. It had been on December 3 that Laurent had stayed, for an entire night, and given it to her. It had to be that night, since he'd spent only one night with her recently—the ninth in two years.

He had come for the ninth time. He had visited and revisited just as he had promised on the station platform, when she had sobbed because she hadn't believed him. But he had come, and each time she had been amazed, telling herself that it might be the last time.

She hadn't told him anything because if Laurent did return a tenth time, she wanted to be sure that it was really for her, only for her. As a lover who couldn't keep himself from rushing to the woman he loved, even if only for a night. Not as the father of a child whose mother couldn't decently be abandoned.

She knew that she was expecting Laurent's child in September, and that Maurice, who was waiting along with her, was already calling it Volodya.

Why Volodya? She no longer really remembered, and had never been able to admit this to Maurice. She should have done so long ago, after he'd left the Salpêtrière, when they had shared the contents of The Family Picture Frame and he had insisted on taking the photo of the handsome saber-scarred man whose history she had forgotten. But even then it was probably already too late to confess. She had realized that from the way Maurice had almost apologetically clutched at the vestiges of a drama that supposedly belonged to the two of them.

She knew that there'd been an old Volodya story, very long, very sad, very complicated. She even knew where, on what day and at what hour Maurice had told it to her, and why she had listened to it so distractedly that November 10 in Chéramy's at about ten o'clock in the evening. She knew because it had been in the afternoon of that November 10 that she had made love for the first time in her life, on a big low bed in a half-darkened room with red curtains, and she could think of nothing but returning there to make love again with the man who had just violated her, as he had himself said, with all the tenderness in the world. "Don't be afraid, my love, I'm going to violate you now," that's what Laurent had said to her and that was what she'd been thinking of while Maurice was telling the people at Chéramy's the story to which she had paid no attention.

She knew that the story began with "Pouett-Pouett" because later, in that big bed, Laurent had said to her that he wished he had known her when she was five years old and had made love to her again, caressing her as though she had been a little girl. She knew that they'd been so crazy that they'd even thanked Hitler for not having let her, Zaza, go off to Germany with Mimi. She knew that she'd returned to the Bonnets' in Laurent's car early in the morning, and that as they were crossing a deserted and flag-draped Paris, Laurent had told her that all the flags had been put out just for them. She remembered that the light had been switched on up on the third floor, in Old Lady Lowenthal's apartment, when Laurent had stopped the car and then the motor in front of the building, and that they'd been unable to bring themselves to part. She remembered that in the morning she had made up some excuse and left the house before noon—she hadn't waited for Maurice, who for once was coming to have lunch with them.

She remembered everything: the gesture with which Alex had replaced a pin in Angelina Crespi's hair—she was looking a little old in Alex's pullover—just as Laurent, his hand resting on her own shoulder, had lightly pressed his fingers down to tell her that he wanted to go back to the room with her, now, immediately, and that he wasn't listening to that endless story either.

She remembered everything, except the never-ending story about Volodya.

But she thought that she could never admit it, now less than ever. And when Maurice called the child Volodya she pretended to know why and made no objection. After all, why not Volodya? Volodya was a pretty name.

Only she thought it was a little early to give a first name to a child who still had no family name. The day before, she'd laughed and said as much to Maurice.

He had once again called on the Christ as his witness: he'd said that carpenters never had any luck with respectable young girls who were always bringing home children who hadn't been fathered by them, and he'd suggested Jesus as a family name for Volodya.

"Too Jewish," Zaza had replied.

"Still too Jewish for the present season, agreed—but this is still only April. Wait until September, Mademoiselle Roux!"

"That's all I'm doing, Monsieur Gauthier-Berthier!"

"True enough, that's all you're doing, instead of learning to read the future in the constellations, as I've been doing since I began studying the stars. You would have seen September as I've seen it . . . And now I know!"

He was sorry that she couldn't climb the tower to read September in the skies with him, but considering her interesting condition, he strongly advised against scrambling up the scaffolding.

As for the name, he was going to tell her what he knew: the child born to Mademoiselle Roux in September '44 would be free to call itself whatever it wished, and that was the big news he had read in the Little Dipper.

Anyway, they could always call it Roux, if by chance the young mama wanted to retain her pretty *nom de guerre*.

Or they could call it Verdon, if by chance the young papa were to acknowledge his child coming along the street.

But, especially and above all, it would have the right to call itself Roginski. "And Roginski, Vladimir—you can believe me when I tell you this—will be very fashionable this autumn: Roginski is Polish, but it sounds Russian, and the Russians will have won the war by then."

Obviously, Vladimir Verdon-Roginski would be ideal. Provided that Verdon was pronounced "Veurdonn," because the Americans will also have won the war. Vladimir Verdon-Roginski: what a ring it has! It'll be a little like Pierre Richard-Willm riding through Colorado in a troika . . .

"Don't you think that's a little heavy for a child to carry, Monsieur Gauthier-Berthier?" asked Zaza.

" 'bsolutely, 'bsolutely, and that's why we'll begin by calling him Volodya. It's light; it makes you think of a man who dances."

"A man, maybe, but not a woman!"

"If you're going to complicate everything, Mademoiselle Roux, you might as well call it Roux-Combaluzier, like all those elevators. Me, I say what I know . . . " Maurice said before giving Zaza a fraternal kiss on closed lips that were wet with tears of laughter.

That had been the night before last; they'd been drinking tea after putting the children to bed. Maurice had poured just a drop of brandy into his bowl and he hadn't gone down to drink all by himself later.

: :

AND NOW this evening he must have finished all of Marcel's bottle, as he always did when he was unhappy. She wouldn't ask him anything tomorrow. She'd say that she had slept soundly, and he'd say, "Me too," and she'd never know why he had been so sad the night before and so happy the one before that. No, not happy: more like amusing, because it had been she who'd been so unhappy that evening.

That was the way they had lived their lives for two years, and it had been fine.

If he brooded about women, he said nothing, and she didn't tell him that at the hospital, when he was all but dead, they had made it clear to her that it would be a long time before he could make love to a woman.

If he brooded about Robert, who had gone off without him, she didn't tell him that she often thought of Alex and Angelina—now in America—with whom she and Laurent could have left when there'd still been time. They had chosen to stay, she to be near Maurice when he returned to the world, Laurent to be near her.

If he brooded about what he had done in Paris before coming to her here, she didn't tell him that she believed there had been some kind of "Jewish move" that was so serious she preferred to know nothing about it, so that she could never possibly reveal anything.

Only once had they been unhappy together, unhappy enough to die together: that had been at Châteauroux.

All in all, they were often happy together—because of the children, because of her own "Jewish action." At least they could talk about that.

She'd been wrong, however, to show him Loulou's drawing that evening: she was sure it was Loulou's, even if the child had had one of the older ones write MAMMA; all those Ms meant MYRIAM. The star on the cardigan was so obvious. And he'd been wrong to bring up the children's letters again. Tomorrow they'd write whatever they wanted to in their notebooks—penmanship exercises if they wanted, or just nonsense. She'd collect the notebooks and grade them. That way, for once, they'd get real responses to their pages of writing; for once, they wouldn't have to begin with "Dear Mama and Papa."

No more ritualistic tossing into the sea of bottles bearing good news from the mountaintop.

Tomorrow, she'd tell them: "No news is good news," as they used to say at home, back on rue de la Mare, when they were children.

It was especially Elie Guttman who would say it. Say it often. Much more often than her own father.

He would say: "No news is good news," and sometimes he would add: "Out of sight, out of mind," and that would irritate Sonia, who would look at Olga—and both women would sigh.

. . . No, it wasn't quite like that: Elie would say "No news is good news" and Sonia would say, "Out of sight, out of mind" and shrug. And he, with his beautiful but somewhat sad smile, would correct her and say: "No, Sonia, out of sight, but maybe very much in mind." Or "Always in mind." Or "Still in mind." Something like that . . . And Stépan would agree, and then they would stop talking because either she or Maurice had walked in.

How kind and vulnerable all four of them had been, with their carefully shared—and carefully kept—little secrets!

She felt like going upstairs and giving Maurice a kiss while he slept. But she didn't. She didn't want to wake the children.

Her own was apparently already asleep. He was sending no more messages. She could go to sleep too.

As for messages, she hoped she'd get one from her lover, sometime before September . . .

Tomorrow she'd have to ask Maurice if he remembered: after "out of sight"—was it "maybe," "always," or "still" in mind? . . .

It would be a game for them, and they'd see which of the two had the better memory.

$\mathcal{O}\mathcal{S}$ HE SHOULD simply have said "out of mind."

Zaza's child was already eight months old and wasn't called Volodya.

She was called Marina, Marina Verdon; and her mama was Elsa Roginski.

She had indeed been born in September: September 15, 1944, at the end of a rainy day—a *September in the rain* as Maurice whispered to Zaza in English in an effort to make her laugh between two contractions as the taxi sped to the hospital maternity ward.

Her father hadn't acknowledged her as she came along the street, but he had very civilly acknowledged her at the *Mairie* of the Ist arrondissement in Paris.

Her mother hadn't chosen to go to the *Mairie* of the VIIth arrondissement to become Madame Laurent Verdon.

Strangely enough, there had been neither melodrama nor victims. It was simply that they'd both recognized they were no longer in love when they met after so long a separation.

They no longer loved each other, but they still liked each other. They had even continued to live together. But now it was Marina who slept next to Zaza in the red-curtained room. Laurent slept in his office whenever he was there, which wasn't very often.

Maurice called Marina Volodyna, but only to himself. Or rather he *had* called her Volodyna, because he soon called her nothing at all. She and her mother left for America. For Hollywood, to be exact.

That had been decided one night after an interminable and probably exorbitantly expensive international phone call, which at about two in the morning had awakened first Laurent, then Zaza and finally Marina.

Alex's voice had faded in and out as he told Zaza to come and work with him, Angelina Crespi, and their *partners*—as he put it, in English —it sounded like an invitation to tennis. Angelina Crespi's voice had followed that of Alex to repeat exactly the same thing, and then there had been another voice—this one completely unknown—on the line just long enough to coo that its owner was dying to cuddle the *baby* . . . Alex had come back on, insistent and definite. She'd be sent money for the trip. She and the child should come as quickly as possible. Laurent had listened on the extension and signaled to Zaza to accept. "I'll come and see both of you there . . . " he had murmured when Zaza had hung up, having said yes to Alex, Angelina Crespi and *partners*.

She had giggled a little when she'd understood, from Alex's follow-up letter, the identity of this *partner* who was so eager to cuddle the *baby* of a mother she'd never known, either as an infant, a little girl, an adolescent or a young woman, and who seemed to be unaware that the young mother herself had had a mother . . . Nevertheless, Zaza had gone. At that very moment she was riding the blue waves.

Soon after her arrival, she would go to work. They had been eagerly awaiting her expert advice on error-free, authentic and realistic costumes for an important film about the great misery of outcasts in Occupied France. Outcasts to whose cause it appeared Alex and Angelina Crespi's *partner* had devoted herself body and soul—from Hollywood, that is—during the terrible years. And, indeed, attached to Alex's letter was a calling card with plum-colored engraving on a salmon-colored background indicating that Vicky Rogin was the *chairman* of the F.J.B.H. Ass. (French Jewish Beating Hearts Association). The initialese had been too much for Zaza, who had idiotically translated it as Jewish Hearts Beaten by the French until Maurice had corrected her version. As he understood it, it meant "Heartbeats of the Jews of France," or maybe "Jews of France with Beating Hearts." And to make sure that she henceforth avoided all such barbarisms and other unfortunate mistranslations, he had gone to the Gibert bookstore and picked up an out-of-print copy of *Alice's Family*, which he'd suggested she reread during the trip.

Her luggage contained little except Marina's bottles and diapers— and, of course, *Alice's Family*. Over there you could get everything that still couldn't be found in France.

Everything. Except a gadget that Alex had asked her to bring him and which she had gone to pick up on rue Campagne-Première, where he had left it when he himself left in 1940.

It was simply a big champagne-colored enamel Easter egg, and when you pushed a small ruby lever it opened to the sound of music into four sections, like an orange.

It was very pretty, but perhaps a little delicate to transport. However, that egg must have done a lot of traveling—in Pullmans, aboard the Orient Express, in a troika, and aboard the Trans-Siberian Railway. There was no reason to think it wouldn't survive the lurching and rolling of a steamship. Especially since it had been wrapped in three pairs of diaper pants and solidly stowed in the middle of a vast leather carryall that Laurent had given Zaza for the trip.

Dressed all in white, on the stern of the *City of New York*—the daughter in the mother's arms—they had both looked very pretty. To have one hand free, Zaza had set her elegant immigrant's "bundle" at her feet, and she was gently waving her child's hand toward the two men she was smiling at whom she was in the process of leaving behind.

Or ditching, Laurent had said on the way back in his car, which he had driven much too quickly from Le Havre to Paris.

Or abandoning, thought Maurice. But he let Laurent say what he knew. Laurent was Laurent; he was himself.

: :

MAURICE didn't leave. First of all because he had the feeling he had just arrived. Even after ten months. Every day it seemed to him that he'd just returned, only the evening before, from a twenty-year trip. To an imaginary and white land, as white as his hospital room had been. Like everyone else, he stuffed himself with sounds, lights, farandoles, kermesses and carousels. Like some, he was astonished that people did so much dancing at night, having done so much formal mourning of the dead during the day. The known dead, that is. Everyone still waited to mourn the others. Waited to know.

They were about to find out. The others began to return. By groups and in convoys. In real passenger cars, but just as jumbled together as they had been when they left in cattle cars.

If Marcel's friend were to see this, thought Maurice, he'd say it was still a mess.

To recognize them at the reception center, you had to do more than simply look for a familiar face in the crowd. You had to scrutinize all of them, one by one; but what you really had to do was show yourself so you could be recognized by people who had become unrecognizable.

Villeneuve was so changed that he had to say, "Hello, Guttman, it's me," twice before Maurice finally clasped and embraced this emaciated, shaven-headed giant, who looked at him and gave a toothless laugh.

Since then, Maurice had come back almost every day, at about noon, to await the arrival of the buses. But he had his own method: instead of losing himself among those who blocked the entrance to the Hôtel Lutétia, he got up on a bench across the way. He would sit on the back of the bench, his feet on the seat, so that he could be seen as well as see. Sometimes, when he wasn't sure, he would stand up before getting off the bench and then hastily elbow through the crowd, stopping to touch a shoulder or shoulder blade jutting up like a breastbone under the striped pajamas or the Red Cross jacket of a stranger who wasn't Sami.

Who was none of the others he was waiting for.

But it was still too soon to say that they wouldn't come back. Except for the Slovak or Bulgarian, Sami's friend. They knew about him: he'd never left; he'd been shot right here in Paris.

Between the arrivals of the convoys, Maurice sat on the bench in order to keep his place.

He knew this bench very well.

He now had all the time he needed to decipher the graffiti that little by little he discovered under its patina.

Placed as they were between the Cherche-Midi prison and the Grand-Hôtel Lutétia, these double benches of green painted oak had provided a spot for all kinds of waiting during the last few decades. Running his fingers over the initials and intertwined hearts, the dates, the diminutives and an incompleted "Down with . . . ", Maurice regretted not having left his own carving in the days when he'd taken up his post there, in the dark, to watch, to spy, to verify schedules, to spot and time the habitual movements of the four Ukrainian members of the Gestapo from the Lutétia. At the time, he'd been too afraid to think of making nicks on a bench, but it was a shame, he now thought. Gashes in wood are more durable than scratches on the skin of a hand, even if those scratches are dignified by being called scars.

For months at a time he no longer looked at his, because months went by without him looking at the palms of his hands. Since that time he had gone back to working with his head, and his hands had gone back to touching books. But here, on this bench where he had left no carving, he opened his left hand, and under the fine May sun the slight brightness reappeared, just as visible as under the ugly Convent lamp.

YESTERDAY, Myriam had come to wait with him. She had never been caught. After Sami was arrested at the end of '43, she had lived hidden just about everywhere—burrowed in a horrible cellar under the bells of Notre-Dame during the last weeks. They had heard the results of the attack against the Ukrainians very quickly, by the next morning: three had died. She had even told him their names, but Maurice hadn't been able to remember them.

She was now working as a secretary in an organization run by her friends. Since she had reclaimed Loulou, both of them had been living in Alex's studio. It would be convenient for Sami because it was close to the Cochin. She hadn't told Loulou that she was waiting for the child's father and all her relatives. Actually, Loulou never spoke of her father. She wanted to go back to the mountain with its Mirador, Miroir d'Or of a Mystère Flore . . .

Dédée, Markus, Luis, Frédo and Dany were in a house in Switzerland, with other children. No doubt they were being told neither the lies nor the truths that he and Zaza used to tell them. They were being told others.

Maurice often thought about them. He missed them, but the Organization didn't want any visits—they were considered "traumatizing," and very courteously told him so by mail.

It was nevertheless the only trip that Maurice would willingly have undertaken. On a Sunday, for example, with Loulou.

During the week, there was too much to do at the bookstore. He was running it, together with Madame Villeneuve and the oldest of the boys. But since Villenueve had returned, his wife had concentrated on looking after him in the upstairs apartment. He was very slowly getting better. He smiled and laughed—always being careful to put a hand to his toothless mouth—ate a little, slept badly and said nothing about what had happened to him.

∶ ∶

AT LUNCHTIME, Maurice closed the store and walked over to the Lutétia. The other day, he'd bought himself a sandwich at Le Dragon. It was all new, both inside and out. The proprietors were new. They had bought the café after the Liberation, but hadn't opened again until the renovations were complete. "When we came to see the place, it looked like Mers-el-Kébir after the British were finished with the

French fleet," the owner had told Maurice. He'd bought it through an agency and had no idea what had become of the former owners. Except that they were surely still alive, since they had been the sellers. But according to what he had been told in the neighborhood, the "Mers-el-Kébir" had been due to the vengeance of another café owner, who'd wanted to teach them not to rake in money by serving steaks hidden under the rutabagas, Swiss chard and Jerusalem artichokes everyone else was living on.

Just a short while ago, practically right in front of the Lutétia, Maurice had run into one of the three "Revenants." He, too, had come in search of news. He had invited Maurice to a memorial meeting for their martyrs. He talked of *our* martyrs, exactly the way Sami's friend had said *my* men. The number of martyrs belonging to the "Revenant's" family was still unknown, but it was staggering if, as he did, you placed them end to end, his comrades who had fallen here in the shadows by the tens of thousands, and his comrades who had fallen elsewhere in full daylight by the millions. "From Brest to Brest-Litovsk it was *our people* who gave their lives . . . Come and join us in Pantin when we honor them on Saturday night at nine o'clock. After all, before you let us drop, you did do a little mimeographing for us, didn't you, Gauthier?" he'd added, giving Maurice's shoulder a paternal tap before striding off.

"Guttman . . . " Maurice had wanted to correct him, but it was too late. The "Revenant" was already going down the steps of the Sèvres-Babylone Métro station.

: :

HE DIDN'T go on Saturday night. Nor did Villeneuve. In any case, on Saturday there'd been a little celebration in the apartment. A "house-warming" for his teeth, Villeneuve had called it. A dentist friend had put together some new front teeth for him, and he'd come to try them on him that morning. They were fantastic. Now all he had to do was get rid of the habit of putting his hand to his mouth when he laughed or smiled. "Back there, I used to do that not because I saw myself, but because I saw the gaps in the mouths of the others," he had explained. It was his only mention of the camp in Maurice's presence.

No . . . he'd also said that *back there*, with the Jews (he had said *your people*), the Russians had been treated worse than the others. And that those poor bastards really hadn't had any luck. Nowhere. And that they'd have no better luck when they got back home, because people there weren't about to forgive them for having let themselves be captured. That's all he'd said about *back there*.

But the day after he returned home, he had asked Maurice to relate the details of what he was the only one to call "the assault." He admitted that when he had found his bed and room empty that morning, it had never occurred to him that Maurice had anything to do with it. Only later, remembering the fire sirens that had awakened him during the night, and then learning of the execution of the three Ukrainian Gestapo men, did he make a connection between that and Maurice's disappearance. He'd never said a word about it to anyone. He thought it would be best to keep it secret even now. Everyone had talked too much, and everyone was getting ready to talk too much again.

"That morning, the first thing that occurred to me was that it had something to do with some woman, and I decided you were imprudent, useless, flighty and a little ungrateful . . . Forgive me!"

Maurice had blushed. A woman . . . He had gone back to see his doctor at the Salpêtrière. Spoken to him of the underbrush, the red skirt. The doctor had seemed interested. Actually, surprised might be a better word. He'd suggested that he fall in love, but that he first try things out with a whore. Maurice had done nothing. In other words, he hadn't fallen in love. As for the rest, or rather the beginning, of the program, he hadn't even given it a thought. Because what really bothered him was just that inability to fall in love. He hadn't even written to London to find out if little Anny was still alive. This lack of love was strange. Zaza was no longer in love either. She no longer loved—that's all there was to it. But at least Zaza had had a child and might have another, perhaps several others.

: :

EVEN BEFORE dinner that evening, he already knew that Villeneuve would make him tell all about the mountain and the children in their hooded capes, Zaza, the snow, the tools, Marcel and the astronomer's tower. He wanted to hear only simple stories. He was tired of History, and of the History of the World. At least for the moment.

One day Maurice would ask him to listen to the story of Volodya. But it was still too soon. Once, when Villeneuve had started to talk about the Russians, those poor bastards, he had almost begun the old story . . . But it was too long and complicated for a man who was so exhausted, and Maurice gave up the idea. All the same, he was aware that Villeneuve was the only intelligent man he knew now who was capable of listening to it, understanding it and believing it.

It seemed so incredible that Maurice himself sometimes wondered if he hadn't invented it or arranged the details.

Or else he wondered if he hadn't attached an exaggerated importance to the life and death of Vladimir Guttman, who had disappeared somewhere around Irkutsk long, long ago. Maybe those old bones of the young convict should be forgotten, now that they had been buried forever under the corpses of millions of true heroes.

Maybe that's what had to be done—forget. Then it would be *farewell, Volodya.*

: :

SO FEW PEOPLE knew the story of Volodya. Zaza had taken it with her, but she would almost certainly lose it on the way.

Who knew if Robert would bring it back with him when he came? Tomorrow? In a week or a month? In any case, soon, since he was coming.

There was no doubt that he at least would be coming back. He'd written. Three pages that could be called "Around the World in 2000 Days with a Deserter." You might say he had told everything about himself—a clandestine traveler wherever he traveled, a sometime dishwasher, ballroom dancer, archaeologist, seminarian, French professor, sari merchant, bootlegger, healer, private secretary and kumquat planter; by leaping from schooner to raft, raft to steamboat, steamboat to pleasure craft, pirogue, junk, canoe and even the bunker of a destroyer, he had crossed all the seas and fled all the continents on which any kind of war had tried to catch up with him. It was an incomprehensible tale, as beautiful as the *Aeneid, Terry and the Pirates, Candide* and *Around the World in Eighty Days* as revised and stitched together by Blaise Cendrars.

The letter ended with "Telegram follows."

The address on the envelope was: "For Maurice Guttman, Possibly at Librairie Villeneuve, Rue de Seine, Paris, France."

The telegram consisted of a single sentence: "There is no Black Cat in Shanghai."

Both the letter and the telegram had been sent from Zurich.

—Autheuil, April 1983–September 1984

ABOUT THE AUTHOR

SIMONE SIGNORET was born Simone Kaminker in 1921 in Wiesbaden, Germany, where her father, who was Jewish, was serving as an officer in the French army after World War I. She took her mother's maiden name, Signoret, in order to escape detection by the Nazis while working in Paris during World War II.

Her career as a film actress included roles in more than forty films spanning four decades, among them *Casque d'Or* (1952); *Room at the Top* (1958)—for which she won an Academy Award as best actress—*Ship of Fools* (1965); *Is Paris Burning?* (1966) and *Madame Rosa* (1977).

Simone Signoret was married twice: to the director Yves Allégret, by whom she had a daughter, Catherine; and, in 1951, to the actor and singer Yves Montand. Her memoir, *Nostalgia Isn't What It Used To Be*, was published in the United States in 1978. *Adieu, Volodya*, her only novel, was a major best seller in France and throughout the rest of Europe in 1985.

Simone Signoret died in her country house outside Paris in September 1985.